MAN DOWN

A ROOKIE REBELS NOVEL

KATE MEADER

This novel is a work of fiction. Any references to historical events, real
people, or real places are used fictitiously. Other names, characters, places,
and events are products of the author's imagination, and any resemblance
to actual events or places or persons, living or dead, is entirely
coincidental.

CONTENT WARNING

This book features depictions of and references to topics that might be sensitive for some readers, specifically a car accident, death of a spouse and young children, grief, and cancer.

1

October

GUNNAR: *Remember when we'd look at each other and you'd ask without saying a word: is this crazy? And I'd tell you silently: probably but do it anyway.*

That's how I feel every time I send one of these texts to you.

I'm waiting for the dots. I'm waiting for those dumb emojis you'd add to every sentence, even though you'd laugh at me because I never understood what half of them meant. Still don't.

Born old. That's what you said about me when we met. Born old but I think I'm going to die young.

I can't do this without you, Kel.

I can't do this without any of you.

The cell service here sucks. Half the time the messages don't go through and when they do, I wonder: is this crazy?

Probably. But I'll keep doing it anyway.

I'll keep sending because if I stop then it's over. We're over which means ... I don't want to go there.

How about I tell you what I did today? I'll take your silence as encouragement

I chopped wood.

Don't laugh. Honestly. There's a mountain of logs out back of the cabin, enough to get me through winter. I've turned into one of those weird survivalists, the kind of nut jobs we used to laugh at, complete with small-animals-a-nesting facial hair and a wild-eyed look that would scare off Grizzlies. Now I'm guessing all those crazies have their reasons because here I am. Chopping wood in the middle of Nowhere, New Hampshire.

Kurt says hi. Actually, that's a bold-faced lie. My brother would summon the men in white coats if he had any idea of the state I'm in. He already thinks it's bad enough I won't stay with them at the lodge. How can I tell him I can't look at his beautiful kids? That every time I hear my niece and nephews' laughter I want to smash something.

How can I tell him I'm currently in a complicated texting relationship with my dead wife?

~

GUNNAR: *Dante Moretti called today. Remember him? The Beast, Italian badass, amazing cook. Used to be the scouting manager in LA but now he's the General Manager in Chicago. Guy's a trailblazer, one of the good ones. I let it go to voicemail so I don't have to talk to him. I don't talk to anyone but you.*

You would put your doctor hat on and tell me it's unhealthy. I can see that elegant eyebrow arching as high as your hairline, see it as clear as if you were standing right in front of me. You've got to go back, Gunnar. You've got to move on.

I have moved on, or as far as this forest. The world's not big enough to disappear into. People will always find you. Moretti wants to talk about bringing me onto the Rebels. All their legends have retired and they're rebuilding.

Perfect timing, *you would say*. Rebuild a team, rebuild a life.

Sounds like Moretti's looking for babysitters. That's not for me.

≈

GUNNAR: *Happy anniversary, Kel. Ten years! Who would've thought it? You didn't think much of me when we met.* Too many pucks to the head, *were your exact words. (I laugh now but I didn't then!) We made it work, didn't we?*

≈

GUNNAR: *Harper Chase called, hot-shit CEO, the Rebel Queen herself. Must be scraping the barrel in Chicago. Tommy's being a dick but then that's what agents do. He sees "potential" in my comeback story, aka dollar signs. I think you'd have a good laugh at that.*

≈

GUNNAR: *I wish I could hear your voice again. I wish we had another day, just you, me, Janie, and Danny. I wish I'd taken your advice and let that asshole pass me sooner on that road. I wish a lot of things.*

≈

GUNNAR: *It's been a few days. Maybe a week? I've lost track of time. Just lost track.*

Kelly: Hello! Sorry, but I think you might have the wrong number?

2

GUNNAR BOND OPENED the drawer and stared at the phone he'd locked away yesterday morning. For two years, it had been a lifeline, a tether between his precious old world and sharp new reality. Now the link was broken. Kelly was gone and the message from the stranger confirmed it.

Recycled. The fuckers had recycled her number.

He should have paid to keep it. A while back he'd asked Kurt—or Kurt had offered, he couldn't remember—to take over some household stuff. Paying bills, selling the house in LA, putting everything in storage. His brother must have changed his wireless account from a family plan to a single man plan because that's what he was: a single fucking man. Why the hell would a man without a family keep an extra line for his dead wife?

Kurt probably thought he was doing him a favor. Another person encouraging him to move on.

Some stranger had been eavesdropping on his private conversations with Kelly. Every dream, every wish, every grievance—he'd typed it into the small screen and watched it bubble and pop into the ether. What was left of his imagination had fired off enough neurons to conjure an alternative reality: somewhere his wife was reading it, smiling down at him. He wasn't stupid or deluded or insane enough to expect a response. He knew she was incapable of communicating with him through a phone, but his heart felt her presence. His soul knew she was listening.

Until she wasn't. Until this other person answered back.

Buzzzz.

He picked up the phone. Only a text from his agent, Tommy Gordon.

Call me when you can. Chicago very interested, but won't be for long.

Well, he wasn't interested in them.

Back on the message list, he touched the line with Kelly's name. So odd to see an incoming text on the other side of the screen, that ghostly gray bubble instead of his life-affirming blue. Her name in his contacts but not from her.

It vibrated again and he dropped it.

A new message appeared. *Kelly: You okay?*

Not from Kelly but from the thief who had taken her place in the mobile numbers matrix. That first message had made it clear this person knew this. Knew they were intruding on a private moment. Knew they were in the wrong. Kelly's number had been recycled and that's all there was to it.

Now here they were asking if he was okay. The fucking nerve.

No, I'm not.

I'm drowning.

Texting my dead wife was keeping my head above water.

You've taken something from me.

He didn't type any of those things. Instead he inhaled a jagged breath, which felt like ice shards drenched in gasoline. So the stranger wasn't to blame, but that tentative "you okay?" texted volumes. This person knew something about him, whether it was from the messages they'd read or the desperation sweating through the phone or the long silence.

He should block the number. Cut the cord that bound him to the past. But something stopped him from taking that perfectly logical step, maybe the fact that none of this was logical. He'd been texting his dead wife for eighteen months. Logic was in short supply.

Gunnar wasn't religious. Not before his world was destroyed and certainly not after. No benevolent being would allow this much pain to befall one man.

But he did believe in ... signs, for want of a better word. Kelly had agreed to go out on a date with him a month into his sophomore year at Vermont and he'd won his next game. Scored two goals after a losing streak of three.

He knew Kelly was not on the other end of the line, but he wasn't ready to shutter that window on his old life. He picked up the phone and re-read that last message.

Kelly: You okay?

He tapped out, *I've been better.*

Delivered, but he had no idea if it was read. Maybe he'd never hear from—

Kelly: Know that feeling. And then, **What do they say? Better days are ahead.**

Something reared in his chest. Hella presumptuous.

Gunnar: Shows what you know.

A short delay. Then, *Yeah, I suppose that sounds like junk. Only if you've been better, you know what it feels like. You know you can get there again.*

Okay, someone must be punking him. What ridiculous after-school special BS was this?

He prepared to tell them so, but took a second to think

on it. Sure, intellectually, he knew that if he was happy once, and that happiness had deserted him, it meant he had the capacity to *be* happy. Everyone had. Gunnar wasn't a sad sack by nature. Circumstances had driven him to hell. Maybe new circumstances could punch his return ticket.

But that required embracing the possibility. The potential.

As long as he was living in the woods, refusing to talk to his brother or his agent or Dante Moretti, and having one-sided conversations with his dead wife, possibility felt improbable.

He didn't want to think about a time beyond the now. Not yet. The pain kept him going.

Gunnar: You don't know anything about me.

The small screen magnified his belligerence.

Kelly: No but I saw your messages.

Gunnar: How long have you had this number?

Kelly: A month. Maybe six weeks.

He scrolled back to check when this cheeky upstart might have started listening in, assuming a month meant at least two. Yeah, plenty of misery fodder there. But not the worst of it. Not the early days when he could barely tap out a few misspelled words and everything was filtered through a haze of Jack Daniels.

Gunnar: It belonged to my wife. She's dead.

Bluntness was the one trait Kel said she enjoyed about her husband but suggested he might want to temper in company. *Not everyone appreciates your searing wisdom, G.* *wink emoji*

Right this minute, he didn't care. Anger surged, a sucking surf in his chest. He wanted to shame this person who had come into possession of something that didn't belong to them. With all the More You Know drivel, he suspected a *her*. She should feel embarrassed for reading those private messages.

No response. That shut her up, though that wasn't relief overwhelming him, more like pettiness. He didn't feel proud of it, but neither did he have it in him to soften.

That would be the last he heard from this stand-in. Though 'stand-in' wasn't right. What did you call the person who took over your dead wife's phone number? His mind was a fog of pain.

He opened up the contacts, ready to expunge it and assign it to the bowels of history. He would be closing the door on his talks with Kelly but that was done. Ruined. After over two years of numbness, he didn't like this new feeling. This rage. He'd gone through this stage in the so-called grieving process, so why was it back? Why did he feel worse?

Just as his finger hovered over the block option, another message came in.

Kelly: Fucking AT&T.

He blinked through the sting of tears. Read it again. His hand shook.

An unfamiliar noise erupted in the dead silence.

It was him. Laughing.

Merely a reflex, a biological reaction to the stimulus of a smart-ass comment, but a laugh all the same.

Fucking AT&T. That was it. That was her response to him gutting out that his wife was dead.

He stood there, frozen, partly because the laugh had cracked something open and partly because he had no clue what came next.

The words were on the screen before he could second guess them.

Gunnar: Yeah. Waste not want not. That was his response. Kind of bland but he had no idea what to say.

Kelly: Still, have a heart, soulless corporation. A (much) wittier comeback.

He added with a shaking finger, *Unreasonable to expect them to never use the number again. Only so many number combinations, after all.*

9 million, this know-it-all said.

Gunnar: Really?

Kelly: Well, 9 million for the 7 digits, not counting the area code. (I Googled it!) So each area code could have 9 million potential numbers. LA would need more, what with everyone being so important and all.

Right. This person was in LA.

And suddenly, out of nothing, in the middle of Nowhere, New Hampshire, Gunnar Bond was enjoying himself. More precisely he wasn't *not* enjoying himself, which while not quite the same thing, was better than the thick, heavy mud of before. The tightness in his chest had eased to the level he could breathe without a sharp draw of pain.

Gunnar: Are we making excuses for the soulless corporation?

Kelly: LOL. I think we are! Coming up with unused numbers is a tough business, even for those fuckers at AT&T.

We. He'd started it but she picked up on it. They were suddenly a team, united in their mutual disdain for a multinational corporation.

Maybe it was a guy. The swearing with abandon to a total stranger hinted as much, though that was probably sexist. And what difference did it make? He wasn't going to be getting friendly with this person.

Yet he found himself not quite ready to quit. He found

himself feeling something other than pain, grief, and despair for the first time in over two years.

Gunnar: AT&T are absolved. Sure they're thrilled.

Kelly: Yes! They're probably reading along. YOU'RE OFF THE HOOK, ASSHOLES!!

He chuckled, the sound so surprising he looked around the room, worried someone might have heard him. That Kelly might have heard him.

There was that feeling again, a lightness of spirit. He couldn't trust it, especially with that crush of guilt nipping at its heels.

Gunnar: Anyway, sorry to bother you, he typed in, needing to end it before … he wasn't sure what.

Kelly: No bother. Just chilling.

Gunnar: Bye … and thanks.

Nothing, then dots. Gone, then dots again.

Finally, from the ether: *Take care.*

He decided to do just that. On a deep inhale, he left the phone on the dresser, pulled on his Nikes, and headed out for a run.

3

"*Now, it's time to get real because you know I'm all about speaking my truth. Let's talk about: Keeping. It. Tight. And you know what I mean by that? Yeah, ya do! Tight-as-a-vise punanis, my friends! And how do you get there? Well, let me tell you a little secret.*

Dried. Fruits.

That's right, dried fruits are your punani's best friend. Daily doses will keep everything nice and snug where we need it. I know it seems counterintuitive to be eating something shriveled and low in moisture for your vaginal health, but the anti-oxidants are amazing! And now, my fabulous punettes, you can buy punani fruit right from my website ..."

"At only $49 a pound," Sadie muttered as she made the cut in the video and pulled in the transition slide that took viewers from Allegra's Malibu smile to the relevant page on her website.

Prunes. The woman was selling prunes, no more or less shriveled than the ones available at grocery stores across the nation, but with one major difference. These were repackaged by one of Allegra's many suppliers of feminine wellness products to appeal to her demographic. Blue state women between the ages of 25 and 49, with hefty disposable income. They adored Oprah, Gwyneth, Michele Obama, Marie Kondo, and Chrissy Teigen in that order. Forty-three percent took Barre and Bowka classes three times a week (yeah, she had to look it up, too). Sixty-five percent believed happy hour appletinis were a constitutional right.

Sadie applied herself to the task of editing the latest video for Allegra McKenzie's YouTube channel, Punani Power. As personal assistant to a lifestyle guru, this was one of the fun parts of a job more often focused on ordering or fetching or smoothing over all the things that made her boss's life easier. She liked the creative aspects of tightening up Allegra's brand (*punani puns? you're welcome!*) and crafting content that appealed to women, even if the message was suspect.

But Allegra was a true believer. She didn't hawk anything she didn't use herself and was a firm adherent to the notion of the feminine divine. Girls rule the world, starting with their vaginas, the source of all power, pleasure, and strength.

After slipping in a cut of a yellow Hawaiian hibiscus to smooth the transition (Allegra liked Hawaiian touches as a nod to Kapo, the goddess of fertility), Sadie saved the video and checked the notifications on her phone. Nothing from LonelyHeart, the nickname she'd given to the guy whose wife's phone number she'd inherited. Or at least, she assumed it was a guy.

Two months ago, Sadie had lost her phone and Allegra had given her a fancier one with a new number. *This way, any future assistant of mine will have the same number, Sadie. Continuity is key!* Money was as tight as, well, Allegra's punani, and it was just as easy to move her contacts into the new phone. Still, Sadie was well aware of the veiled threat in Allegra's comments.

You exist by my favor. You are replaceable.

Feminine divine, indeed.

A message from a Chicago number caught her attention. Her heart dropped into the pit of her stomach. This was it.

She played it back, her shoulders sagging deeper with each word.

Guilty. House arrest. Sentencing at a later date.

John Byron, her father's lawyer, sounded blasé, but then lawyers weren't obliged to have a soothing bedside manner with the estranged daughters of their douchebag clients. She pondered her next move, recognizing that she needed to do something that went against the grain. Talk to the man who was her father in name only. Avoiding it would have been her first choice but she had Lauren to think of. Sadie would put aside her discomfort to make sure her half-sister knew she was here for her.

She dialed with a shaky finger and listened to the rings, hoping fervently it would go to voice mail. It clicked over— yes!—and she waited for her father's outgoing message, but then got a techno-voice telling her, Message box full.

Rats.

She called the lawyer and was put through after a couple of minutes.

"Ms. Yates."

"Hi, Mr. Byron. I got your message and I tried calling my father but his message box is full."

"Well, all his former clients are likely reaching out to tell him where to go."

"Long walk, short pier," she muttered.

"Somewhere hotter," he replied smoothly, as if marching orders to hell were par for the course. She supposed they were for a man who defended people accused of embezzlement and fraud. "We're working on the appeal, trying to play up your father's grief over losing his wife so suddenly and the fact he has a minor child to care for with no likely guardians on deck. He's paid most of the money back and we're setting up a plan for restitution on the rest. Sentencing will be in approximately four months to give time for victim impact statements. Meanwhile your father is under house arrest and the assets are frozen."

Sadie closed her eyes. Somehow, she'd expected her father would escape conviction, the Houdini of hedge funds. "How's Lauren holding up?"

"Still at that boarding school in Wisconsin, though I expect that won't last long. This semester is paid up but there won't be funds beyond that."

There won't be a father to care for her, either. Lauren's mother, Zoe, had died a couple of months ago from ovarian cancer, and Sadie had seen her twelve year old sister for the first time in years at the funeral. Silver-eyed, like Sadie. Like their father.

"If my father gets a custodial sentence, what happens to my sister?"

"Your stepmother had no surviving family so there's no-one—" He cleared his throat. "We're hopeful we can avoid that eventuality. Your father wanted you to know about the court decision but he's still not ready to, uh, reconcile."

What in all that was holy did that mean? Sadie was the one who had been replaced in her father's affections by first, Zoe, then by a half-sister she barely had a chance to know. And now *he* wasn't ready to reconcile?

All that old, biting anger came rushing to the surface and she fought mightily to maintain control.

"Okay, thanks for telling me. If there are any developments, you'll let me know?"

He hesitated before responding. "Ms. Yates—Sadie—I don't know what happened with your father and I don't want to interfere. But sometimes, a cut and run is the best thing for your mental health."

Sadie could feel a grim smile forming on her lips. It sounded like Mr. Byron was well aware of her father's brand of toxicity. The man had bilked millions from his clients' life savings. His status as a widower and father of a minor might garner him some sympathy during sentencing, but there was little doubt as to his guilt. Jonah Yates was not the best person.

She wasn't here for him. She owed him absolutely nothing. No, she was reaching out for Lauren. With her father out of the picture, perhaps Sadie could cultivate a better, or actual, relationship with her half-sister. Not that she wished a prison sentence on the man. That would be rather petty, wouldn't it?

"I'm just trying to do right by my sister, Mr. Byron."

"Understood. I'll be in touch if anything changes."

She hung up, her body shaking, her mind racing with the hot feelings that inevitably surfaced in the cool of the long shadow cast by her father.

Her phone buzzed with a message from ... damn, not him, her sad texter. This was from Allegra.

Make sure the video is uploaded to my channel by 3pm, Sadie! The punettes expect consistent content at the same time each day!

Allegra had been pushing that *punettes* thing for a month now. *Not catching on, babe.*

Getting back to the video, she let her mind stray to LonelyHeart and the dark place he must be in. Before he ended that text exchange yesterday morning by apologizing for bothering her—as if—she'd enjoyed his wit.

AT&T are absolved. Sure they're thrilled.

That dry as dust tone had permeated his previous texts, along with a bone-deep pain. The man spent his time updating his dead wife on his daily routine. It was either weirdly healthy or messed up beyond recognition.

Reaching out the way she did, putting a halt to that conversation with his wife, might not have been one of her best ideas. But those messages had been so private and she needed him to know she was eavesdropping. Then she wanted him to know she was there for him.

Which was strange because she didn't know him from Adam.

If he did want to talk more, he could reach out. But after hearing about her father's conviction and his desire not to reconcile—*which I don't want at all, Dad!*—she itched for something real. To relive the good vibe she'd experienced yesterday.

Surely, it wouldn't hurt to say hello. She scrolled through the contacts to LonelyHeart.

~~Hey~~

~~Hey, how are you?~~

She tried again. *Hey, stranger. What's the weather like today?*

Friendly, no pressure, creating an opening through which he was welcome to walk through any time. That was all.

She waited. Nothing. No indication it had been read, either. That was okay, she had all the time in the world.

But not much before she needed to get this video uploaded to Allegra's Punani Power channel. She pressed play.

"Time for today's *Muff Buster*, punettes! Do you believe so-called scientists who say your punani is self-cleaning? After a strenuous workout or some fun times with your man, do you think it's cleaning without a little help from the goddess? Don't be fooled. You need to take care of business and I have just the thing ..."

4

SADIE PULLED up in her shabby ten year old Honda Civic and parked behind Allegra's new Tesla outside her home in West Hollywood. The old girl was still kicking—like Sadie herself—but the miles were starting to show. A duct-taped side mirror, rusty undercarriage, and careworn leather told the true story.

She took a few cleansing breaths and considered her plan of attack for the day. Allegra would be in her sun room, drinking a kale smoothie (ugh) and checking her view numbers. A quick look revealed one hundred and fifty thousand views in twenty-four hours, with an increase of six thousand new subscribers to a healthy 2.5 million. Sadie kept spreadsheets of the daily numbers so Allegra could plot her trajectory toward influencer stardom. The Instagram numbers were phenomenal as well, growing even faster than YouTube. On there, she was helping Allegra to craft a presence marketed at a millennial base.

If only Sadie put as much effort into her own creative endeavors.

Sadie had to give it to Allegra. She had found her passion and trod her path, not like Sadie, who had floated aimlessly for ten years as a waitress, receptionist, barista, and other assorted jobs until landing a gig with Allegra after she'd bumped into her in a restaurant bathroom in Venice Beach. Allegra complimented Sadie's dress, a design of her making, they got to talking, and Sadie was only too happy to leave her virtual assistant concierge job to work with a woman who was so driven. She thought it would ground her and give her time to get her own design business started, but no such luck. These days Sadie was busier than ever on Allegra's passion, with little progress to date on her own.

At twenty-eight years old, she wished she had it figured out.

She smoothed the skirt of her dress, a cute shift style she'd cut from an old Vogue pattern and paired with a fun, sparkly belt. Placing her hand on the door handle, she grabbed her Kate Spade, gift from her friend Peyton, only to stall at hearing her phone buzz.

"Hold your horses, woman," she muttered, expecting to see an all-caps text from Allegra. Instead it was from someone rather unexpected.

LonelyHeart: It's cold and miserable, like me. How about you?

More than twenty-four hours later, he'd texted back! About the weather, but she'd take it.

Sadie: Sunny with a chance of more sun. Like me!

She cringed at her ridiculousness. *Sadie: Sorry, just being a goof. What's going on? Forehead slap*. He's mourning his wife, that's what.

LonelyHeart: I've been thinking about the 9 million numbers and how it is, you have this one number. Of all the numbers. This one that means something to me.

She had no idea what to say to that. *Maybe it's fate? The goddess? Maybelline?*

The dots started up again and she let him finish his thought.

LonelyHeart: Maybe it means we're supposed to be talking.

Sadie: I think so. It has to be a sign.

Gunnar: So you don't think it's weird?

What? Talking to a man who wished he was chatting with the deceased love of his life. Nah!

Sadie: No, not at all. You don't have to say anything but I wanted you to know I'm here, if you need to talk.

LonelyHeart: Not much of a talker.

Sadie smiled. This man—and she was sure it was a man —was much more of a 'talker" than he claimed.

Sadie: Yet you can't shut up in those texts

LonelyHeart: Kind of chatty when there's only four wooden walls.

Sadie: You have me now.

She sent it before she had time to think about how it would sound. Presumptuous. Needy. A bridge too far.

Allegra: SADIE, WHERE ARE YOU??!!!

Damn. She waited for LonelyHeart to respond, worried she'd scared him off. Her phone rang with Allegra's high-energy smile on the screen (Allegra had energy degrees for her smiles. This one was an eight.) Sadie let it go to voice mail. It seemed incredibly important that she wait for his response. Just a second, just one more second ...

LonelyHeart: I should let you go. I'll check in later if that's okay.

Sadie's heart thundered. *Definitely. I'm dying to hear about the wooden walls. Are you Amish? But a user of phones? An Amish tech-lover?*

LonelyHeart: No. I live in a cabin. In a forest.

Sadie: Like the Unabomber? I'm not really into revolutionary anarchy but I can tell a million jokes about it.

LonelyHeart: Jokes would be welcome during the revolution.

Sadie: Awesome! I'll get my arsenal of bad puns ready. (Arsenal? Revolution? Get it?) Prepare to be entertained.

LonelyHeart: Is that your way of discouraging me from checking in? Because I'm not easily frightened.

Sadie: Wait until you hear my A material.

SADIE: It's your morning funny! Knock, knock

LonelyHeart: Really?

Sadie: Could you play along?

*LonelyHeart: *grumble* Who's there?*

Sadie: A little old lady.

LonelyHeart: A little old lady who?

Sadie: I didn't know you could yodel!

LonelyHeart: Classic.

Sadie: I thought so. Plenty more where that came from!

LonelyHeart: Please God no.

SADIE CHUCKLED, immensely pleased with herself. Who didn't love a good knock knock joke? For the last few weeks, they'd been chatting every day, usually starting with Sadie's knock-knock-icebreakers. Which sounded like a good name for a sex toy.

"Sadie, have you sent out the prizes for the "I Heart my Punani" contest yet?"

She looked up to find Allegra, standing in the doorway to her office at Allegra's house. Allegra's movie producer father had gifted the 3000 square feet Spanish-style home to her as a college graduation present (apparently no one gave out cars anymore). With its gorgeous portico terrace, white stuccoed walls, and sun-drenched great room, it was an inspiring place to live and work.

Instead of playing hooky, Sadie was supposed to be packing up prizes for contest winners. She grabbed a bottle of fur oil and waved it in Allegra's direction.

"Yes, getting the packages together now." Allegra received free products all the time and gave most of them away to her viewers. "And I heard from Ciara at Having It All about that cross-promo opportunity."

"Remind me again."

"You said you wanted to look at opportunities to lift other women up."

Allegra held up her hand. "What are her numbers like?"

"Not as good as yours but she's up and coming."

Vigorous head shake. "What have I said? I can't work with anyone who's below me on the totem pole. If I'm to achieve next level I need to be striving for partnerships with people who can bring in more eyeballs."

Logic alert. If everyone came at it from that angle, then no one would help anyone. "I thought of it as a pay it forward thing? If you help someone below you then someone else might do the same for you. On the shoulders of giants and all that."

Allegra narrowed her eyes, unable to find fault with that. "I'll take a look at her channel." She turned to leave then pivoted again. "So, a little birdie told me that you might be going through some personal issues right now."

Sadie's pulse picked up. How in the hell would Allegra have heard about her father's legal problems? "Not really. I mean, nothing that interferes with my work for you."

Her boss stepped one willowy leg forward and canted

her head in practiced sympathy. "We all have crosses to bear, Sadie. If you need to talk to someone—"

"That's very kind of you, Allegra, but I'd never impose on you like that."

She waved dramatically. "Oh, I don't mean me, Sadie! Boundaries are incredibly important between employer and employee." Said the woman who had asked her on Day Two of employment to pick Allegra's best "vag-shots" for a gallery exhibit in West Hollywood. "I mean that you should talk to a friend or even submit to that relationships subreddit. Names changed to protect the guilty, of course."

Sadie dug her nails into her palm. "Right."

"I need you here giving me 110% because ..."

"100% is never enough," Sadie finished Allegra's mantra for her.

Allegra raised both her fists and gave a half-pump. "Exactly! Now, back to those packages. I'll be filming in the sunroom, so the video will be ready for edit in fifteen." She hovered a moment, then offered a lazy hand gesture toward Sadie's outfit. "That one of yours?"

Sadie stood to give her a better view of the peasant-style dress she'd made last week. Red with white flowers, it had a romantic ruffle that hit just above the knee and flattered her curves.

"It is. What do you think?"

"Pretty." She touched a finger to her chin and waited a beat. "You know, I'm in a book club with Galatea Hughes. We're reading Reese's latest pick."

Sadie swallowed her ignorance. Galatea who? But her know-nothingness must have shown on her face.

"Galatea Hughes? She's on one of those MTV reality shows? Anyway, her brother is married to Shannon Shah. The designer."

"Oh, wow, really." Sadie wasn't a huge fan of Shannon Shah, who made weirdly inappropriate outfits for children, but she'd never turn down an introduction. "Have you met Shannon?"

"God, no. Those slutty outfits for kids are popular, I suppose. Maybe when I see Galatea, I could mention you." Allegra only sounded half-begrudging. She might have felt a touch guilty at closing off her sympathetic ear a moment before.

Sadie smiled. "That would be so nice, Allegra." Her phone buzzed and she ignored it, knowing who it probably was.

"No promises!" Allegra wagged a finger. "I'm all for women looking out for each other but no free rides."

"Got it! I wouldn't dream of taking advantage."

Allegra looked suitably smug and went on her way. Buoyed by Allegra's passive-aggressive promise, Sadie picked up her phone.

LonelyHeart: I didn't mean you had to literally stop texting.

Sadie: Oh, I know. My boss stopped in so I had to pretend I was working.

LonelyHeart: Bosses. Don't miss that.

Sadie considered how to ask without prying about his employment prospects. *You're your own boss, then?*

LonelyHeart: Taking a break.

Her heart hitched painfully. Of course. She took the plunge into a pool in which she might drown. *Are you talking to anyone? About what you're going through?*

LonelyHeart: Doing it right now. With you.

But this couldn't possibly be enough. *Sadie: This is only knock knock jokes.*

LonelyHeart: Never underestimate the power of a good knock knock joke.

Oh, that was nice to hear. Feeling a little smug herself, she got back to the job that paid the bills.

5

December

KELLY: Happy New Year!

Kelly: Hey, have you blocked me or is this an AT&T conspiracy?

Gunnar smiled and started typing. ***Stop seeing conspiracies everywhere. No one's blocked anyone. Happy New Year to you.***

Kelly: Yay! How are things?

Gunnar: You mean, am I still a miserable bastard?

Kelly: Well, I assumed that. More a query as to your general health.

Gunnar cast a look to the clear Maine sky. A burst of fireworks lit up the inky night not far from his current location, his brother's house at the ski resort he ran. Behind him, sounds of muted revelry echoed like ghosts through the windows. He moved further out into the dark of the yard, closer to the forest perimeter. Kurt would come looking for him soon enough. No one could leave a widower alone. He took a swig from the bottle and cursed the fact he was still sober.

Carefully he placed the bottle against the tree and plonked his ass down with his back to the bark. Cold as fuck but he wouldn't be here long.

Gunnar didn't feel his day had started properly without a daily text from the woman who had Kelly's phone number. Usually it was a joke—a morning funny, she called it—which sometimes led to exchanges about other things. Nothing especially deep, though he felt they were hovering on the edge of something significant, if only he'd take a leap from the precipice. He stared at the phone, and that stare seemed to bring in another message.

Kelly: So, what's on your mind?

Gunnar: I haven't figured out how to get back into it.

Kelly: It?

Gunnar: The groove of life. I feel out of step.

Kelly: Everyone's moving forward and you're stuck in one place.

He thought about that. *Not even one place. A million places. Everywhere I look reveals a memory, every memory is a stab to my heart.*

A light dusting of snow had grazed the trees earlier, hardly worth the effort. Now new flakes fell, attempting to stick to the ground and be counted. That's all anyone or anything wanted, even snowflakes. To stick, to make a damn difference.

Danny had loved the visits to Maine, adored making snowballs and angels. Janie, not so much. She was a Cali girl through and through. *"It's too cold, Daddy! Wrap me up!"* And he would, inside his jacket like he was a kangaroo and she was a shivering joey who needed his body heat.

He indulged that sharp-fanged memory for a moment while the phone buzzed in his hand.

Kelly: What can I do to help?

Such a simple question with a complicated answer. He needed a distraction.

Gunnar: Tell me more about you.

Kelly: Oh hell, really? Like what?

Gunnar: What you do. How you got here.

Kelly: Like, on this earth? LOL. My life would bore you to tears. In fact, hearing about me might actually be the kickstart you need, bud, because then you'll be dying to return to reality. Where should I begin my epic journey?

This Angelino was funny. But she probably wasn't from there. No one in LA was.

Gunnar: Where are you from originally?

Kelly: Right into the in-utero stuff, huh? Well, I landed topside in Chicago and after several life changes and big moves, ended up in LA, which is sort of home.

Gunnar: I lived in LA for a while. Pretty fake.

Kelly: Oh, definitely. And I'm contributing to it with my career choice which props up a snake oil saleswoman who sells shit to sheeple who want to be fooled and ... my life is filled with all kinds of suckage. Happy?

She was doing that for him. Selling herself short to make him feel better about his miserable existence.

Gunnar: What would you rather be doing?

Kelly: Be my own boss. But I'm in a competitive field and I need to stand apart from the crowd. Hard for someone who usually prefers to blend in.

Gunnar: You don't seem like the shy and retiring type.

Kelly: On here, we can be whatever we want, right? Much easier than out there, especially in LA where everyone's hawking something.

So true. Texting with someone who had no preconceptions about you—apart from whatever she'd gleaned from his misery-laden messages—was freeing. And oddly safe. In real life, he couldn't imagine connecting with any woman, not even this one, where the reality of a physical presence created a whole other series of expectations. Not being able to see her in the flesh kept it inside the lines.

He aimed for a return to the easy, breezy tone of their previous exchanges. *What's going on tonight in LA other than the usual fakery?*

Kelly: I'm sitting in the booth in the corner of a very trendy bar watching as everyone gets trashed and vows to do better next year. The cycle begins again.

Gunnar: Hey, I'm the hardened cynic here. Stop trying to steal my crown.

Kelly: No, you're not. You're the guy who's a little out of step with life. Who talked to someone he lost long after they left the path you both were on. Nothing cynical about that. If anything, it's lovely to want to keep that connection alive.

That froze his texting fingers. It might sound lovely but the pain definitely diminished the romance of it.

Kelly: I'm sorry I interrupted the conversation with your wife.

He sucked in a sharp breath, appreciating her directness while hating its effect. So many people danced around his pain.

Gunnar: Not much of a conversation if it's one-sided. I need to plug back into this world. Hearing from you hurt at first, but not now. Or not as much.

Was he trying to make her feel better or ... might he actually mean that?

Kelly: I hate the idea I might have inflicted any pain in you. Can we still blame AT&T?

Gunnar: We can and should.

He took another slug of Jack, enjoying the warm burn while his ass muscles rapidly cemented into ice. The fireworks burst in fiery sprays off in the distance. A couple of minutes passed without a message. He wondered if she'd signed off for the night, finally tangled in the revelry of her life in LA.

Then at last: *Sorry about that. I'm trying to fend off the multitudes here.*

Gunnar: Really?

Kelly: No, not really. If you saw me and saw my wing-girl you'd think that comment hilarious. She's a twiggy supermodel, and I'm, well, not.

Gunnar: Maybe you could send a pic.

Shit. What made him text that? He knocked over the half-drunk bottle of Jack, watching as the future of even more poor decision-making seeped into the thin blanket of snow. No more alcohol for him.

Ominous dots blinked on his screen and his pulse rate picked up. He had to admit he was curious.

The next communication was a gif of someone familiar. Ah. The blonde from *Clueless* pushing some loser away.

He smiled, glad she saw the humor in his request and half-relieved that she knew instinctively that sharing photos was not a good way forward. It turned what was happening between them into something where the optics overrode the foundation. This was not what he needed, some weird texting-slash-flirting relationship with a stranger. Sure he missed sex. Mostly he missed the comfort of Kelly. He missed the way she accepted his brute strength and turned it into their joint power.

Yet his cock had stiffened, just like that.

Was he so devoid of a friendly ear that the first woman

to give him the time of day was turning him on? Damn, he was in a bad way.

He ignored the throb of need pushing against his zipper and instead drew on his prime directive: to protect. He used to do it well on the ice. He used to protect his family, even if he'd failed at that final hurdle. Those instincts couldn't be completely dead.

Gunnar: So you're with friends right now? She'd said she was, but he was really trying to nose out if she had a boyfriend.

Kelly: I am. Why?

Gunnar: Just wanted to be sure you're safe. Security in numbers.

Kelly: Aw, so sweet! I'm starting the celebrating early but I think you said once you were on the east coast so maybe the new year is already upon you? I wanted to get in during that special, witching hour when the year has yet to be stained with mistakes. When anything seems possible.

He liked how she phrased it. Possibility flowed around him, energizing, waiting to be drawn upon.

Or the whiskey was finally working its magic.

Gunnar: I've been offered a job. In Chicago, as a matter of fact.

Kelly: Is that a good move for you?

Gunnar: I think so. It feels like the right time.

Kelly: Then congrats!

He had a talent he was currently squandering on gutters and firewood and Jack Daniels. If he didn't do this now, he might go to his grave never having realized his full potential. He had to re-start somewhere.

He couldn't imagine coming to that conclusion two months ago. Before this woman had answered back.

Gunnar: It's a good thing. I need to feel useful again.

Kelly: Ah, usefulness. No one would ever accuse me of that.

Gunnar: You've been useful to me.

Kelly: Really? I hoped but I didn't want to overstep.

Gunnar: You didn't. You haven't. It's easier to talk to someone I don't know. Who doesn't have any expectations.

Kelly: Same. Big time. Which is why I need to go, while there's still a chance I don't screw this up.

This? He wanted to ask what she meant by that.

Stay safe, was all he could text back instead of the orders he wanted to bark: *Don't drink and drive. Don't get into a car with someone you don't trust. Don't die senselessly.*

Kelly: Take care. That was how she always signed off, and he'd been trying to do exactly that. Go easy on himself.

He pulled himself upright, rubbing his frozen ass to get the circulation back in. Before he went back into the house, he opened up his contacts, hit edit on Kelly's name, and changed it to Angel for his guardian angel from Los Angeles.

Swiping at his half-frozen tears, he headed into the warmth.

6

March

SADIE PARKED her car on the side of the road near the entrance to Allegra's gated community, ten minutes before she was due to work. Once on site, she wouldn't get a chance to make any personal calls, so it was now or never.

The phone rang once, twice, and was answered with what sounded like brisk efficiency.

"Good morning, this is Brenfort Academy. How may I assist you?"

Sadie took a quick breath. "Hi there! I'm trying to get in touch with one of your students. My sister, actually. Lauren Yates?"

Slight pause. "Lauren's in class right now. No, I'm forgetting, it's Monday. She'd be in practice. Is this an emergency?"

"Oh, no. Not at all! I just—well, I don't have the number of her personal phone—"

"Who did you say you were?"

Sadie swallowed. "Sadie Yates. I'm Lauren's sister. I was really just hoping to check in with her. Not a big deal."

The ruffle of papers, a muffled voice, then the speaker came back, her tone now more guarded. "You're not listed as an approved contact, Ms. Yates. We have to be mindful of our students' privacy and security. You'll need to contact her father—Mr. Yates—and ask to be added to the list. Or perhaps get her personal phone number." Midwestern disapproval raced across the country.

"Of course. Sorry to disturb you."

The woman hung up. Damn.

Sadie did not want to go through her father to make contact with her sister. Jonah Yates had made it clear long ago that he wasn't interested in cultivating any relationship with his oldest daughter or encouraging a connection between Sadie and his youngest child. But Lauren's mother was gone and her father was about to be sentenced, possibly incarcerated. If not now, when?

She called her father again, for once wishing he would answer so she could have this out with him. While she appreciated the security consciousness of Lauren's boarding school in Wisconsin, she did not appreciate the subterfuge her father was forcing her to undertake. Family was important, and Sadie was only starting to realize how much.

Blame LonelyHeart. Without his wife, the man was broken. In those texts to her, he was trying to hold onto something precious and long gone. What if something happened to her father or Lauren, and Sadie never got a chance to make it right?

The call went to voice mail.

"Hi, Dad, it's Sadie. I wanted to check in and see how Lauren is doing. How you're both doing. I was thinking of coming out to see you, or maybe a visit to Lauren at school. Does she get a spring break?" She floundered, unwilling to beg for crumbs of affection yet needing to do something. "Anyway. I'm thinking of you both. Call me back when you can."

She hung up and stared at the screen, waiting for a sign.

A text came in ... from Allegra. Gah. *Could you stop at Starbucks and get me an iced soy honey flat white with one and a third Splendas? Please ensure they mix the Splenda into the espresso before they make the drink.*

Sadie typed back, *Of course! *Smiley face**

Nothing from her father, which said it all. She put the phone down, but picked it up when it buzzed again. It was from LonelyHeart!

LonelyHeart: Missed my morning funny today. You're slacking.

Sadie: Sorry. Running behind and ... maybe you could come up with the jokes, bud?

LonelyHeart: Me? I haven't got a funny bone in my body. But you're right. I'm putting too much on you.

Sadie: Just kidding! Feeling overly sensitive. It's one of those days that's barely started and I just want to crawl back into bed and sleep through the rest of it.

LonelyHeart: Know what that's like. Sometimes it would be nice to pull the bedcovers over my head and forget about the world outside. Especially these days.

Sadie waited a moment. He had started his new job in Chicago last month and was fairly quiet about it. Maybe it wasn't going well.

Sadie: How's the job? All you expected?

LonelyHeart: It's good. Except I'm being eased in slowly when really it would be better to go at it full-tilt. I have the skills, I just need the bosses to put me to use.

Sadie: And how are things otherwise?

LonelyHeart: Not exactly better. Just different. I feel disconnected from people, especially the ones I work with. Which isn't good because this job requires teamwork and a sort of telepathy. I worry my state of mind is holding me back.

Sadie knew something about that. When you felt frozen in one aspect of your life, it was hard to thaw the rest of it.

Before she could respond, another text came in. *I'm in LA.*

She dropped the phone.

Holy shock to the heart. Did she read that right? She picked up the phone and inhaled deeply.

LonelyHeart: I'm in LA.

Omigodomigodomigod. He was here. In the same city as her. She'd asked for a sign and look what the goddess had provided. *Play it cool, Sadie.*

Sadie: Oh, that's nice.

Nice? She told him it was nice?

LonelyHeart: I leave tomorrow, early. Would you be interested in telling some of those bad jokes to me in person?

Sadie put the phone on the seat and waved her hands over her face, trying to fan away her anxiety. Her heart refused to slow. Her hands refused to steady.

He wanted to meet.

So did she.

At New Year's he'd asked for a photo, in a jokey way, she'd thought, and she had resisted. Too soon for that kind of thing. A photo placed them on some strange footing where appearances mattered. But an in-person meeting? That jibed better with her gut on this. She could wow in the flesh.

Sadie: I take offense at the notion my jokes are bad. But I would love to tell you some brilliant, witty, clever jokes to your face.

LonelyHeart: Okay. I have work this afternoon but maybe we can meet for coffee at 6pm? I'm staying at a hotel near the Staples Center. Could cab anywhere.

She didn't know downtown all that well, but she could figure it out. *6pm it is! I'll scout locations and send you a place to meet.*

LonelyHeart: Sounds good. And if this seems out there, or you're feeling pressured, just say so.

Sadie: I don't. Feel pressured, that is. I'd like to meet. Really.

Allegra: Sadie, where the hell is my coffee?

Sadie smiled, then texted to LonelyHeart. *See you later.*

~

GUNNAR CHECKED his reflection in the mirror. He needed a haircut and a shave, but short of putting his travel day suit back on, there wasn't much he could do to make himself more presentable. What did a clean button-down shirt and jeans say about him? Making an effort but not trying too hard, perhaps. He no longer had that sunken, hollow-eyed look but there was no missing the scar marking the left side of his face, from cheek to chin.

He wouldn't want to miss it.

Maybe this was a mistake. He had a good thing going with Angel right now. Dumb jokes interspersed with deeper dives when he needed it. No expectations. No pressure. A meet in real life would take it to another level—or it might prick the bubble of safety he was living in now. He liked it here.

But the act of deliberately *not* meeting Angel when they were in the same city assigned this thing between them more importance than it deserved. *Not* meeting her meant he was afraid he might be attracted to someone other than Kelly. He would not be, and the only way to know for sure was to meet Angel.

Having talked himself into going through with this for the tenth time today, Gunnar checked his wallet and room key and headed for the door. It opened just as he touched the handle.

"Double, oh!" Theo Kershaw, his roommate for this trip, bounded in like a big puppy. "You headed out?"

"Yeah, I-I'm meeting an old friend."

Theo narrowed his eyes. One of Gunnar's favorite people—though he would never tell him—Kershaw had skated with him three years ago when Gunnar was captain of the LA Quake, the team they were playing tomorrow. Brimming over with self-confidence and good humor, Kershaw had gone through some health problems and had clawed his way back to his peak on the Rebels roster. There was a lot to like about the guy.

"What old friend? Someone in the Quake camp?" Theo grabbed his shoulder. "Are you consorting with the enemy, G-man?"

"No. This is someone you don't know. Not a player. Just a friend."

Theo stripped off his T-shirt, damp from the run he'd just taken. He had a lot of energy he needed to expend after the four-plus hour plane ride. "Was hoping you'd hang with us for dinner. You haven't been the most social since you came on board."

Gunnar had assumed no one had noticed, cared, or was tactless enough to speak his mind. But this was Kershaw. Good kid. Filter, nonexistent.

"It's just taking me a while to get into that groove again. It's not personal."

"Yeah, got it. We're buds, I know you love me!" He hauled his suitcase up onto the bed and started digging around in it. "Just know that I'm here for you if you need anything. I've been trying to do a better job of listening, so I can be—" He stopped short, biting back something.

"So you can be what?"

Theo shook his head. "Some stuff going on. Nothing I can talk about just yet. But when I can, you'll be first on my list because you're in the inner circle."

Gunnar couldn't help his smile. "Good to know. I'll text you later."

"You do that. Let me know if you're staying out late, young man."

Angel had sent a text earlier, suggesting a coffee shop near Pershing Square, a couple of miles from the hotel. In the cab, he tried to relax, but traffic was stop-and-go, and about four blocks out from his destination he asked the driver to pull over so he could walk the rest of the way.

Gunnar had never been a fan of LA with its perpetual sun, dismal air quality, and never-ending sprawl. But he'd built a life here once, a life that was shattered in a heartbeat. Memories of that life had entangled around his nerve endings, so LA was heaven and hell at once. He walked on, toward Angel, each step heavier and heavier.

His phone rang, and for a moment, he hoped it was Angel canceling the meeting. *Fuck, really?* It was his brother, Kurt. Gunnar had been dodging his calls for a week, so now that he wanted to slow his roll toward this meet-up, he answered.

"Hey," he said, stopping outside a shoe shop window. A pair of red heels caught his eye, the kind Kelly would wear.

"You ready for the game?"

That was his brother. Straight into the conversation though they hadn't talked in several weeks.

"Probably won't even get on," Gunnar said. "Coach thinks I'm rusty."

"For Christ's sake! How are you supposed to get un-rusty if they don't play you?" Gunnar let Kurt rant a bit on his behalf while he waited for him to get to the point.

"How are things at the lodge?" The ski season was wrapping up and they were getting ready to switch to hiking and ATV tours.

"All right. Carrie's pregnant."

Gunnar froze. So this is why he'd called. Another niece or nephew on the way.

Kurt went on. "Figured I'd tell you in person. Well, y'know. With a call."

Gunnar found his voice again, though it came out scratchy. "How far along?"

"Due in August." His brother cleared his throat. "She'd love you to come visit—when the season's over, of course. I just mean there's no need to head back to the cabin. You could come here for the summer."

I'd rather dip my left testicle in molten lava.

His reaction horrified him. Why did the thought of spending time with his brother's family make him physically ill? Almost three years later, and his body was still in charge of his heart.

"Let's play it by ear. Listen, I'm on my way out with the guys. Tell Carrie congrats and—just, congrats. And hi to the kids."

"Sure, Gun—"

Gunnar hung up and started walking. His heart was

pounding, the air was soup, his scalp prickled with the heat of the still-warm evening sun.

After a couple of minutes he stopped and looked around. He'd walked in the wrong direction, away from the coffee shop where he was supposed to meet Angel.

He hauled in a breath, then another, and tried to calm his pulse rate. Nothing doing. The people walking toward him were watery blurs, then invisible as darkness edged out the light. A stumbled few feet further, he turned into an alley, just to get off the street.

He raised one fist to the wall and held it there, trying for balance while filling his lungs. He'd always assumed he had a decent pair. Hell, he'd bellowed the fuck out of them when he was trapped in that car, trying to get the attention of anyone driving by. Anyone who would save his family, because he was incapable of doing it himself.

How had he thought he was ready to meet someone new? Because let's face it, that's what he was doing. Angel had become important to him, and here he was, hoping that this connection he had with her could be built upon. He could fool himself that it was a casual meet-n-greet, but no. He couldn't even hear the news about his brother's new baby without having a meltdown. Couldn't find a sliver of joy in his heart for these good tidings.

And now he wanted to meet this woman who was propping him up by text to do what exactly? Use her to make himself feel better?

Can't do this. Can't fucking do this. Just. Can't.

Gunnar stood there for a while, breathing himself out of his panic attack. His pulse rate slowed. His vision returned. And his heart, that useless fist of muscle? It turned a little harder because that's what he would need to get through this.

Scrubbing a hand through his hair, he stepped back into civilization. Then he flagged a cab and headed back to the hotel.

June

"HOW LONG WAS I OUT?"

Kelly reached her hands up to the roof of the SUV and pressed her palms there, earning the stretch. I could almost hear the subtle shifts in her spinal column as she forced her body awake.

"Only an hour."

She glanced at the car's clock. "More like three. You should have woken me to take over."

"I don't mind driving. Gives me time to think."

She smiled, knowing I liked these moments to organize my thoughts. We'd been married for seven years, right out of college, and together for the full three years before that. I met her at a frat house party, though a quality woman like her shouldn't have looked twice at a bruiser like me.

"You're a hockey player?" she'd asked, not with the usual gush I'd become accustomed to when meeting women for the first time at Vermont. Kelly was a studious type, a brainiac, pre-med, and resolutely unimpressed by jocks.

"That's my side gig," I'd said. "I'm pre-law in case it doesn't work out."

But it had worked out. Drafted number five straight into the LA Quake. Assistant captain by year three, full captaincy by year five. No Cup yet, though we'd come close this year, only to be denied a conference finals berth. Our top D-man, Theo Kershaw had an aneurysm on the ice that knocked him on his ass and threw off our dynamic.

But the team, and Kershaw, would rebound. In the off-season, I wanted to enjoy my ten weeks of down time with my wife and terrors—sorry, angels. We'd spent the first month at home in LA, grilling and chilling. Now we were road-tripping, on a slow ride north from LA to San Francisco on the Pacific Coast Highway. Today was July 4th, so traffic was a little denser than usual.

Danny was asleep, making soft, snuffling snoring noises. I checked the mirror, but I couldn't see him. Why couldn't I see him?

Janie let out a huge sigh, distracting me from the mystery of why Danny wasn't in my sightline. She might be his twin but she was determined to be the opposite to him in everything. Louder, funnier, a total daddy's girl. She caught me spying on her.

"Hi, Daddy."

"Hi, baby."

"I'm not a baby. I'm four."

Kelly smothered a chuckle.

"I know you're not," I soothed. "But you're my favorite girl so I can't help thinking that."

Janie considered for a second, then accepted this as her right. Kelly wiped her brow and mouthed "Phew!" Tantrums were a relatively new thing.

"How far to the lodge?" Our next stop was a luxury cabin in Big Sur.

I checked the GPS map on the phone, clipped to the dash. "About forty minutes."

"I can't wait to hit that hot tub." Kelly reached over and squeezed my thigh. "Of course, I might fall asleep before these two."

I smiled through the beard I should have shaved off once our season ended. Kelly liked how it felt against her thighs, and I liked how she tasted on my lips.

"I'll keep you awake, honey."

"I don't know. One glass of wine and a bedtime story for these two ..."

"I have ways, Kel. Let me take care of it."

She gave a small moan of appreciation, and dammit, I was hard already, thinking about fucking my beautiful wife in a hot tub. I was one lucky sonofabitch.

"Maybe, we'll work on Number Three," I said.

"There goes my lady boner."

I wanted more kids. Kelly wasn't sure, given that she was left holding them while I travel so much. But I could bring her around. I had ways.

Traffic was more spread out along this section and I slowed down as the curves of the road turned more winding than before. Though it was only about 6pm, the road ahead appeared dim, the usual summer evening light fighting to filter through the trees flanking us on either side. It was a surprise when the flash of a car's headlights in my rearview momentarily blinded me. The guy had come out of nowhere and was obviously in a hurry.

Tough. He'd have to wait until we got to a straighter stretch to overtake me.

He didn't like that. He made sure I knew with a slam on his horn.

I kept the same speed, steady as she goes. Asshole stayed right on my tail.

Kelly looked over her shoulder, her brow ridged with concern. "Someone's not happy."

"Screw him."

"Gunnar ..."

"He'll survive the next couple of miles."

But that wasn't good enough. Less than a minute later, he spotted a window to pass. He sped up, so I slowed down, suddenly acutely aware of my precious cargo and anxious to get him out of my hair.

It happened so fast. Lights ahead. An oncoming car. Shit. My tailgater jerked back into the right lane ahead of me and barely missed clipping my SUV. I swerved to avoid the inevitable.

No one got hit, thank Christ. But I'd overcorrected, off the road and through a gap between the trees. The lights on the road behind us dimmed, then went dark as we dropped at a sheer angle. We slammed into something—a rock or a tree or a bank of dirt, maybe—and came to a halt. The airbags went off, plastic clouds that knocked the wind out of me.

Instinctively, I reached for Kelly. "You okay?"

She nodded slowly, her head swiveling to take in the twins. Wherever we'd landed was darker than the road.

"Daddy, we crashed," Janie said.

"Just a little bump, baby—"

The car jerked forward, its stop merely temporary, and now we were plunging down, down, down—

Gunnar shot up in the bed, sweat-drenched hair in his eyes, his cheeks soaking wet. Not sweat. Never sweat.

He swiped at his face and tunneled fingers through his hair. Once he'd signed onto the Rebels and moved to Chicago five months ago, he'd stopped having the dreams, his brain more focused on his new team and working his way back to form. Getting into a routine—training, practice, travel, games, hanging with the boys—had driven those demons out. Now with the season over, they'd come back, not just with a vengeance but pissed to all mighty. Returning to the cabin, the refuge he'd sought after his life imploded, was too tempting for his subconscious.

Maybe he wanted the dreams.

Maybe he needed them because he was in danger of forgetting.

Why couldn't he see Danny in the backseat? That was new.

In a fugue, he picked up his phone. A little after six a.m. and already two texts from Kershaw. Since the season's end, his Rebels teammate had taken it upon himself to check in with a 'wakey, wakey, rise and shine' text every morning. Usually it was a link to a video of cats being assholes or a flash mob in a train station in Europe.

Gunnar rarely responded to his texts. Kershaw could see he'd read it, which apparently was sufficient to convince him that Gunnar was okay.

He checked the latest message, a thirty-second clip of a community college version of that showstopper number from *Cats*. Toward the end, Theo's voice could be heard in a stagey whisper. "Double-O, this is only the rehearsal. There'll be a ticket at the box office for the opening and I know Aurora would love to see you there."

Sure, an amateur version of *Cats* starring Kershaw's grandmother was exactly what he needed to pull him back to the Midwest long before the season started. No thanks.

Nothing from Angel this morning, but then he hadn't heard from her in a couple of weeks. It was strange how reliant he'd become on those morning funnies, the opening they created, and even stranger how much he missed them.

He was trying to give her a space after she mentioned she had some family stuff going on. She could have talked to him about it. God knows he'd unloaded on her often enough.

He swung heavy legs out of bed and headed to the bathroom to take care of business. One look in the mirror took him this close to smashing the thing. He needed to shave but the beard partially covered his scar, not that the bullfrogs and bats cared what he looked like.

It was weird to be back to the cabin. In those early weeks in Chicago, he hadn't spent much time on the ice but by the time they made the playoffs, Coach had seen the light and given him the shifts he needed. They'd lost to the Edmonton Chucks in the conference finals. A decent showing by all accounts, given that the Rebels weren't quite as exalted as they once were.

The next day, he was on a plane to Logan. Away from Chicago and the media and people. So he was a surly prick. He wouldn't apologize for it and no-one would call out the grieving widower. Win-win.

He headed to the counter and started the coffee. The cabin wasn't exactly luxury—no hot tubs, four-poster beds, or even a wireless router. A cell tower nearby kept his phone connected, if need be.

The scent of coffee activated the sleep neurons in his brain, and by the time he'd downed half a cup, he felt human again, or an approximation of one. The day stretched out ahead. He had firewood to chop, a gutter to replace, chores to do. Like Little House on the Prairie, but with alcohol and swearing. He'd probably go for a run in the woods later, to kill time and counterbalance the cell death from the ethanol.

A couple of hours later he'd hit his push-up quota,

dunked a couple of chicken breasts in a lime-cilantro mari-
nade, and was whisking eggs for second breakfast when his
phone rang. Recognizing the name, his curiosity bested him
enough to answer it.

"Isobel."

"Hey, Gunnar." Co-owner with her sisters of the Rebels,
Isobel Chase was a great player, whose career was stunted
by injury before she inherited the team with her sisters.
She'd married Russian powerhouse left-winger and Rebels
captain, Vadim Petrov, and now provided skating consul-
tancy for the Rebels. "How goes it at your serial killer
cabin?"

"At my what?"

"That's what Kershaw calls it."

Of course. Angel called it his Unabomber Hideaway, and
the thought of her warmed a spot in his chest. "It's the
perfect, cozy spot for planning murders and cataloging
human specimens."

"Awesome. I'll get right to the point. I need you in
Chicago."

"Pretty sure my contract says you have to give the players
the summer off."

"It doesn't but I can understand why you'd assume your
time was your own instead of your ass being mine."

His mouth curved. He didn't know Isobel well but he'd
always enjoyed her direct approach. "Does your husband
know you're talking about my ass?"

"He loves when I get mouthy about my ownership of the
team he captains. It's a good bedroom dynamic."

"TMI, Isobel."

She laughed, and a flash of those mischievous green
eyes she shared with her sisters popped into his mind. "Now
that I have you squirming, here's what I need. You know I

run the youth hockey camp at Rebels HQ. We usually have a couple of the players visit and spend time with the kids, just a few hours, but we're short one. Kaminski's wife kicked him in the nuts, threw him out, and he's useless. Kershaw's more involved this summer and he suggested you."

Theo Fucking Kershaw. Was there any man's business he didn't think worthy of sticking his nose in?

"Don't you have a couple of brothers-in-law and a husband who could fill in?"

"Vadim had knee surgery and needs a lot of handholding. Kind of being a big baby about it, to be honest. I'd ask Remy or Bren but uh, they're sort of, well, oldsters." At his snort, she hissed, "Don't tell them I said that! Basically, we need someone on the current roster who the kids would recognize. Most everyone else has left town for the summer—"

"As have I."

"Kind of lonely up there, I bet."

"Just how I like it." Was it, though? The dreams were definitely worse when he was alone. Neither was he feeling exactly useful. Rudderless was the word that came to mind.

"That's what all the crazed murderers say."

He played along. "I probably should get back to fixing the gutters in my serial killer cabin."

"For better blood flow and clean-up. Understood." Before he signed off, she jumped in with, "Don't say no immediately, Gunnar. If you find yourself at a loose end, think it might be fun to bond with your teammates, and want to show a future generation how it's done, I will love you forever."

"Not one of those three things is likely to happen. I've no plans to return to Chicago before training camp in August." But the words sounded hollow and Isobel knew it.

"La la la, I can't hear you and if I can't hear you, it means you haven't said no. I'll let you sleep on it and will check in tomorrow. Have fun with your gutters!" She hung up.

TWO MINUTES LATER—LIKE the man knew Isobel had called, or worse, she'd called and told him—Theo was making his case. "Are you deliberately ignoring me, Double O?"

Gunnar sighed. "Hardly. I'm talking to you now, aren't I?"

"So, has Iz summoned you to the Big Smoke?"

"You know she has. I'm not going."

"What? I already told Jason you'd be here! He's a big fan of yours."

Jason was Theo's twelve year old half-brother. They'd recently connected in typically soap-operatic fashion. "I thought he was a big fan of *yours*."

"That goes without saying, but he has access to me all the time. He'll be at hockey camp and he'd like to meet you and get some pointers from a kick-ass center. That's you."

"Way to lay it on thick, Kershaw."

"Dude, usually I'd be back home with my gran in Saugatuck, but I'm in the city because one, my lovely lady is with child and wants to be close to her OB and two, I've signed on to indoctrinate the kids' minds with my unbelievable skillset. I need a wing man, man!"

"Get Hunt."

"He's in wedding planning mode, which is another reason why you'll need to come back." One of their teammates, Levi Hunt was tying the knot in July. Gunnar was looking forward to not attending. "We have to get him shitfaced for his bachelor party. Again, I need someone to help me plan all this."

"He picked you as his best man?"

Theo went quiet. The blissful moment passed too soon. "Nah, he's got some army dude lined up, but you know he'll be useless. No one knows better than me how to throw a good party. So, you'll need to be in town for Hunt's bachelor shindig and wedding, my gran's production of *Cats*, the musical, and the hockey camp. Oh, and the big Fourth of July cookout at Chase Manor." Gunnar envisioned Theo counting all this out on his fingers. "I don't know why you aren't on a fucking plane as we speak. Here, talk to Ellie."

Gunnar suppressed a groan. He liked Elle but he didn't need the soft cajole of a woman. He'd much rather read the acerbic texts of his guardian angel. He hoped she was okay. He worried about her.

Elle came on. "Gunnar? You okay?"

"I'm fine. I should be asking you how it's going." To say the pregnancy had been eventful so far was somewhat of an understatement. But then this was Kershaw Country.

"All good. My back's sore and I can't drink and Theo could really do with some time out of the house, if you know what I mean."

"Hey!" Theo's objection was loud and pointed.

"How's the serial killer cabin coming along? Got nice drapes?"

"All the better to hide my crimes." He was starting to enjoy the joke.

Elle laughed. "Wouldn't it be more fun to hang with your Rebels pals and bond this summer, pun intended?"

"You must really want to distract your guy, huh?"

"Desperately!"

Another *hey* cut across the line, then the sound of a minor scuffle from which Kershaw emerged victorious.

"Please ignore my woman. Her hormones are all over

the place. I'm officially inviting you to be my right-hand educator of the youth during hockey camp. As well as getting to enjoy my most excellent company, you'll also get to see Cats! On stage! Which my grandmother assures me is much better than the movie."

Gunnar shut his eyes. His brother wanted him to stay with them but he couldn't be around all that joy, not with his little ones so close to the ages of the ones Gunnar missed more each day instead of less. He really should be resisting this offer from Chicago but in truth, he liked Kershaw. He was a little tired of his own company, which would have been tolerable if Angel had texted recently. But she hadn't and he was living in a cabin fit for a serial killer.

He was probably going to regret this. "I'll see you in a couple of days."

He ended the call on Kershaw's whoop.

8

Four years.

Even her father's lawyer was surprised. Apparently paying most of the money back, the loss of her father's wife, and the minor child he needed to provide for weren't enough to keep him out of prison. One year, suspended, the lawyer had expected. Four years was a shock.

But not the only one of the day. As soon as Sadie returned from the sentencing to the house in Andersonville, Mrs. Braithwaite, the imperious British nanny/housekeeper had left for good, citing her unpaid salary and general "lack of respect." Sadie couldn't disagree with her. No one should have to work for free.

Sadie looked up at the cathedral ceiling. The house where she had grown up had an eerie quiet, its once buoyant life force dampened to dust. Her father's assets were frozen; the property would be sold at auction to pay legal bills and make restitution to the victims. Mr. Byron, the lawyer, had promised them three weeks, four max, before they had to find alternative accommodation.

Before the sentencing, Sadie's father had reached out—

through his lawyer—and asked that she be on hand "in case." Well, *in case* was here. Sadie was on the hook for Lauren's temporary guardianship, made more difficult by the absence of the redoubtable Mrs. Braithwaite. She had hoped Mrs. B would stick around to introduce, or re-introduce, her to Lauren. It had been nine months since she'd seen her little sister at Zoe's funeral, and then, she'd been stuck like glue to their father and completely resistant to Sadie's efforts to make amends.

Chin up, old girl! (as Mrs. Braithwaite might say) How hard could this childcare lark be? In a few weeks, they'd be back in LA and in the meantime, Lauren was old enough to look after herself. For now, Sadie would drive her places in the car not yet seized by the courts. Food could be ordered. Friends could be bribed. It would be a full-time job, but Sadie would muddle through.

Instinctively, she opened her message app, ignored the twenty-three notifications from Allegra, and scrolled to—no, she couldn't burden him with this. His life was turning around and she'd never been officially part of it anyway. Just a sounding board and a mouthpiece for smart comments. If she had a nickel for every time she'd thought about reaching out to him since she arrived in Chicago, she'd have enough to get her design business off the ground—or pay Mrs. B.

She inhaled a breath and walked into the living room. A brown, decaying Christmas tree, still fully decorated, leaned precariously to the left of the fireplace in exactly the same place the Douglas firs from her childhood had stood. The fireplace was filled with half-burnt and rotting wood and the place had an air of must. Otherwise the room looked the same.

She stepped around the high-backed armchair her

father usually sat in, only to be waylaid by a hockey stick. Looking down, she met the dark, mercurial gaze of an alien pixie shooting fire from behind a helmet with a clear visor.

"Hey, Lauren, how's it going?"

"You shouldn't be in here."

"Oh? Why?"

"This room's off limits. Even *she* knows that."

Meaning Mrs. Braithwaite, Sadie assumed. "Mrs. B's gone out so I'm having a look around."

She perched precariously on the edge of the armchair because the sofa was occupied with stuff. What looked like something moldy—*shudder*—peeked out from under a blue and white comforter emblazoned with the words, Chicago Rebels, and the logo of a sword crossed with a hockey stick. Sadie spied books, Pop Tarts, a half-eaten apple, Skittles, a sketch pad, pencils, an iPad.

Lauren liked art? Her heart warmed at this thing they had in common. Maybe this could work.

"Lauren, I'm going to be around for a bit while we sort out next steps."

Her sister stared with the dark silver eyes they both shared with Jonah Yates. Her gaze dipped down, taking in Sadie's sober courtroom attire: a midnight blue vintage fifties style full skirt with a white wide-lapel blouse, which contrasted nicely with her red-gold hair. With her own designs, she usually went with brighter, bolder colors, that absorbed and reflected the Cali sunshine. Not here. Chicago Sadie needed to look the part and be respectful of the people her father had hurt.

"Is Dad in prison?"

Lying would be pointless. "For now. His lawyer is going to do his best to get him out but it might be a few weeks."

And in the meantime, your home will be sold from under you, decaying Christmas tree or not.

"You're staying?"

"Of course I am!"

"Because you haven't visited before. Except when Mom died."

Sadie snatched a jagged breath. Kids were so skilled at loading on the guilt, and this one had every reason to be pissed at her older sister.

"I actually lived here when you were little. I left when you were about two."

"Why did you leave?"

"I wanted to do my own thing, find my way."

She nodded. "Dad said you were selfish and didn't give us a second thought."

Sadie wouldn't be speaking ill of the recently-incarcerated just yet. Round One to Jonah Yates. "I thought about you," Sadie said quietly. "A lot."

Look up *tween skeptic* in Merriam Websters and you'd get this young lady, right here.

Lauren had made a nest for herself on the sofa, a messy one at that. Something else Sadie noticed: this kid smelled. Her hair was lank and greasy, her clothes had a distinct mildew odor, and was that a sleeping bag on the sofa? Sadie flicked another glance at the tree. It was starting to come together. The first Christmas without her mom, and her dad had tried to make it as normal as possible.

Sadie understood that craving for stability. She'd lost her own mother Heidi, while her parents were in the middle of divorce proceedings. Sadie remembered the screaming, the slamming of doors, the threats to leave. When they finally accepted their marriage had run its course, it had been a relief. Sadie would live with her mother, try to make her happy, and hopefully escape the disdain of her father.

A boating accident on Lake Michigan changed all that. An inexperienced sailor, her mother died after a drink too many along with her then boyfriend. Sadie was thirteen, not much older than Lauren now, and left with her father who saw only the image of the woman who had cheated on him. Who saw only evidence of his own failure.

"How come the tree's still up?" *In June.*

"My dad likes Christmas," Lauren said, her voice hard with challenge.

"It's not going to go anywhere," Sadie assured her. "If you want to go to the bathroom"—and take a long, needed shower—"I'll make sure it stays here."

Lauren squinted at her, then back at the tree. "Fine here."

Sadie sighed. She'd have to pick her battles. Before she turned away, she spotted something out of the corner of her eye. Surely it couldn't be—it was! Benny, a small stuffed bear given to Sadie by her mom when she was little. She'd left it behind with her Chicago life and here it was, a connection to a past she'd thought long forgotten. With one eye missing and the red heart she'd stitched to his chest faded and hanging by a few frayed threads, he definitely looked the worse for wear.

It was like seeing an old pal. God only knew Sadie could do with seeing a friendly face right now.

"Looks like your buddy could do with some TLC."

Lauren snatched the bear up. "That's Iggy. Mom gave him to me."

No, I did. And he'd reinvented himself with a name change. *Good for you, Benny.*

Now wasn't the time to argue about the provenance of a

ratty toy, not while Lauren glared at her from beneath dark matted tresses, shunning Sadie's efforts to connect.

There would be plenty of time to bond. Four years, in fact.

"BUT WON'T THERE BE AN APPEAL?"

Sadie's friend, Peyton managed to look prettily annoyed on the FaceTime call while Sadie kept half an eye on Lauren. Slashing through the air with her hockey stick, she was doing a decent impression of Rey's training montage from *The Last Jedi*. Sadie swore she heard the faint cries of cute porgs.

Seated in her father's high-backed armchair, Sadie absently flipped through papers on side table—bills, bills, and more bills—and tried to ignore the framed photo of her father on his wedding day to Zoe. The family's dog, a tobacco-colored Great Dane called Cooper, ambled in, sniffed at Sadie's knees, then lay down as if she was the master of the house. She remembered him as a gangly pup. *We all get old, buddy.*

Sadie refocused on the phone call. "His lawyer didn't sound too hopeful." With a quick glance at Lauren, Sadie wandered out of the living room and into her father's study, leaving her sister to get her cardio in by slashing at lamps. The dog shuffled in behind her, showing his age. He had to be at least eleven years old.

She sat in her father's leather chair while the scents of her childhood filled her lungs. Cigars and Creed cologne. "The evidence was pretty cut and dried. The appeal before the sentence was denied, so now the only thing might work is to appeal the harshness of it because of Dad's grief over losing Zoe."

"Yeah, but they must have taken that into consideration already."

Sadie agreed but she was scrambling for optimism. "Maybe. Whatever happens, Lauren needs care now."

"So your father was forced to give you guardianship. Quite the turn up after he tried to keep you away from your sister for all these years."

Sadie couldn't believe it either but she had known she'd be on the hook for Lauren's care if her father was incarcerated. Who else was there? The notion that she was in a parental position to any being more sentient than a plant was mind-boggling.

Lauren wouldn't like the upheaval of a cross-country move, but she was a child and didn't get a choice in the matter. It would be awkward—they didn't know each other after all—but someone had to fake being the adult here. Sadie had her job to return to, a cute and expensive apartment in Del Rey, and a wardrobe she missed like a phantom limb. Not knowing how her father's appeal, if any, would go, she couldn't stay here indefinitely with her life in stasis.

Her father had looked at Sadie only once during the courtroom sentencing. After it was pronounced, he turned, his eyes glistening with more emotion she'd ever seen him show. Before the bailiff escorted him out, he said, "Don't take my daughter away."

My daughter, as if he had only one.

"He asked me to stay in Chicago and not to take Lauren to LA."

Peyton waved dramatically. "You're the one in control now, Sadie. What's he ever done for you?"

True. He'd never been a great father, always with one

eye on the prize, a standard that constantly shifted. A better wife, a prettier daughter, a bigger life.

Feeling antsy, she opened the drawers of her father's big mahogany desk. "I'll be here for a couple of weeks while I figure things out."

"What does Allegra think?"

Allegra's reaction to the news Sadie had to go to Chicago for her father's sentencing—and possibly more—was definitely on brand.

How am I supposed to survive without you for two weeks, Sadie? My business could collapse in that timeframe!

"I can still be her personal assistant from here. By the time she wakes up in LA, I'll already have half the tasks she assigns done-zo. I don't need to be on site to do everything."

But it would certainly help. Out of sight was definitely out of mind as far as Allegra was concerned. Being unable to reach her PA twenty-four hours a day would be disastrous to her boss's ego and Sadie's bottom line. Sadie needed to cultivate that relationship to maintain any chance of getting her design business off the ground.

Reading her mind, Peyton said, "And you have to keep in with her. Though she should really have done something by now. It's been almost a year."

"I know, but she's right. I'm not ready and I need a bigger portfolio of designs."

Peyton arched an eyebrow. She didn't have as much faith as Sadie when it came to Allegra's promises to talk her up to designers she knew. Her boss had shown pictures of a Sadie original to that woman in her book club but didn't get a bite.

The goddess knows when you're trying too hard, Sadie. You need to put out more positive energy and watch it come back to you.

"Maybe you can have some fun while you're there."

"Fun?"

Peyton wiggled her blond eyebrows—or at least Sadie thought she did. So hard to tell with her Botox smooth forehead.

"LonelyHeart! You said he was in Chicago."

Sadie curled in on herself, wishing she'd been more circumspect and never shared with Peyton that she was texting a lonely widower. Three months ago, she'd tried to put that positive energy out there, just like Allegra advised, by agreeing to his suggestion to meet up. *His. Suggestion.* A meeting *he* bailed on. Sure, something had come up at the last minute, but she knew the score. Part of her had been relieved. Keeping it in the ether meant they stayed inside the box they'd built to manage this, whatever this was.

"Nope. He'll think I'm stalking him."

She had already told him she'd be incommunicado for a while, ostensibly to keep ugly reality from intruding on what they had, but mostly because she didn't want to force him to make a decision about another meeting. Texting and lying about her location was too much of a stretch. Better to keep it all separate.

Peyton leaned in. "When's the last time you went on a date? The screenwriter?"

The guy dating "girls of all sizes" for his screenplay research. She *loved* when the getting-to-know-you segment of the date focused on her favorite snack foods. What a loser.

"Since that guy, I went out with the modesty sock costumer—remember him? He got up close and personal with Sam Heughan's best bits on Outlander." Great stories, zero chemistry.

"Right! So, you have some odd dating experiences. This should be no different. Keep Sadie weird! Maybe get some hints about LonelyHeart? A social media handle? A nick-name? Stalk him like a millennial, bitch."

Sadie laughed, glad of the release, then waited a beat. "It's gone really quiet in the other room, so I'd better check on Lauren." She bent over, taking her phone with her and checked the bottom drawer. Locked. Hmm.

"I know it's tough. You will get through this, and if you need any help managing Allegra, let me know. I can run point for you here."

"Okay, thanks. Catch you later."

She pressed finger pads to her eyes. What a nightmare. She put LonelyHeart and Allegra and her father out of her mind and focused on Lauren, who had gone through months of upheaval since her mom's death. Now here she was with both parents out of the picture, one dead, one in pokey.

She walked out to the living room, though this time Cooper didn't follow. When she looked behind she saw why —he was too busy taking a big old dump on the Persian rug in her father's study. Fabulous! She couldn't even leave it to Mrs. Braithwaite and the weekly maid service had stopped months ago.

Abandoning the stench with a closed door, she checked on Lauren. A lamp lay overturned on the floor, miraculously unbroken. One of the throw pillows was slashed, as if someone was looking for hidden treasure—or her father's ill-gotten gains. If only.

"Were you using something sharp?'

Lauren ignored her and continued carving up the air with her hockey stick.

"Lauren! What happened to the cushion? And could you pick up this lamp?"

Her sister carried on with the ninja demonstration.

Sadie peered down at Cooper who looked on the scene with a weariness Sadie felt in her bones, then promptly threw up like a champ.

Perfect.

~

THE NEXT MORNING, Sadie headed toward the Dead-Tree Room, her eyes unavoidably drawn to the beautifully-framed photos of the perfect family that lined the hallway's walls. While there were a few pictures of the three of them, most of them where of Zoe and Lauren together. The happiness was tangible, a bright spot in this sad house.

She pushed the living room door ajar and watched Lauren for a moment.

This kid was a stranger to her. Totally Sadie's fault. She understood that. Sadie reminded her father of her unfaithful mother, and for the years after she died, he'd only ever looked at her with disdain. Once Zoe entered the picture, they became a united force in building a bubble for the two of them, one that excluded Sadie. Zoe wasn't awful. She just didn't have the patience for a teen double-whammied with grief and puberty, and her priorities were clear. Her marriage and her newborn child.

Sadie had let her misery at being abandoned by her father poison her life for the last ten years. It had blocked any chance of developing a relationship with Lauren. There was no room for sibling love, not when Sadie needed all the space in her heart for bitterness.

"Hey, you okay?"

No answer, which was enough reason for Sadie to invade Lauren's space. No kid could expect privacy—that she remembered from her own childhood no matter how much she screamed at her father and stepmom.

Lauren sat in one corner of the sofa, a pencil in her hand as she shaded in a section on a drawing pad. They needed to talk about a plan for moving. Sadie would need Lauren's help to pack up the house before the auction in less than a month. So far she had left the living room only to use the bathroom or get food from the kitchen, mostly cereal and Pop Tarts, even though Sadie had made a gorgeous salad last night.

"I'm going to put in an online grocery order. Anything you want?"

Nothing.

"Maybe you can download the app and we can share a cart? That way you can add stuff when you think of it and I won't forget anything."

Lauren said, "'kay."

Progress! "So what are you drawing?" Art had saved Sadie as a child and her heart lifted at the possibility they could bond through this. She moved closer, happy that Lauren didn't make any effort to hide what she was working on. It was well done, a caricature of Disney's Maleficent, somewhat bloated yet oddly familiar.

"Who's that?" The words were hardly out of her mouth and she knew. Sadie, a fat Maleficent. "Thanks for giving me cheekbones."

Lauren's lips curled beneath her dark wave of hair.

"Mrs. Braithwaite left." Yesterday, but Lauren hadn't asked about her.

"Good," was Lauren's response, but then she looked up, her brow wrinkled. "I need my hockey gear washed."

"Hockey gear?"

"Hockey camp starts tomorrow."

Sadie perked up. Camp? That sounded like an overnight thing, possibly multiple overnights. With any luck it was already prepaid. Not that she wanted rid of her sister but ... she wanted rid of her sister. At least while she packed up this mausoleum.

"Where's this camp?"

"In Riverbrook, with the Rebels." Excitement tinged her voice, a significant change from her usual bored state.

"So, you go and stay there for a week or two?"

"Two weeks. You have to drive me there, every day."

Damn, a day camp. Riverbrook was in the suburbs. "I don't know, Lauren. We have to start thinking about next steps. Like going to LA."

"My life is here with dad. You're not part of it."

"It's not as easy as that. You're my responsibility now. Unfortunately I have other responsibilities, back home. My life is there and for a while, you'll have to live with me."

Lauren looked mutinous or like she was going to cry. Sadie wasn't sure which she'd prefer. Tears might be more liberating. Let them have it out.

"I'm not living with you. I'm staying here and waiting for Dad to come back."

"Could be a while," Sadie muttered and instantly regretted it.

Lauren grabbed a box of Pop-Tarts from a spot on the sofa and ripped it open.

"Is that the regular diet of hockey players?"

"It is of this one," Lauren said.

Sadie snorted. *Okay, hockey girl.* She needed to make a concession here. If Lauren wanted to do this camp, she could, but she would be doing her own laundry.

"You'd better find your gear, then."

9

THE CHICAGO REBELS hockey camp was run by a team of youth coaches, with the pro players dropping in for a couple of hours on one of the days. This camp was different because Kershaw specifically asked Isobel if he could spend the entire week of this session with the kids as his little brother had signed up. They were also a couple of men down in the trainers' roster. Despite what Isobel said, Gunnar suspected these kids wouldn't know him from a hole in the ice. He'd been out of hockey for years, kids had the memories of gold fish, and he'd had barely any skating time with the Rebels for the three months of the season since he'd signed on.

Still, he was glad to pitch in. He liked kids. He missed being around his own and even though these kids were older, there was something comforting about watching all that potential.

Jackson Callaghan, brother to Ford, the Rebels right-winger, ran the camp. He went through the welcome, the rules, and introduced the pros. "No doubt you guys know Theo Kershaw, Rebels D-man. He's here to help with blocking tactics and defensive plays. Anything to say, T? Try to keep it under thirty seconds."

"Yeah, good luck with that," Gunnar muttered.

Theo elbowed him affectionately. "Welcome, guys, we're thrilled you're here, and we can't wait to see who's got what it takes to go all the way to the big time. This lump beside me is Gunnar Bond, formerly center with the Quake, now with the Rebels. G?"

Gunnar sketched a salute. "Good to see you here."

A couple of the kids nodded, obviously shy at the notion of hanging with real pros.

Jax spoke up. "Okay, let's run some skating drills to get warmed up. I'm going to split you into two groups."

"Hey, Jason," Theo called out. "C'mere."

One of the kids skated over and accepted Theo's fist pump. "G-man, this is my brother, Jason. He's gonna be a defenseman like me."

Theo sounded so pleased, and Gunnar's heart checked, remembering that feeling. Pride in one's family.

Gunnar held out his fist for the bump. "Great to meet you at last, Jason. Your brother never shuts up about you."

"Really?" The kid's green eyes went wide behind his helmet visor.

"But then he never shuts up about anything, you know?"

Jason laughed. "Yeah, that's true."

Theo threw up his hands. "I'm right here, gentlemen. Okay, Jase, you'd better get going. And don't think I'm going easy on you!"

Jason rolled his eyes and headed off to his assigned group.

"He looks like you."

"Yep." Theo grinned and uncharacteristically, didn't elaborate. For once, there was no need. Things were going good for Kershaw, and no one deserved it more. Talking about your happiness had a habit of jinxing it.

For the next hour, the kids were put through their paces, mostly sprints, drills, and puck-handling. Every few minutes, Jax would invite Theo and Gunnar onto the ice to show them a particular skill, from circle skating to skating transitions.

Theo's brother was pretty good, with nice pick-up skills and a smooth skating motion, but Gunnar had his eye on a different kid: small, lightning fast, and way ahead of the others.

"See that?" he muttered to Theo after Fast Kid had yet again dispossessed another boy with at least six inches and twenty pounds on him.

"Yes, I do. Got ourselves a flyer there."

About half-way through, Jax set up one-on-ones and that's when it all went south.

One of the rules for kids this age was no checking allowed. They could get a little pushy but not overly physical while they were still so young. One of the kids—Fast Kid—went all in and practically mowed Jason down on his way to the goal.

Theo shot up, ready to defend his kid brother, and skated over with Gunnar following. Jax was already there, picking up Jason.

"You okay?"

"Fine. I'm ... fine." He sounded winded.

Jax skated over to Fast Kid and said something, to which FK shook his head and skated away. Jax followed, said something else; this time, FK heeded the words and skated back over.

"So, we're not checking during camp. This is a no-body-contact zone." Jax turned to FK.

"He got in my way," was the kid's response.

That was a surprise. Gunnar looked closer at the kid's eyes through the visor.

"You still need to apologize," Jax said. "No need to go at it so hard on Day 1."

"It's okay," Jason said, sounding as easygoing as Theo. "She didn't do any damage."

"She?" Theo jerked his head to FK.

"You gonna tell me I'm good for a girl?" FK said defiantly.

Theo grinned. "Wouldn't dream of it. We got any other girls here?"

Jax shook his head. "Lauren's the only one."

"You're pretty quick out there," Gunnar said to her.

She twitched her nose, but otherwise remained silent. Her right foot moved back and forth, a nod to her eagerness to escape censure. It had to be tough being the only girl in the group, though Gunnar doubted this kid would ever admit it. Show any sign of weakness and they'd be on her like vultures.

Jax would keep an eye on her but it wasn't his job to give special consideration to particular players, not in a group of twenty rambunctious tweens. Gunnar watched as she skated away, her head held high, her motion easy. She fronted well, that was for sure. Smiling, Gunnar took a seat back on the bench.

GUNNAR OPENED the sandwich that came with the catered boxed lunch. The future was bleak: two bites and this would be history. "Not sure this is going to be enough."

Theo shook his head. "Vittles for littles. Growing pro hockey players can't be expected to survive on this."

"Looks like everyone's fed. I'll grab us another one."

Gunnar headed up to the table the top of the lounge. There were three turkeys left and Fast Kid—Lauren—was hanging at the table, reading the ingredients on the box. Her dark hair had fallen out of a messy braid. Janie had loved when he braided her hair.

Shoving that memory deep, he asked, "You okay?"

Lauren nodded and returned to scrutinizing the ingredients.

"Not a turkey fan?"

"I'm a vegetarian."

"Well, turkey is most certainly not vegetarian. Didn't you tell them before you got here?" The kids' parents had to fill out forms with dietary restrictions before they arrived.

"My sister screwed up." Her tone was monotonous.

Gunnar called over one of the assistants and asked him to check on the food options in back. While they waited, he made small talk. "You play hockey regularly?"

"I used to."

"But no more?"

Stormy silver-blue eyes met his gaze. "You don't have to talk to me."

"I don't? Good to know. Hate doing stuff I don't want to do."

Not a hint of amusement. Tough crowd.

The assistant returned. "Sorry, Gunnar, we don't have anything, but we could remove the turkey from one of these."

"That's not the same. Don't worry, I'll sort it. Come on, Lauren, we're taking a walk."

Three minutes later, they cut through the players'

lounge and into the kitchen. Several of the guys were still in town—yet Isobel had recalled Gunnar, which he was starting to think was some sort of front-office-mandated-let's-fix-Gunnar shit—and came to the practice facility's gym to work out, so the fridge was usually well stocked. "You eat cheese?"

Lauren nodded while Gunnar made a Gouda sandwich with lettuce, mayo, and red peppers. Not the most exciting combo, but better than nothing.

Gunnar whipped up a chicken breast and cheddar combo for himself, grabbed a couple of water bottles, and took a seat at the high-top counter. Lauren sat beside him and picked up her sandwich. Her mouth twitched, but before she took a bite, she muttered, "Thanks."

"No problem. How come you went so hard out on the ice?"

"Just seeing what I'm up against."

"And what do you think?"

She eyed him over her sandwich. "None of them are as fast as me."

"True. Where did you play before?"

"At school in Wisconsin." At his eyebrow raise of query, she added, "Brenfort Academy."

Anything with academy in the title was likely a fancy prep school. "Good hockey program?"

Lauren shrugged and went back to eating.

Fair enough, the kid wasn't chatty. But she was talented, and that made Gunnar curious.

"Who's your favorite player in the NHL?"

She squinted at him. "Not you."

Gunnar laughed at her honest reaction. "Not fishing for a compliment, just wondered."

"Vadim Petrov," she conceded. "I hoped he'd be here."

"He's resting up after knee surgery."

"I heard he won't be back in the fall. Or ever." Evidently she took this as a personal slight.

"Knee rehab is the worst. He might still be back, and if he is, he'll want to be in peak condition for another Cup run." Though Vadim hadn't officially retired, the rumor mill about his fade-out was grinding hard.

"They haven't won big in four years. Everyone says this team isn't good enough for another shot at it."

The cynicism of youth. And hard not to feel slighted as part of "this team." "Petrov might have something to say about that. The last time he had to rehab, he had his wife training him. Isobel's a great player. You ever see her in action?"

"Yeah, on YouTube, from years ago. But women's hockey is going nowhere."

"Wouldn't say that.."

"When I go pro, it'll be on a guy's team. Or nothing."

So, Fast Kid had something to prove. He liked that. He liked her, despite the surliness.

"What do your parents think about your ambition to be in the NHL?"

It was the wrong question. Her face crumpled and a mottle flush overtook her skin. "I live with my sister. For now."

"Oh, yeah?"

"She wants me out of the house so she can spend all day with her boyfriend."

"I'm sure that's not the case."

"Yeah, it is. She doesn't know I hear everything she says to him. How I'm a brat. How she wishes I was out of her way." She took another bite, chewed it. "And she's usually doped up to her eyeballs, so I suppose all the crap she thinks about me has to come out."

Gunnar froze. "Doped up to her eyeballs?"

"Her boyfriend's a dealer. Pot's legal now but she'd rather get it from this loser. She drops me off, then goes back home to toke up all day."

Words failed him, and Lauren stepped into the pause, suddenly the chattiest thing on the block.

"Coop's at home, though. He's helpless. Needs constant looking after."

Gunnar's lungs tightened. Jesus, a baby being looked after by a stoned sister and her dealer boyfriend? That did not sound good. That sounded terrible.

"So tell me more about your sister and her boyfriend."

10

Sadie turned into parking lot at the Rebels facility twenty two minutes late. Allegra had sent her a long rambling, text-voice message of things to do, and Sadie had spent the last two hours trying to fulfill her mistress's bidding. Who knew purple roses were so hard to come by? Allegra had been most displeased to hear only lavender ones were available from the usual suppliers in LA.

It doesn't go with the theme, Sadie. This dinner party is supposed to be a celebration of Prince's life!

Wait until she heard doves didn't actually cry.

Sadie was skating on thin ice when it came to her job, but she just had to stall for a few weeks more. Pack up the house, pack up her sister, close the loops and cauterize the wounds ...

Another reason for her delay stemmed from a disturbing discovery she'd made among her father's papers. Getting a head start on packing up his study—still no joy on that locked desk drawer—she had come across an envelope addressed to her father, written with a Sharpie. There was something loud and belligerent about the handwritten script. Curious, she opened it.

Burn in hell with your dead wife, asshole.

Sadie's heart had pounded as she sorted through the rest, mostly bills and account statements she would pass onto the lawyer. At least three other envelopes had handwritten addresses, which was unusual enough in this day and age to put Sadie on notice. She had opened another.

You've ruined my life. All my savings are gone and my wife left me. May you rot in prison.

More polite, that one. No signature on either. Of course people would be angry at losing their money and the collapse of their dreams. While Sadie doubted Lauren would open the mail, she needed to do a better job protecting her. So much to think about when your life started revolving around a child.

Only as Sadie was leaving the house did she realize she didn't have contact numbers for the camp. She was failing epically here. She'd tried calling Lauren, only to find her sister's phone on the sofa among the rest of her detritus.

Outside the facility's entrance, she spotted Lauren sitting on the curb with a mountain three times her size. As they stood, Sadie's eyes came to rest very easily on this giant with huge shoulders, untidy, dark blond hair, and a full beard. She parked—sloppily—and jumped out of the SUV.

"Lauren, I'm so sorry! I didn't take the rush hour traffic into account and—"

"Doesn't matter," her sister cut her off. She turned to the giant. "Thanks for waiting with me."

The giant nodded, all his focus on Lauren, and helped load her gear, a big bag and a hockey stick, into the trunk. He even opened the back door, watched while Lauren clambered in, and cast a beady eye over the seatbelt situation, making sure her sister was suitably restrained. Okay. He muttered something too low for Sadie to hear, but whatever it was made her sister smile. A real honest-to-God smile! Closing the door, he turned to Sadie.

The full-on view was even better than the profile. He wore black sweat pants and a gray tee with the slogan "I like hockey and maybe like three people." Cute. Thick forearms were currently getting a nice flex on as he fisted his hips. Blue eyes rimmed with a hazel-gold fire stared back at her. His mouth was set in a stern seal that matched the scarring along his cheek, only partially covered by that hot beard. A story there, no doubt.

"Thanks for—"

"Miss, we need to talk."

Miss? That sounded rather sexy coming from those forbidding lips. "Okay."

Of course today she looked like one of Cooper's turds. If she'd realized she'd be meeting some hottie hockey camp guy, she'd probably not have gone with the baggy, spaghetti-sauce splattered tee that pronounced her 'CUPCAKE WHISPERER.' Not that it was even that baggy, or inaccurate. In fact, it clung to her generous hips and did not cover nearly enough of her ass, which were lovingly hugged by yoga pants. (The most action she'd seen in months.) The different-colored flip-flops were the perfect finishing touch.

If she'd shown up to work like this, Allegra would've fired her on the spot.

To compensate for her *just tumbled out of a bag of Doritos* appearance, she smiled at the hockey camp guy. It was her best feature and usually got her out of trouble.

"You're late."

The harshness of his tone took her off guard. "Excuse me?"

"You're twenty five minutes late."

She couldn't argue with that. "Are you one of the camp counselors?"

His eyebrow raise had a rather superior inflection, she thought. "Something like that."

"Well, Mr. ..." He left her hanging. Charming. "I actually have multiple demands on my time these days so I'm going to drop the ball on occasion. I'm here now so thanks for your time." Shaken by his attack, she turned to leave. He might be hot, but she didn't need this level of aggravation.

"I'll have to report this."

She pivoted, annoyed as all hell he was still speaking to her. The waves of judgement rolling off him almost flattened her.

"Report it? What business is it of yours?"

"When one of these kids is in harm's way, it becomes my business."

She could feel her mouth gaping. "Harm's way? I was twenty minutes late, you asshole. I know it's not cool but I'm juggling a lot of balls here."

"Boyfriend one of those balls? Or is he home ignoring the other kid?"

"The other ..." *Boyfriend? Harm's way?* She shot a look over her shoulder to Lauren, who was nose-deep in her phone, oblivious to whatever she'd put in motion. Or completely aware.

The lying minx.

When Sadie turned back, the giant was closer. He leaned in ever so slightly, which would have been pleasant if he wasn't such a dick, and ... sniffed. It wasn't one of those inhaling the fragrant scent of my lover sniffs, either. More like "is that an open sewer I smell?"

"What are you doing?"

He stopped suddenly. Cast a sharp glance at Lauren, who was doing a stellar job of avoiding his gaze. Back to Sadie. Surprising emotional range was showcased as he parsed a number of thoughts flying around his hockey lug brain.

She helped him get there. "Believe every word out of a twelve year old's mouth, do you? I guess training for the camp counselors is slacking big time."

He rubbed his beard, aw-shucks embarrassment transforming his expression from stern to sexy.

Then he spoke and ruined it. "Maybe I jumped to a conclusion or three there."

Worst apology ever.

"Maybe you did." *Great comeback, Sadie. Stellar burn.*

She turned away, furious with him, with Lauren, but mostly with herself for taking this crap. As if she didn't have enough going on. She was trying to do the right thing by everyone.

Screw this guy and the high horse he rode in on. Hot people thought they could get away with anything. Whirling to face him, she asked roughly, "What exactly did she say to you?"

"She spun quite a tale. Abandoned kids, high-as-a-kite guardians, drug dealer boyfriends. Apparently you're glad to have her out of the house to carry on with your, uh, activities. A social services visit might have been mentioned." He rubbed his mouth, clearly finding humor in the situation, and why couldn't she? "I should have known it sounded weird, especially the boyfriend stuff. Thinks she's too good for the rest of the class. Gets better workouts at her school."

He passed over the boyfriend comment so quickly, but not quick enough for Sadie. Anyone with two eyes, especially ones as amused as this guy's, could see that she wasn't girlfriend material, at least not how she looked today: too many pounds, a bit of a frump, a hot mess.

"Interesting. She'd have to actually attend said school and not be expelled for fighting for that to be true. What else?"

"What I said about you wanting her out of the way—"

"To spend time with my boyfriend. Right. That's the weak part of her story, the part that tipped you off. Because that couldn't possibly be correct, could it?"

His brows drew together. "I have no idea. I was waiting here and annoyed on her behalf and put two and two together—"

"And got never in a million years."

"Hey, wait a second. I feel like we're having two different conversations here."

Unbelievable. "I need to go."

He stepped forward. "I apologized for going off on you."

"No. You didn't. But I truly believe that you think you did, so I suppose we have that to be grateful for. Thanks again for waiting with her. Enjoy your evening."

She walked around the other side and with trembling hands, yanked at the car door handle.

"Put on your seat belt," she barked over her shoulder, even though Mr. Safety First had taken care of it. Then she left that parking lot with as much dignity as a woman in a spaghetti-sauce stained cupcake-themed tee could manage.

BY THE TIME she stopped at the Wendy's drive-through, she'd calmed down by about fifty percent. In the absence of In-and-Out burgers—stupid Illinois—she had to go for the next best thing because she had no intention of cooking.

May as well laze around getting high with her imaginary boyfriend.

"What'll it be?" When Lauren didn't answer, she turned around.

Her sister regarded her with suspicion. "Aren't you mad?"

Furious. "Why should I be?"

She shrugged, confused. "I know Gunnar spoke to you and you looked mad at him."

Gunnar. Of course he'd have some weird superhero Viking name to go with the massive shoulders, unreasonably attractive beard, and pillage-her-village attitude.

"Because I'm trying to cut you some slack. I can't stop you from having negative thoughts about me. If you need to lie about me because you can't think of any actual abuse, then we're probably okay."

Lauren looked out the window. "I don't want to go to LA. I want to stay here with Dad."

Sadie closed her eyes for a second. "Do you know what could have happened if that hockey guy hadn't spoken to me first? If he'd reported me to the authorities? If they believed it?"

"I wouldn't have to move to LA."

Grrr. They reached the ordering window. "What would you like?"

"Taco salad. No chili."

She put in the order for that—though she suspected a Wendy's salad was probably awful, serve her right—and a Baconator for herself.

"And a vanilla milkshake?"

"Alright." Only because Sadie wanted one, too. "So, how was camp, apart from the false abuse allegations?"

"I got into a sort-of fight."

"What?" The Viking could have mentioned that, but then he was too busy being a judgmental ass.

"I checked someone and they didn't like it."

"Checked someone?"

"Pushed with my shoulder. It's a big part of hockey but they don't like it when kids do it." She sounded annoyed. God forbid the child's desire to destroy was inhibited. "He's a good player, the kid I checked. Just not as good as me."

Sadie smiled privately at the tone of grudging admiration she heard in her sister's voice along with the confidence in her own abilities.

"That guy I spoke to? Gunnar?" The name sounded strong, like a medieval fort or eighty proof liquor. "He said you thought you were too good for this class. Is that true?"

"That I thought it or that I am?"

"Either."

"Both."

What must it feel like to be that good at something and unafraid to tell the world about it? Sadie had felt like that years ago when she moved to LA, filled with hopes and dreams, fueled by an urge to prove her father wrong. *Drawing pictures of dresses isn't a real job, Sadie.* The classic, *You'll need to find a rich husband to support you.* And the cruelest, *You're not unique enough to stand out.* After marrying Sadie's flighty and artistic mother, a woman who couldn't be tied down, he'd been determined to stamp out any of her mother's traits.

Perhaps he had. Ten years later, she had little to show for it.

She refocused on her sister. Coco Chanel in Heaven but was she smiling back at her?

"I'm sure we can find a school in LA that knows what to do with someone of your talents."

The smile vanished, taking the good vibe with it. "I'm not going."

Sadie drove to the pick-up window. "Let's try to end the day on a positive note. You're about to have a taco salad and a milkshake, you've established you're better than your peers, and you made me look like a drug-addicted crack-head. What a productive day for you!"

Lauren squinted at her again, probably trying to assess if Sadie was being sarcastic. She was but she was also being kind, which made Sadie a doormat, she supposed. Same difference.

Thank the goddess she had a Baconator in her future.

11

"HEY, what are you doing here so early?"

Gunnar turned to find Isobel Chase standing before him at the entrance to the Rebels practice facility. Tall and well-built, with a shock of dark hair tied in a ponytail, she cut quite the imposing figure, reminding Gunnar of her late father Clifford more than any of the Chase sisters.

"I wanted to chat with one of the hockey moms—well, hockey sister. If that's a thing." With the Chase family, owners of the Rebels, he supposed it might be. He was still confused about what had happened yesterday with Lauren's sister but he'd been married long enough to know when he'd stepped in it, rolled around in it, and ate it.

"Oh?" Isobel zeroed in on him with green, all-seeing eyes. "What happened?"

"One of the kids, Lauren, said some stuff about her home life that put me on alert and when her sister was late to pick her up I might have been a bit sharp with her."

"Lauren? That'd be Lauren Yates. Tough situation."

"It is?"

"Her father was recently sentenced to prison in some

major fraud case. And she lost her mother several months ago. Cancer, I believe. I was kind of surprised to see her name on the list. I was sure they'd cancel."

That sounded like a clusterfuck of epic proportions. No wonder Lauren had looked so wounded when he asked how her parents felt about her NHL ambitions. Right after that, she came up with the tall tale. *Nice work, Bond.*

The sister looked a good deal older so maybe they were only half-siblings. They definitely weren't close, judging by the way those lies slipped so easily from Lauren's mouth.

Something about the older sister had put him on edge. Not her defensiveness. That he understood. She came off as holding onto her pride by a thread, and not all that surprised to be the subject of her younger sister's fabrication. She'd expected trouble.

With her unmatched flip-flops, figure-shaping tee, and a chip on her shoulder the size of a rink, she'd certainly made an impression. Beneath that red-gold hair tied in a messy topknot, she'd looked harried and annoyed until she smiled at him. A great, hooky smile that had almost prevented him from screwing up. Almost.

Her eyes shone like silver stars.

He realized that Isobel was still speaking to him and he hadn't heard half of what she said while he was thinking of Lauren Yates's sister and her wicked smile and storybook eyes.

"What's that?"

Isobel frowned. "What did she say about her home life? We have a mandatory reporter status here, so if we suspect something is wrong ..."

"No, the kid's lashing out, trying to make trouble for the sister. They don't get along, which is one thing. And the kid thinks she's too good for this group, which is another."

"She sort of is," Isobel said with a knowing grin. "I remember what that was like. She has great skills for a twelve year old, but that doesn't mean she can't learn something. Maybe we can talk to Jax about putting her in the U14 group. Thing is, she'd get crushed by those bigger kids." She put a finger to her chin. "I'll take a closer look at her today and let you know if I have any ideas. We only have four days left but she's also signed up for next week's session as well, so I'd hate to think she's not getting the most out of it."

"Okay, I'll talk to the sister."

Isobel folded her arms. "I'm happy to take care of that. You didn't sign up for heart-to-hearts with the parents."

In this case, more like an ice pick to the heart. "I didn't sign up for any of this but someone dragged me back to Chicago to make me work in the off-season."

"Your boss sounds like a real asshole." She grinned. "I can talk to this woman you've pissed off."

Passing the buck was attractive, but he wasn't one for shirking his duty. "I made a mistake and I'd like to own it."

She looked a touch too gleeful at his admission. "I'd be the last person to ever prevent a man from owning up to a mistake. Good luck, G-man!"

"Ms. Yates?"

Sadie turned at the sound of a deep, rumbly voice, only to be greeted by *him*, the hockey camp guy. Where was a sinkhole when you needed one?

"Could I have a word?"

She exchanged a glance with Lauren, who she was pleased to say looked worried. She banished that petty thought. Last night Sadie had resisted delving too deep into why Lauren would so blatantly lie. Better to not know how much her sister must hate her.

"Sure. Lauren, I'll see you here at four. Don't be late, you whippersnapper!"

Her sister ignored her and went inside the glass front doors. *Whippersnapper*? What was she, eighty? She'd be handing out boiled candy next.

Hockey Viking loomed expectantly, waiting for her to speak. How refreshing.

"Can you make it quick? I have a lot of errands to run."

Next stop was a visit to the vet with Cooper, currently slobbering over the back seat upholstery. All that pooping and now, vomiting, had to be for a reason. As soon as she dealt with the marble statue in front of her.

Tree-trunk was more apt. Viking even more so. Olaf? No, that was the goofy snowman. The other guy, the broad-shouldered hero. Kristian or something.

"I won't keep you long. I wanted to apologize properly for yesterday."

Never mind that. "I heard she got into some sort of fight. And *you* didn't tell me." She moved closer, pointing a finger in the general direction of a defined pec. "Is my sister safe doing this?"

Hockey Viking stared at her. He was awfully handsome, even with that piratical scar down the left side of his cheek. Or perhaps because of it. That and the beard gave his all-American good looks an edge of danger.

And now she was staring.

As was he.

"Is she? Safe?" Sadie managed to choke out into the weird silence. Her skin was heating up while she was the focus of his regard.

He shook his head, like a man trying to wake himself

from a deep sleep. "She's safe. Being the only girl, I'm keeping an eye on her—"

"Only girl?" She should have known that, but she was too busy trying to pack up their lives and avoid the difficult topics. Guilt consumed her. Whatever Lauren had told this guy about Sadie's negligence wasn't completely off-base. She might not be hanging with a drug-dealer boyfriend but Lauren had obviously picked up on Sadie's attitude and internalized it. "She could really get hurt doing this!"

"She won't get hurt. There's no checking allowed and now that she's been warned, it won't happen again. If anything, the rest of them are in danger from her." This seemed to amuse him because child-on-child violence was hilarious, apparently. "You could stop in and watch a practice any time. See how it all works."

It sounded conciliatory, a way to soothe the rift between them and put her mind at ease about Lauren. But it didn't soothe her. It made her heart speed up a thousand times more than was safe. Only she wasn't sure if it was her worry about Lauren or the strangely tangible energy connecting her to the man before her.

"I-I'm kind of swamped with work. Maybe on the last day of camp. It ends Friday?"

He nodded. "And then the advanced skills session starts up next week, which Lauren is signed on for. Plenty of time for you to visit."

Lauren was hurting, Sadie knew that. She just didn't know how to make it better. Judging my her secret smile when recounting her prowess yesterday, Lauren seemed happiest on the ice, around other people who appreciated her talent. Having spent the last few years in boarding school, she didn't have friends in the city so the camp was a godsend, temporary though it might be. Sadie needed this to work.

"Sure. Anything else?" She knew she came off as rude but her skin was tingling and her heart was hammering. She needed to escape.

"Yeah. Isobel and I have been talking—"

"Isobel?"

"Isobel Chase. She runs the camp and is one of the team owners?" At her blank look he returned another critical one. "Lauren's really talented and we think that maybe she's bored with some of the stuff we're doing. A lot of the kids are here because they love hockey and exercise is good but very few of them have the talent and drive to take it to the next level. The regimen is pretty circumscribed by age group but we're thinking of ways to keep her interest." He paused and rubbed his beard. Good God, she'd play a gif of that over and over, if she could. "I understand she's had a rocky few months."

So he knew. She didn't feel his judgment anymore, only a quiet understanding that almost undid her.

"It's been hard for her. Still is. I moved here temporarily to look after her while we come up with a guardianship plan. She's my half-sister and I don't know her very well. The first order of business is getting her into school in LA. We should be there now but I have some financial stuff to tie up and I promised we'd stay for the camp ..." She stopped talking, realizing that she was babbling, but when Hockey Viking wasn't being a jerk, he came off as incredibly soothing. Something about those blue-on-blue eyes ...

Snap out of it.

"Anything you can do to maintain her interest would be fantastic." *But please stop whatever it is you're doing to maintain mine.* "I need to get going."

"Sure." He remained still, nary an eyelash flutter.

Her muscles felt heavy as his eyes landed like weights on every inch of her. She'd made more of an effort today, wearing a cheery sundress with flirty cap sleeves and a full skirt that flattered her curves. She was especially proud of this design, a homage (okay, rip-off) to a 1930s dress pattern she'd found on her search through vintage pattern books. Its warm green gingham was Rockwell Americana in fabric form. Not worn for him, though. Just so she didn't feel like a complete frump while she did the camp drop-off. She looked forward to Cooper puking on it later.

She walked around to the driver's side and pulled on the handle. And pulled. Her eyes were drawn to the car keys, currently in the ignition.

Ah, hell.

12

"COOPER, honey, don't worry. I'm going to get you out of there."

Cooper raised his head, a sliver of drool hanging off his jaw, not a care in the world.

Sadie tried the car door again, but the situation had not magically resolved itself in the last thirty seconds. The big dog was still locked in a rapidly-warming car. She turned to Hockey Viking who had dialed up the intensity and disapproval to epic levels. "This is your fault."

He tried the car door himself, obviously not trusting her to do that simplest of tasks.

"How is this my fault?"

"You distracted me the moment I showed up with your "let's have a chat" spiel and I took my eye off the ball for a second. A second!" She grabbed the car handle, this time taking in more details. The key in the ignition, her purse in the passenger seat, her phone peeking out of it like it was giving her the middle finger.

"Coop, I'm here."

Cooper didn't even acknowledge her that time.

"He's getting lethargic."

"He's not getting lethargic," the Viking—the useless, annoying, why-aren't-you-helping-Viking— muttered.

"My phone is in the car so could you call someone? Preferably a locksmith rather than the authorities so they don't take my sister and her dog away from me."

"Is everything okay?"

A dark-haired woman appeared out of nowhere. Great, another person on hand to judge. "Oh, hi, Gunnar," the new arrival said. Two hundred percent better, they knew each other.

"She's locked herself out," Gunnar said, with an edge to his voice.

"Oh, I've done that a time or five." The woman waved cheerfully at Coop, who remained unimpressed.

"He's been ill and I was taking him to the vet when I became distracted"—she shot a look at the source of her distraction who was now on the phone, speaking in hushed, non-emergent tones. Was she supposed to feel calmed by this? Because she ... didn't. Not in the slightest.

"We can always break a window if we have to," the woman said blithely.

Easy for her to say. Sadie couldn't be without the car for any length of time while she was chauffeuring Lauren around the suburbs. Broken windows cost money.

"Help's on the way," the Viking said a moment later.

"What kind of help?"

"Unlocking-door help." Cupping his face, he squinted through the semi-tinted window. "Sure, it's a grand adventure for him. And it's not that warm yet."

"Coop, you okay?" Sadie leaned in toward the window again, her arm brushing against the Viking's. A sizzle of heat she'd prefer to credit to the big, bright ball of gas in the sky coursed through her and she stepped away.

The dog gave her the sad eyes, which were better than the dead eyes.

"I can't believe this is happening. I just need one thing to go right today and you couldn't give me this."

"Who are you talking to?"

She turned to the oaf. She meant him of course but she didn't want to get into it with his lady friend present. "The universe. Ever heard of it? The puppeteer that pulls the strings."

There it was, that dismissive glare again. "You think someone else is calling the shots here? That's not how it works." He said that last part with a vehemence that surprised her.

"I know I didn't ask to be dropped into this situation."

Clearly she was projecting here. For "this situation" read instant parenthood. Her life uprooted. Everything she thought she knew overturned. Perhaps she was being dramatic but she couldn't see a way forward that resulted in her returning to her previous, stable existence. That life was gone. As she hadn't chosen for that life to be blown to smithereens, someone else must be responsible.

Her father. But she refused to think he had this much control over her destiny. She'd worked her ass off to ensure he did not, so to have her life upended by his mistakes made her mad.

A crowd of hockey moms had gathered. Sadie was glad Lauren wasn't here to witness this, but she could have done without the whispers slithering into her ear. She heard her father's name. When she looked, a couple of women held her gaze, but most of them were staring at the Viking.

She turned to him. "Who did you call again?"

"This guy."

A man in overalls appeared with a toolbox. Two minutes later, he'd unlocked the car and thirty seconds later, Sadie was hugging her savior—the toolbox guy—a lifeline in this cruel, unfeeling world.

"Thanks so, so much, Mr. ..."

The man blushed. "Dennis. I work in maintenance."

"Dennis, thank you! You have done a good thing here."

"Happy to help," he said with a diffident smile. "The lock shouldn't be damaged, but you might want to check. After you have your keys outside the vehicle, of course."

The Viking shook Dennis's hands, and possibly gave him something? Was that a hundred dollar bill? The last thing she needed was to owe this guy anything.

Sadie opened the back door. The stench hit everyone at once.

"Cooper the pooper. Of course." She looked around helplessly.

"I've got some wipes in the car," the dark-haired woman said, backing away quickly and wisely. This was also the signal for the rest of the rubbernecking crowd to disperse.

Gunnar remained at a stench-safe distance. "I guess your dog is stressed."

"We all are."

"Here we go! I'm Jenny, by the way. Jenny Isner." She handed off a large cylinder of wipes along with a brown paper bag.

"You're prepared."

"It happens a lot. We have a Border collie that's very highly strung. Let me help—"

"Oh, no, you've done more than enough. I mean, you've been very helpful already." Sadie grabbed a huge wad of wipes so she could return the container and not be obliged to have witnesses for her poop-scoop method.

"Sure," Jenny said. "Do you need the name of a vet? We have one."

"No, it's okay. I have one and I'm hopeful he can give him a pill or something." She handed off the container, and added politely but dismissively, "You've both been amazing."

So amazing that neither of them were leaving. Cooper decided now would be a good time to exit the car, which was probably not a terrible idea so she could clean up without trying to lift him.

"Hold up, Coop, I need to put you on a leash."

She found it and attached it, then looked around for some way to keep him tethered to the car.

"I've got him." Gunnar took the leash from her and her as-yet-unstained-by-poop hands brushed with his. Bit of a zing there, she was sure. Oh, Lord, why?

"Thanks," she said, only because Jenny was still here.

She cleaned up as best she could, all with half an ear to the conversation behind her. Something about a production of Cats, and a couple named Theo and Elle, and one of them being a diva. Jenny found this hilarious. Mr. Fun-in-a-Beard did not.

When she turned, she found him hunkered down, using the wipes to clean up Coop who had obviously rolled around in his own poop like the genius he was. Gunnar cleaned his hands with more wipes, gave Cooper a good old scratch behind the ears, and whispered something to him. Coop loved it, of course.

Sadie deposited the dirty wipes in the paper bag, which Gunnar took from her and filled with his own soiled cloths.

"I can show you where to wash your hands." He handed off the leash to Jenny. "Couple of minutes?"

"Of course. I'll keep an eye on him."

Oh. She had to follow him? He deposited the bag in a trash can, which was really nice of him.

"Uh, thanks." She was getting sick of thanking him when the words were not naturally formed on her lips.

Up ahead, he walked with a loose-limbed grace that came from being an athlete, she supposed. His sweatpants should really have been less tight because no way should she be appreciating the stretch of fabric across those taut, muscular buns.

Think about anything else. The dog shit she'd just cleaned up was the perfect antidote to the sight of a lovely male ass.

Thirty awkward seconds later, Gunnar pointed toward a door. "Here you go."

She smiled sweetly. "Thank you. You've been wonderful."

He raised an eyebrow, acutely aware of her attitude. Whatever.

Two minutes into a very vigorous hand wash, her phone rang with Darth Vader's theme (switched while here in Chicago as no way could she get away with that in LA). Allegra's face appeared on the screen, and Sadie answered her on speaker because she'd already let three calls go to voice mail on the ride over.

"Hi, Allegra, I'm—"

"Where have you been? I've been calling forever! Never mind. I need you to book my flights to New York for the Selfie Expo."

"I already did that a month ago."

"Yes, but did you get a flight for Ramon? He'll be with me to check my energy levels. He thinks they're much too low and that all this stress is the problem."

Sadie bit her lip and counted to three. Ramon had insinuated himself into Allegra's life as her chakra guru in the last three weeks, so no, she hadn't booked Ramon's flight before he was even present in her boss's life. If she had time travel as a marketable skill she sure as hell wouldn't be using it to manage Allegra's love life.

"I'll get on it. Business class?"

"I'm not going to have him sitting separately in coach, Sadie. I mean, really." Sadie could see Allegra shaking her head.

"Of course!" *Cheery, cheery, keep that smile.* Allegra had a sixth sense for negative energy. "Consider it done. Anything else?"

"Have you listened to my voice mails? I've told you all the things I need to happen today to make sure the dinner party goes off without a hitch. The liquor delivery hasn't arrived yet. Did you verify the time? And I have that meeting with that production company in Century City so I need you to call a car service for pick-up at 11:30. It's all in the voice mail, Sadie." She sounded exasperated.

"I know. I've got everything on that list and I will take care of it all, I promise."

Allegra tutted. "You know I still have my doubts about this remote working situation. I feel like your attention is divided, you know? I need you to be my right-hand woman, Sadie."

"It's only for another couple of weeks. I'll be back in LA soon and you won't even realize I was gone. We do so much of our work on our phones anyway."

"It's really not the same," Allegra said, sounding miserable. "But I suppose I have to acknowledge you have personal issues. Ramon says that your energy is probably misaligned. People with your kind of problems are usually magnets for bad karma. All this negativity in your life is likely playing havoc with your chakra."

I'll play fucking havoc with your chakra.

But maybe Allegra had a point. She needed to think positive, and that started with putting better energy out there. Bring the good to her. "Allegra, did you get a chance to talk to Andie's assistant about the clothing line? You said you, uh, might."

Andie Caswell was a full-figured model/influencer with a huge following and a quirky design aesthetic that matched Sadie's. Allegra had met her assistant at her candlelit yoga class and had dangled it before Sadie like a Magnum ice cream bar.

"Not yet, it's on my list," Allegra said, which Sadie supposed she deserved.

"Oh, okay, thanks."

"You know, you sound stressed, Sadie." Of course she did. Her world had imploded. "I expect it's not doing good things with your diet. We'll check the yeast levels of your punani when you come back and—"

"Allegra, are you there? I think this connection is bad. I can't hear you!" Sadie put the phone near a gush of water and ended the call.

Then she screamed, a Valkyrie yell that in an alternative universe would unleash hellhounds or mortal enemies. The mirror in front of her appeared to shimmer under the force of her decibel levels.

Gripping the sink's sides, she expelled several yoga-quality breaths. It did no good.

There was nothing wrong with the yeast levels of her punani, not that anyone cared to find out in a meaningful way. Allegra enjoyed having an assistant who could never be a threat to her in the attractiveness stakes. She rarely missed a chance to tell Sadie how she could be treating her body better. (Sadie and her size 16 ass were not part of Allegra's demographic.) Sadie didn't care. Happy with her curves, she ate and felt healthy, and looked good when she made an effort. Like today.

Neither did she care for the power plays Allegra employed to keep a stiletto on Sadie's neck. Holding the promise of her fashion contacts over Sadie's head and never quite getting around to doing that favor. But for all that passive-aggressiveness, Sadie needed this job. Keeping on Allegra's good side, especially as she now had to support another human in her household, was imperative. The last thing she needed was Allegra bad mouthing her all over town and damning Sadie's efforts before she'd begun.

Sadie spent a few more minutes scrubbing every inch of her hands until they were raw, then headed outside. Her new bestie was waiting, casually leaning against the wall with his hands in sweatpants pockets. The supremely masculine pose drew her gaze to his trim waist, strong hips, and all that action in his groin area. She couldn't help herself—his hands were right there!

She raised her gaze, the heat in her cheeks surely making her glow. He couldn't have missed that unworldly bellow on the other side of the bathroom door but nothing on his face hinted at a reaction or even an acknowledgment that she'd been checking him out. He probably had women doing that all the time, like those hockey moms outside.

He asked evenly, "All good?"

"Never better!"

Curt nod, which instinctively drew her babble to cover her awkwardness. Maybe they could start over.

"I appreciate your help out there. That was kind of you."

"Not particularly."

"Well, it probably goes beyond the regular job description of a hockey camp counselor. Is that what they call it?"

His expression changed to something like surprise. Had she got it wrong? She took a closer look at him. Shadowed half-moons bloomed like bruises under his eyes. He wasn't sleeping well. The scar on his cheek seemed more pronounced, everything about him exaggerated in both a worrying and beautiful way.

"Sure."

Why so cagey, mister? He'd had plenty to say when he was telling her off.

"So I wanted to ask a favor. You said that Lauren was good but she gets bored easily. Could she get extra coaching or something? Maybe personalized lessons?" Before today, before realizing that Lauren must be picking up on Sadie's ambivalence about being her guardian, she would never have dreamed of asking for a new way to throw her money down the drain. But she needed to do something for her sister. She'd take another advance on her credit card so Lauren could have this experience.

"I'm sure you could hire someone. Coaches aren't hard to find, especially for the right price."

"Could I hire you? It would only be for a few extra hours over the next couple of weeks because then we'll be gone."

"Gone?" With those dark blond eyebrows dipped in a V, he considered her for a long beat.

"Yes, I have to move back to LA. That's where I live and I'm only here to tie up some loose ends. Your services would be short-term. I just want Lauren to—" *like me and*—"get as much out of this experience as possible because I'm not sure how soon I can set her up playing in LA. So could you?"

"Could I what?"

Good Lord, the man might be gorgeous but he'd obviously been hit by a puck or three. "Could you give my sister Lauren—little diva, mouthy liar, bad attitude—extra lessons?"

"No."

She recoiled. "No?"

"I'm not for hire. I don't coach."

"Then what the hell are you doing here? Aren't you coaching the kids during this camp thing?"

He scowled at her introduction of pesky logic. "This is a temp gig. Coaching's not my usual job. I'm just helping out." He dug his hands deeper into the sweats. "Maybe I can find someone to recommend."

"Oh, could you?" Her hand shot out and grasped his upper arm, a cylinder of heat and muscle and fire.

His face crumpled. That was the only way she could describe it. Maybe it was what she'd been doing before she entered that bathroom, or maybe it was that scream that must have been heard all the way to LA, or maybe it was her. Whatever the reason, his discomfort at her physicality was genuine. Realizing her mistake, she drew back.

"Sorry. I shouldn't have—listen, I need to get going. Dog. Vet." She turned to leave.

"Ms. Yates?"

Could he not let her slink away with her last shred of dignity? "Yes?"

"Do you need help? At home?"

She blinked in disbelief and tried to speak but words refused to take shape. Was he for real? She'd just *asked* for his help.

"Isobel mentioned your situation."

The sainted Isobel again. "There have been a few bumps in the road but nothing I can't handle. And yes, I know how it looks when my sister hates me enough to pretend I'm abusing her or I lock a dog inside a car on a hot day or I scream like a banshee after a call from my crazy boss. Not all of us are blessed with a cool, no-fucks-given temperament like a Viking robot in EPCOT, if that's a thing, and if it's not, it should be. I might look like I'm losing the plot but I'm actually enjoying each chapter's cliffhanger. Go me!"

He stared at her, struck speechless by her outburst.

Immediate shame overcame her and she backed up. "I appreciate your help—and I'm not being sarcastic. That's the God's honest truth. I appreciate you keeping an eye on Lauren so she gets the best out of this experience. It's good to know people have her back. She needs that right now."

She walked away, listening for his sure step behind her. Go. Away.

"I didn't mean to imply you're not managing. I just know kids are hard enough for one parent—"

"Do you have kids?" she snapped as she spun to face him, her patience finally in shreds. "I mean ones you don't have to give back at the end of your work day?"

In the space of a thundering heartbeat, his face drained of all color.

"No. I don't."

"Then please don't tell me how hard it is! Now, you can get back to whatever it is that you do here. I've got this."

Jenny walked toward her with Cooper. She must have taken him for a stroll to one end of the lot, and that little kindness almost unraveled Sadie. Not the blow-up she'd had with Gunnar.

Trembling, she took the leash from Jenny. "Thanks so much. I really appreciate it."

"Any time. Do you live in Andersonville, by the way? I only ask because I saw the Ann Sather's box on the passenger seat. Love those cinnamon rolls."

On guard, Sadie said a cautious, "Yes, we live there."

"So do we! Lakewood and Thorndale. Maybe we should swap numbers. We might be able to work out some sort of car pooling arrangement. Jason said Lauren was doing the next session as well. If we're practically neighbors, we could switch off the kid drops."

What the hell? Were people gossiping about her, finding ways to be "helpful" to the tragedy-stricken Yates crew? She slid a glance toward Gunnar, who looked uncomfortable, like one of those whatchamacallit Gambini ice machine trucks had rolled over him.

"I've got it in hand, thanks." She knew she was deliberately misunderstanding this woman's likely benign intent, but she could feel everyone staring holes into her head.

Censorious eyes watched as she bundled Coop in the back seat. He could fill it with shit to the windows and she would not be stopping here a moment longer.

Then *he* was there. Right beside her. Gunnar opened the car door for her and when she stumbled slightly on the tread-board, he cupped her elbow, or rather her new erogenous zone. God almighty, it was the hottest thing to happen to her in months, even while co-mingled with embarrassment.

She shook her head. If she was allowing this critical dipshit to get under her skin like this, then she seriously needed to get laid. Because this was unacceptable.

His palm lingered. She pulled away and uttered a far too loud, "Got it, thanks!"

And then she drove off without another glance at his hypercritical ass, both the actual and metaphorical.

13

AN HOUR LATER, Sadie had a prescription for Cooper—fixable digestive issues, thank God—and she'd dropped him off at the dog groomers because some things were worth going into debt for. She needed a bath herself but mostly she needed a big glass of wine.

It was probably good that Gunnar had turned down her offer to hire him. She really couldn't afford it. After a few more calls to knock out Allegra's to-do list—apparently the dove-handler for the Prince party had brought gray instead of white doves—Sadie headed up to the attic.

The house would go on the auction block in mid-July after which the new owner would likely take possession immediately. That was three weeks away. Three weeks to wrap up several lifetimes. Gazing on the boxes, she was tempted to throw it all out into the alley dumpsters. After all, thirteen years had passed since she'd seen it.

Sadie wouldn't have been surprised if Zoe had thrown Sadie's belongings on the trash heap. Yet here were old diaries (mortifying), book reports (terrible), art scrapbooks, toys and knick-knacks. Even her Hello Kitty comforter.

Every remnant of her childhood was here, yet Sadie felt so distant from it all. She'd been shy and overweight, and wanted her parents to see her as the funny, bright person she knew was inside her, if only that girl could get out.

But her parents had been too wrapped up in their failed marriage to pay Sadie much attention. Heidi hadn't been all that happy with Jonah Yates, a man who thrived on fickle adoration and wasn't willing to work on his marriage. Likewise, Sadie's mom thought her husband was just another "working stiff." She liked the money, but she liked her freedom more.

Blinking back a tear, Sadie refocused on her task. She moved a box and ...oh. A small noise escaped her throat.

Her trusty old Singer, a gift from her mom on her thirteenth birthday before everything turned to crap. Heidi had recognized that her daughter's creative outlet of art should be encouraged in myriad ways.

She ran a hand over it, not minding the dust. The one she had in LA was a marvel of engineering but this one, fifteen years old, had fed her love of sewing and taught her so much. She might not be able to control her life, but she could craft a fabric shell to gussy it up.

Her phone rang with Darth Vader's theme. Sadie switched it off.

Back home, she found comfort by creating something, and uncovering her old sewing machine certainly seemed like a sign. But that was an old habit, a warm bath she slipped into when the world was beating down her door. What she really needed was a friendly ear, or better: a kind word or two.

She opened her contacts and scrolled.

～

GUNNAR WALKED into the lunch room and looked around, unsurprised to see Lauren Yates eating alone. She'd mouthed off at a couple of the other kids earlier on the ice, though Gunnar hadn't seen or heard what started it all. Either way, this kid did not make it easy on herself. Not unlike her sister, Sadie, which he now knew because he'd looked up the registration records. An old-fashioned name, but pretty.

The vulnerability she'd shown today had surprised him, and when she touched him, his body had gone haywire.

So odd. Women had touched him since Kelly. Hugs from family members or co-workers, even the odd fan in a bar. Nothing had set him off like this woman's fingers on his forearm. Like his body was a desert suddenly sprinkled with precious rain.

But then she'd shut down when he offered help, or maybe he'd shut down when she asked if he had kids. The question had thrown him, not so much because of the pain of the answer—the pain was always there—but because she didn't know. She had no clue who he was or what had happened to him. For the last three years he'd lived in a world where everyone knew his business and here was someone oblivious to that, who had no idea that he was Gunnar Bond, tragic hockey player.

He didn't know how to feel about that. Relieved, perhaps. Maybe even liberated from expectation. Kind of like how he felt texting with Angel.

He strode over to Lauren. "So you found something to eat."

She looked up, a curious flicker in her silver-gray eyes. That same spark he saw in her sister's gaze intrigued him.

"Someone must have said something."

That someone was him. He took a seat. "Not made any friends yet?"

"They don't like when a girl beats them."

She meant her speed and feints on the ice rather than physicality. She'd never win in a checking contest against anyone with an XY chromosome—at least not against older boys—but she was good enough to skate and slash her way out of trouble. He'd seen examples of it several times this morning as she scurried her way across the ice, zig-zagging like a demon.

He wasn't here to pat her on the head, though. "How come you lied about your sister?"

"I didn't!"

He threaded his arms over his chest. "She's not a pothead. She's not neglectful. Does she even have a boyfriend?" He found himself a touch more curious than he should have been about the answer to that.

"I don't know. But she wants to go back there when she could live anywhere. I'm not going to LA."

"Well, she had a life before you. So if not LA, what's the alternative?"

"Here or back to Brenfort."

"The school you were expelled from?"

Surprise that he had this information lit up her eyes. "They can pay to get me back in. Cassie Langdon set off fireworks in the bathrooms and got expelled. Her father donated the new science wing and she's back. No problem."

"Is that likely?" He knew Lauren's father wouldn't be donating anything to anyone anytime soon. This kid didn't seem like dim bulb; surely she understand what that meant.

Her next words confirmed she did. "They could give me a scholarship. I'm good enough for them to pay me to go there."

A solution that encapsulated sheer once-rich girl entitlement and overwhelming confidence in her abilities. Had he ever been that young and cocksure?

Yes, when he first met Kelly. When he was drafted into the league. No barriers existed, no problem could stand in the way of his future. He was talented as fuck, blessed with a woman who adored him, going places as fast as his skates could carry him. He had it all.

This girl had felt the same way once, not so long ago. Before her mom died. Before her father was ripped from her world. Now this sister she barely knew was in charge and she had no control over her life again.

Hell, he'd been there. He was still there, only there was here.

"I'm sure your sister has your best interests at heart."

"Are you?" Never had two words sounded so skeptical.

"She wants you to be happy." His family wanted the same for him. Kurt had left a couple of messages since he'd returned to Chicago, urging him to check in. Gunnar understood the push-pull of families who thought they knew best and wouldn't leave it alone.

"She wants whatever solves her problem the quickest," Lauren said, warming to her topic. "Right now, I'm her problem."

Pretty astute for a twelve year old. Every time he met a kid in this age group, he felt old because they were all so damn wise and knowing.

He changed tack. "LA has a good hockey team. The Quake."

"Yeah, better than the Rebels these days. You didn't play much this season." Her own problems forgotten a moment, she latched onto his with the precision of a sharpshooter. "Guess Coach thought you'd gotten fat and lazy."

Give these kids an inch ... "I was neither fat nor lazy. I'd just been out of the game for a while."

"Rusty, then."

"I suppose."

She took a bite of her sandwich and chewed. "Did you give up hockey when you were away?"

"For a while." He eyed her, wondering what she knew. The sports media had spent enough time on his story to take it from tragedy to the returning prodigal to what-was-the-point. They needed the Christmas tree topper of a good season to be sure he was worth their ink. "I lost my family and gave up on myself for a while. I know what that's like."

She nodded. "My dad didn't want to come to my games anymore. He kept missing them after—" She paused as some force got the better of her for a second. Only for a second. Kid was a fighter. "I figured if he couldn't watch, I couldn't play. Seemed pointless."

He understood that. The joy left the game for him without someone to play for. Someone to strive for. He wasn't much good at striving for himself.

"What happened at school to get you kicked out?"

"I hit someone in my class with a puck. She had it coming."

"Why?"

"She said stuff about my mom and dad. I didn't like it. They threw me out. Zero tolerance. I stopped playing for a while."

He raised an eyebrow. "Got fat and lazy."

Half-hidden behind her long hair, her grin was a slow burn. "Yeah, but I'm here now," she said quietly and with surprising force.

"Yep. Me, too."

ANGEL: *[gif of moving dumpster fire]*

   Gunnar: That good, huh?

   Angel: You wouldn't believe me if I told you. So how's your day going?

   Gunnar: Interesting. Surprising. All things. It's good to hear from you. Been a while.

   Angel: Good to be heard from. Sorry for the radio silence. Stuff.

   Gunnar: I've wanted to reach out but figured you needed space.

   Angel: I'm sorry. It's been a rough few weeks and today was peak shitty. Literally.

   Gunnar: Need to talk about it?

   Angel: Maybe? But first I have some news. Not sure if I should share.

   Gunnar: Uh, this vague-texting or whatever the kids are calling it will not do. Out with it.

   Angel: Okay. So here goes ... I'm in Chicago! For a visit. And if you're still in Chicago, I thought we could maybe, possibly, perhaps, meet up? Or not. I know it didn't work out before, probably for a good reason. I understand if you're not keen but I'm just throwing it out there. No pressure, I promise.

GUNNAR STARED AT THE SCREEN. He knew three things about Angel. She was a woman. She lived in LA. And she'd steered him through the worst period of his life.

He'd wanted to meet her since the beginning, almost eight months now, but he was too chicken to follow through the last time this had come up. Upsetting the balance between them was a risk. He liked what they had now, the intimacy of it, which was much easier to manage without looking someone in the eye.

But she hadn't been in touch for a while. He'd missed those daily chats. He'd missed his angel.

Theo sat beside him on the bench, one eye on the kids who were doing sprints.

"Who's Angel?"

Gunnar turned over his phone. "A friend."

That million dollar grin stretched wide. "A text buddy?"

"It's not like that. Neither is it any of your business."

As usual, Theo was incapable of taking offense. "I've been thinking of who I could set you up with but sounds like you might have it in hand. Better that than your dick."

Gunnar sighed. "I don't want you to set me up with anyone, T. I'm not in the market for anything."

"Not even a summer fling with Angel? What does she look like?"

No idea. The thought of meeting her made him uneasy, like he was cheating. And the weird thing is he wasn't thinking of Kelly—or not only Kelly. He was thinking of her, Sadie Yates.

Lauren's sister was a striking woman, with those fall-into-me gray eyes and that strawberry blond hair and the curves that would feel just right in his hands. The dress she wore this morning made her look like a naughty fifties housewife. He'd already imagined peeling it off her slowly. Or, given his lack of sexual interaction for three years, not so slowly.

Well, howdy, libido. Welcome back!

He hadn't thought about sex with another person in such a long time that the shock of it made him drop his phone. He picked it up, turned it over again in his lap. Of all the women he'd met since Kelly, why was he interested in the one who was clearly not a fan? Maybe their friction added to the attraction.

"Listen, I need a favor." At Theo's grin, he added, "Not that kind of favor. I need you to talk to Jason about making an effort with Lauren. Sitting at the same table with her at lunch, maybe even invite her over for video games or whatever. She lives in the same neighborhood."

That would make Lauren feel more included and might remove that streak of worry in Sadie's silver-starred eyes. Completely altruistic. He certainly wasn't doing this so he could find out what was going on under that dress.

Stop thinking about her dress or curves or great rack ...

Theo shrugged, not even questioning it. "Consider it done." He stood and stretched. "Come on, time to show the kids some of your moves."

Gunnar turned over his phone, thinking on how he wanted to proceed. Sadie Yates might be the stuff of wet dreams, but Angel had seen him through one of the hardest times of his life. She made him laugh and he wanted to meet her. No expectations.

He typed, ***Name when and where. I'll be there.***

14

SADIE SAT in the parking lot after the hockey camp drop off, scowling at the unrelenting perfection staring back at her. Not the Viking, though. An obnoxiously early riser, Peyton was showered, made-up, and already on her second soy milk latte.

"Hey, girl!" Her smile blinded from the screen. She really needed to lay off the teeth whitening. "When are you coming home?"

"A couple of weeks? I hope. The house is going on the block soon." She still hadn't told her father about the move, though he had to have some idea. Not that his new zip code gave him much say over how she should be raising his child for the next four years.

"I miss you," Peyton said, "and I'm worried you're sacrificing a whole lot of your life for this father that has never done a whole lot for you."

That stung a little—not the sacrifice comment but the jibe about what her father had done for her. True, they weren't close, but she couldn't abandon her blood. "Lauren's a kid and she's hurting. Someone has to be on her team and that's why I'm here. I just have to get her through the next few weeks and then find a school in LA that will take her." Did high schools have hockey programs or was that a separate thing? Another thing to research.

"Listen, thanks for helping me with the purple roses." Peyton worked at the virtual concierge service were Sadie had been employed before Allegra hired her. "And for vetting the new dog walker. I managed to keep my job. Just."

"You've got to be careful there. She could find anyone to take that position."

Maybe. None of Allegra's previous assistants had lasted more than a couple of weeks while Sadie had put up with her boss's mercurial personality for ten months. Theoretically Allegra could find a replacement, but then theoretically Sadie might beat Serena Williams in a US Open final.

She changed the subject to a topic she knew her friend would appreciate. "So I did it."

"Did what?"

"I set up a meeting with LonelyHeart."

Peyton perked up even more, though it should have been impossible. "No! You've been so against it. What changed your mind?"

"I had a rotten day." She told Peyton about Cooper and how she'd ended up elbow deep in dog poop. "And this hockey camp guy was there, one of the counselors. Mr. Judgment-in-Sweats, dying to weigh in with his opinion. I offered him cash I don't have to coach Lauren but he shut me down, then had the gall to ask me if I needed help. I asked you for help, dingus, and you told me to take a hike."

Peyton tilted her head. "So ... is he cute?"

"I haven't met him yet."

"Not LonelyHeart. The hockey guy."

"Oh, God no. He's the opposite of cute. He's like a cross

between an Orc and Ent. He has the big, brutish body of an Orc but he got some Ent genes, probably from his mother's side. Basically a tree-trunk with good hair."

Peyton's nose twitched. Lord of the Ring references were not her jam. "You've given this a lot of thought."

"He flinched when I touched him."

"You touched him?"

Not the point, Peyton. Even now, she cringed at the memory. "He said he'd ask around for coaching help for Lauren and I was so stupidly grateful at someone saying a kind, freaking word that I grabbed his arm. And my touch disgusted him! He has these very expressive eyebrows, kind of a brown-bag blond, and this scary scar, half-covered by a beard. Because of course, bearded. My Kryptonite. So it lulled me into a false sense of security, which had me accidentally touching him only to get the eyebrows and scar and lips all twitching in revulsion. I was mortified."

Peyton looked appropriately sympathetic.

"Anyway, I haven't had a moment to myself, but I've been thinking about taking chances, putting myself out there, YOLO, and all that jazz. If it turns out to be a disaster, I can chalk it up to one of those things that was never supposed to be, and not worry about seeing him again."

"Like any other date."

"Not a date." A brief flash of Gunnar Bond's stony stare froze her brain for a couple of seconds. *No, no, little gray cells, I will not think date and you will not return "Gunnar Bond" with a straight face.* The guy was a one person game of fuck, marry, or kill, minus the fuck and marry options.

"Sounds like a date to me."

Sadie sighed. "Maybe we should swap names before we meet. That way we can do our due diligence and go in with full disclosure."

Peyton shook her head. "No! This needs to be as blind a date, uh, meeting—" She added a theatrical wink. "—as you can make it. See if it's possible to build off that chatty text attraction. If you guys work out, what a cool way to say you met."

Cool? She doubted he'd appreciate his private tragedy being known. Neither was she thinking 'date' but the mere mention of it made her uneasy. What if she ruined the good thing they had going? There was a reason it hadn't happened already.

"So you had a bad day and to wipe the sour taste from your mouth you decided to reach out to LonelyHeart. That's pretty brave of you."

"Is it? I don't know. I might be reacting to the wrong stimulus here." She wanted to think her big life changes were driving her motives, yet her mind was full of a pair of blazing blue eyes that disapproved of her every move.

Peyton guessed right. "So Hockey Camp Hottie is stimulating?"

"No, my pearly-white-toothed friend. He's an asshole, and I'd like someone to be nice to be for a change, which is why I've reached out to my text buddy. He's sensitive and kind and wounded, so he's already 99% perfect. As a friend."

"You have friends. You need a man."

"Nope. My lonely texter-slash-platonic-soulmate will suffice. Kindness. I need kindness."

"Yet ..."

"What?" Sadie bristled, prepared to dislike her friend's conclusion.

"You've spent most of this conversation talking about the Hockey Camp Hottie and very little of it talking about how excited you are to meet your text buddy. Hormones will out, m'dear."

"Oh shut up. I'll keep you posted."

As soon as she hung up, the age-old doubts about being good enough tried to wheedle their way in. LonelyHeart was the only decent thing in her life right now and she wanted to ruin it by ... meeting it in *real* life? But she also knew that she was tired of standing still. Tired of waiting for life to happen to her instead of the other way around.

She was going to do this.

For the second day in a row, Sadie screamed so loud she might have shattered the ice on that practice rink. Damn, it felt good to let go and act against her safety-seeking instincts for once.

A small sound caught her attention and she turned her head. Jenny, Provider of the Wipes, stood outside the SUV. Oh boy.

Sadie lowered the window. "Hi, there."

"Hello! Everything okay?"

"I just stepped outside my comfort zone and it felt really good. And scary."

Jenny's mouth dropped open. "Oh, wow, congrats!"

As it was a day for moving forward, Sadie prepared to humiliate herself. "Listen, I wanted to apologize about my abruptness yesterday. You were so kind with the wipes and watching Cooper and I was a complete troll."

Jenny's eyes widened, lovely hazel ones with inky black eyelashes. "Not at all! You were understandably over-whelmed. How's your doggy today? Is he with you?" She glanced toward the empty backseat.

"God, no. I will never put him in a car again." No matter how much Febreze she sprayed, the scent still lingered. "He's on a pill regimen to help with his tricky tummy and is probably pooping the house to death as we speak. "

"Aw, poor baby!"

"Yes, poor stinky giant baby. I'm sorry I wasn't receptive to the car pool offer. To be honest, I wanted to escape because I was embarrassed."

"About the dog poop?"

"The dog poop, the dog, my banshee wailing, the gossip girls, that camp counselor being a jerk—"

"Camp counselor?"

"Right, the Judgy Viking." *Nice work.* Stepped in it again, and she didn't even need the presence of actual shit. "Sorry, I know he's a friend of yours."

Jenny's mouth quirked. "Pretty casual. I know him through my husband. Well, my stepson. Listen, do you want to go for a coffee? I could do with a pick-me-up."

Sadie had the attic to clear out, photos of her father's preferred family to bubble-wrap, and Allegra's groceries to order. "That would be great."

15

GUNNAR WALKED into a quiet Empty Net, playing the part of an off-season hockey watering hole to perfection. He raised a hand in greeting to his teammates, Levi Hunt and Vadim Petrov over in the corner before stopping to grab a beer from bar owner Tina.

She waved away his money. "Drinks are on your captain tonight."

Gunnar pulled out a chair and sat across from Petrov, who has holding court with his knee in a brace and up on a chair.

"Thanks for the drink, Cap. How's the knee?"

"Not as bad as post-op. Then, it felt like a million hot pokers were piercing my patella looking for a way to destroy me."

"It hasn't changed your tendency toward the dramatic, I see," a drawled voice sounded behind them. Gunnar looked up into the shining blue eyes of Remy DuPre, former Rebel and now husband to the team's owner, Harper Chase. He took a seat beside Gunnar, nudging with his elbow as he did so. "Good to see you, Bond."

Unspoken was the slight admonishment that Gunnar had not been much of a mixer these last few months. Though nothing sounded truly negative when said in Remy's warm Cajun tone.

Gunnar tipped his bottle toward Remy. Within minutes, the remaining seats were filled by Erik Jorgenson, the Rebels goalie, recent addition to the roster Cal Foreman, D-man Cade Burnett, left-winger Tate Kaminski, and Theo, who sat next to Gunnar.

"Okay, gentlemen," Theo said, his tone grave, "we're gathered here today to discuss something of prime importance."

"Cereal is not soup, Kershaw," Cade said.

"Not that, but it is."

Erik snorted. "This from the same person who thinks the meat should go in the taco first instead of cheese." Jorgenson had strong opinions on all things food, as did Remy.

"Cheese first, of course," the Cajun said, "so it's properly melted. Kershaw, is there any taboo you won't violate?"

Theo held up a hand. "I know in my heart what's right, DuPre, and you can't change what's in a man's heart. Now, what I want to talk about today is not food-related, though I'm guessing it might end up being because every gathering needs a good spread, in which case—"

"Move it along, T. We're not getting any younger," Tate said impatiently. He looked like shit, bleary-eyed and unkempt. Still on the outs with his wife, apparently.

Theo assessed him with undisguised pity. "Right. It's about Hunt's bachelor party. What are we doing and how fucking off the chain is it gonna be?"

Levi's brow wrinkled. "I'm okay with something quiet. You know, like this."

Several unquiet groans followed that. Theo gave a sad headshake. "You want to go against the wishes of the group, Gigi?"

Arcing a gaze over those seated, Petrov mouthed, "Gigi?"

Who knew? Theo's nicknames for people were often torturously byzantine in their origins. Gunnar sometimes went by G-man, which he assumed was because of his first name and Double-O because of his last, as in James Bond, 007.

"Perhaps he should get to decide," Erik said, not unreasonably, "as it's his final night of freedom."

This outburst of logic was dismissed as patently ridiculous.

Theo focused on Hunt. "The problem is this Green Beret buddy of yours, the best man."

"J-Bird?"

"He's from out of town, so how the hell can he organize a shindig when he doesn't know the players or the lay of the land or the best wing joints? You need someone on site."

"Yeah, like a local concierge," Cade said, egging Theo on. Remy shook his head.

"Exactly!" Theo pounded the table, shaking the glasses enough to have everyone grabbing theirs. "Which is why you should leave the bachelor party to me. I'll keep it classy and will not let you down."

"Aw, let the guy throw the princess party," Cal said, with a pat of Theo's head. Formerly a right-winger in Quebec where he and Petrov were a dynamic duo, Foreman had played Division One hockey with Gunnar at Vermont. He'd been on the Rebels injured reserve list for a couple of months. "What's the worst that could happen?"

Petrov muttered something in Russian, and locked eyes

with Remy, who despite his retirement had retained elder statesman status.

Remy said diplomatically, "You shouldn't have to do it all by yourself, Kershaw."

The big Russian raised an aristocratic brow in query in Gunnar's direction. That was a call to action if ever he'd seen one. Still, he kept quiet, not especially eager to play babysitter.

"Don't worry, we have an adult on the job," Theo chimed in. "Bond's helping me out."

"Oh, alright then," Hunt said with a look of relief Gunnar's way that almost made him laugh.

Before he could protest—and what would be the point? —his phone rang with a call from his brother.

"Sorry, got to take this." He stepped away and headed for the corridor that led to the restrooms, then canceled the call. Guilt churned his stomach. Kurt meant well, but Gunnar knew how the conversation would go. The awkward pauses. The strained patience. The unsubtle hints to move on.

The love was there, the chains heavier than ever.

He scrolled his contacts, thinking about Angel. They would meet tomorrow and he was starting to worry. About expectations. About mistakes. But mostly about how much he was looking forward to it.

It wasn't a date. He'd told himself that a million times. But it was a step away from Kelly—and that terrified the fuck out of him.

～

"DAMN, THAT SMELLS GOOD."

Dante smiled and stirred the fragrant sauce on the stove in his kitchen, then put a lid on it. "Wine or beer?"

"Whatever you're having."

Dante grabbed a wine glass by the stem from a rack above the kitchen island while Gunnar scanned the chef's paradise, loaded with gadgets and knick-knacks. The fridge door held signs of his life with his partner—now husband— Cade Burnett, the Rebels defenseman. Photos of them looking goofy together, magnets from cities they'd probably visited, a baby's ultrasound picture.

He mentally traced the blurred outline of new life. Dante and Cade would soon be parents of a baby currently cooking up in Violet Vasquez-St. James, another Chase sister. All very cozy, even incestuous. It was the first thing he'd noticed about the team dynamic when he arrived. One for all and all in each other's damn business.

There's the heartbeat ... ah, two heartbeats. Look, one of them is hiding behind the other. That's often the case. One twin is more dominant, even in the womb.

"A nice Cab." Dante passed off a glass, and Gunnar painfully hauled himself back from the memory brink.

"Don't know much about wine." Kelly did. Kelly knew it all.

"Well, I taught Cade and now he thinks he knows more than me. The confidence of youth." Dante flicked a glance to the ultrasound image, his expression even. "We're having a girl."

"That's great, man." He meant it, too.

"Surprised to hear from you."

"Because I've been so responsive to all your other invites."

"Something like that."

He and Dante went back to their days at the LA Quake,

when Dante had been the scouting manager. They'd hit it off then and usually tried to get together for a drink when they were in the same city. Dante was a large part of why Gunnar had accepted the offer to play in Chicago. Since his arrival in January, he'd been keeping to himself, but tonight he'd wanted to talk to his old friend.

"I was down at the Empty Net. Surprised you weren't there."

Dante's grin was wry. "I try to keep the business and personal separate, except when I obviously don't. But yeah, I don't usually drink with them."

Gunnar had drained his beer back at the bar, then left his raucous team mates arguing over whether a hot dog was a sandwich (three guesses as to Kershaw's views on the topic). He should have been fine with the mindless trash talk and nonsense of a boys' night out, but he'd felt disconnected from it all. Floating above, unable to engage. He needed to talk to someone who knew him on more than a surface level and wouldn't judge.

"I took a chance you might be lonely and need company."

"Instead of enjoying a little peace before my life turns upside down with the baby?" Dante sipped his wine. "Sure, I don't need a quiet night in."

Gunnar could feel his smile crumbling around the edges. "I shouldn't have assumed."

Dante held up a hand. "Amico, I jest. I'm very pleased you're here. Let's eat."

They did, an amazing meal of pasta—thick noodles Gunnar didn't know the name of—and a meaty tomato sauce he'd happily eat every day for the rest of time. They chatted about the team, the rebuild, their chances next season, and after dinner, took their glasses of wine out to the patio overlooking a perfectly-landscaped back yard.

"You work on this?"

"Cade does. I used to get someone in but he likes to mow grass and trim hedges and plant stuff."

Gunnar appreciated that. He'd always been a fan of yard work. "What's your plan when the baby comes along? A nanny?"

Dante looked at a point beyond the trees at the end of the yard. A smile curved his lips.

"I'll be staying home. We haven't made any official announcement yet because we don't want to jinx the birth. But if all goes well, I'll give up my job."

Gunnar shook his head in disbelief. "But you love being GM. You used to talk of nothing else."

"I love Cade more. We can't both travel the way we do and still be there for a family. I'm not the first spouse to give up a job and my husband is a star defenseman who earns more money than I do. It makes sense. Harper thinks I could still be GM and not travel to games but that's a pipe dream. Even she realizes she couldn't do it without Remy being a stay at home dad. Besides if Cade were traded, I'd be out of a job anyway."

Kelly was a pediatrician, who had never enjoyed the sword of trade hanging over their heads. Gunnar's career had been with LA until the accident so they were never tested that way. Of course, she was a good doctor and would have had no problem getting a job wherever they went. But UCLA wasn't really her first choice for med school or residency. She'd made that sacrifice for him.

"Enough about me." Dante put his glass down on a side table. "How are you doing? Really."

"Really? I like being busy. I like playing. To be honest,

that's the only reason I took on the summer camp gig because it fills my time. I don't have to think too hard, or that was the plan." He took a breath. "It's turned complicated."

"The summer hockey camp gig has turned complicated?"

Because of her, Sadie Yates. But he didn't want to talk about her or the fizzing energy between them. So tangible. So wrong. He turned his mind to a safer topic: Angel.

"I've been texting with someone and tomorrow I'm meeting her for the first time." He didn't explain how they'd crossed paths.

"That's ... interesting."

"She's—"

"You're sure it's a she?"

"I am. She's easy to talk to. There's something there, an affinity. I'm not sure what I'm doing."

Dante smiled. "Doesn't sound so complicated after all."

"I'm not interested in a relationship."

"Maybe she's not either. Doesn't mean you can't both indulge in an attraction."

Gunnar stared at his friend. "I haven't been with anyone since Kelly. I don't know if I even want to do that with anyone."

"Ah. No sex forever, then."

"It's not that simple." He'd had a couple of short-term flings before his wife but once he'd met her that was it for him. "I'm not really built for casual."

Dante's eyes warmed with understanding. "Lots of guys who go through tragedy react in ways that might be considered self-destructive. Booze, drugs, sex. What did you do?"

"What did I do? When my wife and—" He cut off, the mere notion of expressing it aloud too painful.

Dante pressed gently. "Did you go to counseling?"

Did communing with nature count? "I moved away so I wouldn't have to inflict my moods on anyone. My brother and his family. My friends." He'd never been the most social, but everyone wanted to help and he knew if he was around people and all their well-meaning notions, he'd say things he might regret. So he went dark. Worked at the cabin. Kept busy. Drunk a lot.

"Sounds like you cut yourself off so you could maintain everything at status quo. You wouldn't need to have a hard conversation with your brother. You wouldn't need to talk it out with a therapist or friends. That's okay. You found a way to cope. But now you're back in the real world and the status quo is only going to get you so far." He put his glass down and leaned forward, elbows on his knees. "You might not like the next thing I say."

"Okay." But this was why he'd turned up, wasn't it?

Dante interlaced his fingers. "This attraction—this affinity—you feel for this woman you've been texting, I'm guessing you feel guilty about it? Like you're betraying Kelly."

Of course he did. "I don't want to be attracted to anyone who's not my wife."

Sadie Yates and her damned storybook eyes. That barbed hook of a smile. Attraction was impossible to reconcile with this crushing guilt that he was enjoying a conversation with a stranger and now, lusting after another woman he barely knew when Kelly and his beautiful kids couldn't enjoy anything at all.

"Sounds like you're finding your way back to the messy dramarama of sex and relationships."

"Don't want that," Gunnar gritted out, wishing he'd not

said yes to this meet up with Angel tomorrow. He should cancel, especially now he was in this strange mood.

"You don't want it, yet here we are. Being interested in someone who's not your wife is perfectly natural, Gunnar. Hell, I know all about being attracted to the wrong person. But the wrongness here isn't so much about the person as about your guilt that you're attracted to *any* person who's not Kelly. I'm not going to tell you it's just sex, because that first time since your last time is never just anything. You might not want to be attracted to this person but you are. So what are you going to do about it?"

"I was kind of hoping to hear a good argument for 'nothing'."

Dante picked up his wine glass. "You don't have to do anything. It's not like you're going to run into this woman in your usual circles. Sounds like any interaction would have to be purposeful."

Gunnar rubbed his mouth. "Yeah, no accidental falls on my penis."

"Hey, who's accidentally falling on Gunnar's penis?" Cade strode out to the patio, placed his arms around Dante's neck, and kissed the top of his head. "Hi, honey, I'm home."

Dante's smile was almost one of relief at seeing his SO in one piece. Gunnar remembered that feeling, the way his body tensed when he didn't have Kelly in his immediate sightline and how it relaxed when he knew she and the kids were back in the shelter of his arms. For the last three years, he'd held his body as taut as a bowstring. He couldn't imagine ever feeling at ease again.

That was one more reason why the notion of sex with someone new was so difficult. Letting go like that required a level of surrender he wasn't sure he had it in him to give.

Trust in another person to see you at your most vulnerable and not take advantage.

Dante looked up at Cade. "You want wine? Grab a glass."

Gunnar stood. "I should get going."

"No, stay, Double-O," Cade said with that Texas drawl. "I'll let you guys get back to it, though we did miss you after you left tonight. Theo assumed you were sick of him."

"I won't say I'm not."

Cade chuckled. "The kid needs a lot of attention. You know how he is."

"Yeah, I guess a million plus Instagram followers, a woman who puts up with his antics, and brothers who adore the ground he skates on isn't enough." Jesus, bitter much? This was why he shouldn't be around people. He turned to Dante. "Thanks for the meal and the wine. Sorry we didn't do it sooner."

"Any time, amico."

They accompanied him to the door, and Gunnar could tell from their sly looks at each other that they weren't all that sorry to see him go.

"I'm going to walk home, clear my head. I'll pick up my car tomorrow."

"You can stay the night if you want," Cade said. "We have a guest room."

"I'm good." His apartment was only ten minutes away. "You two enjoy your alone time before the baby cramps your style."

Dante walked him to end of the drive. "About what we were discussing before. It's okay to have feelings, and that includes lust. Lust, or the indulgence of it, is often a great gateway drug to other feelings."

Indulgence. That was a curious word, and strangely apt. That's what it felt like. A luxury he didn't deserve.

"I'm happy to stop at lust. Not sure I should even go any further than that." Fantasizing about someone might be enough.

Sadie Yates and the way she filled that dress. Her soft hand on his arm ripping his hormones from a deep, numbing slumber.

"Sure, but if you do act on it, don't be surprised if it takes you to places you haven't visited in a while."

"Okay, thanks, Doc."

He saluted his friend and headed off into the night.

16

ONE TROUBLEMAKING CLOUD scudded across the summer sky, trying to ruin an otherwise perfect day. A little like the bad feeling Sadie had about this whole enterprise.

"This is a terrible idea."

"Which? The dress or the date?"

Sadie should not have Facetimed with Peyton, whose fashion claws were out. It was also obnoxious to be chatting so ostentatiously with someone on your phone in public, but she needed the boost before she headed into the coffee shop for her meet-up with LonelyHeart.

"What's wrong with this dress?" She'd worn another of her designs, an A-line pink and black satin frock with a boat neck that showed off her collar bones and a hint of shoulder. Along with her smile, Sadie's shoulders were one of her better features.

"Nothing! Just kidding. Very appropriate for a date."

"Not a date." Sadie peeked in the coffee shop window. Would she recognize him? She felt in her bones that she would. He'd be sensitive, maybe dressed in a suit and glasses. Yes, definitely glasses. "He's just a friend." Though that sounded strange on her lips. They'd never really defined what they were to each other.

"Sounds like the plot of a book. The story you'll tell your grandchildren."

"This isn't a date," she growled. "It's a friendly meet to put a face to the texts."

"Uh, right."

"Less of the dismissive tone, young lady. I get plenty of that during the hockey camp drop-off."

Fantastic. Now, all she could think of was Gunnar telling her off, assuming the worst about her. So she'd locked Cooper in a hot car—she hadn't left him there! So her sister was spreading rumors about Sadie's Cruella tendencies. Untrue, but it obviously spoke to a breakdown in communications on the homestead. Thankfully she'd not seen him this morning and Jenny was handling the pick-up, so yay.

"Why aren't you going in?"

"Because I'm five minutes early. And I'm reserving the right to bail if I feel hinky about this."

Peyton smirked. "This whole business is hinky."

"As always, it's been a pleasure."

"Oh, shut up. I'm trying to help. I miss you, bitch."

"I miss you, too. Oh, wait, I think I see him."

There he was. Sort of nerdy, hand-wringing, wearer of Buddy Holly glasses, a little bit lost. And early. She'd missed him at first because he must have been in the bathroom, probably throwing up with nerves. Her heart panged for him.

"What's he like?"

"Exactly as I imagined him. I'm going in."

～

SADIE'S IMAGINATION must be on the fritz. This was not the guy.

Three minutes in, she'd figured it out, but by then Buddy Holly had already bought her a coffee. She really needed a coffee, or something stronger, so she didn't speak up immediately because this was the kind of day she was having.

Buddy Holly smiled at her tentatively. "You're a really good listener."

Yep, she was, but then the man was a talker. He had already regaled her with his views on coffee shops—so cozy and neutral, whatever that meant—though he found the coffee expensive. Possibly a subtle hint that she now owed him? He'd also unloaded on the weather (too warm) and the ice water (too cold). All because she'd sat beside him with a breathless, "Hi there!"

She'd practiced it in the car, looking into her cell phone and trying a number of different greetings to project normal. Texting was so much easier. People claimed that nuance was lost in e-communications but Sadie did not agree. There were so many ways you could spin a conversation in text: the perfectly-chosen word, the need to say it succinctly and not over-explain, a well-appointed emoji, a nicely-apt gif.

Now her "hi there!" to whoever the hell this was had locked her into an interminably boring conversation about umbrellas.

"The British call them brollies," said Buddy Holly. The strains of *Peggy Sue, Peggy Sue* wormed in her ear.

"Do they?" Her eyes did double duty: ensuring BH felt acknowledged while checking the door for incoming customers.

"The British have a better word for everything."

"Actually the Germans do."

BH looked doubtful.

"Like *schattenpaarker*, which means wimp, but really refers to someone who parks in the shade. Isn't that perfect?"

"I suppose."

"Or *backpfeifengesicht*, which means a face that literally deserves to be punched."

BH looked alarmed. Time to call this.

"Listen, I'm sorry for being weird, but actually I came in here to meet someone—a particular someone—and I thought you were him. Kind of like a blind date. That's why I sat down."

"I bought you a coffee."

Fair enough. "So you did. Let me give you money for that." She took a five dollar bill from her purse and placed it on the counter. "You seemed excited to see me so I thought we were on the same wavelength, as in both expecting each other. My mistake." Sadie stood and reached for another, final apology. "Again, I'm sorry I messed up."

"Is this your usual MO? Sit beside unsuspecting men and get free coffee? Then leave when the situation is no longer to your liking? When you've gotten what you want?"

Oh, for fuck's sake. "Yes, you've figured out how I've managed to remain caffeinated all these years without opening my wallet. I hit on lonely men in coffee shops and pretend I know them."

"I object to the characterization of me being lonely." He added air quotes as if *lonely* was some strange, invented word that could never, ever apply in this situation. "Probably the only way someone would be interested in you."

Hoo boy. That escalated quickly. She'd given this man

five minutes of her time, five dollars from her purse, and far too many words of comfort. "Like I said, my apologies."

"Sure, bitch." He turned away, dismissing her with more than words.

Shock rooted her to the spot while she searched for a suitable response. Was he one of those incels who hated women? Had his mother not breastfed him? Gearing up to give him a piece of her mind, she made the cardinal error of looking around.

Others were listening in. She caught the embarrassed gaze of the barista, who lowered her eyes, not willing to get involved in what looked like a domestic situation. After all, she had been happily listening to him wittering on about umbrellas less than five minutes before. A woman sitting at a table further along the window stared, then looked away. *Thanks, sisterhood.*

The moment to react and defend herself had slipped away now that the world was watching. When push came to shove, she was merely a *schattenparker.*

Humiliated, she turned and slapped right into a wall of warm steel. Looking up—and this required significant neck strain—she met deep blue eyes, a crop of dark blond hair, a full beard, and soft-looking lips. A strikingly handsome and familiar face, and a complete *backpfeifengesicht.*

"Sorry I'm late, honey," Gunnar said. "Traffic was killer."

"Traffic?" *Honey?*

He glanced over her shoulder, his eyes darkening to pin pricks. "Was this guy bothering you?"

"Uh, no. I made a mistake and bothered him." A generous interpretation, but she wanted to escape this situation with as much as grace as possible.

Good luck with that. Gunnar stood between her and the door, and given that he'd stepped in to alleviate her embarrassment—rather unexpected, that—she really couldn't leave without him.

She would play along for a few. "Maybe we could sit over here?"

Gunnar was still staring over her shoulder at her date mistake.

"So. Let's move." She placed a hand on his chest—mercy, so solid—and gave an unsubtle push.

He took a step back and stood aside to let her lead. Acutely aware of him following her, she took a seat on the other side of the coffee shop.

"Listen, thanks for stepping in there. It was my fau—"

"Sure, just a sec." He left her mid-sentence and headed back the way they'd come.

BH was rearranging his trench coat and umbrella—sorry, brolly—moving his coffee cup a quarter inch until it was just so, and likely congratulating himself for his nasty set-down. Gunnar placed a hand on his shoulder. BH squirmed and tried to extract himself but the Viking was having none of it. Whatever was said was for BH's ears only, and was enough to make him blanch and scurry out the door like a bespectacled rat.

The coffee shop had clearly not had this much entertainment in years. Everyone present gave one hundred percent of their attention to this exchange because, one, it had the makings of a fight and two, Gunnar was so damn watchable. He had what Hollywood agents called presence. Someone that tall would always get a second look, but it was more. An intimidating, brooding, don't-fuck-with-me solidity. No sweats today—in fact, he cleaned up really well. He wore a French blue shirt tucked into black jeans and black hiking boots. It was close to eighty five degrees outside but he looked cool and unfazed.

His audience, including Sadie, remained glued to his easy amble back.

She tried to be as cool and unfazed as him, but you know, *how*? "What did you say?"

"Told him he needed to leave."

Exit stage left cool and unfazed. "What? You don't have the right to throw people out of a business!" She only wished she'd had the presence of mind to deal that kind of blow, but in a feminist way rather than a damsel way.

His brow wrinkled like this didn't compute for him. "He had to be dealt with."

"I did not need that from you. I was handling it just fine when you showed up with your white knight act."

"Everyone needs a little help now and again. You needed some help yesterday when you locked your dog in that car—"

"That was an accident."

"Still needed help." He moved in, bringing with him the scent of sandalwood and musk and probably a locker room somewhere. Her nose searched for that top note to ruin the rest but failed to find it. Very disappointing.

"I know you're embarrassed," he said quietly, protecting her from the nosey public with his low-key strength and high-impact body. "He was rude and he needed to be told that. Now would you like me to buy you a coffee?"

"Given that it's my MO to lure unsuspecting men into my web?"

"I'm not unsuspecting. Know exactly what I'm getting myself into."

Those dangerous blue eyes twinkled, though given their past dealings, she couldn't be sure. Was the Viking robot flirting with her? Worse, did her body like it?

Because her mind and morals did not.

"No need. I have to go but ..." She cast a small wave over the rest of the coffee shop, still watching, now waiting with bated breath for the next installment. The woman who had been sitting nearby approached and placed a hand on Gunnar's arm.

"Oh my God, it's you, isn't it? I'm such a huge fan. Would you sign a napkin?"

Practically elbowing Sadie out of the way, she put a napkin down and offered Gunnar a pen. She wanted his autograph. She was a fan. Of the hockey camp counselor. This universe sure *seemed* like the one Sadie must have teleported in from.

Equally curious was Gunnar's reaction. At first, he had the beginnings of a smile for the woman—as if he expected someone else—but as she continued, his expression morphed to something closer to disappointment.

"Happy to," he murmured, sounding not happy at all. He took the pen and scrawled an indecipherable scribble on the napkin.

"They really should have played you more this past season and by the time they did it was too late!" The woman flicked a dark look to Sadie, seeking her agreement, perhaps? As she only got confusion on Sadie's part, she turned back.

"Tell it to Coach," Gunnar said with grim humor. He passed the napkin back.

"Oh, I will! And ..." Moving closer, she offered a business card and lowered her voice. "I work in financial services so if you ever need advice or a shoulder or *anything*, don't hesitate to give me a call. I'm a very sympathetic ear."

He held up a hand to the card, a gentle but firm rejection. "I have people who take care of all that. Thanks, though."

She squeezed his arm again and pressed a little closer, employing the side boob strategy. This involved her getting in between Gunnar and Sadie, and really getting on Sadie's tits. "I just want you to know that I'm—*we're*—here for you. Everyone is rooting for you to get back to your peak."

His eyebrows drew close together. "Thanks, that's nice of you. Though before I get back to my peak, I really should get back to my date."

"Your ..." Her head swiveled. "Oh, right. Of course! Sorry to intrude." With one last longing look at Gunnar and a less than civil one at Sadie, she moved away.

Sadie repressed her first instinct to demand what the hell that was all about and then all instincts went bananas as he closed the gap between them, his focus on her completely.

"What were you saying?"

"Saying?"

He tilted his head, again with that unexpected humor curving his lips.

"Before? About having to go."

Did she say that? Why on earth would she want to leave this cozy bubble made for two? Then she remembered that she really did want to leave, to escape the humiliation wrought by Buddy Holly, who had called her a bitch in front of an entire coffee shop.

Mostly, she was also curious about why people recognized Gunnar. *Coach, season, play* ... Oh! He was a sports person. A *hockey* sports person.

"I'd offered to buy you coffee and you wanted to leave," Gunnar said, his low, husky voice inviting a shocking intimacy. "But unless I go with you, it looks like I was rescuing a complete stranger. Quite the dilemma."

He had to go remind her of what he'd done for her.

Recognizing she had little choice, she hissed, "Go get the damn coffee. Non-fat latte for me, extra foamy. And a chocolate croissant."

There was that unexpectedly sexy grin again. She made sure not to watch his ass perfectly hugged by denim as he walked away. Instead she checked her phone for any messages, annoyed with herself for making assumptions about Buddy Holly. *That'll be the day.* It was twelve—no, thirteen minutes—past the meeting time with LonelyHeart and she'd been stood up. Maybe he'd spotted her before she came in and ducked out at the sight of her. She probably was not who he had in mind.

You're being too hard on yourself. He might merely be running behind.

Her phone vibrated. It was from him.

LonelyHeart: Just arrived. Was running late but looks like you're later than me. Your ETA?

Her ETA? He was here?

Frantically she looked around. This must be the wrong location because no-one here looked remotely likely. Still, she'd already made that mistake. Two women were clearly meeting for a girls' catch-up. Financial Planner/Swim Fan was on a computer in the corner. But she'd been here for a good ten minutes, so even if Sadie had completely misgendered her LonelyHeart, that didn't look like her coffee date.

Other than the staff, there was no one else except Gunnar ... who had just pocketed his phone.

Grave walk chill right over her heart.

No, no, no.

She looked at the message thread again, checking the location of the coffee shop. She was in the right place.

Gunnar had put in their orders. Surely, if it was him, he wouldn't be buying someone else coffee while he waited for a date? Except it wasn't a date. It was merely a hey-how-are-ya-let's-put-a-face-to-the-texts meet-up and Sadie was the sad rescue he needed to expedite in the meantime because that's what a guy like Gunnar did. He rescued damsels who did not want rescuing.

Only one way to be sure.

She inputted a message: *Still a few minutes out. Can't wait to meet you!*

She hit Send.

The Viking robot didn't even flinch. Not him. Phew.

Or not-phew? She checked her body's reaction—surely that wasn't disappointment? She didn't want it to be him. Under no circumstances could she imagine having anything in common with this superior know-it-all, or that he was the person she'd been joking, chatting, and yes, flirting, with for eight months.

He paid for their coffees, and she was happy to say, a chocolate croissant (good boy), and moved to the pick-up location.

Whereupon he pulled out his phone.

Whatever he saw on the screen conjured a smile that hit her full-on, a photon torpedo to the chest. He typed something and ...

... The bomb in her hand went off.

LonelyHeart: I'm currently with another woman at the coffee shop. Long story ;)

Oh, yes, it was.

17

OF ALL THE coffee shops in all the world ...

Gunnar walked back to where Sadie was sitting. Her head was bent low, her nose practically stuck to her phone. Interfering in strangers' business was not his style but the moment he saw her, he'd been curious. Walking by, he had overheard her conversation with that asshole, and a firecracker had gone off in his chest. A need to protect ... though no woman had ever given off an I-don't-need-you vibe more than this one. So, this was his problem, his desire to right a wrong while he saw it.

She looked exceptionally pretty today. Those red-gold waves fell over shoulders that were half-bared with the wide neck of her dress. And that dress ... it was gorgeous, hitting just above her knee, revealing an expanse of creamy leg that tapered to strappy sandals. It was a date outfit, of that he had no doubt. So why the hell was she wasting it on that dickweed?

"Here you go." He placed the latte and the croissant down on the bar along the window.

She stared at the cup, like it had offended her honor or something.

"That's what you wanted? A foamy nonfat latte?"

"Yes! Yes, it is!" Her voice was high, her cheeks flushed.

He took a seat. "Listen, don't worry about that jag off."

"I'm not." She looked away.

"Have I done something wrong, Sadie?"

Her snapped her head back. "You know my name?"

"Yeah. When Isobel and I were talking about Lauren, it came up."

"I don't know yours. Well, I do, because Lauren mentioned it, but it's just a name, isn't it? I don't know a thing about you."

She sounded bitter about her lack of knowledge, as if it was his fault she was out of the loop. Perhaps it was.

"I'm sorry. When we first met, I launched right into you and I guess we never got a chance to make proper introductions. I'm Gunnar Bond."

"Right. People recognize you." Her nose twitched. So damn cute. "What's that about?"

"I play hockey for the Chicago Rebels."

She nodded slowly. "I don't really follow team sports. More of a tennis person. Do you know Serena and Venus?"

"I've met them a couple of times. Charity gigs. They're really cool." He licked his lips, feeling strangely nervous around this woman. "It was kind of nice when you thought I was a run-of-the-mill jerk instead of a pro-athlete jerk."

"I don't enjoy being kept in the dark." There was that tone again, a veiled accusation of some crime he was unaware he'd committed. Neither did she push back on the jerk thing. Fair enough. "It sounds like you know all about me. I suppose my family's misfortune has been doing the rounds at hockey camp."

He studied her. Her mouth quivered with emotion, her jaw stubbornly set in opposition. Those gorgeous silver-blue eyes shone with anger, daring him to piss her off more than he apparently already had.

"All I see is a woman trying to do right by her sister."

"Ah, now I have your pity. Because of my criminal father and that asshole earlier? What exactly did you say to him anyway?"

"I explained how his teeth could be easily detached from his gums if he didn't leave in the next thirty seconds."

She shook her head. "I do not need that."

"Really? Because it sounded like you were apologizing for tricking him into buying you a coffee."

"Just a misunderstanding."

"You seem to be at the center of a lot of those, Ms. Yates."

"That's me. Fooling men into buying me coffee by mistake since 2009. Look, you don't have to stick around. Any embarrassment I felt has vanished and your duty to this charade is at an end. Thank you for your service, kind sir."

Why the hell was this woman so prickly? More important, why did it make his skin sizzle like he was flying too close to the sun?

"We got off on the wrong foot. Maybe we could start over."

She squirmed. Literally squirmed.

"Or not," he added.

"Like I said, I appreciate you striding in here to do your manly man thing." Her eyes were drawn to somewhere below his jaw, possibly his shoulders.

He was so confused. But he also knew that this was the first physical interest he'd had since ... well, there'd been that time with Angel, last New Year's Eve, in the bitter cold in Maine. When he'd asked for her picture and the thought of knowing who she was and what she looked like had ignited something below the waist.

Angel, who would be arriving any minute.

Sadie stood and hovered for a second, as if about to say something. "Thanks for the coffee."

Not that. She hadn't even touched it or the croissant.

"Sure, any time." What else could he say? He couldn't demand that she stay, not when the person he was meeting would arrive any minute. He needed all his bandwidth for that because how could he explain to anyone how he knew Angel?

Oh, just the woman who answered the texts to my dead wife.

He watched Sadie leave, enjoying the sway of her hips while she did her level best to exit his breathing space as quickly as humanly possible. Which made him feel incredibly creepy.

Taking a seat and a sip of his now-cooled Americano, he tried to parse what had happened. Anyone might be embarrassed to be insulted in public like that, but Sadie was surely made of stronger stuff. She'd stood up to Gunnar just fine when he made that false accusation of neglect.

Only one conclusion made sense: this woman hated him.

Sighing, he checked his phone, which had vibrated this second with a message from Angel.

Sorry, something came up and I have to take a rain check. Later!

That sounded about right.

~

OUTSIDE JENNY ISNER'S HOUSE, Sadie sat in her car and did

what she should have done the minute she found out who Judgmental Viking was. She employed her Google-fu.

Gunnar Bond, aged thirty-two. Youngest son of a Finnish ski champion mom and American hockey player father, both now living in Finland. Former captain of the LA Quake. Lost his wife and four year old twins in a traffic accident in California almost three years ago.

Sadie dragged in a choppy breath. *There it is.* She had inherited his wife's phone number.

She scrolled through links to news items, most of them with pictures, usually the same one. A clean-shaven Gunnar in a LA Quake hockey jersey, carrying a beautiful blond little girl, all smiling eyes and smug contentment. And why not? He'd had it all. Beside him his wife stood with a blond boy in her arms. His wife, Kelly.

Yet again Sadie felt like a trauma tourist, spying on this man's pain.

Gunnar Bond was Sadie's LonelyHeart. Not hers, she shouldn't say that. Shouldn't even think that. What forces had aligned—or misaligned—to produce this crazy coincidence? More to the point, why had she fled the coffee shop instead of fessing up? It would have been so much easier to rip off the Band-Aid there and then, tell him who she was. Instead she'd panicked and allowed a situation to get *more* complicated. As if that were possible.

Fifteen minutes later, sitting in Jenny's kitchen, she tried to calm her brain and make conversation like a normal person. Lauren was in the Isners' den playing a hockey video game with Jason and Jason's fourteen year old brother, Sean. Sadie really wanted to go down there and drag her home—put an end to this miserable day—but Lauren didn't seem to have a lot of friends, so she left them alone.

Jenny gave a TV commercial mom smile. "Coffee or tea?"

"Tea would be nice. Thanks."

This woman would know more about Gunnar. Sadie considered how to play it and decided to go direct.

"So what's the deal with Gunnar Bond?"

Jenny filled a cup with hot water. "What makes you ask about him?"

"He was kind of nosey about Lauren yesterday, so I figured I could be nosey back."

"Do you like him?"

Her cheeks heated. "God, no. Forget I asked."

Jenny passed a cup of tea over. "I'll let you steep that to your preference. In case you like it thick, strong, and bearded."

"Oh, can it," Sadie said with a nervous giggle. "So he's good-looking, but that doesn't give him a pass on being an ass. The man accused me of abusing my sister. As if I don't have enough to deal with."

"He was probably feeling overprotective. Do you know his story?"

She nodded. A man who lost his family might overcompensate when he suspected another child in trouble. "What happened to him was awful. I can't imagine the pain he must have gone through. Must still be going through."

Jenny considered this. "Theo's worried about him. That's why he persuaded him to come back from that cabin in the forest." Over coffee yesterday, Sadie had heard all about Theo, who was Jenny's husband's son from a previous relationship. At Sadie's quizzical look, she added, "Gunnar went sort of off grid and lived in the middle of the woods in New Hampshire for a few years after the accident. Goes there when he's not here."

The Unabomber cabin! Another puzzle piece slotted in. "Oh. That sounds lonely."

Jenny smiled. "Yeah. The Rebels are big on brotherhood and bonding. No one's allowed to be lonely, according to Theo."

Sadie liked the sound of Theo. She also liked knowing that LonelyHeart had people looking out for him, even if the beneficiary of their kindness was a jerkwad like Gunnar Bond.

But they're the same person, her brain chimed in.

I know! I'm still trying to wrap the old noggin around it.

Jenny sat at the counter and lifted a tea cup to her lips. "How are things with you? It must be tough with your father—"

"Behind bars? Not the best. To be honest I have no clue what I'm doing."

The other woman squeezed her hand. "It's a lot, I know."

"It is! I don't have the parenting gene. I don't even have the big sister gene. I haven't even visited since I left Chicago ten years ago, when Lauren was two." She clamped her mouth shut.

Jenny did one of those quiet nods, guaranteed to get Sadie to spill.

"I'm not that close with my father and we fell out a while ago. My parents were about to divorce when Mom died and my father has always felt he got the short end of the stick. Left with me." It didn't help that she looked like her mother, a constant reminder of the woman who hurt him deeply. "I don't know Lauren that well, or at all, and it shows in every choice I make."

"That sounds *soooo* stressful. I'm happy to tell you that kids are the worst—it's perfectly okay to think and say that!" She chuckled. "Listen, why don't you stay for dinner? Nick will be home in a few and there's more than enough for all of us."

Frozen pizza, a trip to Wendy's (again), or a home-cooked meal? If Sadie didn't worry she'd look like a weirdo, she would have hugged this woman.

"Thanks, I'd love that."

18

THIRTY MINUTES and two cups of tea later, a man Sadie didn't recognize walked into the kitchen and stopped on seeing this strange woman making herself at home.

"Hello," he said cautiously. "I didn't realize we had a guest."

"Nick, this is Sadie Yates, Lauren's sister. Sadie, my husband, Nick."

His brow lined at the mention of her name—her father's reputation must have preceded her—but he recovered quickly and extended his hand. "Nice to meet you, Sadie."

"You, too. Your wife makes a mean Earl Grey."

"So, how are things?" he asked.

Jenny had mentioned that her husband, a lawyer and a Chicago alderman, was rather concerned with appearances and had even rejected Theo at one point, who he'd categorized as "a youthful mistake." Of course the alderman wouldn't be too pleased to have criminal-adjacent elements in his home.

"Nick," Jenny warned. "Not now. Or ever."

Sadie appreciated the defense though she didn't need it.

Turning on her sweetest tone, she said, "Lauren's having a tough time, so I really appreciate you being kind enough to include us in dinner." To Jenny, she added, "Can I help with the salad?"

Before Jenny could respond, a sudden movement caught Sadie's eye and then her sorry eyeballs were filled with the last person she expected in the Isners' kitchen.

"What are you doing here?" she blurted out.

Gunnar Bond's superior eyebrows slammed together. "Lovely to see you, too, Ms. Yates."

Ms. Yates. *Shiver.* "You seem to be everywhere."

"That's his talent on the ice," another voice said.

Sadie clapped eyes on an exceptionally hot guy with perfectly waved black hair, moss green eyes, and a puckish grin. He looked vaguely familiar.

"Hi, I'm Theo. Your sister is a wicked fast player, by the way."

"Pleasure to meet you and, uh, thanks." She turned back to Jenny. "I'm sorry, I didn't realize this was a big family affair. Maybe we should ..." She waved ineffectually behind her.

"Nonsense," Jenny insisted. "More than enough for everyone. Red or white, Sadie?"

"White, please." Because she was weak.

"I'm Elle." A dark-haired woman had appeared, heavily pregnant, and with a bright, mischievous look. "I'm with Theo."

"With. Theo." Theo murmured. "Such enthusiasm."

"How else should I describe it? I'm carrying *the* Theo Kershaw's super-child? Living in sin with pro hockey's gabbiest player? Knocked up by an Instagram influencer?"

That's where Sadie had seen him. "You did that hockey butt pants video! My girlfriends in LA were obsessed with it." Sadie might have looked at it once or fifty times herself.

"Just doing the Lord's work." Theo laced an arm around the waist of his mama-to-be and pulled her close. "As for how to describe me, I kind of like 'NHL's Top Hottie.' It's an award I received today."

"That's not a real award, Theo!" Jenny passed a large pour to Sadie, then muttered to Elle, "Is it?"

"Yes, it is, sweet Jennifer," Theo answered before anyone could deny it. "They went with a pretty revealing shot of my hockey pants slung really low. Excellent hip flexors action. Kind of raunchy. No idea where they got those photos."

"I have an idea," a deep rumble sounded. Gunnar Bond, LonelyHeart himself.

Sadie still couldn't believe it, and now that she knew all the details, she had no idea how to act around him. Not that she'd known how to before, but at least then she could roll along on a wave of dislike and antipathy. Now she knew this secret, she felt heartsick and fraudulent. *It's me*, she wanted to scream. *The woman on the other end of the texts.*

The conversation swirled and she tried to focus on it. It was interesting to track the undercurrents as Nick and Theo edged around each other with Elle and Jenny oiling the way.

Or at least, Sadie kept a finger on the pulse of that so she wouldn't have to pay any mind to Gunnar Bond.

GUNNAR WASN'T sure if Sadie's presence at this dinner was a blessing or a curse. After their run-in at the coffee shop a few hours ago, and realizing that she was not his biggest fan, he was anxious to improve her opinion of him. The woman was taking up valuable real estate in the—let's call it how it is—*lust area* of his brain. Every time he saw her, every time she popped into his head, his pulse thumped and his blood raced and his cells screamed in desire.

He hadn't wanted anything this much in a long time. Not even hockey.

Sure, he'd come back to the game, mostly out of a utilitarian need to earn a living at what he was good at. To be less of a mope. And texting with Angel didn't require any great effort on his part. He enjoyed it, but it didn't have this crazy, visceral effect on his body. A burning need that had to be sated.

Sadie Yates might not like him but her body language told another story. While she'd been in a hurry to get away from him today, he'd also seen the tell-tale signs: that flare in her silver eyes, the dipped gaze to his mouth, the obvious appreciation of his physique.

She wasn't completely unmoved.

She might be doing her best to ignore him, but she'd yet to go pro at it. Over dinner, he caught her looking at him for a nanosecond or two before she would quickly avert her gaze. A faint blush would appear on her creamy skin along with a sharp intake of breath.

"So, Sadie works for Allegra McKenzie," Jenny said after the dishes had been cleared away. "She's her personal assistant."

"Really?" Theo asked. "She's such a nutj—I mean, a fun personality."

Sadie laughed. "It's okay. She embraces the nut job she knows she is."

Theo grinned. "I'd love to have her Insta numbers."

"Sorry," Elle said. "I have no idea who that is." Gunnar could have kissed her because he had no idea either.

"She's Gwyneth-lite," Theo said. "With an emphasis

on"—he cupped his mouth and stage-whispered —"vaginas."

Both Jenny and Elle exclaimed, "Theo!" which was a standard reaction to the junk that often emerged from Kershaw's mouth. Thankfully the kids were in the other room watching TV and eating pizza.

Nick's mouth was shaped in a disapproving downturn, which was also pretty standard. Gunnar had met Nick a couple of times. He understood that the man was now trying to do the right thing, but for years he'd known Theo was his son and ignored him. His own flesh and blood. What a tool.

Sadie laughed again. She had an easy laugh, light and musical, and Gunnar felt it like a caress over his skin. "No, it's okay, he's right! Allegra aspires to be Gwyneth but rather than do everything that goop does, she's honed her market to vaginal wellness."

"Vaginal wellness?" Gunnar asked.

Sadie's smile faded and now she looked annoyed with him. Again.

"Allegra's core belief system centers on the punani as the start and end of all female wellbeing. She's built an empire around it."

Elle was scrolling through her phone. "Detox pearls? Sounds sort of sketch."

Sadie grimaced. "Not everything has been evaluated by the FDA, so yeah, I wouldn't stick half the stuff she promotes up my—well, you know. But she's a firm believer and she has the revenues to prove it. She's very LA."

"I liked living in LA," Theo said. "It's got a cool vibe."

"Fake." Said by two people at once—Sadie and Gunnar.

Sadie caught Gunnar's eye for what felt like the tenth time tonight. She might be fighting it, but this connection wasn't completely in his imagination. He hid his smile of victory while something pinged in his chest. Angel had commented on LA's fakeness, too, though given that she'd bailed on their meeting today he wondered if maybe she was more ingrained in that superficial culture than she claimed. Or maybe it was payback for canceling their get together in LA back in March.

Sadie picked up the thread. "There's a lot of focus on appearances, that's for sure."

"I couldn't live somewhere like that," Elle mused. "Everything seems so surface. Bet it's hard to make real friends."

"It was at first, for me. I moved there when I was eighteen and it was tough for a while." She looked lost for a second, but quickly recovered with a smile that was no less beautiful for being forced. "It always is in a new place, but I figured it out. Made connections. Friends."

"Sadie's trying to get a dress design business of the ground," Jenny chimed in. "She makes all her own stuff!"

Elle and Theo were suitably impressed. Gunnar was, too, but he'd never been a gusher.

"I'm hoping to get a business going but right now, I have to pay the bills. I have a few things to sort out—financial things, the house—and then we'll be in LA."

"Got to pay back all those people your father cheated?"

"Nick," Jenny said to her husband. "Really?"

"Cheated?" Elle looked on with concern.

Sadie blinked away her obvious discomfort. "My father was recently incarcerated for embezzling a hedge fund he ran. A lot of people lost their life savings."

Elle said with feeling, "You can't choose your family, that's for sure."

Theo squeezed her hand, and they smiled at each other.

He turned back to Sadie, and lowered his voice. "Jonah Yates? You're related to that guy?"

"Blood only."

"Hell, Tate lost a bunch with that business, or his accountant did. Tate's wife kicked him out."

Tate Kaminski was their Chicago Rebels teammate, the one with marital issues. Gunnar hadn't realized the connection.

"Small world," Nick said.

Sadie's silver-eyed gaze met Gunnar's for a heartbeat, and Gunnar swore he saw regret there, and something else he couldn't discern. The moment passed as she moved to tackle Nick head on. "Yes, the house will be sold soon. Every account in my father's name, even Lauren's college fund, has been frozen and will eventually be liquidated to make restitution. Mostly, I'm worried about my sister's mental health since both her parents have been ripped from her life through no fault of her own. That's why I'm here. For my sister."

"You're taking responsibility," Gunnar said. "She's lucky to have you."

Sadie's mouth, with that attractive pouty lower lip, parted slightly in surprise. Should she really be so shocked? Okay, maybe, after their first meeting. And the next.

"I don't know about lucky. We barely know each other. I didn't get along with my father and haven't been in Lauren's life much up until now. This is new for both of us."

"But as soon as she needed you, you stepped up." Gunnar shot a withering glance at Nick. Fucker. "That's the definition of good parenting."

He caught Sadie's eye again, and this time she held his gaze a little longer. Half-baffled, half-annoyed, but that extra second felt like progress.

19

"Thanks so much for inviting us," Sadie said, hugging Jenny. "It was so lovely to meet everyone."

"Except me," Gunnar said, no change in his tone so she couldn't tell if he was joking. Not that she was ready to joke with him. Something weird had transpired over dinner, an odd simpatico between them that had nothing to do with what she knew about him and everything to do with what she didn't.

"Well, I've already met you and I was unimpressed."

"Whoa!" Theo swung his head to Gunnar, his eyes alive in amazement. "What the hell did you do, Double-O?"

"Put my foot in my mouth. Thought we'd moved beyond that, though."

"Did you?" Sadie gave her most sugary smile, but even that felt like she was playing a part. *It's me, LonelyHeart. It's me!* Turning away, she kissed Elle on the cheek. "I'll make sure to drop off some of that body butter at the hockey rink."

"By body, we're talking punani, right?" Elle whispered. At Sadie's chuckle of agreement, Elle went on, "Or we could meet for coffee or lunch some time if you're not too busy.

Theo's hanging at camp during the day and he won't let me bartend anymore. I'm taking some online finance classes, but I have time. You too, Jenny."

Jenny looked pleased to be included. "Now how are you getting home?" she asked in a mothering tone, a clear nod to the fact Sadie had imbibed two classes of wine.

"We'll walk and I'll come back to pick up the car tomorrow." It was only six blocks. "Hey, Lauren, come on!"

"Nick can drive you home."

Nick opened his mouth, though whether he could drive them home would never be known because a deep, rumbly voice spoke for him.

"I'll drive you," Gunnar said.

"Oh, no need!" Sadie insisted cheerfully as Lauren arrived from the other room. "Have a good time?" she asked her sister.

Shrug of indifference. She'd take it.

Two minutes later, she was outside with Lauren and Gunnar, arguing her case for walking home. "This neighborhood is perfectly safe and I have a rabid tween who'll protect me."

Not even the hint of a smile from the Viking. So much for that simpatico. "My car's right here," he said.

Six blocks lasted several lifetimes. Lauren had her headphones on so Sadie took a chance.

"Was it my imagination or was there a bit of an atmosphere between Nick and Theo?" Nick and everyone, to be honest.

"Not your imagination. Did Jenny explain their relationship?"

She nodded, and Gunnar went on. "Theo's giving him a ton of slack but Nick needs to prove himself. Taking pot shots at people who aren't responsible for their parents' actions is not the way to do it."

Sadie could feel her color rising. "Thanks for that. You didn't have to say anything, but it was nice to hear I'm not getting it completely wrong."

No comment from Gunnar, just his eyes steadfast on the road. She sneaked a look at his profile, so strong and virile. Was driving tough for him after the accident? Was he nervous with other people in the car? Did she weird him out by staring at him like a, well, weirdo?

His blue eyes flickered in the mirror, catching her gaze, and she looked away quickly.

"Theo and Elle are a sweet couple. They must be so excited about the baby." Gah! Why did she have to bring that up? The last thing he needed was to be reminded of his friend playing happy families.

"They're a good fit. She keeps him grounded, which is a full-time job in itself, and he worships the air she breathes. I've never seen a guy so besotted."

Not even you? Of course, he wouldn't recognize that in himself, the man who adored his wife and kids and the life they'd built together. It would have been completely normal. Maybe he couldn't even remember the good because the pain had more of a hold.

"Back there, I didn't mean to sound ungrateful for the offer of a ride."

"It's okay. You're still pissed at me for my multiple sins."

"I'm—I'm not. It's just ..." She had to come clean.

Knock, knock.

Who's there?

Butter.

Butter who?

Butter tell you who I am before you lose your freaking mind.

"Here we are." He pulled up outside the house.

"Great, thanks so much. Hey, Lauren, say thanks to Gunnar for the ride."

It was the first time she'd said his name aloud in his presence and it tasted strange on her tongue. Also sweet and sexy and—nope. Not going there.

Oblivious to her inner trauma, Gunnar jumped out of the car, opened the back door, and held out a hand for Lauren.

"Milady," he murmured as he helped her down.

Her face lit up, and there it was, that rare ray of winter sun from Gunnar in return. "See you at camp tomorrow, Lauren."

Confession time. "Lauren, could you give me a second to talk to Gunnar?"

Her sister's smile vanished and she scurried up the steps of the brownstone.

"I'll be there in a sec," Sadie said sunnily as if Lauren cared. "I can't believe you got a smile out of her. She's been so dark lately."

"Tough time for her. You, too."

His compassion warmed her through, but she quickly chilled as she realized she didn't deserve it. "I need to tell you something. To explain my behavior at the coffee shop."

He moved closer, placing his palm on the stoop's newel post. The streetlight glinted off his knuckles, momentarily distracting her from her mission. How could knuckles be so attractive? Because they were attached to big, capable, talented hands ... *stay on target.*

"I was sort of abrupt with you. And tonight. You see I'd just found out something and ..." She stopped, licked her lips, and looked up. Big mistake.

He was so tall, so disruptively handsome. That beard did

things to her, and she didn't even like him. Except she did. She liked the guy in the text messages, the man who shared things with her with no agenda.

But she could be all wrong. Everyone had an agenda.

"I'm sorry," she murmured, because she was about to upend his life. He'd had a lot of that so far, and here she was making it worse.

"I'm sorry, too," he said, and now she knew he was closer because those blue eyes glowed and she could feel a shift in the air's energy around them.

"For what?"

"This." And then he bent his head and touched his lips to hers.

GUNNAR MUST BE LOSING his mind. This woman infuriated him, yet he couldn't stop thinking about her. About her lush curves and bright eyes, that mobile mouth and stubborn chin. A part of the attraction was how much he obviously pissed her off—which was somewhat his fault and somewhat hers. After years of numbness, the novelty of feeling something, *anything*, was so electrifying that all considerations about the fact he was kissing the wrong person were easily set aside.

The wrong person? Why had he thought that?

Possibly because she wasn't kissing him back.

Fuck.

She wasn't kissing him back.

He stopped. "I shouldn't have done that."

"No?" A question rather than outright agreement.

"This isn't what you want. I—" He scraped a hand through his hair.

She peered up at him, her eyes big and round as silver moons. No censure, only ... confusion.

"You surprised me. Big time." Her lips curved into that slayer smile and his heart kicked hard against his rib cage. "I thought you didn't like me."

"I don't." It was out so fast that it could only be true. "But then like doesn't have much to do with this, does it?"

"This?"

He waved between them, indicating the *this* he meant.

"You're ... attracted to me?" Her eyes grew impossibly rounder.

"That is usually why someone kisses someone."

"But you don't like me?"

"I don't know you. To be honest, we seem to rub each other the wrong way."

"We know why that is. You accused me of being a neglectful guardian and frankly, your apology was not good enough."

Here we go again. "I apologized, but some people prefer to hold grudges because they enjoy being mad at anyone other than themselves."

"That's what you think this is? I'm misplacing my anger and directing it at some poor guy who doesn't deserve it?"

"Why else would you hold onto it?"

"Clearly because I'm annoyed at wanting you!" Her hand flew to her mouth. "That's not what I meant to say."

A pleasant shiver of surprise rolled through him. He had been right. There was something worth pursuing here. "What did you mean to say?"

"That I don't buy your psychobabble. I can be mad at you for several reasons. I am woman. I contain multitudes."

He rubbed his mouth, hiding his smile. Sadie Yates was going to be a lot of fun. Only that's what he'd thought about Angel, who had ignored the couple of texts he'd sent her.

Sadie reared up on tip-toes, all fire and indignation, and pushed at his chest. "Don't you dare laugh at me."

"Why not? You're being funny right now."

"I'm not. I don't even like you and ..." Her brow furrowed. "I want to."

"You want to? Why?" A weird statement and a weirder question, but he needed to know.

"It's like when everyone reads the latest New York Times bestseller and loves it, but you're all 'who cares? Why are people loving this junk?'"

Comparisons with junk. Definitely on brand. "So you're wondering why your opinion of me is so out of step with the masses. Maybe because you like to go against the grain to be contrary."

"Maybe because I have taste. As far as I can see, you're a judgmental dick who happens to be tall and bearded. That's all you have going for you. Unreasonable height and killer facial hair!"

"Poor me." He felt another smile coming on. "Sadie?"

"What?"

He stepped in closer. "You don't have to like me. You don't have to think what everyone else does. Half the time, I can't tell if people are being nice to me because they like me or because I'm a famous hockey player or because I have a sad backstory that invites pity."

She chewed her lip. "I didn't know your story before we met. Not even after because I didn't know who you were so I couldn't look you up. I found out today. My dislike of you comes honestly."

Either she was the most forthright woman he'd ever met or ... that. She was honest. Her candid nature was as much of a turn on as those curves and eyes and hooky smile.

"So we've established you don't like me. I'd like a chance to change that."

"And you don't like me, though I'm not sure how that could be. I'm very likable."

He was starting to agree. She'd gone sky-high in his estimation in the last five minutes. "My problem with you stems from the fact you're holding a grudge. That's it. I could like you if you dropped it."

She threw up her hands. "Why are we having this conversation? Do we need to establish we like each other enough so we can feel better about wanting to kiss each other? Are we so afraid of sheer animal lust that we have to pair it with, ugh, *respect*?"

He laughed, enjoying himself immensely. It was supposed to be just a kiss. How had it turned into a thesis on likability and lust?

"Don't need to like you to want you, which I'm pretty sure I said about five minutes ago. But I do need you to be interested rather than ... bored."

Surprise brightened those pretty eyes. "Who said I was bored?"

"You didn't kiss me back."

"Because I was shocked."

"Because you're not interested."

"God, you are such a dumbass." And on the expiration of "ass" she curled a hand around his neck and pulled his lips to hers.

Electric. That's how it felt. Tingling and chemical and hot. All those dumb, dormant cells in his body came alive, re-sparking into existence. She tasted like cinnamon and heat, a brand new, intimate flavor.

His hands couldn't help themselves. One cupped her hip, the other her magnificent ass, and both pulled her tight to his straining erection, the one he'd been fighting to contain all evening. She went with the move, adapting to the flow of their bodies fitting together as if it was the most natural thing in the world.

He pulled back an inch, merely to get his bearings. A voice in his head sounded a warning: *stop now. Stop before you cross a line there's no coming back from.*

Her silver eyes gleamed, her mouth glistened with the wetness of his kiss. No woman had ever looked more wanton or sexy.

The voice screamed. *No woman? Did you really just think that?*

She pressed a hand to his chest. "It's okay, Gunnar." Soft, knowing, a wealth of compassion. He wanted to weep, but mostly he wanted to kiss her again.

A yell cracked through the night, the sound of a child in pain. *Janie?*

Sadie jerked back and looked over her shoulder. "Was that Lauren?" She raced up the steps of the brownstone and pushed open the door, calling out for her sister. Gunnar was fast on her heels.

"Lauren?" Sadie rushed through a hallway and entered a room near the end. "What happened? Are you—what the hell?"

When Gunnar arrived, he noticed three things: Lauren hunkered down, soothing the big dog with the shitting problem; a broken window; and a Christmas tree that had seen better days.

Lauren turned, her cheeks red. "Someone threw this through the window." She picked up a flat, smooth rock, about the twice the size of a puck.

"Wait here," Gunnar said. He headed to the back of the house, though the kitchen, and out the door. The room with the broken window faced the back yard, which was large and shrouded in darkness except for the faint glow from the house. No security lighting and no evidence of anyone sticking around to view their handiwork. He remained still for a second, listening to the night. Nothing spoke back.

He took a circuit of the garden. On the east side, a few feet from the house, a flowerbed surrounded by a rock border looked like a tooth had been pulled. He picked up one of the border rocks, the same as what he'd found inside. So a crime of opportunity rather than premeditation.

He headed back inside, where Sadie met him in the kitchen. "You should call the police."

"Maybe it was a kid, some vandal." She frowned, something else tripping through her mind.

"You still need the police report to make an insurance claim for that window."

"I don't even know where the insurance information is. All my father's papers are such a mess. I'll have to call the lawyer."

Gunnar touched her arm gently. "Police first. I'll call a glazier."

"No, could you wait on that? I don't have any—" She cut off. "Whoever it is won't be coming back, will they?"

Probably not. "Window still needs to be fixed."

She nodded and headed back in to her sister.

Thirty minutes later, the police had arrived to take the details. Like Sadie, they pegged it as random vandalism, or would have if Sadie hadn't mentioned the letters.

"What letters?" one of the officers said.

She opened her purse and took out a few envelopes, all with cursive addresses in varying degrees of neatness.

"They're postmarked a few weeks ago, from before my father's sentencing."

Gunnar took one from her hands before she passed it off to the cop. Unpleasant, but generic. Still, threats in writing seemed to carry more heft. He gave it to the questioning officer, who, from his expression, resented his interruption.

"You should have reported these before," Gunnar said to Sadie.

"I haven't had time to worry about it. Besides, we'll be in LA soon."

Not satisfied with that response, he turned to the police. "You think this is related to the property damage?"

"Probably a coincidence." Cops didn't like being told how to do their job. Exhibit A, the California Highway Patrol and their endless questions about the accident, looking to assign blame to the man before them instead of the one who drove away. Law enforcement preferred their conclusions wrapped up in a bow. Less paperwork.

They never found the driver who, in his hurry to overtake him, had driven Gunnar's car off the road and into a ravine. How would they? Gunnar's brain had pushed certain details to some deep, unknowable recess. As easy as it was to blame this phantom, Gunnar knew who was truly at fault here. He'd overcorrected, lost control, doomed them all. The only reason he was here was because fourteen hours later someone—not CHP—had spotted tree damage on the curve where the car had left the road and went to investigate.

"Let us know if anything else happens," one of the cops said, to which Gunnar snorted his disgust.

Lauren seemed to be taking it in her stride. There'd been some resistance to leaving the room—apparently she slept there with the dead Christmas tree—but when Sadie explained that the glass could hurt Cooper, she relented. Now she was somewhere else in the house.

The cops left and if Sadie had her way, Gunnar wouldn't be far behind.

"Thanks for sticking around," she said, her hand on the open front door.

"I'll wait for the glazier."

"You don't have to. You've already been a great help."

"Sadie, I'm not leaving until that window is boarded up. They said they'd be here any minute."

No sooner were the words out of his mouth when a van pulled up with Glass Doctor on the side.

"I can wait until—"

She placed a hand on his arm, and there it was again, his body glittering with new-found life. "Gunnar, it's fine. You've been really helpful but I've got it from here."

He wanted to kiss her again, but the message was clear. *Not now. Let's forget about what just happened.*

The Gunnar of before would have agreed. New Gunnar —alive Gunnar—was not ready to call this quits. But he recognized she needed time after a stressful night, so he merely nodded and headed down the steps.

20

"HOW CAN YOU BE SURE?"

This was the third time Peyton had asked the question. Unlike Sadie, she hadn't had time to weigh and absorb each evidential fact that pointed to one thing: LonelyHeart and Gunnar Bond were one and the same person.

"I'm sure. The more I read about the hockey player, the more I'm sure that this is my text buddy."

This morning, she'd hunted down every scrap of information she could find about his tragic loss. Now she understood why he'd sometimes said "them" in his texts. He hadn't lost only his wife, he'd also lost his children. He'd lain in that car, pinned and unable to move or help them while their lives slipped away. Not that he'd ever given an interview or recounted the events in such heart-wrenching detail, but the report of the accident had made it clear. The autopsy had pieced the accident together, established timing, who went first, who lasted the longest, and the tabloids had woven a story of horror.

He was trapped for hours and his family didn't die immediately.

"So it's him."

"And I knew this but still kissed him."

Peyton wagged her finger. "Yeah, so why is that? Why did you let it go so far?"

"Because he makes me mad! He's not like how he is on the texts. There, he's this lonely, sensitive, aching soul who needs my soothing words. Who listens to my problems—such as they are." Not that they could compare to what he had endured.

He had texted this morning, to his wife's old number, asking if she was okay and she didn't have the guts to respond. All she could hear was Gunnar's voice. All she could see was Gunnar's beard and eyebrows and that blazing blue gaze.

He didn't even kiss like the guy on her texts would have kissed. This version of Gunnar Bond kissed with a lusty desperation that surely he shouldn't be wasting on the likes of Sadie Yates. To compound her confusion, he'd been the man on the spot last night, taking charge. "But the real guy —that guy infuriates me. He came right out and said he's attracted to me, but doesn't like me. Who says that?"

"You don't like him and it sounds like you're attracted to him."

"But I wouldn't say it." Except she did. She'd told him he was a jerk but she still wanted him, which made her no better than him.

"What are you thinking?" Peyton squinted at her.

"That maybe they are two different people. Maybe I've got it all wrong." She wanted to have it all wrong. She hated to think she'd been wasting her efforts on someone like Gunnar Bond, which made her a terrible person. Grieving assholes needed a shoulder to cry on, too. She just wasn't convinced it should be *her* shoulder.

"You have to find out. You can't go on like this especially if kissing and more is on the horizon."

"No. I'm putting a stop to that. I can't be with someone I don't like, it's ... seedy. And I'll be back in LA soon anyway."

Peyton rolled her eyes. "Oh, please. That makes it perfect. You have a hot, sexy athlete who wants to have his wicked way with you."

The thought of Gunnar's mouth on hers—and other places—heated her from the inside out. What else might have happened if they hadn't been cut short last night? Her ass had fit perfectly in his hand, or at least, that was how it had felt. With her bountiful body type, she never felt comfortable with most men, but with Gunnar, she'd slotted into the concave spaces of his frame with ease.

As for his taste, it was sweeter than anything she'd ever experienced. Intoxicating. She'd have happily let him ravage her—*ravage*? Really? Uh, yes, and let the fates fall where they may.

In the wake of the window damage, there'd been no time to analyze next steps. All she knew is that they couldn't return to what they had before and she wasn't sure they could make any moves forward. Stuck in lusty, lying limbo.

She had to get to the bottom of it. "I'll set up another meet with LonelyHeart."

"Or ask his name. If it was really him coming to meet you he would have told it to you eventually. He's a famous hockey player. He has to know he couldn't hide it once you met up." Peyton waved madly. "Or call him. Surely you'd know his voice?"

Like her own. "I'm going to call him."

"Really?" Peyton shrieked.

"That's what you said I should do."

"Yes, but—I didn't think—really?"

Sadie bit her lip. "I need to know."

Peyton nodded gravely. "When? Now?"

"If it *is* him, he's at hockey camp, so there's a good chance it might go to voice mail. Which would be even better. I could hear his voice and he would know the person he's been texting had called but not that it's me. Sadie."

"And if he answers?"

"I'll worry about that if it happens. Whatever feels right." She had to fess up eventually. "Wish me luck."

"Good luck." But she sounded like she was sending Sadie off to war.

Sadie scrolled through her messages. She could text but she needed clarity, and the cold, shock of hearing Gunnar's voice would provide all the clarity she needed. In that moment, she'd know if she was glad it was him or profoundly disappointed.

She dialed. It rang once, twice, three times. Yes, bring on the voice mail. She would know and he wouldn't know and then she could decide what to do.

"Hello?"

Not a voice mail but a live, speaking, gravel-voiced Gunnar Bond. Shock constricted her vocal cords. She held the phone away from her ear, her finger hovering over the end call button.

Hang up, her brain screeched. *Hang the fuck up.*

"Hello—Angel, is that you?"

Angel. Why would he call her that? Did he think she was someone else?

"Hi, it's me. Sadie."

∿

SADIE.

Gunnar blinked, confused as all hell. He checked the name on the incoming call. Angel. She had yet to respond to any of his texts. It had bothered him but then he'd had that exchange with Sadie—of words, of lust, of hot kisses—and Angel, the woman who had helped him through, had gone clean out of his brain. A clear case of his little head ruling the big one.

How could Sadie be calling from Angel's number?

"Sadie Yates?" It was her voice, and Sadie was a unique enough name. He felt stupid fumbling for confirmation. "Lauren's sister?"

"One and the same."

"How did you get this number?" He wasn't even sure if he meant his number or Angel's.

"Ah, that's quite the story, which I only realized was a story when I ran into you at that coffee shop yesterday." She cleared her throat, then added, "You were planning to meet someone there."

"Yeah, but—wait, how did you know that?"

A sharp inhale of breath preceded her next words. "I'm that person, the one you were supposed to meet. I'm the one who got your wife's number."

His heart plummeted, a free-fall with no apparent end in sight.

He couldn't speak, so she spoke for him. "Fucking AT&T, remember?"

"No, that's ... not right."

"Might not be right, but it's the truth."

Sadie was Angel, Angel was Sadie. The shock had subsided, and something else had taken over. That feeling of knowing something innate, in his bones. Like it was meant to happen like this.

A chill crept over his skin. "When did you know?"

"While you were buying coffee. You texted me that you'd arrived that minute but you might be hanging with another woman and ... I put two and two together."

"So you knew when we were at the Isners last night for dinner? And when I drove you home? And kissed you?" And waited with her for the police to arrive. This was completely ass backwards. "You knew through all that and decided not to tell me?"

"I screwed up. I was reeling with the news and what was I supposed to say? By the way, the woman you've been flirt-texting with for the last year is actually the woman you think is a terrible parent and bad sister and incredibly annoying person—"

"Flirt-texting?" That was not what they were doing. "This is fucked up. You should have told me the second you figured it out instead of stringing me along like some sort of game. Unless you've known longer. And this was—I don't know—*planned*."

"That's not—that's not what I did! And planned? What do you think I did? Bribed someone at AT&T to give me your wife's number so I can stalk you for a year and then finally surprise you *after* I find out you're a complete and utter jerk? You think this is some sort of long game? I should have known you'd be like this!"

She ended the call.

No. She didn't get to end this conversation. This was not even close to ending.

21

SADIE WASN'T sure how long she sat in the kitchen, staring with unseeing eyes at the phone. Ten minutes? Thirty? Peyton had texted a couple of times, Allegra had called her usual twice every fifteen minutes, and Gunnar had called once, after which Sadie decided the best course of action was to turn off her phone altogether. Because ignoring the problem always worked.

Gunnar Bond was definitely LonelyHeart. And he'd been a jerk about it, just as prophecy dictated.

Well, not prophecy. Sadie had known he wouldn't react well. She should have hung up when he answered, then texted the details. Reading it on the screen might have softened the blow. As it was, hearing Sadie's voice with the news was never going to endear him to her.

Was that her intention? Push him so far that he would be pissed off at her and they could pretend the attraction between them was really too hard to overcome? After all, there was no way they could return to that previous state of affairs, the messy I-don't-like-you-but-boobs-and-pecs-are-nice option. It had seemed so much simpler last night when all that existed between them was unabashed chemistry.

Now they had baggage. They didn't have a relationship but whatever they had already came with pre-packaged cargo weighing them down and dooming anything more.

It probably would have been awful anyway. The man looked like a Viking god and she was about as far from warrior queen as it got. That mouth, though. And his kisses ... *Reel it in.* She was not in his league—and now she needn't worry about it.

She might want to worry about that insistent doorbell.

It had to be him. She didn't know how he'd made it from Riverbrook in twenty minutes, but she knew it was him. She could ignore it like she'd ignored the phone call but they really needed to have this out face to face.

Shooting titanium into her spine, she marched to the front door and yanked it open. He stood there wearing black sweatpants, a gray tee, and a scowl.

Never had anything sexier appeared on her doorstep.

Give him a chance to speak, Sadie. Expect the hot vibe to be ruined in three, two, one ...

He opened his mouth. She opened hers. Neither of them said a word.

Standing back, she motioned him inside impatiently as if she had gossiping neighbors to consider. "Shouldn't you be in hockey class?"

"I was running errands in the neighborhood when you called."

Sure you were. He had arrived fairly quickly, though.

"Listen, I'm sorry for how this went down," she started, eager to move off the back foot. "I've been in a state of shock since I figured it out."

"But you did figure it out." His eyes burned into her. "You

knew and you still chose to stay silent. You had a chance to speak last night. Instead you kissed me back!"

"If you recall, I didn't kiss you. I didn't react at all, and then—okay, I did. But only because you drive me nuts. You're such a jerk but apparently my hormones don't care!"

He rubbed his forehead. "Jesus. This is fucked up."

"Yeah, you said so on the phone. Can we assume that's all entered into evidence and skip to the part where we figure out how we're going to deal with this going forward? We know it's a mess, we know it's really awkward, and we know it shouldn't have happened."

"What shouldn't have happened?" He took a breath-stealing step closer. "You having Kel's phone number? Us talking to each other for months? Sniping at each other from the minute we met?" Another step. Another hitch in her throat. "Or kissing? Is that what shouldn't have happened? Because a lot of things have happened here."

Kel. He called his wife Kel.

"I guess what I mean is that if we hadn't given into our baser urges, we wouldn't be having this problem. You liked the woman on the texts. You don't like the woman before you."

"You're the same person," he said, King of the Obvious.

"And you wish I wasn't."

He narrowed those stunning blue eyes. "I didn't say that. I just wish you'd told me as soon as you knew instead of keeping it to yourself."

"Do you think I hid this from you for some dastardly plan?"

"I don't know. I just know I don't like it."

Typical male response, instinct telling him what his brain couldn't compute. That was all very well on the ice or in a foxhole, but instincts tended to get people like her into trouble. She should have played it safe, not agreed to meet. Knowledge was dangerous. Putting all that can-do energy out into the world had come back to bite her.

He was thrillingly close now, his eyes flashing in fury, blue brightening with golden sparks.

"You can't even admit why you don't like it," she said, going on the offensive again. "We know it's because you don't like *me*."

"I never said that. Are you forgetting that kiss?" His eyes dropped to her mouth. Mentioning the kiss created a warm bloom in her core that spread outward to all extremities.

"I'm—I'm not forgetting it. I'm saying you didn't like me when you kissed me. I mean, you liked my mouth and maybe you liked touching and tasting me"—all things she liked about him—"but you didn't like *me*, the person those lips belonged to."

"So we got off on the wrong foot, you annoy the hell out of me, and I like kissing you. It's possible to not be crazy about someone's personality and still want to kiss the living daylights out of them. Finding out that we know each other in this alternative universe is weird. I *am* allowed to think that."

Of course he was. Just as she was allowed to think about kissing and tasting and so much more.

"You want to kiss the living daylights out of me?"

"Sadie—"He stopped abruptly, making her name sound like a curse. He rubbed a hand cross his mouth, a big meaty paw that drew attention to that sexy beard and those gorgeous lips.

It was suddenly very hot in here.

They seemed to be at a crossroads, where they could only deal with one thing at a time. The facts so far:

1. They liked the texting versions of each other.

2. They did not like the IRL versions of each other.

3. Kissing each other felt really, really good.

Points one and two canceled each other out, which left point three.

"There's a lot going on here," she murmured, "but the one thing I'm hearing is: Kissing. Good." *Woman echoes prehistoric ancestor. Verbs no longer necessary.*

He must have agreed because he set about proving that kissing was indeed good. His mouth on hers was heaven, hell, and all points in between. It was everything.

She didn't want to desire someone this much, to be so focused on another person's mouth and feel and taste, yet here they were with a kiss that blocked out everything else. All problems were null and void. If this was everything, what was left?

He backed her up a few steps, clearly seeking some sort of leverage. A wall, a stair, a—yes, that would do. The backs of her knees hit the edge of the chaise. *Don't ask why there's a chaise in the entryway to the house, Sadie, just be thankful it's here!* She flipped their positions and pushed him down. He landed with a thud.

Their mouths separated and now he peered up at her from beneath those forbidding brows, his eyes alight with something she hadn't seen before: undiluted want. Oh, she'd seen garden variety lust and plain old I-bought-dinner-so-you-owe-me lust but never such need. To inspire that was heady and for a moment, she hovered over him, unsure of her next move. Unsure if she could live up to the expectations she saw in those blazing blues.

He made the decision for her with his big hands on her butt, pulling her astride his lap.

"Oh," she ooffed. She took a moment to study him, placing a hand at the back of his head, another at the side of his face. The facial hair was surprisingly soft. He must condition it.

His lips shone wet with her kiss and she couldn't help herself: she licked the corner of his mouth, then along the seam until he opened to let her in. The frenzy of the kiss had subsided, and in its place was an awareness that there was pleasure to be had. It crackled between them, a special brand of knowledge.

Gunnar Bond was a wonderful kisser. He applied himself with deliberate thoroughness. This was a man who enjoyed giving the full experience. A light tug of the lips, a protracted nibble, a flick of his tongue, a guttural sound to indicate pleasure. Gunnar Bond kissed with gusto!

That made her giggle—and not just in her head.

"What?" He whispered, pausing long enough to blow the word into her mouth. It didn't stop this kiss. Nothing could stop the kiss. It merely morphed into a different phase. Nibbling continued. Nuzzling took over.

"Admiring your technique."

He spread a large palm over her ass and yanked her forward over his erection. Yep, perfect technique.

"You usually laugh when you're admiring a man's skills?" More nibbles, now to her jaw, her earlobe. This kiss had legs.

"All the time," she breathed, though that wasn't true at all. She was usually so tense, wondering what the other person was thinking, was she slanting her mouth correctly, was she enough for him.

His beard tickled. His lips amazed. And his hands ... wow.

Her skirt had ridden up, flashing quite the expanse of thigh, and now he was pulling her closer, which only forced her hem higher. More skin, more heat, more—oh, he was so hard beneath her.

Closer. More. Please.

She didn't have to ask. Wordlessly, he pushed the hem up so she could settle her thighs easily on either side. Wordlessly, she ground against him, yielding groans from them both. No need for anything verbal. Those groans were unmistakable affirmatives.

His erection dug into the sensitive fabric-shielded flesh between her thighs. She used the friction to spiral higher. He slipped his thumbs over her underwear, a light, maddening stroke.

The new, faintly surreal pleasure produced a shiver. Pressing down, she encouraged him to continue, to give her more, to join skin with skin. One thumb slid past the border of her panties, traveling a lustful route through slick heat.

She pushed back, seeking a more deliberate motion, demanding her due. His thumb brushed her clit. A moan ripped from her throat.

"Yes, yes, please," she whispered, her eyes closed, and when she opened them, he was there, right *there*, staring at her with those blue, heated suns. He pushed her panties aside, and rubbed a rough palm through all the wetness between her legs. Like he needed to verify the evidence of her desire.

Her entire body shook with sheer, crazy, fucking need, and then she was riding his hand, grinding on it while he watched her so carefully. Kissing had ceased, their focus on the race too important. If his hand didn't do it, his eyes would. Heat bloomed and pulsed and exploded in a crescendo of body-wracking pleasure. She made an embarrassing noise she would block out in future re-lived fantasies of this moment. His mouth met hers once more, kissing her through the descent and keeping her centered while her body flew apart.

Wow. Fucking wow.

His hand remained in a possessive grip between her thighs, gently teasing, building a fire once more.

"What about you?" she asked shakily because it was incredibly selfish to let him take her there again without repaying the favor.

He went stiff. A shadow crossed his face, a ghost of remembrance, and she watched in growing horror as each moment hit him in quick succession: knowledge, guilt, sorrow, regret, a soul wrecked. His color rose quickly and his eyes softened with a depth of emotion that knocked her back. This couldn't possibly be his first time since ... no, she refused to believe that.

But if it was, he needed to be reminded that there was no comparison. She wasn't Kel, the woman of his dreams. Far from it.

"Gunnar, it's okay."

He swiped a hand across his mouth, its tremble unmiss-able. So was the conclusion: he was removing the taste of her from his lips. She stood awkwardly. She preferred to stay seated over his strong thighs, but he was definitely giving off vibes of got-to-get.

Or perhaps not. He didn't move a muscle. His head was dipped, his stance taut.

Taking a chance, she placed her palms on his broad shoulders and held on as they sank in dejection. She kept her hands loose, giving him every opportunity to slip her grip.

It's okay.

Leaning in, she kissed the top of his head. His body shuddered, his shoulders heaved. She applied more pressure with her fingers. *I'm here.* He raised the heel of his hand to his eyes, a motion that could mean only one thing.

He was crying.

She got the orgasm, but he'd fallen apart.

She inched closer until his bent head touched the soft folds beneath her breasts. Never had she been so glad to have a few extra pounds, all the better to pillow his head. His arms circled her waist and pulled her close, absorbing a strength she hadn't known she possessed.

They stayed like that for a while. She wasn't sure how long, just that she didn't regret a single second.

Finally, he leaned back, his hands loosely cupping her hips. He looked up at her with eyes wet and raw.

"That was embarrassing."

She sat beside him on the chaise. "I can't help that sound I make. You wouldn't believe the number of guys it's sent fleeing into the night."

A whisper of a smile teased his lips. "I'm sorry for that. I wasn't expecting this—you—and it took me by surprise."

She had a million questions but prompting him to explain his reaction might close him down. It seemed easier to take some of the pressure off and apologize for her sins of earlier.

"I'm sorry for not telling you as soon as I figured out who you were. I didn't do this to trick you. I swear I was just as shocked when I worked it out but I needed time to think about it. So I called you today to make sure. I didn't expect you to answer. I thought you'd be busy at camp and then I could super-sleuth and work out a plan. I should have hung up—"

"No, you—you did the right thing."

Surprise took her aback. "I did?"

"Of course. Because the wrong thing would be for you to

have hung up and not told me who you were. I was annoyed because you had information I didn't have and no-one likes being kept in the dark. It makes them feel stupid. But I understand why you did it."

"You do?"

"Just said I did." He frowned, and grumpy was super hot on him. No surprise there.

"I'm sorry I haven't been so polite to you, especially when you were trying to help with Lauren. I shouldn't have snapped, asking if you have kids."

His eyes froze, the blue the chill of Arctic ice.

She continued digging her grave. "I-I lashed out at you and of all the things to say, that was terribly cruel."

"You didn't know," he said, the words a whip against her skin. She shouldn't have brought it up. She hated that she could ever have hurt him with such a thoughtless comment. He was obviously still in a bad place.

"I didn't. But it was no excuse."

"It was the perfect excuse. But now you do know. You read those texts I sent and we've been sharing something for months. Neither does it help when a man breaks down after making a woman come. I'd say it's shifted our dynamic."

Hell yeah it had. How could she not be moved, knowing who he was along with the additional insight she had from the man she knew as LonelyHeart? And how could she not be affected by a man who gets so emotional after sex?

Was I your first since Kelly?

"It bothers you. This shift."

"Might have preferred when I was just the jerk you hate-lusted after."

"I didn't hate-lust after you."

"Didn't you?"

She rolled her eyes. "So the dynamic is different. People

learn things about other people all the time. Layers are peeled back. Mysteries are revealed. Would you really rather we knew nothing about each other—oh."

A cold gust of knowing washed over her. He'd given her an orgasm that sent her into a different stratosphere, had a good cry, and now felt foolish. She'd thought it brought them closer but he saw the gulf for what it was: unbridgeable.

She struggled to a wobbly stand. He peered up at her.

"What are you thinking, Sadie?"

That she already missed LonelyHeart. At least, that guy had been honest.

"I think it's best you leave."

"Leave?"

She slid a glance to the door, the one he'd been so anxious to walk through a while ago. "I need to pick up Lauren."

He stared at her, incredulous. "Are you mad at me?"

"No. Not at all. I—well, I liked what we had on text. I liked where that was going but this isn't the same."

He blinked. "No. It's not. It can't be."

But they were friends before. They were opening up to each other.

She wanted that back.

"I'm not sure what you expected to happen here," he said.

"You're right. This situation is too weird to have any idea how it would play out. But I know that we were friends and what's just happened has changed that. Possibly for the worse, and not because it wasn't good because it was." Damn, it was. "But because you don't like that I have this insider knowledge about you. That you've shared pieces of yourself with me. And you especially don't like that what we did here tapped into some part of you that might have been previously inaccessible. You don't want to be known, least of all by me, and that's okay."

"I suppose that's not wrong," he muttered. "When it was just sniping and lust—"

"It didn't seem all that important."

He looked uncomfortable at the reveal of this strange truth.

She wasn't here to be his guide back to himself. She could barely figure out her own problems. A man like Gunnar Bond came with far too many complications. She was accusing him of holding back but maybe she was scared of what exploring this might mean for her.

"I should leave." He screwed up his mouth, and even that was attractive. He needed to go before she did something more stupid than rutting on him.

She nodded, choosing silence, worried that any words out of her mouth would be the begging kind. He left without a backward glance, and she slumped against the door, telling herself it was sweet relief and wondering why she hadn't asked:

Who's Angel?

22

"SWEETHEART, *are you alright? Can you hear me?"*

I reached over to the passenger seat, blindly because of the dark liquid in my eyes. Blood. I hauled my hand back and wiped, taking a few seconds to allow the scene to come into focus. The air bags had gone off. There was a dripping sound—the fuel line?— and a metallic-oil smell.

Kelly's head was at a weird angle but her eyes were open.

"Kel—Kel! Can you hear me?"

She tried to move. Nothing happened. But I saw the effort in her eyes. Her body refused to cooperate.

"I-I can't feel my legs. Can't feel any-anything."

"Just stay still, sweetheart." I turned my head, shifted in my seat, doing a quick check of my body for injuries. The side window had caved in and some of the glass must have slashed my forehead and cheek. It stung but other than that, I was remarkably intact.

Except I couldn't move.

I pushed at the airbag but behind it, the entire dash had lurched a foot forward, trapping me in place.

"Janie! Danny! Can you hear me? Can you hear Daddy?"

Nothing for a second, then a wail. Janie. That's my girl.

"Daddy, my leg hurts."

"I know, baby. Daddy's gonna take care of it." I hauled a breath into lungs restricted by imaginary steel bands. "Danny, you okay, buddy?"

Nothing. Panic set in, not like before, but bone-whittling fear. Why wasn't my son responding?

"Danny! Wake up, Danny!

"G-man, it's okay." Someone shook Gunnar's shoulder and his first instinct was to lash out and connect.

"Fuck!"

He bolted upright and realized his mistake. Theo stood over him, holding his jaw, looking as wounded as a just-kicked puppy.

"Theo? What are you doing—?" In his bedroom. Only, this wasn't his bedroom. He looked around, taking in Kershaw's living room. Memories of last night rushed back for a morning meet-and-greet.

Sadie. They had—Jesus. And after, weighted down with shame, he had needed unchallenging company. Three beers later, he'd taken a snooze on Theo's sofa.

"Shit, did I hit you? I'm sorry, T."

Still rubbing his jaw, Theo said, "Yeah, you hit me! Have you any idea how much this face is worth?"

Gunnar swiped the sleep from his eyes and swung his legs to the floor. "Your beautiful face will survive. Now you know not to approach a man in the middle of a bad dream."

Theo sank into the sofa. "Was it about your family? The crash?"

Kershaw would never be known for his tact, but that's what Gunnar liked about him: he was a straight shooter. A tactless straight shooter.

"Yeah. I haven't dreamed about them in a while. In fact, here in Chicago, I haven't been dreaming much at all."

Except about Sadie Yates's lush curves. That had to be why the dream was returning: soul-crushing guilt. Giving her that orgasm, the sensation of her unraveling in his arms, had felt so good. He'd forgotten how amazing it felt to give someone else pleasure, to watch that sweet surrender.

But it had meant another shift in the sands of time. Another door shut on his old life. Another vow broken.

For a few stolen minutes, he'd lost himself in this woman's taste, her sounds, the feel of her wet heat. Only when she asked what she could do for him did he realize the depth of his betrayal. As if the act wasn't bad enough, he'd broken down in front of her, then pushed her away because he was so mad at himself.

This wasn't how a man should grieve the loss of his family. For all intents and purposes, he was still married, still had two beautiful children, even if it was only in his dreams—or nightmares.

"I guess dreams pop in because of something else that's going on," Theo said.

"Uh huh."

"Or someone else."

Gunnar stared at Theo. "Don't hold back now."

"At dinner the other night over at Nick and Jenny's, you couldn't take your eyes off that Sadie chick."

"If you'd been paying proper attention, you'd have noticed that we weren't exactly enjoying each other's company."

Theo grinned. "Yep. Classic symptoms of the love-hate connection. Summer lovin', had me a blast ..."

"There will be no summer lovin'."

"Why were you so pissed when you stopped by last night? Because you're sexually frustrated?"

"Leave him alone, Theo," a soft voice called out. Elle walked into the room in a Rebels jersey, one hand on her hip, the other protecting her protruding belly. "Go start on breakfast."

"Yes, my commandant!" He saluted then hopped up to kiss her, adding a belly rub at the same time. His attention squeezed a smile from her lips.

"Sorry if we woke you," Gunnar said as Elle took Kershaw's spot on the sofa. He hoped she hadn't heard his moaning, or whatever he'd been doing.

"I can never sleep these days. And Theo is usually up all night, talking about the future and all the things he wants." She looked embarrassed to be caught in such domestic bliss. A daughter of con-artists, she'd had an unconventional upbringing, so this was new to her. "You okay?"

He shrugged.

"Gunnar."

He flicked a glance to the kitchen, where the strains of Kershaw singing "I'm Too Sexy" filtered through. "I screwed up."

"Find that hard to believe. Want to tell me what's going on?"

No, but he could use a woman's perspective. "I'm interested in someone."

"Go on."

"It's kind of more complicated than it should be. You see, I've known her for a while but I didn't know who she was." At Elle's quizzical frown, he explained how he'd first "met" Sadie and described their argument without going into too much detail.

"I did not have 'recycled phone number of my wife' on

my bingo card," she finally said. "Theo's going to love that story."

"You have to tell him?"

"I do." She chuckled at his weary sigh. "So, you enjoyed texting with Sadie."

"Angel."

"You felt a connection."

"I suppose."

Elle smiled at his cagey response. "Then you met her in real life, and underneath the backbiting and snark—which believe me I know all about relationships starting out that way—you were attracted to her."

"Excellent summarizing skills."

She made a face. "In other words, Mr. Sarcastic, you have all the right kinds of chemistry, so what's the problem?"

What was the problem? He actually understood why Sadie kept it a secret, at least for a while. He didn't blame her so what exactly was the true source of his discomfort?

When it was just sniping and lust, it didn't seem all that important.

"She knows things about me." Things he hadn't told other people, things he would have only told Kelly, if even that.

"You're worried she'll use it to what—tell all to a tabloid?" Awareness dawned on her face. "Ah, you're worried it'll make the sex too good."

"What? No!"

She smiled. "She knows these things and it makes you feel vulnerable. Vulnerability tends to open the floodgates of emotion. Emotion and sex together is a pretty lethal combo. That bothers you."

Yes, it bothered him. He'd already made a damn fool of

himself. "I'm not like Theo. I'm not an open book. I don't want any woman to feel she has to be my therapy, the one that cures me of my grief. I don't want to overpromise anything. But at the same time, I'm not really a casual hook-up kind of person."

She squeezed his thigh. "That's quite the dilemma. But maybe look at this way: has it ever occurred to you that she's not interested in a deep, open-your-heart connection with you either?"

Way to tear down his ego. But Sadie *had* seemed hurt that he was reluctant to spill his guts to her now that they had met in real life. Surely she saw what a terrible idea it would be for him to use her as his sounding board. Yet, he didn't want to stop what was happening here.

"She's only going to be in town for a couple more weeks. She's moving back to LA." Something lurched in his chest at the thought.

Elle's eyes brightened and she grabbed his arm. "Which makes it perfect for a fling. I know that's not really your style but this could be your means of inching back into relationships. You're not built for casual. You might want to get serious with someone again. Not this summer or next, but eventually. No harm in exploring with someone who you already have a connection with even if it can go nowhere. Even better *because* it can go nowhere. It's time- and geographically-limited and then neither of you will feel any pressure to take it more seriously."

A brief fling, a short affair. Could he do that? And more to the point, would Sadie want that? He'd have to come clean with her and ensure the expectations were clear.

No future, no past, only living in the present.

No more tears.

And especially, no exchange of hearts.

23

THE PLACE SMELLED like institutional death and decay. Sadie wasn't sure what to expect. Something like *Silence of the Lambs* perhaps, a walk by a row of cells with cat calls. Or glass screened carrels with germ-ridden phones.

She was surprised to be shown into a room with tables where visitors sat across from inmates. There were signs about touching—as in no touching—but she could see people holding hands.

She'd rather obey the rules, thank you.

She took a seat at an empty table and waited. Low-hummed voices comingled with muffled sobs. Her father appeared at a nearby door, clad in orange, stooped like Quasimodo. Her heart wrenched at seeing him dragged so low. He had screwed up his life and Lauren's, but he was still her father.

"Hi Dad."

"Sadie." He took a seat, clasped his hands. He'd turned completely gray since she saw him last, no longer able to rely on the hair color that kept him looking youthful. Finally, he was showing his age and then some.

"How's Lauren?"

"She's fine. Playing hockey at the Rebels summer camp, wiping the rink with them. Her coach says she's really talented."

"She stopped playing after Zoe left us. She got mad at school and ..." He broke off, rubbed the bridge of his nose. "Don't bring her here. Please."

"Of course. But Dad, we need to talk about what comes next. I have to go back to LA—"

"Why can't you stay here?" His sharp voice drew attention from tables around them.

She lowered her voice. "I have a life in LA. Friends, an apartment, a job."

"For that D-lister? You can get a job anywhere."

"My skillset is difficult people. LA is my hunting ground, Dad." She smiled, but he didn't return it.

Jonah Yates had never liked her. Parents didn't have to like their children, but they should try to love them, at the very least. Once her mother had cheated, then died (which her father saw as another form of cheating), it had doomed any chance of love from Sadie's father. All he saw was her mother, all he knew were her faults. For five years, they'd both counted down the days until she turned eighteen and any semblance of duty could be abandoned.

Now duty had brought Sadie back. Not to her father, but to Lauren.

Her father's eyes were cold steel. "So you want to take my daughter away from me? I'll be out of here soon and then you'll have upended her life for nothing."

You upended her life, Dad. This is not my fault.

"Dad, if your appeal works out, of course she'll come back. But for now, I have to do what's best financially. I don't have a job here and there's no money. The house is being sold for restitution."

He shook his head. "That lousy leech of a lawyer. Couldn't stop the judge and what'll happen when I win my appeal? Too late then. Too late for everything."

The evidence had been overwhelming, the paper trail a million miles long. The appeal would fail.

"What grounds do you have for appeal, Dad?"

"That judge had it in for me. Bitch. Probably can't get laid and takes it out on all the male defendants."

"Dad ..."

"Zoe would have known what to do. She would have made me look sympathetic. She shouldn't have left me." He buried his face in his hands. "And now you're taking my daughter away." He raised his head and threw a look of sheer hatred at her. "You never understood."

Oh she understood alright. That she wasn't good enough to be his daughter but had her uses now. That she was a distant second once her father remarried and Lauren was born. That she would always remind him of the wife he couldn't lock down.

"So like your mother. You couldn't wait to leave and now I suppose you'll have the last laugh."

Shock tied her tongue. Sadie had learned a long time ago that her father didn't think like other parents. Even now, he hadn't acknowledged Sadie as his daughter or thanked her for her part in coming to the rescue. It was always Lauren.

Worst of all, her father was right. Jealousy, cold and sharp, cut through her. She hated feeling this way about an innocent, troubled girl. Lauren was not to blame.

"I'm trying to do what's best for Lauren. So you and I didn't get along, but that's all in the past. We'll be here for a few more weeks while I pack up the house and settle up here. I'll bring her to see you. She'll want to see you."

"I won't sign over parental rights to you."

"You won't have to. The state has appointed me her temporary guardian. I make the rules for now."

The words out of her mouth sounded bitter. She didn't want to get wrapped up in using Lauren and guardianship for revenge. She just wanted it to be over.

SADIE WAS NOT A SPORTS PERSON. She saw the appeal—winning, camaraderie, tight pants on muscular butts—but she was hard-pressed to appreciate the work involved. She also worried about creating tiny assholes who would turn into bigger assholes. As if Lauren didn't already have enough problems when it came to their father's genetics.

The final day of the week-long hockey camp session was upon them—the longest week ever, it seemed—and apparently the kids capped it all off with a game to showcase their skills. Sadie would finally get to see her little sister in action, and Gunnar Bond, too.

It shouldn't be a big deal as Lauren had signed on for the advanced skills camp next week, but she'd been a bear all morning. Scowling, general teen rudeness. She'd even pushed Coop away when the poor thing was looking for a hug. Sadie put it down to nerves. Rather that than admit this was how the rest of the summer was going to go.

"Anyone sitting here?"

Sadie looked up to see Jenny coming down the row toward her, a large bag in tow. She'd thought about saving seats for the Isners before she realized that none of the other hockey moms wanted to sit near her anyway and the space remained wide open. Nothing subtle about the disapproval wafting her way either.

"Best seats in the house! No Nick today?"

"Oh, he's down in the locker room giving a pep talk." Jenny unloaded a giant tray of cupcakes and passed them over. "Here, get started on these."

"Okay." Next came a tupperware container of brownies, followed by a five-liter box of Franzia Pinot Grigio.

"White for you, if I remember correctly."

"Uh, yeah. Wow, thanks!"

Jenny waved to a spot behind her and Sadie turned to see Elle and two other women entering from the other side of the row.

Elle sat on Sadie's other side and let out a huge sigh of relief. "Damn, this baby is pissed at me." She thumbed to the woman to her left, a redhead with perfect skin and pretty freckles. "Sadie, meet ace sports reporter, Jordan Cooke. And this is Mia Wallace. She plays pro hockey except they don't pay her enough."

"Hey there!" Jordan, the red head offered an easy smile. "I heard your sister is a flyer."

"Vadim showed me a video of her," the other woman— Mia—said, reaching out to shake Sadie's hand. "Amazing for her age. Vadim Petrov's my brother."

That name was familiar, but Sadie wasn't sure why. Another hockey player, perhaps? This woman looked young, maybe early twenties.

Jenny passed plastic wine glasses along the row and a ginger ale for Elle. "You should have her on the podcast, Jordan. Get Isobel and Mia and do a next-gen women's hockey episode."

Jordan's eyes went wide. "I love that idea!" To Sadie, she

said, "I'm a sports reporter for Chicago Sports Network. I also have a hockey podcast."

"I don't know anything about hockey. Sorry. But I'm learning!"

Elle held her hand out for the fist bump. "Speaking my language. I know zilch as well, which really bugs Theodore. Fun times. How's Lauren?"

"She's nervous. And I chatter too much around her." Sadie found herself nervous as well, mostly because Gunnar Bond had given her an orgasm and they'd parted on such weird terms.

"Jason was a mini-wreck this morning," Jenny said. "They're all like that."

"I love that dress," Elle said to Sadie, then to Jordan added, "Sadie designs all her own clothes."

"Really?" Jordan snagged the wine box from Sadie. "Woman, do you make wedding dresses?"

"I haven't but—"

Elle cut her off. "You're getting married in three weeks. You already have a wedding dress."

"Yeah, but it's kind of frou-frou, almost too much for a second wedding."

Jenny scoffed. "It's amazing! But Sadie, you should definitely make wedding dresses, just not for Jordan who already has one. Maybe in this vintage fifties style you're wearing."

"Yes!" Elle and Jordan agreed, and soon everyone was giving opinions on Sadie's rockabilly dress, a black-and-white polka dot skirt with a green scooped-neck bodice and a wide black satin sash that forgave all manner of sins. One of the whisper-formation a couple of rows in front of them turned to glare because they were getting a little raucous. Mia asked outright what they were looking at, only to be shushed by Jordan, which everyone thought very funny. Sadie knocked back her wine, with not a care in the world. This was the most fun she'd had in months.

On the rink, a band of teeny-tiny children in the under-7 class, weighted down with pads and helmets, kept falling over. Everyone found this hilariously adorable.

Her phone pinged with a text from an unexpected source: Gunnar. Though in her contacts, she still had him labeled as LonelyHeart.

Lauren dropped something called Iggy (??) somewhere. She won't play without it.

She fired back a quick, *I'll check the car.*

"When do they go on?" Sadie asked Jenny.

Jenny checked her phone. "About fifteen minutes. Who's LonelyHeart?"

"Um, no-one. I'll be right back."

In the lobby, she found Gunnar, looking unreasonably handsome in sweats, but then gray had never looked better on a man. On her approach, he smiled the most gorgeous, heartbreaking grin that all Sadie could do was stupidly grin back.

"Hey," he said, as if things hadn't devolved into awkwardness yesterday and they were old friends, maybe what they might have been if they'd stayed the course and hadn't ruined everything by meeting in real life.

"Hi," she returned, the soul of wit.

"Thanks for checking. Lauren's wigging out about it."

Right, her sister. "Is she okay? She was nervous earlier and this can't be helping."

"She's fine. Or will be." He held the door for her and followed her outside.

She opened her mouth to tell him there was no need to

accompany her but he was already walking. She had no choice but to lead the way toward the car.

"You okay?" he asked.

"Okay?"

"After yesterday."

For a moment, she thought he was talking about the visit to her father before it dawned on her.

"Don't worry, I've recovered from your superior orgasm delivery, Gunnar." Best to frame it all as a grand joke. Without waiting for his response, she opened the back door and leaned in, scouring the seat and floor area for the bear formerly known as Benny. After a couple of seconds, she spotted something peeking out from beneath the seat's overhang.

"There you are!" She snatched at it and turned. Gunnar's eyes quickly darted away from where they had been previously engaged. Her rear.

"Find it?"

"Yes." She turned the bear—Iggy—over in her hand. A little ragged, the fabric heart she'd sewn on faded to a dull pink, it conjured up memories of another lifetime. Sadie's mom had bought it for her at Disneyland. It was the last time they went on vacation together as a family. The last time she remembered being happy with her father.

She marveled that Lauren had it after all these years, but especially that Zoe had let her keep it. Sadie had crept into Lauren's room and left it in her cot before she packed up her Toyota Civic—the same beater she had now—and drove cross-country to LA two days after her high school graduation. With school over, her father had made it clear that their minimum parental responsibilities were at an end.

"Must be important." Gunnar said, calling her back to the present.

"It used to be mine."

"Family heirloom."

"Something like that." With ridiculously bad timing, a tear leaked from the corner of her eye.

"Hey, it's okay." He curved a hand behind her head, his thumb extending to catch another tear.

"I'm—I'm not upset about—" How could she explain? Her father and sister hated her. She felt like she was spinning her wheels, unable to get her life firing on all cylinders. To top it all off, she'd gone and ruined this burgeoning connection with LonelyHeart, the one person she thought she could rely on. "Everything's upside down. I can't seem to get a grip on what's important."

He nodded, waited.

"Lauren's not happy with me. I'm here but I haven't always been. I'm the enemy and she won't forgive me." Neither did Sadie think she should. All those years and she'd made no effort to reach out to her sister because she hated Zoe and her father too much. She shook her head, not wanting to get into the specifics, but something about his solid strength standing in front of her loosened the knot behind her breastbone. "Sorry. That's not what you're here for."

"You'd tell me if we were texting."

She might, but that was over now. They couldn't go back to that.

"What do you wish you could say to her, if she wasn't a raging pre-teen who hates your guts?" He asked it gently, and that care unlocked something in her chest.

"That I'm sorry I let my bitterness toward her mom and dad get in the way to being a good sister. I'd tell her that I wished I hadn't been so stubborn. That I wished I wasn't the kind of person to hold a grudge. That I wished I was a different person."

His face fell. "Don't ever wish you were a different person, only that you might handle things differently."

That held a ring of truth. "I worry that I spent thirteen years holding onto that resentment because maybe I like it. Maybe it defines me. And now I'm making Lauren bend to my will because it's all about me." She turned to him, matching his intent gaze. "Regret is the worst emotion."

"Not the worst."

That was thoughtless of her. "I'm sorry. I can't seem to get it right with you."

He cupped her chin. "I should apologize for what happened yesterday," he said, lowering his voice to a level that made her anxious to move closer. To place her cheek on his pec.

He regretted what happened, and who could blame him? She'd behaved atrociously in the aftermath.

"I might have overreacted."

"No, not at all. It's been a strange few days, don't you think?" His eyes darkened to black smoke. "This energy between us—it's more than I'm used to."

"More what?"

He held her gaze, unblinking, unyielding. "Emotion, I suppose. The last few years—well, I don't have to tell you." *Yes, you do. Please.*

He didn't. "I haven't been attracted to anyone since my wife died. I haven't wanted to even think about that, but with you, it's burning through my veins. A buzz of need that's almost ... painful."

She couldn't breathe. These words, their naked honesty toppled her.

"Which version of me are you attracted to? Because you don't think much of the one you dislike."

"Are we back to this? You know, when it comes to sex, I've had offers—"

"Congratulations."

"What I'm trying to say—badly—is that it would be easier if I could fuck some woman who hits on me in a bar, if I could get my rocks off that way. I would love if the easy option worked for me. Instead..."

"Instead what?"

He looked pained. "Instead it's you. And you are the opposite of easy. But this last week, I-I can't get you out of my head. My body goes haywire when I see you. When I'm near you. It's like a live current running through it."

Like her body was going bonkers here and now.

His eyes burned the brightest blue. "Thing is, I can't offer you dating or romance. I can't offer you anything more permanent. But I will tell you this: I'm on fire for you."

Swoon. Except ..."Even though you're not a fan? Of me." The words sounded small and pathetic.

He considered her, like he was gearing up for something important.

"Sadie, I think you're funny and smart and gorgeous and doing an amazing thing in upending your life to take care of your sister. We got off on the wrong foot and that's my fault. I totally own it, and I totally own that I've been attracted to you from the start. Add in our weird history and it seems crazy that we wouldn't do something with this energy between us. It'll burn out soon because sex can't be the glue of anything ... real. If you're looking for something more permanent, I can't do that."

It had to be the longest speech she'd ever heard from him, and there was so much to unpack. She placed both hands on his chest, needing to both steady herself and determine if he was real. "Are you proposing some no-strings-sex thing with me?"

"Yes."

Again, his honesty sliced through her, rapier-sharp. He wanted her. For sex. That was nice, wasn't it? Who didn't want to be acknowledged as attractive to someone, especially someone as sexy as Gunnar Bond?

But she'd had something else with the guy on the other end of those texts. A real connection, that glue he mentioned. Gunnar wanted to put that aside and indulge in something visceral, a meeting of bodies, not minds. *Don't even think of indulging your pesky feelings, you crazy woman.*

She could get really hurt here.

But she could also see that he needed her, and God knows it felt good to be needed.

"I don't usually embark on hook-ups with a bunch of rules in place." Or hook-ups at all.

"Not asking you to sign anything, Sadie. But I think you liked what I did to you yesterday. I think you liked how I touched and kissed you. I think you liked my fingers inside you and how wet I made you." He leaned in, his breath a heated whisper against her lips. "And I know you liked how hard I made you come."

"Well, everyone likes orgasms." *A meme for the ages!*

His smile was wry. "They do. So if we keep it within those lines and don't stray outside them, then maybe we can enjoy more of them."

Another week, maybe two. That's how long it would take her to wrap up the house, let Lauren finish her next hockey camp session, and return to her life in LA. The offer of a pro-hockey player's hard body for her personal use was undeniably tempting. Neither would there be enough time for her do something stupid like fall for him.

What it meant for the texting, she had no idea. Or she suspected that was already fading into their history. It had already changed, and not necessarily for the better. She might want LonelyHeart, but for now she was getting Gunnar.

He still had his hand on her hip, his presence all up in her space. She could feel his heat, his vitality, his burning need. The want in his eyes matched the throb between her legs and the desire raging through her veins.

She pressed a hand to his chest, ostensibly to push him away so she could think without the scent of him invading her nostrils and curling like sex smoke into her chest. But that didn't work. It merely highlighted his undeniable maleness and how sexy he was.

He inclined his head. "Just a little taste. Let me show you how good it could be."

She moaned, and he took. His lips on hers were fire and magic. She threw her arms around his neck and cleaved her body to his, needing to assure herself this sensual connection between them wasn't a figment of her overwrought imagination.

She had to touch him everywhere. She grabbed his ass because she'd had that number one on her list for a while and she hadn't had a chance to yesterday. He returned the favor but upped the stakes by slipping beneath her skirt and clamping tight on her left butt cheek. His mouth slanted, his tongue slipped in and tangled with hers. Together they groaned at how good it felt. How honest this desire made them.

She fell back against the back seat—or maybe he gently shoved her—and within heated seconds, his hands were roaming along her inner thighs and her panties were half-way down her legs.

"Gunnar," she gasped.

His eyes darkened with lust. "Take 'em off, Sadie," he ordered, but before she could respond, he'd hunkered down, pulling her underwear with him rather efficiently. He even lifted her foot, one at a time, and like a sheep, she let him.

He stood and stared, something like disbelief in those shocking blue eyes.

"We need to get back," he murmured.

"We do?" She tightened her grip on—oh, Iggy. *Cover your eyes, you poor thing.* "We need to get back!"

His smile knocked her over. "That's what I said."

"But—but you just took off my panties ..." She lowered her voice and hissed, "in a public place in broad daylight. I'm going to need those."

He popped them in his pocket. "Think I'm going to need them more." Then he steered her to the side, closed the car door, and took charge of Iggy. "You should lock the car."

"Gunnar, you can't hold onto my panties. That's —you can't."

"Lock the car, Sadie."

She did, then followed him as he started heading back to the rink.

"Gunnar, could you—?" Good Lord, his legs were long. "Could you wait up?"

He pivoted suddenly and she bumped into him. Strong, wicked fingers curled around one of her arms and held her still.

"Be careful with Iggy's heart," she whispered.

"Excuse me?"

She touched the fabric heart on the bear's chest. "I need to mend it, but for now, be careful with it."

He nodded. "I'll see you after the game."

"I haven't agreed to any of this."

"Your lips agreed, the wetness between your thighs agreed, and the way your eyes are shining at me ... are you saying you don't want this? Tell the truth."

So direct. Of course she wanted it, but that was the problem. She might want it too much and he might not want it— or her—enough. Could she manage her emotions as efficiently as he did?

Because that's the vibe he was giving off. Efficiency. Biological imperatives. Hearts of stone.

"If it's the only way to get my panties back," she grumbled.

His mouth kicked up at the corner. "It is." Then he dropped a light kiss on her lips and steered her inside.

24

Sadie was nervous.

She had a host of reasons. Her sister was on the ice surrounded by rough boys with sharp weapons on their feet and clubs in their hands. As for the puck, wow was it fast and likely lethal. Why were children allowed to play this again?

Team L'il Rebels (Sadie's nickname for them, which—shocker—didn't seem to be catching) were playing well, and even Sadie could tell that Lauren was amazing. So quick and deft, and every time she bumped against someone, Sadie's heart stuttered and stopped. As if knowing she couldn't be there to comfort her—not that Lauren would want it—*he* was there instead.

Gunnar.

Sadie watched him almost as closely as she watched her sister. He wasn't as vocal as Theo who spent most of the time on his feet hollering like a madman at the team, much to Elle's amusement. No, Gunnar had that quiet, forceful solidity Sadie could feel from all the way across the rink and twenty rows up to where she was sitting.

When Lauren was on the ice, he followed her motions intensely. When off it, he sat beside her and pointed to things happening on the rink. During these interludes, Lauren didn't look at him, just kept her eyes on the play, but Sadie could tell her sister absorbed every word into her heart.

He must have been a wonderful dad.

The sharp catch in her chest made the connection. All that loss, yet here he was hanging with kids and giving back. Perhaps he was further along in the healing process than she, or even he, had thought. Perhaps ... *no, don't think you can be his harbor.*

For some reason, this man wanted to bed her. Her, Sadie Yates.

Well, a bed hadn't been mentioned but an offer of mind-blowing, no strings sex with a hockey god was on the table. She assumed he was a god in the physique stakes; her eyes and fingertips didn't lie and no man filled a T-shirt like that without being able to back it up. The appetizer orgasm had been wonderful, though the antagonism between them had definitely helped, and the teary afterglow had only added to the tenderness she felt toward him.

It was also hard to hold a grudge against a man who had taken her sister under his giant wing. Yet Gunnar Bond still managed to irk her with how he'd phrased his offer of multiple orgasms.

Don't look for any relationship vibes here, Sadie. I'm a Viking Robot and don't do emotions. Ignore those tears behind the curtain.

She reached into her bag and took out a pad and pencil. Her nerves could do with some soothing, and sketching might help. A few quick lines, a swoosh of action, and Sadie managed a smile.

"Oh, that's good." Jenny leaned in. "Could you get one of Jason?"

"Sure." She drew a few sharp lines, softened the ones around his feet to indicate motion, and pulled up his visor so she could add a dimple. "Here, what do you think?"

"You've captured something there," Jenny said. "There's something truthful about them. Did you go to school for design?"

Art had been her bedrock when she was a kid, a way to stay in her head and ignore her body. She might not feel beautiful but she could control it on the page. That love of lines naturally flowed into design and making her own clothes instead of relying on plus-sized, shapeless bags.

"I thought about going to design school, but it didn't work out." Actually her father had refused to pay her tuition unless she majored in something "useful." Besides she couldn't hate his guts and take his money at the same time.

"You don't need it if you're already designing your own stuff. I know you probably don't have the time but I'd love to have one of your dresses." She rolled her eyes. "Not one of *your* dresses, but a Sadie Yates exclusive. For me."

"Me, too," Elle said. "Give me something to look forward to after I lose all the baby weight."

"Oh, I haven't done anything for anyone before."

"But that's the plan, isn't it?" Jenny sipped her wine. "Make a business of it? I'd pay you, of course. You could take my measurements and then send it to me when you're back in LA. Whenever you have it done. Unless I've completely overstepped here."

"No, not at all. I mean, that's what I want to do." Having people wear her designs might be even better than trying to get investors. Maybe she could start a portfolio on Instagram. Real women in Sadie Yates Originals ... "I'd love to."

"Awesome," Jenny said. "So what are your plans for the Fourth?"

A week from Sunday was Independence Day. Usually Sadie would be helping Allegra host a cookout and taking photos and video for her social. She'd promised she would be back in LA but that was looking less and less likely.

"Packing, packing, and more packing."

"Would you like to get out of the city for a night? Theo's grandmother is in a play in Saugatuck. It's a couple of hours drive away, and we've been invited."

"Oh, but that's a family thing, surely?"

Elle leaned in. "Theo has bought out one night of the show and wants to pack the house. We can't get out of it, so why should you?"

Sadie felt warm at their easy acceptance of her. It might be nice to skip town for a while, and especially escape the house with its chatty walls and ever present ghosts. "I don't really have any money for a hotel …"

"Don't worry about that," Elle said. "Theo also bought his gran a big house years back with his signing bonus. There's plenty of room and you're going to love Aurora. She's a hoot!"

"Looks like I've run out of excuses to refuse. We're in!"

"Excellent."

Team Li'l Rebels won 6-3. Lauren scored a goal and helped with two more—assists, Jenny said—which apparently counted almost as much as goals in bragging rights. After the game, they headed to a lounge in another part of the complex for a camp graduation party.

She found Lauren, went for a hug, but stopped at the look of horror on her face. In that moment, she looked so like their dad that Sadie had to fight the lump in her throat.

"You were awesome! I can't believe how good you were. Good thing we found Benny."

"Who?"

"Sorry, I meant Iggy. I snagged him from the car."

"Uh, thanks."

"So, did you have fun?"

"I suppose. I'll be back next week anyway."

"Yes, you will! Off you go and get some pizza," she said, though Lauren was already heading for the food and her new friends. It was good to see her acting her age around other kids. Anything Sadie could do to take Lauren's mind off the family's issues, she'd make it work.

As for her own issues, her greedy eyes sought out the man of the hour. Gunnar stood near the door—oh dear— watching her like a ravenous wolf spotting his prey. He took a long draft of beer from a bottle. The sight of it traveling down his throat should not have had any impact on her whatsoever, but she was weak. She wanted to lick that throat and more.

"Here you go." Jenny passed her a bottle of water. "Figure we should be responsible and sober up. You okay? You look a little flushed."

"Me? Oh, fine. So how long does this thing last?"

Jenny raised an eyebrow. "In a hurry?"

"Not at all! Just wondering what the etiquette is."

"This is the first year we've done it." She checked her phone. "Probably another hour or so."

Sadie's phone buzzed with a text message, and her heart skipped at the name of the sender: Gunnar.

Edited from LonelyHeart, which she'd changed after a quick visit to the restroom. Out in the parking lot, he'd become someone else and in that moment, she'd become someone else. Someone desirable and good enough to break a man's sex fast.

Gunnar: Make an excuse and meet me outside.

She shot her most meaningful glance his way and made a face to indicate this was nuts and she couldn't possibly and did he not realize there were children present, for crying out loud.

With eyes raking her body, he placed a hand in the pockets of his sweats and pulled out something pink. No, he wouldn't dare.

He would. Another inch of fabric.

The. Fiend.

She turned to Jenny and squeaked, "I need to make a phone call. Work. Could you keep an eye on Lauren?"

"Of course. Say hi to the Punani Queen for me!"

"Will do!" Ignoring Gunnar, she sauntered right by him and out the door.

FOR FORTY THREE excruciating minutes after the game, Gunnar watched Sadie from across the room, enjoying the way his body changed in her presence now that he'd given himself permission to indulge this desire. She was throwing her hands around, explaining something to Jenny. He checked her out furtively, getting a kick out of her vibrancy.

Why did he say all that stuff to her about connection and feelings? He wasn't a big talker—he hadn't been with Kelly—and now he found himself needing to explain to this woman something unexplainable.

He wanted her.

Badly.

Telling her why and how and all the ways he wanted her

had assumed a weird importance. He could say it was to avoid any confusion about what this was, about the potential for more than the physical. He was explaining for her sake.

Not true.

He was doing it for himself. He needed to say aloud that this was merely biological, a raw physical need. *Rest assured, Kel, nothing more than my dick will become involved.*

Yet he found himself in a bind. Because he wasn't an asshole, not really. His factory setting was good guy. This cranky, brooding version was a placeholder, a shell he'd created to pour his pain and hurt into.

These dueling versions of himself were as far apart from each other as Chicago was from LA. He and his useless emotions were in flyover country. What was left of him, the rubble of his existence, was all he had to give. He hoped it was enough to satisfy Sadie for a brief time.

He waited a couple of minutes after she left then turned for the exit.

Theo materialized like a phantom. "You're leaving?"

"Do I need permission to take a leak?"

"No, but you might need condoms. Got any?"

Gunnar went for the bluff. "Why would I need condoms?"

"Because Sadie just left and you've been making eyes at her for an hour. Going to give her a tour of the facilities?" He shuffled closer. "And by facilities, I mean, your—"

"I know what you mean, Kershaw."

The man had a point. He hadn't even thought of protection, hadn't thought for a moment he'd pounce on Sadie in the parking lot, demand possession of her panties, and then text her to meet him for sex in the middle of a hockey youth camp graduation celebration.

Who was this person?

"You prepared?" Theo raised an eyebrow. "I have a condom in my wallet."

"Is this from the same batch you used when you knocked up your woman?"

Theo grinned. "No, actually. Those condoms—and you'll note I used the plural—belonged to Elle. She picked them up at the army base where she used to serve, so you could say Uncle Sam is responsible for that cock-up. Though really, it all worked out for the best because without the baby we probably wouldn't be together. So thanks, military-industrial complex—"

"Just give me the rubber, Kershaw."

"Sounding impatient there, Double-O! Try to give the poor woman a good time before you blow your load."

Jesus. "Forget it."

Theo zigged when Gunnar tried to zag. "Hold up, man! Just kidding around. Here you go." He slid a foil into Gunnar's hand, who slipped it into his pocket with Sadie's panties. He was fifteen years old again.

"I'll cover for you while you're gone."

"No one will ask—okay, thanks." The kid meant well but Christ, he was exhausting.

At the end of the corridor, Sadie was circling a spot. On hearing footsteps, she quickly put a phone to her ear. Acting. When she spotted him, she lowered the phone and smiled.

His cock stirred and his heart flipped over. Both of them, just like that. *Ker-ist.* That should not be happening.

He closed the gap and took her hand. "Let's go."

"Where? We can't stay away for long. I have to ..." She thumbed over her shoulder.

"I won't say I'll be quick because that's not a good look."

She giggled, and that sound released a coil of tension inside him. He turned and kissed her because to not do so would be a missed opportunity for joy. He found himself craving it all. Craving her.

"What was that for?" she whispered when he let her up for air.

"I'm glad you're here."

She blinked in surprise. "Oh. I'm glad I'm here, too."

He tried a door, pleased as fuck to find it open, and pulled her inside. Coach Calhoun's office. He turned the lock behind him.

Their breaths mingled as he moved close enough to kiss her, yet he held off. Waiting for her to give him the go ahead. The last time, he'd lunged at her like an animal.

"Gunnar, who's Angel?"

"Angel?"

"When I called you yesterday, you asked for Angel."

Ah. "What I called you in my contacts. The girl from LA, Angel." Tying it to the other reason, how she'd saved him, would be too much.

She smiled. "Mystery solved. Now are you going to kiss me?"

"Do you want me to?"

She placed a hand on his chest and he damn near lost his mind. How did she do that with one simple touch?

"I want you to make good on all that orgasm talk. And I don't need any seduction. I'm all in."

She stroked his jaw, her touch soft. He captured her mouth roughly, with a hunger he'd kept at a simmer below his boiling surface. His veins—and other parts—bulged with desire.

Something she said pinged him. "What do you mean you don't need any seduction?"

"You've already said what the expectations are. So no need to play games. I'm a sure thing."

He liked the no games thing and he *had* explained what this was about. That didn't mean they had to forego a build-up. Did she think she didn't deserve to be told how sexy and desirable she was?

"I know I'm rusty but that doesn't mean I can't make it good for you."

She trailed a finger down his chest to his sweats, then brushed the back of her knuckles over his straining cock. Not going to last.

"How rusty?" She mouthed an O. "Sorry, I shouldn't pry."

"It's okay. But to make it good for you, I need you to ... not touch me until I say so."

"You mean anywhere?"

He pushed her back toward Coach's desk. The man would kill him if he ever found out, but Gunnar couldn't wait a moment longer. He placed her on the edge, jerked a chair forward, and sat down.

"Pull up your skirt."

She inhaled sharply. "You mean—"

"I need a taste of all the sweetness, Sadie. And once we've taken care of you, then you can touch me. I've only had the company of my right hand for the last three years, so this is the best, the only, way to make me last."

The tenderness he saw there almost broke him. He figured he could be honest about sex. About desire. This was the first woman he'd been with since Kelly and there was no point lying about it.

She looked over his head at the door.

"Don't worry, Sadie. No one's coming except you."

Her gaze smoldered and she pulled at the fabric of her

dress, a pretty black skirt with white dots. Raising one foot shod in a cute low-heeled sandal, she placed it on his thigh. He moved the chair closer while curling his hand around her ankle.

The skirt inched higher, oh so slow. This woman had claimed not to need seduction, but these moves were seducing them both.

"That's it. Gimme a peek of all that sweetness."

He'd never been much of a dirty talker, but this was good. It separated the *now* from the *then*. Family man Gunnar was gone and in his place, a harder, unencumbered version remained. His cock thickened at the words coming out of his mouth, the flash of desire in her eyes, the skirt creeping higher until finally—fuck, all that pretty pink heat came into view.

He scooted closer, lifting her other leg to slot in at his waist. The move forced her to balance her palms on the desk.

"Wider, honey. Show me everything."

Her breath came in shallow pants now, and as he watched that beautiful sight, she turned wetter under his intent gaze. His mouth watered. He spread his palms on that silky soft skin inside her thighs—which always felt like the most vulnerable place on a woman's body—and coasted his palms north.

Peering up, he found her lips parted, her silver eyes wild.

"Need to see more of you, Sadie. Take off your blouse."

With shaky fingers, she unbuttoned, revealing a pretty cream bra, edged with lace. Her tits were the stuff of every male fantasy. Full, voluptuous, waiting to be sucked deep and long.

"Uncup them, Sadie. I want to see your breasts. I want them ready for my tongue."

But first, he needed to feast on all the pretty before him. His thumbs strained closer and then he gave one light swipe. She shivered all over.

"Like that, honey?"

"Yes. Gunnar, yes." Her voice sounded strangled.

He ran a finger along her soft seam. "You're so fucking wet. Ready for me to taste you?"

"Jesus, yes. Please."

Her impatience made him chuckle and lightened the situation. Inclining his head, he gave the lady what she needed. What they both needed. So sweet, the perfect treat. She cupped the back of his head, urging him closer, and he gave her his all. Sucking, licking, feasting on her in a frenzy. She came quickly, and he was disappointed it was over so soon.

But it was only the beginning.

He stood to find her panting and still in her bra.

"What did I say, Sadie, about needing you naked?"

"I haven't had a chance! You got me off so fast I can barely catch my breath never mind follow your precise orders."

He kissed the indignation off her lips. "Not my fault you've got a hair trigger clit."

"Not usually. But damn, you've got skills, Bond. Thought you were rusty."

He kissed her again, feeling freer than he had in years. "I guess you bring out my A game."

"*Now* can I touch you?" She looked down between their bodies. "Though at the rate that thing's expanding, it's going to be touching everything in the room soon."

This woman was funny. He'd forgotten how funny she was.

He reached around and unhooked her bra, releasing

her breasts. As perfect as he expected. Ripe, teardrop-shaped, with perfect, rosy peaks. She gripped his sweats and pushed them down so his cock sprang free. She was right—the damn thing was big enough to need its own zip code.

Her soft hand curled around him. *Not Kelly, not Kelly.* He willed the panic away.

"How long can I play here?" she murmured.

Not long. Not long at all. "I'll let you know. Yeah—yeah, like that."

She stroked along the length. With every pass, his balls grew heavier along with his heart. "Sadie," he whispered. "I need to be inside you."

The thought terrified him, but he tried not to dwell on it by doing things. Fumbling for the condom. The tear of the package. The roll-on. Some skills were innate.

And then he was moving close, probably going too fast, making a mess of it. But he would never know from how she responded. Sadie Yates smiled, that hooky grin, the one that gave him hope that this was right even when it felt all wrong.

"This okay?" he asked, more so she could tell him.

"It's more than okay, Gunnar," she whispered and he sank into that hot, wet welcome. He touched his forehead to hers and held it there.

This woman is not my wife.

He waited for his cock to deflate but it obviously didn't love Kelly the way his heart did. No, his treacherous body loved that they were back in business.

That's okay, he told it. *Lead the way.* No need to overcomplicate this. No need for remorse.

He withdrew an inch, thrust again, raised his head.

Still that beautiful smile, but those silver-starred eyes

wore a lusty glaze. She was waiting for him to get over himself. Her patience floored him.

"Sorry," he murmured. "I'm no ..." *Good at this.*

She kissed him, a gentle press to the edge of his jaw. Her lips found the corner of his mouth and applied another shivery touch. He groaned, acutely aware that this tentative exchange was even sexier than the connection of their bodies.

Sadie Yates knew this about him.

This is what he'd been afraid of.

They kissed, mouths seeking, tongues in a dance of forgiveness and forgetting. His body moved with the flow, pushing and pulling, giving and taking. He cupped her ass and stroked deeper. The kiss took on a life of its own, urging them on, pushing them further past the point where his vows became meaningless. In this moment, he had no regrets, but he knew he'd feel like shit tomorrow. Like thinking one more drink won't hurt because you've forgotten what a hangover feels like.

He touched between them, a tender press against her clit, needing to end it. Needing to return to that old version of himself, if he even existed anymore.

She fluttered and froze, and made that funny little sound in her throat. It was so sexy. She was so sexy. She tightened around him, milking him hard and long and *fuuckk*. It went on and on as he emptied everything he had into her.

So long with only his hand for company, that was why it felt so good. Not her sweet mouth. Not her forgiving kisses. Not her god*damn* understanding.

His dick was happy, that was all.

25

SADIE DROPPED Lauren off at the Isners after the hockey party. She'd hoped her sister might be in a good enough mood to want to hang with her for Thai food tonight, but no. She wanted to spend time with her new friends "while she still could." *Guilt attack, ten points.*

Sadie supposed it was okay. She'd have four years to get to know her sister in LA, but only a few days to keep her current employment. Allegra had left a million messages while Sadie slipped away for those stolen moments with Gunnar. She would spend the rest of the evening working the phone and online to satisfy her boss's every whim.

Speaking of being satisfied ... sex with Gunnar Bond was as amazing as she expected once the man had given himself permission to let go. Then it was shields-up as soon as it was over. No mention of when they might see each other again. He hadn't been rude, just distant. She understood, even though it hurt.

She pulled into the driveway of the house and froze in shock.

THIEF SCUM

THE WORDS BLARED in large red painted letters across the front door. A chill rolled through every cell. Plenty of people hated her father, but whoever was doing this had to realize he had a young daughter. Anger evicted itchy panic.

Those fuckers were messing with the wrong chick. She dialed 911.

An hour later, she answered the door, assuming the cops had forgotten something after a frustrating session of *you don't have security cameras? Not much we can do, then*. Gunnar stood there, arms crossed, mouth grim, attitude dialed up to eleven.

"What are you doing here?"

He made a rather melodramatic eye swivel to the grafitti'ed door. "You really have to ask?"

"Wow, the Rebels grapevine is on fire today." She'd asked Jenny to keep Lauren for a couple of hours longer so she could head out to Home Depot for paint.

He invited himself in with one last glare at the door. "Why didn't you call me?"

"I didn't think of it." Lie. The first thing she'd wanted to do, before she even called CPD, was reach out to Gunnar. But that wasn't their relationship. He'd made it clear they were a sex-only deal and while he'd come to her rescue before, she wouldn't want to get used to it.

"Where's Lauren?"

"Still over at the Isners. I was going to buy some paint and try to fix this before she gets back."

He reached for her arms and coasted rough palms down them. "You're not seriously thinking of staying here."

"This is Lauren's home, all she's ever known. In a couple of weeks, she'll be ripped from it. The least I can do is ease her out of it gently."

"At the risk of someone going too far, Sadie? The letters, the rock, now this." He shook his head. "Pack a bag, You're coming home with me."

Home. That felt a little too nice. She stepped back. "This is not your problem to solve, Gunnar. I appreciate you've helped me in the past, but I'm not leaving this house. It'll be auctioned in two weeks and I need to have packed up everything. At this rate, I have to work through the night, every night to get all of it done. I don't know what the hell I'm doing sneaking away to hook up with you—I literally do not have time for that. And neither do I have time for your white knight business. I'm holding on by a thread here."

"Hey." He gathered her in his arms and while she claimed she didn't want it, her body took the comfort gladly. "I'm just worried about you. The both of you. What can I do? And don't tell me nothing."

She closed her eyes against his chest and inhaled all that clean, masculine goodness. He wanted to help—not for her, but for Lauren. That protective instinct won her over. "Could you get a can of paint from Home Depot? I'll give you the money. I need to make some phone calls for my job, so that would really help right now."

"Okay, but you'll have to come with me and make the phone calls in the car."

"Gunnar—"

"You can't stay here alone, so that's the deal."

She inhaled a breath. Compromise, that's what needed to happen. That's what she'd not done with her father and look how that turned out.

In the car, he kept his eyes on the road. She'd noticed

that was his MO and who could blame him. He remained silent, letting her get on with her work, and went into Home Depot while she stayed in the car, finishing up calls about Allegra's appointments, her reservations, her favorite champagne, travel plans for her upcoming trips. Finally she called her when she had it all done because a text to confirm wouldn't be enough. Her boss needed the human touch.

She put on her happy face. "Hey, girl, how are things?"

"I'm in a living nightmare, Sadie! There was an earthquake here!"

"Oh, no. How bad was it?" Sadie did a quick check online and saw it registered as 4.4. Barely a quiver.

"7.6 or 7.9. I don't know! Anyway, a couple of my Waterfords fell from the shelf so I'll need you to file an insurance claim for me ..." Sadie half-listened as the sight of Gunnar walking toward her with a paint can arrested her attention. God he looked good. But then he always did.

He caught her ogling, and his mouth kicked up in a wicked grin that made her warm all over.

"... so Raj said he'll take a look but he can't make any guarantees."

Gunnar put the paint and other supplies in the trunk and climbed in. She could make out the thick musculature of his thighs against the sweatpants fabric. One lovely squeeze ...

Allegra was still on speaker, so Sadie switched to regular audio. "Sorry, Allegra, were you saying that Andie's assistant wants to look at my designs?"

Gunnar raised an eyebrow and reached over to squeeze her thigh. She glared at him but it might have come off as a smolder because he slipped a rough palm beneath the hem of her dress and traveled north.

"No promises, but I gave him your portfolio. We'll see if anything comes of it. He said florals are not really in this year, especially on bigger patterns like yours, but Andie has been known to go against the grain. Oh, I sent the prizes for the Come As You Are contest. Did you get those?"

"I did." A box of Moregasm spray bottles—exactly what it sounded like—and other assorted products related to self-love had been waiting on the stoop, and missed being tagged by the stalker. "I'll work on those tonight."

"Okay, I suppose." Allegra sounded peeved. "Now, the insurance information is all here, so I don't know how you're going to manage."

Gunnar's hand crept its wicked way up, up, up.

"I scanned everything months ago. It's all in the Dropbox folder, so if you could send me some photos of the damage—" Gunnar hit paydirt. She pushed back against his hand like the wanton woman she was. In a Home Depot parking lot, no less.

"Send me the photos!" She hung up. "That was my boss."

"She sounds awful."

"There was an earthquake in LA this afternoon."

He rubbed a thumb over her dampening panties, moved his lips to her jaw. His beard against her skin was divine. "Oh, yeah?"

Oh yeah. Meanwhile a Midwest quake was building to erupt. A quick nibble of her ear and she was putty. "I have to get back and paint the door."

Now he added two, then three fingers, still over her underwear but no less effective for it. "If we weren't sitting out here in the open in broad daylight, I'd have you in my lap now, Sadie. But for now, I need you to help a man out.

Pull up your skirt, move those gorgeous thighs wider, and let me see how pretty you are."

"But we already did, uh, it, a couple of hours ago." She sounded like the natural prude she was.

"I've got some catching up to do. Just do as I say."

She did, every delicious thing he asked, knowing this was crazy and wild, and not caring one bit. Even here in the middle of a public place, he took his sweet, damn time.

It felt like they had all the time in the world.

THERE WAS nothing quite like watching a man drinking something down. *Water, gutternsnipes!* The way his throat bulged as it navigated that tan column set Sadie's pulse racing.

"Thanks so much for helping with the painting."

Leaning against the kitchen sink, Gunnar raised an eyebrow.

"Okay, doing *all* the painting. But you did insist, with your claims of better technique, etcetera." She moved closer and ran a hand over the front of his paint-specked sweats. "However can I repay you?"

"I'll think of something. Always happy to help out with both painting and orgasms."

"I see an Instagram account in the making."

He snaked an arm around her waist. "This business bothers me. The police—and you—need to take it more seriously."

She was worried. Who wouldn't be? But she suspected someone wanted to let of steam rather than truly cause harm.

"We'll be gone in a few more weeks."

"In an awful hurry to leave, aren't you?"

"My life's not here."

He looked like he was about to say something when the kitchen door opened. Lauren came in, with Jenny behind her. "Why is there a wet paint sign on the front door?"

Sadie moved out of Gunnar's arms and met Jenny's ah-that's-how-it-is gaze over her sister's head. "Needed a fresh coat of paint and Gunnar was offering."

Lauren eyed them both with suspicion, then zeroed in on Gunnar. "But why are *you* here?"

"I'm pretty handy with a paintbrush."

"Oh." Lauren frowned, not satisfied with that non-answer. "Thanks for the ride, Mrs. Isner." She grabbed a box of Pop tarts, a can of coke, and headed to the Dead-Tree room.

"What did the police say?" Jenny asked once Lauren was out of earshot.

"Probably kids."

Gunnar snorted his disgust. "Kids who know your father was recently convicted of fraud?"

He had a point, not that Sadie appreciated it.

"They recommended I set up a security system or pay for the one we already have. Unfortunately that's a bill I had to let go." She smiled at Jenny. "Do you want some tea?"

Jenny flicked a glance at Gunnar, a secretive smile brightening her eyes. "I think I'll let you get back to what you're doing."

"We're not—I mean, we are, but we don't have to be—" Sadie waved at Gunnar's chest as color rose to her cheeks. "Are you just going to stand there?"

"Where else would I stand?"

That made Jenny laugh, then she turned serious. "You're sticking around, Gunnar?"

"I am."

Sadie whirled on Gunnar. "No, you're not. My sister is here."

"All the more reason for me to stay." He spoke to Jenny. "Don't worry, I've got it in hand."

"Glad to hear it. Oh, and don't forget brunch tomorrow, Sadie."

"Brunch?" Now she remembered. Jenny had invited her to brunch with Elle and Jordan. It had seemed like a good idea after half a box of Franzia. "I don't know if I can—I've so much work to catch up on." Plus she was broke. Friends cost money, especially friends with connections to high-salaried pro-athletes.

"We'll see." Jenny surprised Sadie with a hug and then another for Gunnar. Her expression was disgustingly approving.

The minute she was out the door, Sadie turned to Gunnar. "You can't stay."

"Worried the neighbors will gossip?"

"I don't know my neighbors."

"Might be a good idea to check in with them. See if they saw anything." Gunnar headed over to the fridge. "How about I make us something to eat? You must be starving."

"I appreciate the offer to stay but I thought we were supposed to be coloring inside the lines here." She lowered her voice. "The *sex* lines."

He found a bowl, cracked some eggs, and started whisking them. "I can't ignore what happened here."

"Ah, but you can. It's one thing to help me out as a friend. Staying the night is a little too relationship-y, don't you think?"

"Maybe I like the idea of sneaking around."

She sighed. "While doing your good guy impression and keeping the damsel safe."

"Two birds, one stone." A heart of stone, more like. She wondered, though. For all Gunnar's claims to being unable to offer more, he certainly didn't have a problem being here for her in a way that counted. It was confusing.

In the pan, he stirred slowly. He made eggs like he made her come—with a great deal of patience.

"It all feels a little too paternalistic."

He considered that. "You're right."

"I am?" She loved being right.

He smiled at the surprise in her voice. "I sometimes go overboard when I worry about people. Kelly used to tell me I went too far with the kids."

"Dads can worry about their kids. It's dad law." Not that her father ever worried about her but he was obviously trying to get it right with Lauren.

He kept stirring. "I didn't worry enough when it mattered. I should have—" He bit off the words and turned to face her. "Sadie Yates, if it's okay with you, I would like to make you something to eat. And if it's also okay with you, I would like to stay over tonight in your bed and fuck you to within an inch of your life."

Well, then.

"We'll see how the eggs turn out."

Smiling, he continued with the eggs. His shoulders seemed to relax by degrees, and the oddest thought struck her: *He's more like the man in the texts. He gets closer to that man by the hour.*

What had he meant about not worrying enough when it mattered? She wanted to ask, but Lauren wandered into the kitchen and stood by Gunnar at the stove. "Are you cooking?"

"Knew you were smart."

"Mrs. Isner makes all her meals from scratch."

"Drag me, why don't ya," Sadie murmured.

"What's the plan for tomorrow, Lo?" Gunnar opened the fridge and pulled out a loaf of bread. *Lo?*

"Nothing."

"We could go to the practice rink. You're dragging your heel, so we should fix that before it becomes a problem."

The look of yearning on Lauren's face cracked Sadie's heart in half. "Just you and me?"

"Sure, unless you want to invite Jason. But that means we have to invite Kershaw, and you know how he is."

"Loud. It'd be cool. I mean, just the two of us."

He nodded. "Start toasting the bread, Lo. Six slices."

As Lauren hopped to it, he turned and winked at Sadie. *Nicely done, Bond. Nicely done.*

26

As LUCK WOULD HAVE IT, Saturday's lunch with Jenny and the girls was in Riverbrook, a stone's throw from the Rebels practice facility. Jenny had chuckled and said, "Oh, you can make it after all?" Gunnar dropped Sadie and Jenny off at a cute brunch place called Gallery before heading to the Rebels practice facility with Lauren. This way, Sadie wouldn't be alone in the house while a crazed tagger was terrorizing the neighborhood. She knew she was being manipulated by both Jenny and Gunnar, but sometimes it was nice to have someone else call the shots.

Elle and Jordan were already seated. Allegra had arranged that all the freebies she gave out should be shipped to Sadie for distribution, so Sadie played fairy godmother while they waited for their mimosas.

"Ooh, is the punani cream you were talking about?" Elle twisted off the lid and sniffed it. "Nice and smelly!"

"For external use only. Unlike this doohickey to help with pelvic muscle strength."

Jenny's eyes went wide as she held up the silicone pod.

"So you put it inside and it—oh my God. It's connected to Bluetooth!"

Sadie laughed. "Looking to improve your pelvic thrust? We have the technology."

After a few more giggles about vagina-related products, Elle turned to Jordan. "So, everything we say here is off the record, Cooke. No sneaking it into your column or your podcast."

Jordan smiled and crossed her heart with her fingers. "I'm marrying a pro-hockey star in less than three weeks. Every conversation is in the vault." She eyed Elle. "Which assumes you have something worth keeping the lips zipped for."

Both Jenny and Elle turned to Sadie, and Jenny gestured with a wave. "Meet the woman who is saving Gunnar Bond one orgasm at a time."

"What?" Sadie sputtered. "That's not what's happening."

"Isn't it?"

She shook her head vehemently. "No one is being saved. It's just mindless, what's-your-name-again, don't-bother-calling-in-the-morning sex."

Jordan took a sip from the mimosa that had just arrived. "The best kind."

"No," Elle said, glaring at her friend.

"No?"

Elle waved at Sadie. "Gunnar has been grieving for three years. He went off grid and lived in a cabin in the middle of nowhere to try to outrun his demons. Now he's met someone who makes him want to—"

"Want to what?" Sadie asked, looking at all of them.

"Grab life by the horns again." Jenny grabbed a bread-stick by the horns and bit down on it.

Sadie saw what was happening here and she needed to nip it in the bud.

"You've got the wrong end of the breadstick. Gunnar and I have a very clear arrangement. It's clothes off, straight to business, zero cuddling." Last night, she'd insisted he leave her bed after the orgasms because she was trying to set a good example for Lauren. And maybe she didn't want to risk waking up wrapped in those studly arms—and liking it too much. She was no dummy. "The only talking is instructional and directional. I'm not saving him."

Even if he was playing white knight and saving her.

She gulped down her mimosa, annoyed with Gunnar, who was being awesome with Lauren. He even had a nickname for her. But this insistence on rescuing Sadie while forbidding her to reciprocate was unfair, especially as she'd been there for him when they were text buddies. Sex was great and all but ... one step forward, two steps back was hard.

"Look," Jenny said. "You might not want to label it that way and perhaps neither of you want to overthink it, but this is a big deal."

"He doesn't like casual," Elle said, leaning in with a grave expression. "Sex means something to him. He told me."

Sadie's heart gave a treacherous leap. *Quiet, you.*

"He and I have discussed this at length."

"Thought you didn't talk. At all." Jordan zeroed in, her reporter senses in overdrive.

"Before it started, he told me exactly what I needed and what I should expect. No emotions would be engaged. And I'm glad of it. I'm leaving in a couple of weeks." Though she had to admit, Chicago was growing on her. Or re-growing on her. She felt more welcome here than she'd ever felt in LA. But she had to be realistic about her finances and prospects.

"Even if I wanted more, even if Gunnar wanted to give more, a lot of ifs, then it still wouldn't happen because my life is elsewhere." She knocked back half a Mimosa.

"Now, who wants this pubic hair conditioner?"

GUNNAR RACED down the practice rink, the puck Velcro'ed to his stick, and slapped the board with it so it boomeranged around the net. Two seconds later, he watched with satisfaction as Lauren slapped it forward and bulged the twine.

"Yes!" He skated over to her and offered a gloved high-five. "Nice work, Lo."

"Thanks." Her smile hit him hard.

"Let's do some work on your skating motion. As you get older, it'll change because your weight distribution will be different, but we should set good habits now. Watch me."

He skated a few figure eights, demonstrating the power position of knees bent, butt out, chest and head up. Posture was important and junior players tended to bend at the hip instead of the knees, like little hunchbacks.

"Okay, now you."

He could tell she'd paid attention but she was inconsistent. Down the rink, she'd keep it low but back up she'd rest and let her legs do all the work.

"Not bad. But to get the proper depth, you'll need to keep your knees bent and push though on each stroke to get maximum extension."

They worked on that for about ten more minutes before moving onto puck drills. He figured thirty minutes should be the maximum—she wasn't a pro skater yet.

They sat on the bench, catching their breath. He handed a bottle of water to her.

"I know a few people in LA who could work with you," he said.

She scowled. "My dad won't let her take me."

Her dad had no choice. "You've talked to him?"

A flush crept over her skin. "She won't let me see him." She tapped her stick, hitting the wall of the Plexi. "Why did you stay over last night?"

"That rock that came through your window last week? I don't like it." She didn't know about the graffiti and he didn't want to scare her.

She turned to him. "She's not good enough for you."

"That's not a nice thing to say."

She shrugged. "If you like her so much, why don't you ask her to stay in Chicago? That way she won't even think about moving."

"Not as simple as that."

"Hey guys!" Sadie's voice cut in from behind and they both turned. "Wow, it's chilly in here."

"Because of the ice," Lauren deadpanned.

"Yeah, I got that." She smiled. "Elle dropped me off. She was headed into the city anyway so she took Jenny. I hope it's okay. I can sit here and watch. You won't even notice me."

Gunnar smiled back, feeling foolish for being so happy to see her. He wanted to see her safe, but damn if she didn't look pretty as a picture in a blue dress with a dipping neckline. Her designs were amazing, and while he knew nothing about fashion, he could tell she was talented.

"We were finishing up. Lauren made great strides with her skating motion today."

"Oh, that's fantastic." She held out her hands as if to say, *isn't it*? Lauren refused to look at her. "I would be a complete mess out there."

"Have you ever skated?"

"Ah, negative."

"Would you like to?"

"Also, negative."

He stood and picked his way toward her. "I'm going to grab you a pair of skates and take you for a spin."

"Gunnar, that's such a terrible idea. I will fall down. I guarantee it."

"So what if you do? A few stumbles shouldn't scare a woman like you."

Two spots of color appeared high on her cheekbones. "I'll give it a shot," she whispered.

"Atta girl. What's your shoe size?"

"Seven."

Two minutes later he was back with a couple of pairs of skates. The sisters sat on the bench, backs stiff. Sadie was obviously trying to initiate conversation and Lauren wasn't having it.

He knelt down in front of Sadie and unhooked the strap of her sandal. He couldn't help himself. He curved a hand around her heel, up her calf and enjoyed the silky smooth skin there. She shivered.

"Cold in here," she whispered.

"Yeah, ice rink, dummy," Lauren said.

Gunnar gave Lauren a hard look. "Hey, don't disrespect your sister."

Sadie squeezed his shoulder and flashed her eyes at him. "It's okay. I don't know anything about ice rinks, so yeah, I'm a dummy."

"Put this jersey on." He'd grabbed one of his extras from the locker room. While she did that, Gunnar rolled two pairs of socks on, then fitted the first choice of skate. "Toe down. How does it feel?"

"Sort of snug."

"That's how it should feel." He put the other one on, then grasped both her hands. "On your feet, Sadie."

He pulled her upright and she froze in place. "Not sure I should do anything more than this."

"Oh, we're doing much more than this." As the words left his mouth, they felt applicable to more than a leisurely skate around a practice rink.

"Come on, Lo, let's show your sister how to skate."

"Don't think so."

"Lauren."

She looked up, conscious of his tone. "Okay, okay."

A few minutes later, Sadie was treading tentatively over the ice near the bench, moving back and forth along the wall. She looked so cute and sexy in his jersey, just like ... but not like ... He shook the memory away.

"Now hold the wall with one hand and me with your other."

"I don't know ... oh, look I'm doing it!"

They traveled a few feet, then pivoted, and headed back again. Lauren skated back and forth, showing off, really, but it was more encouraging than sitting on the bench. After a few minutes, he took a chance.

Placing his hands on Sadie's hips, he moved in close. "Do you trust me?"

"Should I?" She tilted her head, and smiled that knockout ray of sunshine that had reeled him in from the beginning.

"You can."

"Okay. Gimme a reason, Bond." More words, multiple meanings.

Still with his hands on her hips, he coasted backwards slowly, bringing her with him. "We're just dancing, Sadie. That's all it is."

She glided with him, three feet, six, nine, until they were in the center of the rink. "That's it, no need to even move your feet, let me guide you."

"I can't believe you're skating backwards," she gushed, her eyes bright as the ice.

"Do it all the time. Second nature." He turned to Lauren. "What do you think? Not bad for a first timer, right?"

Lauren sniffed. "She's okay."

"Ooh, you hear that?" Sadie grinned. "I'm okay." And then her feet went from under her, she grabbed his jersey—the one on his body—and they both crashed to the ice.

She made an *oof* sound. "Sheesh, thought you had a handle on it, Bond."

"You distracted me with that smile of yours." He wouldn't have minded sitting there with her but the ice was chilling his ass and probably worse for her. He picked himself up and pulled her to her feet. "You want to call it?"

"Are you kidding? We're just getting started!"

27

Gunnar watched Sadie as she slept. She still wrinkled her nose, and she still made those cute, sighing sounds, as if he was kissing her in her dreams. Last night he'd sneaked in, given her three orgasms, and took advantage of her bone-tiredness by staying the night in her bed.

He'd moved in to keep her safe. When people lost things, they got angry. He understood that feeling, the need to lash out. Few people truly acted on it in a way that hurt others but he saw no harm in hanging around. If someone saw him on the property, all the better. Let it be known that Sadie and Lauren had a support system.

She stirred and he reached for her. Gunnar held her close, enjoying the soft round curves of her body and how they perfectly aligned with the dips and dents of his. Mornings had always been his favorite time with Kelly, that brief half hour of bliss while he slipped inside her and made her scream into the pillow before the kids crashed into the room.

Another memory assaulted him.

Janie afraid of a thunderstorm, sneaking into bed with them.

Janie tucked under his arm, her fair hair a golden crown of curls. Janie telling him he was the best daddy in the world.

Not so great in the end. Not so great because he couldn't protect them.

He'd gone a while, maybe even a whole night without thinking of them. His stiff body mirrored his guilt.

"You okay?" Sadie whispered.

"Fine," he murmured.

She made a noise that sounded like "oh really?"

"I am," he insisted.

After a few moments of quiet, she murmured sleepily, "You can tell me about her. If you like."

How did she read his mind like that? "Why?"

"Because your family were a big part of your life and—"

"They're still a big part of my life. They *are* my life."

"Of course." She said it so simply that he regretted snapping. Again, her patience made him edgy. He'd offered nothing to her. Why was she so accepting of it?

It was the same with Lauren, who was pretty rude to her. Sadie just took it.

She waited a beat before speaking again. "Do you miss what we had?"

"What *we* had?"

She twisted to face him. "That version of us on the texts. It seemed more ... honest."

He held her gaze. "Desire isn't honest? Kissing you all over, fucking you until you scream, making you come over and over, that isn't honest?"

"It can be, I suppose."

This is what he'd been afraid would happen—a deep dive into emotions. Yet only a moment ago he was lamenting how she'd settled for so little.

"The texting was easier when we were strangers," he

said. "That kind of honesty was easier because we had no preconceptions, no expectations of the other person."

"We still don't."

His smile was wry. "Multiple orgasms not enough?"

"Oh, they're lovely." Her smile was dreamy. "But that version of us, the pre-meet-cute version, or the other meet-cute version, felt different. Like progress."

I still feel it, Angel. That's what he wanted to tell her. He felt it in every half-smile, every deep kiss, every all-consuming thrust. Just because he wasn't pouring his heart out didn't change the closeness.

She tilted her head. "Why did you answer back?"

"What?"

"Once you figured out someone else was listening in to your texts to Kelly, you could have stopped. Blocked the number. You didn't."

"Fucking AT&T." At her quizzical look, he explained. "That's what you said and it made me laugh. I hadn't laughed in a long time and it felt good." This felt good. "Why did you reach out again? After?"

She took a moment. "I was in a weird place. I'd just heard about my father's conviction and I wanted to connect with someone, I suppose. And I thought I could be useful. Be there for you."

Be there. She wasn't asking about the texting versions to make him feel better, or not only that. She needed comfort for herself—and all this time he'd been making it about him.

"Back then you didn't talk about yourself much," he said, testing the waters.

"Sure I did."

No. He'd gone through the texts. Read the entire exchange so he could convince himself it had meant nothing. That he wasn't emotionally cheating on his wife. Angel had always been concerned with his feelings, his needs.

"Just because I'm not dying to unload doesn't mean you can't tell me what's on your mind. With your dad, your job, Lauren. Unless all your problems vanish when I touch you." He brushed the back of his hand against one rosy nipple and yielded a husky moan.

"You're good at the sex, Bond. There, I've said it!"

He laughed, and they spent a few moments kissing and stroking, not with any particular destination in mind.

"I don't need to tell you about Lauren," she said after a few moments. That was Sadie. He could plant the seed, but she needed time to let it sprout. "You see how she is with me. I'm just trying to keep my head above water until I can get her settled."

"You shouldn't let your guilt about not being around when she was growing up give Lauren a pass on the attitude."

"That's not—I've only been here a few weeks. I have to cut her some slack, be the cool sister, because I'm not actually her parent, you know. That pain is still too fresh for her." She leaned up on her elbow. A pillow crease he wanted to smooth away had appeared on her cheek. "I'm not fishing for a shoulder to cry on, Gunnar. I just liked listening to you before, being there for you. I'm offering to be that for you again."

"If I wanted to talk to anyone about it, it would be you." He hoped it was enough for her to know that. What she gave him was a balm to his soul, but he refused to start relying on the woman who would soon leave Chicago in her dust.

She shook her head. "Pot, have you had the pleasure of meeting kettle?"

He pulled her close and kissed her softly, then more deep. "Sadie."

"You think that's going to work to fob me off?"

"Kissing and orgasms as distraction from our problems? Oh, yeah."

She chuckled, and he was so in love with her joy that he almost forgot why they were arguing. If he could only hold onto this, let it heal him without being pushed to talk about his pain. About Kelly. About Janie and Danny.

She traced a finger along his scar, then through his beard. "Will you text me when I move back to LA?"

His heart squeezed painfully. He didn't want to think of a time when she was no longer around. "Yes." Because even though it had all changed, he wanted to talk to Angel again.

Something sad appeared in her eyes. She didn't believe him, and he wondered if maybe she knew more than he did.

SADIE UNFURLED the fabric from the board and let the memories wash over her, swift and sharp.

Swedish love birds. Petals and vines. Years ago, she'd spotted a similar design in a shop window in Andersonville —Midsommar-chic without the human sacrifice—and bought five yards at Hancock Fabrics. Here it was, wrapped in plastic, as fresh as the day she purchased it. Sadie's mind swirled with possibilities. Something or someone more demure, she thought. She snapped a photo and sent it to Jenny.

What do you think of this fabric? For your dress?

The answer came back fast. *Love it!*

Hmm, Sadie had sort of hoped she could keep it for

herself. Two different designs with the same fabric perhaps? Or perhaps a dress for Lauren.

Gunnar was right about one thing. She was ignoring Lauren's disrespect because she didn't want to rock the boat. She wanted to talk to her sister, tell her she was sorry for not making more of an effort. But she didn't want to speak ill of her mom or bad mouth their dad. She'd missed all these birthdays, holidays, special events, and now she had twelve years to make up.

No time like the present.

With the sewing basket she'd dug up from her belongings (*why didn't you burn everything, Zoe?*), she headed downstairs to the Dead-Tree Room, aka the living room. Man, that tree was a mess, and if she wasn't such a coward she'd drag it out to the back yard now.

She glanced out the recently-installed window—a serious blow to her finances—and watched Gunnar putting his boot down on a pitch fork in the flower beds. He'd dived into yard work, not that she'd asked, but he said he liked keeping busy. *Sure thing, Viking. Anything to avoid talking about your feelings.*

A patch of sweat had dampened his T-shirt and molded to those amazing back muscles. He wore faded jeans today, maybe an old pair he dug out for work like this. They looked amazing on him.

Lauren was kneeling in the grass nearby, readying a pallet of pansies for planting. Sadie wasn't sure they should be putting this much effort into a property they wouldn't see a dime on, but watching the two of them together did such good things for her heart. Gunnar looked up then, and that smile ... oh, boy. He must have said something to Lauren because ten seconds later, she gave a tentative wave. Sadie waved back like a lunatic.

She turned back to the sofa and tidied up as best she could without looking like she'd been snooping—which was really hard to do! She knew so little about her sister. She liked art, but what kind? She played hockey, but did she have ambitions in that direction? She missed her mom, but what had their relationship really been like? She loved her dad, but … That's where Sadie's brain switched off. Where the envy took over. Where she became the person she didn't want to be. The bitter, resentful sister.

Benny/Iggy was here, thank God. Beggy? Biggy? Beniggi? Well, he was Iggy now. Iggy who could do with some TLC and would gladly let her care for him. She took a swatch of bright red from her basket, a sheened polyester that would launder well (Iggy could do with a wash), and chalked out a heart shape. A steady cut and several hidden stitches later, and Iggy had emerged as good as new from heart transplant surgery. She placed him in the recovery room (on the sofa against a cushion) and let him take it all in.

"You're going to be just fine, Iggy."

Her phone rang with a call from … Oh, shit … Allegra!

She answered. "Allegra, I'm working on—"

"Where is it, Sadie? 3pm. That's when people expect my daily videos. You're supposed to just, whatever, *schedule* it!"

"Right, I know. I haven't forgotten, I'm running a little behind." She'd yet to actually edit it. It was usually the first thing she worked on after dropping off Lauren at camp but today being Sunday, and having a hot guy in her bed, all bets were off.

"Do I need to start looking for someone else, Sadie? Someone who understands the commitment level I need here. One hundred and ten percent …" When Sadie didn't finish, Allegra screamed, "Because one hundred isn't enough!"

"Right. I get that. I do."

Allegra was on a self-righteous roll. "And I've been helping you with my contacts, Sadie. I have to say, it feels like you're taking advantage. Have I not been understanding?"

"You have."

"Have I not gone above and beyond as a boss?"

"Yes—"

"There are a million people who would want this job but I've been exceptionally gracious about your situation. Ramon said this would happen. That all that negative energy with your father's legal problems would come back to haunt me. You know what that negativity leads to, don't you?"

"Um—"

"Toxic. Punani," Allegra bit out. "If that kind of bad energy infiltrates my chakra and descends into my core, I may as well say good bye to my health, my sex life, my business. I need to call Sienna to see if she can fit me in for a hot yoga session. I have to purge this. And when I come out, I'd better see that video online."

Sadie swallowed. "You will, I promise. I will work on it now."

Allegra hung up and Sadie flopped on the sofa. She needed to get it together. She had no money, no prospects, a sister to feed, clothe, and educate, and a life in shambles. The orgasms, while wonderful, did not pay the bills.

"What the hell did you do with Iggy?"

Oh, rats. She looked up at her sister's wounded expression.

"His heart was falling apart, so I thought I'd give him a refresh."

"You had no right to touch him!" She scanned the sofa. "And have you been in my stuff?"

"I only tidied up, that's all." For God's sake, it was a health hazard. "I haven't changed anything. It's all here. And Iggy, well, he used to be mine. I gave him to you years ago. Before I left."

Lauren's eyes filled with tears. "No, you did not. My mom gave him to me. And now you've ruined him, like you ruin everything."

"Lauren—"

But she was gone. Four more years of this? Sadie wasn't sure she could do it.

28

A NEW WEEK, a new advanced hockey skills session. Gunnar slid into the slot next to Theo's in the parking lot and readied himself for the inevitable questions.

"Hey guys!" Theo high-fived Jason, then Lauren as they exited Gunnar's car. "New driver this morning?"

"He's sleeping with my sister," Lauren said. Jason snickered, Theo went wide-eyed, and here we are.

Gunnar grabbed Lauren's gym bag though really he should let the little blabbermouth carry it herself.

"Really?" Theo was agog, as if he'd completely forgotten his "encouragement" of three days ago.

Lauren shrugged and muttered to Jason, "Come on."

Theo took Jason's bag from him. "Go on ahead so I can talk to your uncle Gunnar."

While the kids walked on, Gunnar shut the trunk of the car.

Theo shook his head. "I give you a condom and you already have your feet under the table. Nice work."

"I stayed over because someone's giving them hassle. Property damage, threatening letters."

"Because of their jailbird dad?"

"Yeah, he pissed off a lot of people." He took a few steps, then stopped and turned to Theo. "I like Sadie. But there isn't anything more to it."

"Okay."

Theo sounded neutral but Gunnar didn't believe him because Theo wouldn't know neutral if he was wrapped in the Swiss flag.

"She knows the score," he insisted. Even if she was trying to get him to open up, a pointless exercise. He didn't need anyone to psychoanalyze him. He was already in a relationship with the family he lost, and what he was doing for Sadie and Lauren was what any decent human being would do. Nothing special about it.

"I'll tell Aurora to put you guys in separate rooms. So there's no confusion."

"What?"

Theo's grin was big enough to fuel the Rebels' rink lights. "For the weekend in the Tuck? Jenny invited Sadie and Lauren to see Cats this Saturday. Well, I told her she could bring whoever she wanted and I sort of had an idea that she'd invite Sadie because they're all buddy-buddy now, which is good for Jenny because I think she's a bit lonely with the stay-at-home-mom thing. And Nick being Nick, y'know. So Sadie and Lauren will be there because the more the merrier, right?"

"You're such a fucker, Kershaw."

They reached the entrance to the Rebels practice facility and Theo opened the door. "After you, G-man."

"I don't mind. Because if she wasn't going, I probably would have stayed in Chicago and not come at all."

"Sounds like it worked out, then."

Gunnar shook his head. "Be prepared for me to shut

down every one of your dumbass ideas for Hunt's bachelor party."

"About that, I've been thinking of maybe skydiving? Or axe-throwing?"

Gunnar walked on ahead, cursing Theo and team dynamics and the social contracts that required him to participate while Kershaw yammered on without taking a breath.

Driving down to Saugatuck (or up, according to Gunnar) was a strange affair. Lauren was still mad about Iggy's heart transplant and wanted to go with Jason and Sean, so Gunnar and Sadie were alone for two hours—two hours she filled with calls to and on behalf of Allegra, bickering over the music choices, and sneaky efforts to get Gunnar to talk.

It wasn't awkward, though. Whenever Sadie hit on a topic Gunnar didn't want to discuss, he'd raise that famous eyebrow, she'd roll her eyes in response, and he'd smile to soothe her ruffled feathers. The man was good at diffusing and deflecting. He didn't get mad, he got quiet.

An hour in, she tried another tack. Twenty questions, or more like a hundred, about favorite movies (*The Dirty Dozen* for him, *Back to the Future, Part 3* for her), last binge watch (*Babylon Berlin* and *30 Rock* respectively), and desert island keepers. All very surface, until Sadie asked about his childhood.

"Are you close to your brother?"

"I am—well, used to be. He's a ski instructor in Maine, followed in my mom's footsteps. She was a champion skier."

She played it like she *hadn't* read every scrap of knowledge she could find about him on Google. "Cool, cool."

"Yeah. Met my dad at the Sarajevo Olympics in '84. He stole her medal."

"Is that a euphemism?"

The corner of his mouth kicked up in that way she loved. The reluctant smile. "Nope. They hooked up in the Village and the morning after, he took her gold medal for the downhill slalom, then left her clues to track it down."

"A treasure hunt? For her own medal?"

"Yeah, kind of an asshole move now that I think of it. She thought it was romantic." His mouth twitched. "We grew up in Maine because that's where Dad was from, but once Kurt and I were in college, they moved to Finland to be with mummo and papa, my grandparents."

She had a million more questions but let a pause take over. Gunnar spoke again, this time quietly.

"My brother has two boys and a girl, eight, and six, and four, with another one on the way. They're great kids but I don't see them much. Kurt's a bit of a clucker."

"Clucker?"

"A mother hen. He worries a lot."

"Nothing wrong with a little worry." She slid him a look. "Sure why else would you be insisting on playing Kevin to my Whitney, if not for concern? Mother clucker."

That made him laugh. "Think you've figured me out, huh?"

"Not at all. You're not exactly indecipherable, but a little mystery keeps it interesting."

He frowned. "And there I was thinking you wanted to know all my secrets."

"Why? Because I asked you to tell me about your wife?"

"I suppose." Slight bafflement colored his tone. "I don't want you to think you have to be my healer, Sadie. That's the kind of emotional labor I shouldn't burden you, or anyone, with."

"That's considerate of you." She hadn't intended it to sound snarky, but he sent her a quick, assessing look anyway, checking for sarcasm. "I mean it," she insisted. "I don't have the bandwidth to worry about your problems as well as my own, and not much point when I'll be out of your hair soon."

He remained silent for a few minutes. "Why do you put up with that woman in LA?"

She burst out laughing. "Really? Thought we were on a nothing deep basis?"

"How deep can it get with this chick and her punani?"

"Oh, pretty deep. It's what makes the world go round, mister."

He reached out and squeezed her thigh. "I can listen. It's just bitching about your boss, right?"

"You first. Hit me with your office politics and who stole who's lunch out of the Rebels lounge fridge."

He groaned but it was half-hearted. "Okay. So, I was pretty pissed that Coach didn't put me on sooner than the playoffs this past season. They wanted to ease me in when really the ice would be the best place for me. It's where I could give it my all. Prove myself."

"What do you have to prove?"

"That I still have what it takes. That a couple of years off has only made me hungrier. That I'm not defined by my mistakes. Why bring a guy on, a former captain of an NHL team, a center with more experience than half the players on this team, if you're not going to use him?"

My mistakes. Did he mean professional or personal?

"Did you play well when you made it on?"

"I thought so. Petrov and Burnett thought so. Anyway, I

guess part of the reason why I agreed to help with the hockey camp was so I'd look like a team player. Show the powers that be I can step up when asked. I haven't always been the best at mixing. I married young and I liked it. I liked the company of one person more than anyone else, then the company of a couple more little ones." He inhaled a deep breath. Sadie held one of her own. "Team dynamics are a lot to manage when you're an introvert. But on the ice, I get out of my head and put it all out there. Not even sure what I'm trying to say here."

Neither was Sadie, but she liked this version of Gunnar. Sort of like texting, stream-of-consciousness Gunnar when he wasn't thinking too much and just letting it out.

"Starting over with a new crew can be tough," Sadie said, "especially when you come into the middle of it. It's like you entered a conversation half-way through."

"Yeah, some people are more adept than others. You seem to have a good handle on it. Being thrown into the deep end."

"Adapt to survive. Sometimes it's the only way. I felt pretty alone when I was a kid, with my parents always fighting and heading for divorce when my mother died. My dad—he didn't like being left with the reminder of his unfaithful wife. I look like her, you see. So when Lauren came along, it was his chance to get it right. A do over. And when I moved to LA, it was my chance to start afresh."

"And you've done that. Made your way."

Had she? She thought she was doing it, plugging away at a life, accepting scraps while trying to build something. But all the while, she was afraid. Of not being enough for her father, Lauren, Allegra, the world, and this man beside her.

"I'm trying. Every day, I try to figure out how to adapt, which decisions will shape this life I'm striving for. We can do it incrementally or we can smash it to pieces and start over." Obviously she was a fan of the baby steps approach. "While you were away from hockey, you were sort of hibernating. It can take a while to figure out how you fit into a world that went on without you. You have to play catch-up. You can do it incrementally or overthrow the status quo in one fell swoop."

"You sound like Moretti."

"Who?"

"Dante Moretti, Rebels GM. He said something like that once, how I've been existing in this frozen state, avoiding change and confrontation and conflict because it's easier. That I'll need to take a chance or stay still, I suppose."

This Moretti guy had the right idea. "Sounds like a smart fella."

"Oh, he'd agree with you there."

SAUGATUCK WAS A PRETTY LAKESIDE TOWN, a former artists' colony, with a lazy, summer vibe. It reminded Sadie of Carpinteria or Laguna Beach, and made her homesick a hundred times over. Sadie and Gunnar pulled into the drive of a low-slung ranch style house at the same time as Theo and Elle. Three gray-haired women stood on the porch, dressed in pink jackets.

"'allo, tarts!" Theo yelled as he jumped out of the car and hugged each one of them in turn. They turned to reveal "Thirsty for Theo" on the back of their jackets.

"What's happening here?" Sadie asked.

Gunnar shook his head. "Theo's gran is kind of out there, and she leads a crew of Kershaw uber-fans. This weekend will be completely about her baby boy, which suits him to the ground and pretty much gives everyone else cover." He hopped out of the car and grabbed Sadie's suitcase and his own much smaller, overnight bag.

A glamorous granny with a silver bob and fire-engine-red lipstick approached them.

"You must be Sadie! My Theodore told me all about you and your NO GOOD FATHER." Thankfully Jenny and Nick hadn't arrived yet with the kids. "Don't worry, we don't hold anyone's relatives against them here. Lord knows, Theo would be DAMNED TEN TIMES OVER with the blood running through his veins."

"Gran, stop it." Theo called over his shoulder while one of the other grannies felt up his bicep. "You're scaring her."

Theo's grandmother ignored him. "And as for Elle, if we were to judge her by that Bonnie and Clyde nest of vipers she climbed out of, she'd be in BIG TROUBLE." Bonnie and Clyde? Sadie shot a frantic look at Gunnar who was rocking that grin-fighting move she loved. "Oh, where are my manners? I'm Aurora. And this dress of yours is DIVINE."

"Made it herself," Gunnar murmured. "All her stuff is gorgeous."

"You did?" Aurora pulled at the sleeve of her pink jacket. "See the stitching quality there? What do you think? My friend Marguerite did it but she can't SEW FOR SHIT."

It was a touch sloppy. Not that Sadie would ever say so or even have a chance to get a word in.

"Of course, she's making the costumes for the show so we have to be nice to her. She's all we've got! HAVE YOU SEEN CATS?"

"I have not."

"You're going to love it! Much better than the movie. But Marguerite's costumes make us look like something from the ISLAND OF DR. MOREAU. Human-animal hybrid lab experiments!" She switched her attention to Gunnar. "Now there's a face I've missed. Come here to me, gorgeous."

She barely came up to Gunnar's pec, so the hug was awkward yet clearly heartfelt. Gunnar kissed the top of her silver head.

"How's it going, Aurora? You still making those killer brownies?"

"You betcha! And now that it's legal, I'm adding some extras to the adult-only versions." She gave a hammy wink. "Just kidding. They're exactly the same as before. I fought the law and my brownies won!"

She directed her attention to Sadie again. "You know, this bruiser here took my Theo under his wing when he first played out in LA after Theo was drafted. My poor grandson, ALL ALONE in the city, miles from home, and his captain made sure he didn't get into any trouble. Especially with girls. Theo's too nice for his own good and so DARN HAND-SOME. Girls will always take advantage. Gunnar would call me once a week to keep me in the loop." She reached up and stroked Gunnar's cheek. "Such a good man."

Gunnar blushed. "Anyone would have done it."

"But no one else did, Gunnar Bond. That was you and it goes to show what a decent person you are. Now, I've put you two in the coach house out back because I figured you're a new couple and you could do with the privacy. The rest of us will be in the main house and WON'T HEAR A THING! You can moan and scream to your hearts' content."

Gunnar's complexion deepened even more, while Sadie laughed her head off.

Aurora took Sadie's arm. "Theo says you work with a PUSSY EXPERT in Hollywood! I want to hear all about it!"

29

AURORA HAD SET up a large movie screen in the yard with top billing a highlight reel of Theo's best moments of the season—"It's as if she thinks you win all the games single-handedly," Gunnar commented to Kershaw. After they suffered through that, she rolled out the *Toy Story* movies for kids and adults alike.

He'd worried it might be awkward, with people asking him constantly about his intentions toward Sadie. But no one made a fuss. Theo and Gunnar were on cookout duty, which gave Theo an opportunity to test his ideas about Hunt's bachelor party.

"Some people do scotch tastings," Theo said. "Do you like scotch?"

"Not really. More to the point, does Hunt?"

"I don't know." Theo prodded a burger on the grill.

"Quit touching it. Let it cook."

"Okay, Dad." He blinked, then shook his head. "Sorry."

"Don't be."

Theo nudged closer. "Is this weird for you? Hanging out with us?"

Gunnar assumed he meant hanging with someone else's family. The kids were older, so he didn't feel that same gut-wrench of his memories. But neither did he jump in to touch Elle's bump like everyone else did whenever she mentioned the baby kicking.

Daddy, brush my hair. I want the pink barrettes with the ponies on them.

"No. I wouldn't be here if it was."

"Wouldn't you though? Sounds to me like you're here to protect Sadie and Lauren. You might choose this as the lesser of two evils."

He glanced over at Sadie, currently licking the salt on the rim of her margarita glass in a way that had to be illegal in several states. She caught his eye and added a wicked smile, and he looked away because Jesus, any longer, and he'd be hard.

"They'd have been fine without me here. I don't think whoever is hassling them would follow them to Saugatuck."

"So you're here for me?"

"Yes, Theodore, it's all about you."

"Knew it." He poked at the burger again because he couldn't leave well enough alone. *That's what's known as a metaphor, kids.*

"I'm going to cut some onions," Gunnar said, resigned.

"So you can hide your tears of bro-joy. Understood."

Sure. Gunnar headed to the kitchen, wishing he could be alone with Sadie. Despite the embarrassment Aurora's "good deed" had caused, he actually appreciated the idea they'd have more privacy later. If he hadn't worried about questions, he'd have stopped somewhere on the way to Saugatuck and brought her off like he'd done in the Home Depot parking lot. Instead, they'd talked and it was as easy as the texts with Angel.

Slicing onions and pickles, he thought back to the conversation on the ride down. He really should call Kurt, or at least shoot him a text to say hello this holiday weekend. He took out his phone and scrolled to the contacts, but didn't get any further than the A's. He inputed a message to Angel:

Could do with some help in the kitchen.

The reply came back in a flash. *Sorry, on vacation.*

Damn. That was cold.

Gunnar: Actually I could do with some "special" help.

Angel: While Toy Story 2 is on? For shame, sir.

That had him smiling like a loon and his cock stirring with interest. That's what Sadie did to him. Made him laugh and turned him on.

Gunnar: I hope you're having a good time.

Gunnar: Sorry if Aurora is being nosy. She and Theo are

He took a deep breath and tried again.

Gunnar: I'm thinking about calling my brother. It's been a while.

He'd probably love to hear from you, she texted back. *Bet he misses clucking.*

Gunnar: Sometimes that degree of care feels like dead-weight. I don't want to be a burden to him. To anyone.

Angel: You could never be. Not for family. And then after a pause, *Not for people who care about you. Family, team, friends.*

The team had been there for him. His family were always there for him, even as he pushed them away. He and Sadie were friends, just as he and Angel were. He wanted to talk to her, like they had before.

Gunnar: I've been dreaming about my daughter. Easier to pretend it was a dream, rather than an unbidden vision.

Angel: What is she doing in the dream?

Gunnar: Making me brush her hair. She loved when I did that. Fifty times, Daddy, she'd demand. Sometimes I'd worry about brushing it right out of her skull. It was so golden and fine.

Angel: Sounds like a princess.

Gunnar: She was. I spoiled her rotten. Danny was more sensitive and—shit, he hadn't thought about this for a while, but the truth of it caved his chest in. *I don't hear his voice. At all.*

A full minute passed before she answered. *Probably because your daughter was louder. Her voice still carries. He's still there, only quieter.*

Perhaps. He worried it was because Janie was his favorite. Of course, he adored Danny but Janie had always had more of his attention.

Her screams were the loudest, but Danny hadn't screamed at all. He was already dead.

Gunnar: Sorry, get back to Toy Story.

Angel: Okay. But you might want to come out soon because Theo's just burned the hot dogs.

"*MIDNIGHT AND THE KITTIES ARE SLEEPING ...*"

"Those are not the words," Lauren screeched from the back seat.

Gunnar's eyebrows rose in that way Sadie adored. "You sure? My favorite was *Magical Mr. Rhinocerous.*"

"Not his name. Or the name of the song," Lauren said, half-grinning.

"I don't know," Gunnar slid a look to Sadie. "Because that's about as sensible as any other cat name in the Cat Show."

It turned out that Lauren knew all about it, being a fan of Taylor Swift, and wouldn't hear a word against the play or the movie.

"Still don't know what it was about," Sadie said.

"It's about getting to Heaven," Lauren said, as animated as Sadie had ever heard her. She didn't even get this excited about hockey. "One of the cats will be chosen to go to Heaven at the Jellicle Ball."

"And every one of them got a song," Gunnar deadpanned.

"Aurora was really good," Sadie offered. "Even when she stood on that other cat's tail. She handled it like a pro."

"Unlike the other cat who screeched as if her actual tail had been stood on." Gunnar rolled in his lips. "That whole thing was pretty wild, though."

"It was!" She shot a glance at Lauren in the rear view mirror. "But good. You liked it, right, Lauren?"

"I suppose." Back to the sullen version. She returned to her phone and ignored them for the rest of the ride back to Aurora's house.

The hour was late, and everyone was soon heading to bed, worn out by the activities of the day. Sadie sat out on the back deck, gazing at the stars.

"It's pretty around here. Quiet, too."

Gunnar sat beside her on the sofa and tangled a finger in her hair.

"Maybe tomorrow Lauren should ride with us on the way back," Sadie said, thinking on how she could connect with her. "She seems to like you. She's different around you than she is with me."

"She's just having a rough time. It's not personal."

"It certainly feels that way."

He released a curl, started on another one. "You two

have a lot in common. You both lost your mom young. That could create an opening."

Perhaps, but she didn't want to force Lauren to talk about her mother, just so Sadie could assure herself she was doing something. "I worry about everything blowing up. Making it worse."

"You're not big on confrontation."

She thought about that. "Challenging other people tends to strip an argument to the bone. And it opens you up to truths you might not like to hear about yourself. Sometimes it's easier to go along to get along."

"Settle."

"Depends on the situation. I don't usually put up with crap. I didn't from you."

"No. Why is that?"

She smiled. "I guess I'd had a bad day and I didn't know you. It was easier to push back because I didn't owe you anything. I didn't care about your butt hurt feelings. All I knew was that you were wrong, I was right, and I wasn't going to put up with your nonsense."

His mouth twitched.

"Oh shut up, Mr. Know it all! Of course it's easier to push back against a stranger."

"But it shouldn't be. It should be easier with the people you know and love. You shouldn't feel you have to present a different, more palatable version of yourself to your father, your friends, your boss. These people take pole positions in your life. They should see the real you. The person you showed to me on those texts. The person you were when we first met and I screwed up. Don't tiptoe around Lauren. She wants you to talk to her straight."

"She won't like what I have to say."

"She doesn't like what you have to say now, this LA or

bust idea. Tell her what's in your heart, Sadie. She'll get it. She's a smart kid."

Sadie slumped in the sofa and folded her arms. "When did you get so wise?"

"I've had a lot of time to think."

She bet. "What was it like, living in that cabin?"

"Perfect, for a while. Everything I needed was there. Wood, coffee, self-flagellation." He gave a wry smile, a testament to self-awareness and progress, she assumed.

"But people wouldn't leave you alone. Your brother. Your parents. Pro hockey came calling. Everyone wanted you to get on with it."

He assessed her for a beat. "Grief is embarrassing for most people. They want to think it has a set timetable, that one day, it will go away and you're ready to live again. Everyone has been telling me that sex is a great first step. That it will open up the floodgates of emotion. That it will heal me."

She waited, her heart in stasis, knowing what would come next. Dreading it.

"I don't want to be healed, at least not in a way that makes me forget about them. I know that's unhealthy, but I can't help how I feel. Holding onto the pain keeps me connected to them."

There it was, in the starkest terms imaginable. If she was thinking of getting any high-falutin' ideas, she'd better think again. He was not for her.

It irked her that he might think himself so irresistible and her so weak.

"Have I given you the impression I want more?"

"No." He blew out a breath, studied her. "I was trying to be honest. I know you understand. You're pretty damn understanding." Was that a criticism? She was seeing it everywhere. "This isn't personal, Sadie. I can't give any woman a hundred percent right now."

"Hundred percent of your penis will suffice, Bond." That's what he wanted to hear, anything that kept it light and kept the demons at bay.

His shoulders eased. He'd stripped off a layer, revealed some inner turmoil, and re-established the status quo. He was probably embarrassed about their earlier text exchange.

He couldn't hear his son's voice anymore.

It had taken every ounce of her willpower not to rush into the kitchen and comfort him. Instead, she'd played it the way he wanted, with cool detachment.

"C'mere." He reached for her and pulled her into his arms, greeting her lips with a kiss for the ages. They were back in his playground with the fences in place and the sand plenty neat, waiting for the games to begin.

He swiped a thumb across her bottom lip. "You're an incredible woman."

She heard the *but* in there. Just not incredible enough for the broken Gunnar Bond.

She wanted to be. She might not be enough for her father, but she could be for Lauren.

And she could be for this hurting man before her.

30

Before sunrise, Gunnar left a sleeping Sadie—and man, that woman loved her zzzz—and headed down to the kitchen of the coach house to start coffee. He already had a visitor.

Theo was sitting at the table, a smoothie in his hand and a smartass grin on his face.

"Double-O, how'd you sleep? That mattress is pretty awesome, isn't it?"

Gunnar opened the cupboard and let him prattle on about Elle's snoring and waffle irons and the new moisturizer he was hawking on Instagram. Once he had the coffee measured out and the drip started, he turned and folded his arms.

"I'm guessing Aurora reminded you."

Theo made a face. Busted. "She mentioned it last night. Hell, I've been so wrapped up in everything that it never even occurred to me that this would be the worst weekend to drag you to watch some community theater on the beautiful shores of Lake Michigan."

Every July 4th, on the anniversary of his family's death,

Aurora checked in with him, usually with a voice mail because he never answered the phone on that day. She just wanted to acknowledge the lives of these beautiful people taken too soon.

His brother had texted this morning already, letting him know he was available to talk. A similar concern was likely behind Dante's text last night, encouraging Gunnar to stop by Harper and Remy's big cookout on the way home from Saugatuck. For some strange reason, Jorgenson decided to say his piece with a DM on Twitter—Gunnar never even updated his Twitter so that was a surprise. Finally Isobel had called to say Vadim would very much appreciate if Gunnar would show his face at Chase Manor.

No one wanted him to be alone, and for the first time in three years, he didn't want that either.

"I'm okay, T. Really."

Theo rubbed his mouth. "Is there anything you'd like to do? Some way to acknowledge the day?"

"I'd like to make Sadie a cup of coffee, then sit out on the deck and watch the sunrise." He would like to live in the moment instead of the past.

"Got it." Theo stood and held out his arms. "Bring it in, big guy."

"Kershaw."

"Don't leave me hangin', brother."

Jesus. He gave Theo the physical demonstration of affection the man needed, then curled a hand around his neck. "You're going to make a great dad, Theo."

"I sometimes wonder. With Nick and everything."

"Not genetic. It's all down to you and what's in here." He bumped his fist lightly against Theo's pec. "You've got this."

His friend's eyes went soft. "Thanks, man."

As Theo headed out, Gunnar said, "Do me a favor, T."

"Anything."

"I know you tell your girl everything but could you hold off on mentioning what day it is? I'd rather not make Sadie feel awkward if I don't have to."

Theo's brow rumpled. "You sure about that?"

"Positive. Let's keep it to ourselves."

Theo nodded his assent and headed back to the main house. Alone at last, Gunnar took a few deep breaths and watched the coffee squeeze out the last drip.

Why the secrecy? Sadie was a giver to the core, the kind of person who would expend all her energy trying to be there for him. He saw how it would go. If he cracked even a little, the floodgates would open, driven by a torrent of pain and remembrance. Better to keep her sheltered from the storm that might rage if he let it. As it stood now, he could lose himself in her body and draw the line—though these days it looked more like faded chalk on the sidewalk.

Three years ago on this day, his wife and children were torn from this world. Others might mourn on his behalf, but he would do his grieving alone.

"Oh, wow!" Sadie made her appreciation for Chase Manor known as they headed down the drive. "This is some spread."

"Lots of money in pro-sports, especially for owners."

The mansion fronted the water in Lake Forest, a tony suburb north of Chicago. A sign on the front door instructed guests to walk around the house along a side path to the back yard. Music and voices got louder as they moved closer and the scent of grilling assaulted Gunnar's nostrils.

Lauren had walked on ahead and made a beeline for

Jason and Sean, who were hanging with a group of kids at the far end of the pool.

Sadie turned to Gunnar. "She'll be okay, right?"

"Course she will." He made a few small circles on the small of her back. "The only one who bites here is me."

She shivered, a sexy little move that made Gunnar's cock twitch. "C'mon, let me introduce you to some people."

"Really? You want—oh, okay."

Did she think he wanted to keep this under wraps? Or maybe that's what she'd prefer? He didn't mind that people saw he was here, getting on with his life. After all he was! Maybe he'd get less of the sad eyes from the WAGs and fewer offers to set him up. He hadn't thought of Sadie providing that kind of cover, but he had to admit it appealed.

"Gunnar Bond," a smooth, sultry voice said behind him. He turned to find Harper Chase-DuPre, the Rebel Queen herself. "I hoped you'd show your face. Playoffs are over though." She made a vague gesture at his beard.

"Harper, good to see you." Usually he wouldn't be kissing his boss, but Harper was a tactile woman who made a point of treating every player as family. She held the embrace a beat longer than usual, and he hoped that would be all she had to say on the subject of his loss.

"This is Sadie."

"Sadie, the dress designer! Everyone's raving about you. Lovely to meet you."

"She's amazing," Gunnar said.

Harper gestured to Sadie's dress, a candy-striped number with a full skirt and a bodice that shaped her breasts perfectly. "Is this from a pattern?"

"Actually, yes, one of my own. I usually like to adapt vintage styles I find in old magazines."

"Mommy!"

Gunnar looked down to the source of a small yet powerful voice. A little blond girl clung to Harper's skirt.

Harper cupped the girl's cheek. "Honey, what's wrong?"

"Giselle won't give me Robby."

Harper grimaced in sympathy, then turned to Sadie and Gunnar. "This is Amelie, my oldest by about five minutes. She and Giselle are always fighting over Robby the Turtle."

"He's a tortoise," Amelie said.

"Thought he was a turtle." Harper raised an eyebrow. "I don't know the difference but my niece, Franky, who's a wildlife expert, insists there is one."

"Tortoises live on land, turtles are aquatic." Sadie pointed at her head with the index finger of one hand. Only when she wrapped her other hand around Gunnar's did he realize his pulse had spiked. "Dumb facts reside here."

"A woman of many talents. Do you have a portfolio?"

"Of dumb facts? Not officially."

"Your designs? The dresses."

Sadie laughed, that soft tinkle that gutted Gunnar's insides. "Oh, right! I do?" She made it sound like a question. With a negligent shrug, she turned and smiled at Gunnar. His heart was racing. That little girl, she was so like Janie ... But Sadie tightened her grip, her clasp the only thing keeping him from doubling over.

He didn't hear what they said because all he could see was the blond doll in front of him. She was pulling on Harper's dress just like Janie used to do with Kelly. It took a moment for him to realize that Sadie was speaking to him.

"Hey, babe," Sadie said, her smile soothing. "Could you grab me a white wine? Sauv blanc, if they have it."

He blinked at her. She kept the smile fixed and squeezed his hand again. She was covering for him.

"Sure. Harper?"

"I'm fine." She turned back to Sadie.

He headed to the bar and ran into Dante, looking strangely casual in a Hawaiian shirt. "All your suits at the dry cleaners?"

"Funny. Who's that?" Dante jerked a chin over Gunnar's shoulder.

"None of your business."

"Rude."

It was, but he wasn't feeling like himself. Or maybe he was feeling exactly like himself. Old Gunnar. Pre-Sadie Gunnar. The sinking feeling in his chest was dragging him down. His pulse rate was rocketing and he hauled air to get it under control.

He'd known there would be kids here, some of them even close to the ages of his own children. Harper and Remy had three kids, two of them adorable twin girls aged three and half or four. He'd seen them in the owners' box from a distance. He'd seen pictures of them on the team's social media. But here, up close ... He hadn't been to a big gathering like this and he wasn't sure he could do it.

He flexed his hand, missing Sadie's touch. "That's Sadie," he said to Dante. "Her sister is in the youth hockey camp."

"Would that be the *complicated* youth hockey camp?"

"We're just spending time together."

"What happened to the woman you were texting?"

Gunnar shook his head. "You wouldn't believe me if I told you."

"It's good to see you." Dante's squeezed his arm. "I mean it."

Gunnar mumbled his appreciation at being appreciated, rolled back his shoulders, and did his best imitation of a man not losing his shit. How had he thought this was a good idea? It was one thing to hang with that small group in Saugatuck, where all he could think about was taking Sadie into that cottage and ensuring she couldn't walk straight for a week. But this was too much. He should be at the cabin, chopping wood, fixing that damn gutter, communing with fucking nature. He wasn't fit for this kind of company.

His gaze tracked the partygoers, like players on the ice, the goal his woman. Sadie was now deep in conversation with Harper and Jordan Cooke, Levi Hunt's fiancée. She spotted him staring and gave him that hooky smile, along with something else.

You've got this.

He took a deep breath. *Okay, you can do this. It'll be over soon.*

It would be over sooner if he could expedite the proceedings. He pulled Lauren away from a bunch of kids. "C'mon, time to meet the Rebels captain."

"Oh, okay!" She picked up a messenger bag filled with items she had brought to be signed.

They passed more kids on the way, several of them splashing about in the pool. With adult supervision, thank God.

Daddy, look at me. I'm swimming!

I see, baby. You're doing great.

Vadim held court at one end of the pool with a few of the players in a semi-circle around him. Lauren hesitated but Gunnar placed a hand on her shoulder.

"It's all good, Lo." He guided her forward. "Hey, Petrov, this is Lauren Yates. She's a big fan."

"Lauren!" Petrov held out his hand for her to shake. "Sorry I can't get up but you know ..." He gestured to his knee in a brace. "I've seen video of you."

"You have?"

"Sure, your coach, Mr. Bond, sent it to me. You have fire in your skates. Amazing for what, a fourteen year old?"

"I'm twelve," Lauren said in a gush. "Almost thirteen."

"Wow, even better. So talented." He gestured to the players around him. "You know these jokers, Lauren?"

Everyone shook her hand and made her feel welcome.

Cal Foreman spoke up. "You'll have to come to a game when the season starts, Lauren. I know someone who can get you good seats."

That would have made any kid happy but this one. Her face crumpled. "I won't be here. I'm leaving town." She looked up at Gunnar, then back at Petrov. "I thought you were retiring."

"The Great Petrov hanging up his skates?" a woman's voice cut in. "You'd have to rope him to a Zamboni and drag him off."

Gunnar turned to a smiling Mia Wallace, Petrov's sister. There was another dramatic Rebels story with a soap opera wash to it. Mia was a college hockey star, a pick for the next Winter Olympics, and the perfect role model for Lauren. "Hey, Gunnar."

"Hey, Mia. Have you met Lauren?"

"No!" She held out her fist for the bump. "Saw you play last week, but I had to leave right after. You were amazing. Wish I was that fast at your age."

"You are fast enough now, sestra," Petrov said darkly to his sister, which drew a snort from Cal. Mia glared at him, earning a wink from Foreman. She made a face and Cal chuckled.

Petrov seemed oblivious to the undercurrents. "I'm not quite ready to call it a day," he said to Lauren. "*Nikogda ne sdavaysya bez boya.*"

"What does that mean?" Lauren asked.

"Never give up without a fight."

"Don't forget to get your stuff signed," Gunnar prompted.

"Right!" She opened her bag and fumbled around in it. Several items fell out. A notepad, pencils, a Petrov jersey, a game program from a couple of seasons back, Poptarts, Skittles, a phone, and that teddy bear she carried around everywhere. She'd been pissed when Sadie stitched it up, but it had sounded more like she was going through the motions. Pushing back on every kind gesture from Sadie because it was expected.

She handed a Sharpie to Petrov. "What was that you said again? The Russian thing?"

Petrov smiled that billion-ruble grin. "*Nikogda ne sdavaysya bez boya.*" He wrote something in a Cyrillic script on the inside of her program.

Lauren repeated the words, mouthing them until she committed them to memory.

Someone nudged Gunnar. He turned to a haggard Tate Kaminski, the picture of sleep deprivation. Gunnar remembered embodying that look himself once.

"Hey, Tate."

Kaminski angled a look around his shoulder. "Is that Jonas Yates' kid?"

Not liking the sound of that, Gunnar moved to block access to Lauren. "What if it is?"

"You have any idea what that fucker has done? He stole from me."

"Yeah, I know. He's hurt plenty of people, including his daughters."

His lip curled in a sneer. "Heard you were banging the other one."

Gunnar placed a hand on his chest. "You do not want to start this, Kaminski."

"Oh, yeah, why the hell not?" He pushed back.

"Problem, gentlemen?" Cal Foreman appeared at Tate's shoulder, his expression as hard as cut glass.

"No problem," Gunnar said. "Kaminski needs to exit my personal space before he does something he might regret." He didn't trust him around Lauren and Sadie. His wife had kicked him out, cut him off from his kids, and left Tate in a bad way. Gunnar understood the man's pain. It was why he stayed away from people when he was at his lowest.

"You don't get a say here," Tate said, but Cal was already steering him away toward the house.

Gunnar checked in on Lauren who was talking to Mia. She smiled shyly, and he gave her a thumbs up which obviously ruined it because she shook her head and rolled her eyes. At least she was safe. For now.

Putting Tate Kaminski out of his mind, Gunnar tried to enjoy himself. All these people, and he was doing okay. Because of Sadie. Sadie, who set his body on fire and smoothed his anxiety with her calm.

He sought her out, needing his fix. His heart erupted when he saw her, fixing the hair of one of Harper's girls. Sadie in no way resembled Kelly but that little girl was so like Janie. And a twin, as well.

Daddy, my head hurts.

I know, baby. Daddy's here. He's going to make it better.

Except he didn't make it better. He didn't do a damn thing.

31

SADIE WAS ENJOYING HERSELF IMMENSELY.

She had attended tons of LA pool parties, though usually they were more opulent than this and more often than not, she was working them for Allegra. Here she didn't feel she had to watch every word she said or try to blend into the sago palms like the help.

Her heart lifted at the sight of Lauren having fun. Earlier her sister had met the Rebels' captain, a Russian guy with supermodel cheekbones, and now she was showing the items he'd signed to Jason and Sean. She'd even smiled at Sadie about thirty minutes ago and Sadie took that inside her heart and held it there. Maybe it would be okay.

The talent on display rivaled a Hollywood pool party, for sure. Plenty of man candy caught Sadie's eye, between Harper's tasty husband Remy and his Cajun drawl to a forbidding brooder with a Scottish accent the team's general manager, Dante Moretti, who had to be the hottest guy she'd seen in real life.

But none of them drew her in like Gunnar.

They weren't tied at the hip but it seemed they were

aware of where the other was at all times. Every half hour or so, he would stop by to replace her empty glass, brush his fingers against hers, or just to say hi, all subtle gestures of caring that made her heart grow three sizes.

Similarly, she tried to look out for him, watching for any interaction with blond angels that would remind him of his children. If she couldn't soothe him with words, she would use every tool in her skillset to keep him safe from those demons.

With one ear on the conversation between Elle, Jordan, and Isobel Chase—a spirited discussion about why there were so many mattress stores in Chicago—she kept her remaining focus on the man she'd fallen for in the worst possible way.

Good thing she was leaving Chicago soon. Better if she was leaving sooner.

Getting Lauren settled in LA and making up for the time away from Allegra would fill every second and stop any ridiculous brooding over her sore heart. Still, like a junkie seeking her fix, she sought him out because no man here could compare.

He was looking at her, an eyebrow raised in query. *Was she okay?* She smiled and he smiled back, and she felt a surge of such affection it almost knocked her over. They were a team, fighting all the slings and arrows shooting their way. He might not want to talk to her about his pain, but she could protect him this way, assure him with a glance that she was here for him.

Another handsome hunk she didn't recognize said something to him that diverted his attention. She checked back into the conversation, which had moved on to another topic.

"Some people have rated it 1-star?" Jordan was saying. "For Stonehenge!"

Sadie's phone buzzed with a message from Gunnar.

Ready to go soon?

Whenever you are. Everything okay?

Yeah, I want some alone time with you.

She closed her eyes. This wasn't fair. He shouldn't say things like that, not when they seeped into her chest cavity like the fog from that horror movie and turned her into a Gunnar-Zombie.

Preparing to say her goodbyes, she became aware of a presence at her shoulder. A tall bearded man with red-rimmed eyes stood beside her, thrumming with energy.

"Your father's a fucking prick."

Sadie started at his tone more than his words. "Can't say I don't agree."

He evidently was expecting her to concur. Quickly he recovered. "You think you can wheedle your way in here, pick up where your asshole father left off?"

Jordan placed a hand on the man's arm. "Tate, let's go get you something to eat."

He shook her off and got in close to Sadie. Whiskey breath sprayed in her face with this next words. "Your father's trash and I'm guessing you're not much better."

Sadie opened her mouth to speak but didn't get far. Gunnar appeared behind him, his expression livid.

"I told you not to start anything, Kaminski. One more word and you'll wish you never opened your mouth."

Sadie gaped at how quickly this had escalated. There was history here, and not just because this Tate guy was another of her father's victims.

"Gunnar, it's okay. He has a right to be angry."

"Yeah, Bond, listen to your woman." Tate pushed against Gunnar's chest, and that was all the tabloids wrote. Gunnar grabbed Tate's T-shirt with both fists and pulled him away from Sadie. The next few seconds went by in a blur. Punches were thrown, though only Gunnar's landed. The group Sadie had been talking with made collective gasps, then several sets of hands intervened to separate Gunnar and Tate.

One of those hands was finely manicured and belonged to the Rebels CEO.

Harper stood between them, all of five feet one, her mouth set in a pink slash of disapproval. "Do I need to remind you this is a family event and not the hockey rink?" Without waiting for a response, she turned softer eyes on Tate. "Kaminski, please go into the kitchen. I'll talk to you in a second."

After some grumbling, Tate rubbed his sore jaw and ambled away in the company of a couple of his teammates. Harper turned to Gunnar.

"I'm going to give you a pass because of the day that's in it. I will see you in my office on Monday at 11am."

"Harper—"

"Don't try me, Bond." She shook her head slightly and switched on a smile. "Okay, everyone, back to celebrating. We'll be starting the fireworks soon, and I guarantee they will be a lot better than what you've just witnessed." With that she headed toward the house to tear one of her players a new one.

Sadie stepped toward Gunnar and splayed a hand on his chest. "You okay?"

He nodded. "Time to go."

~

LAUREN WANTED to stay to see the fireworks and Jenny offered to drive her home later. This worked out because Sadie needed to discuss what had happened with Gunnar and his teammate at the party and it was best to do it when Lauren wasn't around. But before they left, Jenny pulled Sadie aside and told her something she wished she'd known sooner.

Today was the anniversary of his family's death.

She must have missed that in her research on him. Why hadn't he told her? If she meant something, anything, to him, surely he could have shared that. But maybe she wasn't as important as she thought.

For the thirty minute drive, she tried to get him to speak, but he merely grunted, so she left it until they got home.

Home. The word popped into her thoughts a little too easily, and not because she'd lived here for the first eighteen years of her life. Gunnar protecting, cooking, sleeping, doing yard work, for God's sake. All that gave the word extra heft.

He parked the car in the driveway and hopped out quickly, his eyes scanning the exterior for anything different. Still assessing, he moved toward the door, subtly blocking her until he was satisfied she could put the key in the lock safely.

Once she'd turned it, he blocked her again—gently—and entered the house before her. She rolled her eyes, even though she liked it a little too much.

"Stay here," he ordered, though she could've told him the house was empty. Its sounds were as known to her as a favorite piece of music. No one was here but them.

He returned, held up a finger, and moved upstairs, while she walked into the vetted kitchen and took out a glass and an open bottle of wine. She'd head over to the Isners later on foot and hope that walking the ten minutes back with Lauren would create a space for them to talk.

Gunnar returned to the kitchen. "All clear."

"I know."

He frowned. "I just want you to be safe."

Why? They weren't his family. And while she understood a protective streak, he wouldn't be here forever. She wouldn't be here at all.

"Want to tell me what happened back there?"

"One of my teammates mouthed off and I took care of it."

Sadie shook her head. "He wasn't doing much and he has a right to be angry."

"To the point of threatening you?"

She waved that off. "He didn't. So what happened to him other than my father?"

"His wife kicked him out. He's estranged from his kids."

Her heart bled for another survivor of Jonah Yates's schemes. "You shouldn't have hit him."

"What would you have me do? Let him 'talk' to you or Lauren? Not going to happen."

"I talk to people all the time. Using words is generally a good thing."

He made a sound of disgust. "Is that what you'd like to do with whoever threw that rock or painted your door? Talk to them?"

"Maybe! I know you don't buy it because it smacks of therapy. Better to talk than defaulting to your id in times of crisis. Sex and violence only works up to a point."

"You've lived too long in California, Sadie."

"So you don't want to talk? About anything?" She shoved a finger in his chest, angry as a swarm of bad-tempered bees. *Confide in me. Open your heart. Love me.*

"No, Sadie, I don't to talk."

His nostrils flared, his eyes darkened to smoke and sin. She could feel his anger. His hurt. That skirmish back at Chase Manor had failed to take the edge off his pain. There was only one thing for it.

"Here or—"

"Upstairs," he finished as he took her hand.

She didn't have to be dragged but his urgency fueled that impression. Rather than undress themselves, they stripped each other with jerky, angry movements. Even annoyed, her desire was plain. A flush across her chest, pebbled nipples without the slightest touch, the slickness between her thighs.

He pulled on a condom and she pretended not to see that slight shake of his hands. Lying over her with that hard length pressed to her feminine softness, he cupped her jaw. Turbulent emotion in his gaze gave way to something gentler.

She wasn't having it. If he couldn't speak it, she didn't want to know.

"Don't go soft on me now, Bond."

Anger flared again in his eyes. She embraced it with her parted thighs and a grip of his perfect ass. Still he hovered, waiting, for what—she had no idea. *This is all you want from me, so just do it, do it, do—oh!* The thrust took her by surprise, its reach deep and pure. There, there, *yes.*

She kept her eyes open so she could dare him to look away. He didn't break, merely maintained eye contact to a scary degree. No more anger, only lust-stoked intensity stared back at her.

Bravery deserted her and she turned her head, but his big hand gentled her jaw to return what he was giving her. Fury leeched from her body, replaced with love. Maybe it was the same thing. She could feel it flow through her, giving her strength, bringing her closer to him.

"Gunnar," she whispered. "It's okay."

He shook his head, sadness she absorbed through her skin in that gesture.

"It's okay," she repeated. "Because I love you.

He stopped mid-thrust and stared at her in sheer disbelief.

"I love you," she repeated.

"Sadie." His mouth claimed hers. *Shut up*, that mouth said. *Don't say it. Don't need it.* But she kissed him back with every ounce of love she had in her heart to give, and even the ounces she didn't.

Her bruised heart belonged to him anyway.

32

NOTHING WAS BROKEN. *I knew that much. I wasn't even in any significant pain, or at least I couldn't feel it. Probably adrenaline. I knew my face was cut up as the window was smashed and a thick branch was inside, pretty close to my eye. My body was held flush by gravity, pinned against the blown, deflated airbag and the dash, with the car at a forty-five degree angle in the ravine. A tree had stopped the descent.*

I must have passed out. It wasn't dark yet, but the shadows of the late evening were reaching inside the car. I turned my head. Kelly's eyes were closed while she slept.

I hoped she was asleep.

"Kel, can you hear me?" Nothing. "Kel, can you—?"

She moaned, coming alert for a second. "Are they here? Is someone here?"

No. No one was coming. No one had seen the accident.

"Not yet. But someone will come soon." The lie felt like ash in my mouth.

"I can't breathe, Gunnar. I know it's not—not good."

She was a doctor, but I didn't want to hear this. She couldn't know for sure. "You've got to hold on, babe."

"Janie," she called out, though it sounded like she was speaking with her mouth full of water. She coughed up blood. "Janie, are you awake, honey?"

We'd stopped calling Danny's name a while back.

My phone had fallen to the floor or at least, I assumed so, knocked from the holder while we used it for its GPS. My arms were pinned. I tried to turn my head to see if Janie was still awake, but she looked different.

Not Janie. Where was Janie? This wasn't—it was someone else. Amelie, Harper's daughter. But—

I turned to Kelly but she was gone. Sadie sat in the passenger seat and that's when I knew I was in a dream.

Euphoria flooded my veins. Kelly wasn't dead. Janie wasn't here. This, I could control, a video game where I could select the outcomes.

"Sadie, you shouldn't be here."

She gave that wicked smile, the one that hooked me from the start.

"I love you."

He shook his head. "No." And then again, "you shouldn't be here."

"This is your dream. Make me go away."

I could do that. I had the power to win or lose, save or damn. I could think a thought and send her packing. Bring Kelly and Janie and Danny back.

Sadie wasn't injured. She didn't even look like she'd been in a crash. She could leave at any time.

She would. Back to LA. Back to her real life.

"I don't want you to leave," I said, which was all wrong because I did. She wasn't Kelly and this would get her safe. Or maybe Kelly would be saved. I was so confused.

I needed to take action. Find my phone. Get help. I needed to—

GUNNAR FLEW AWAKE, jerking to consciousness quickly. Sadie was there, watching him carefully.

"Hey," she said softly.

He lay back, his forearm shielding his eyes while he got his bearings.

She spoke again. "You said my name."

"Just a bad dream."

"You also called out your daughter's name."

He leaned up on his elbow. "For months after, I dreamed about the crash. It always ends the same way, with me waking up and them not here." At her stricken look, he added, "That's not a dig at you. I'm glad you're here. How long was I out?"

"Not long, maybe an hour." She rubbed his bicep. "Was I in the dream?" The tremble in her voice was barely discernible.

He didn't need a psychology degree to figure it out. Sadie in the same seat as Kelly. Sadie telling him she loved him.

He nodded slowly.

"Oh. Well, the broad you're bopping is probably going to figure in your subconscious, not matter how much you try to resist that."

"You're in my dream because you're in my life, Sadie." She'd told him she loved him, not only in the dream. Before, while he was inside her.

"Right, but you don't like that I'm there, do you? In your dream." Her silver eyes glittered, hard as icicles.

"I don't think anything of it." Lie. "You're there because you're here. Because you're part of—" *Me.* "—my life."

"You can't have it both ways," she said quietly. "I can't be important and unimportant."

She was right, but he wasn't ready to acknowledge it. He wanted her to fight to assume the role she deserved—with Lauren, with her boss, with her father.

But not with him. She didn't deserve that and he didn't deserve a woman like her.

"We should go to pick up Lauren."

Her eyes filled with hurt. "That's it. You have a bad dream with me in it and we're not going to talk about it?"

"It's only a dream, Sadie. It doesn't mean anything." He reached for his jeans and pulled them on.

"I know what day it is," she said. "You should have told me."

"Why?"

The cant of her head said it all. *Gunnar, you fool. Because you'll feel better. Because you'll start to heal.*

"I'm not putting this on you."

"You said that before, that you didn't want me to be your therapy. But it's okay for you to be our protector, to listen to my complaints, to give me advice? And I can't be there for you?"

He jerked his tee over his head and closed his eyes, wondering if he could find his way back to the dream. Where he could control the journey. With Sadie, control was a slippery fish. She made it impossible.

"You don't need to hear this." He didn't want to say it aloud. *Keep it inside. Keep it in his dreams.* His heart beat so violently he worried it would jump right out of his chest.

"I do. I want to."

He could so easily rely on her. He already did, taking her to the Chase Manor party, a crutch for his rotten social skills. Stepping in to defend Sadie and Lo was another crutch, a means to fake it as a family man.

But he wasn't a family man. He had a single line phone

plan. His actions on that road three years ago had ended all that. What would Kelly want for him?

"I wish I could still talk to her," he whispered.

She reached for him and he jerked away, jumping to a stand like a scalded cat. "What kept me going was texting Kelly. Talking to her every day kept me sane."

"Until I texted back."

"Yes." It was cruel, a streak he never thought he had in him.

"I stopped that. The conversation with your wife."

She did. The resentment should have passed, but now he wondered if it had. Or if he resented the fact he felt better with Sadie. Not whole, but getting there.

"You did. I miss her like crazy. I miss my kids and every fucking day it hurts that I'll never hear or see them again. Thing is, talking to you brought me comfort. I looked forward to every text, analyzed every word, trying to learn who you were, what you were about. But then I realized what a mistake that was. What a mistake *this* is. I can't depend on that going forward. I won't."

There it was. The crux of the problem.

Her eyes went soft and shiny. "You don't want to depend on me?"

"On anyone."

"I'm not trying to replace Kelly."

"You can't."

Her breath caught. Harsh, but it had to be done.

"This isn't going to happen," he said. "Us."

She flinched again. Jesus, he'd known he had the capacity to bear pain but had no idea he could inflict it so well. The things you learn about yourself.

There's a knot in my chest. A hard, tangled, ugly lump that can't be unraveled. Not by you. Not by anyone.

He should temper it. *You're an amazing woman, Sadie. You deserve someone who isn't weighted down with all this grief.*

But he didn't say any of that. She'd only respond with a good argument and worse, he might actually listen to her. Instead he watched the play of emotion on her face, the creeping awareness that this wasn't fixable.

"You shouldn't have moved in here," she whispered.

"Sadie—"

She raised a hand. "I didn't want you here. I knew having you around all the time would make it worse."

"Make what worse?" But he knew. He just wanted her to know, too.

"How I feel about you. Because while you've been going out of your way not to depend on me, I've been starting to depend on you. And you did that!"

"I told you how it was. What this was about." The words sounded robotic, spoken by someone else.

"Right. Sex. Pleasure. No talking about anything important, except sometimes you broke your own rules, Gunnar. We can talk about it if *you* think it's okay." She pointed at him, and spoke in a lower, ragged voice. "You can't intertwine yourself with someone's life and then pretend that it means nothing. Not even you could be that stupid."

He'd never promised a thing. He was clear about the expectations. Okay, so he'd moved the pipes a touch when he moved in, but it shouldn't have changed the fundamentals. They had no future.

"You're moving back to LA. That was always going to happen."

"I know. Do you think I don't know that? Did you think the promise of cross-country separation would keep me safe from your masculine wiles, you—you asshole?" She waved a hand, then slapped at her eyes to wipe tears. He wanted to go to her but he was the wrong person to offer comfort. The wrong person to offer anything.

"I would have been fine if you hadn't gone all Mr. Protector for us. If you hadn't held me when I slept or touched my back when we walked into that cookout or made funny faces at me during Cats. I would have been totally okay if you had showed up with your penis and your beard and did your business and headed out. But no. You had to be a good guy, painting doors and cooking eggs and doing yard work and telling me how to fix Lauren, and I had to be an idiot, enjoying the hell out of someone having my back for once."

He had no words, but that had always been their problem.

"I'm sorry." He could say that. He could mean that.

"I know you are. And what's even more stupid is I still want to be there for you. Call me a trauma junkie, what have you. I won't be here in Chicago but I'll always be a text away. When you're ready to talk, you know where to find me."

After she'd told him she loved him? After he'd taken that love and stomped on it? There was selflessness and there was sadism.

She would still be here for him. But he could no longer be here for her. "I should go."

And so he did.

33

"Okay, punettes, I have a secret. A couple of years ago, I did not have the strongest punani muscles. I mean, sometimes I ... leaked! Now I wouldn't admit that if it weren't true. That's generally an older woman problem. But I figured I needed to start working out down there, so as well as exercises, I started using Kegel balls. Look at these—aren't they amazing? You just insert and go about your day, letting the joy of passive contractions do the work. Soon you'll have vag muscles that can crush a diamond ..."

Sadie went through the motions on Allegra's latest video. A cut here. A transition there.

Failure tasted bitter on her tongue. She had thought Gunnar's shell would melt in the face of her empathy and understanding. That showing—and telling—him he was loved would toggle a switch in his brain. They had history! The texts! The connection! But it wasn't enough. She wasn't enough.

Not for her father and not for Gunnar. But she still had Lauren, who needed her because she was a minor and had no choice. Fabulous.

Her phone rang with Darth Vader's theme.

"Hi, Allegra, working on it now!"

"Sadie, we have a problem."

Her heart sank. Allegra's problems were not like the problems of other mortals. Everything was magnified a hundredfold, usually in her imagination, and Sadie was starting to hit a wall.

"What's happened?"

"Someone made some very rude comments on yesterday's video. They're still up there."

"Oh, I can take care of those." Part of Sadie's job was stifling dissent in the ranks of her fans and haters. She checked the video and found a comment that had been liked over two hundred times.

You're a hack. Stop telling people what to do with their vaginas!

Pretty tame and not completely inaccurate. "I'll just delete it."

"You can't do it now! It looks like I'm trying to shut down anyone who disagrees with me."

"But you are. That's what you hire me for." *Oops.*

Sadie could feel the chill from two thousand miles away. "You're supposed to stay on top of it before it gets out of hand. Remove the negativity before it has a chance to flourish."

"Be the Monistat to the yeast infection. Got it. I have a lot going on, Allegra, and I missed this. I apologize."

"Right. And how is that going to change, now and when you come back? With a child, Sadie." Allegra sighed. "I've given you a lot of latitude here ..."

"I know, I know." *But I just had my heart broken so could you give me a little more?* "I'll be back in a few days. Everything's almost wrapped up, I promise. Now let me take care of this comment stuff and get today's video up. I'll check in later. Bye!"

Sometimes it was better to overwhelm Allegra with action. If she really had a problem with Sadie's approach, she'd call back. Sadie indulged in a spot of comment censorship, finished the video on Kegel balls (yes, this was her life), and scheduled it for publication in a couple of hours.

When she got back to LA, she was going to look for something else. While a job in hand was better than the nothing, she needed to make a change because she had more to offer than this.

She headed down to the Dead Tree room to see if any packing progress had occurred. Folded-up boxes were perched against the wall where Sadie had left them a week ago. Lauren hadn't made a dent. "The auction is in three days, so you need to start packing now."

Her sister scowled. "And if I don't?"

"Then your stuff will be dumped on the street, without boxes, and I won't be able to put it in storage."

Lauren perked up. "You're putting stuff in storage?"

Sadie winced at the hope she saw in her sister's eyes. "I have to for now until I can afford to ship it. Storage for a month is cheaper."

Rather than deal with the guilt her sister's eyes made her feel, she walked to the window. Gunnar's car was still there, the morning after he'd left. The sun glinted off his Aviators.

"Knew he was too good for you," Lauren said, her voice filled with the hurt of the prior months. "Knew it wouldn't take long for you to drive him away."

Out of the mouths of babes.

When Sadie didn't say anything—couldn't say anything —Lauren continued twisting the knife in. "He's only sticking around because he feels guilty. We're not in any danger, not really."

Sadie knew that. She also knew that Gunnar's savior complex, the one he'd contracted after he couldn't save his real family, was chronic and not fussy about the particulars. He saw a pathetic woman who couldn't look after her sister and he acted.

"Start packing or I'll hire somebody to do it for you. Is that what you want? Some stranger going through your things?"

Lauren's glare would have cut precious gems. "Better than a stupid cow like you."

Sadie had heard worse. It hurt, but no more than the pain she was already enduring.

"You know something, Lauren. I've been trying my best with you but sometimes you are a real pain in the ass."

"I know you're just doing it out of duty. You already left years ago. You never even visited!"

"Only because your mom made my life a misery and Dad never had my back. So yeah, I'm doing this because no one else will have you!"

Lauren flinched, and Sadie immediately regretted her words. "Lo, I'm—"

"Forget it. And you don't get to call me Lo. Ever. " Lauren abandoned the sofa and headed upstairs, hopefully to pack. But at what cost?

Lauren was right about one thing. They weren't in physical danger. Gunnar's presence here was only detrimental to her heart.

She sent him a text. *You don't need to be here.*

Gunnar: It's a free country.

Sadie: You can't do this for twenty four hours. And I'm not feeding you. Or giving you access to a bathroom.

Gunnar: Doing it crazy astronaut style. Adult diapers for the win.

She refused to smile even though he wouldn't see it. A minute ticked by. Two.

Another text came in. *I'm sorry, Sadie. I wish I could be a different person.*

Sadie: Someone once told me to never wish for that.

Gunnar: Sounds like an idiot.

Yes, but he was her idiot. She didn't want a different person. She wanted this one, damaged heart and all.

Most of her packing was done, but she had some cutting to do for Jenny's dress. First, she needed a moment to decompress. She went to her father's study. All that remained was the desk, the chair, and her father's papers in boxes. She slumped in the chair, stretched out her legs, and closed her eyes. What she wouldn't give to talk to Gunnar about Lauren. They might not agree on everything, but he had an instinct when it came to Sadie's sister that Sadie herself couldn't master.

Once they were in LA and settled, she would figure it out. Standing quickly, her phone slipped and fell to the floor. When she bent down to retrieve it from under the desk, she saw it.

A tiny cubby. She placed a finger inside it and felt the hard, metal outline of ... a key! Oh, God, it couldn't be. That locked drawer?

She tried it, her heart thrilling when it turned easily. What would she find? Hidden illegal proceeds? A ledger of his crimes? Something more unsavory?

Envelopes. She picked up the first one, recognizing instinctively what it was—and knowing that there were likely eleven more just like it.

Her birthday cards to Lauren, each one unopened. Each

one a handmade piece of Sadie's art with a fun, quirky animal wishing Lauren a happy birthday. A duck, a meerkat, a piglet. The cuter, the better. Each one a chance to tell her sister how much she loved and missed her. Each one a broken promise.

Why would her father do this? Had he hated her that much?

There was another envelope at the bottom of the pile, this one not addressed to Lauren, but to Sadie. Just her name, but not in her father's handwriting.

She opened it with trembling hands, her suspicions on high alert. One page in a shaky script, signed by Lauren's mom, Zoe.

Hɪ Sᴀᴅɪᴇ,

I hope you don't immediately trash this. Maybe you won't read it today. But in a couple of weeks, maybe even less than that, you'll get some news and you might want to read this. I hope you do.

I know we both made mistakes, but mostly me. You were in a lot of pain when I entered your father's life. I tried to connect with you and you weren't interested. I know now that I should have tried harder. When your father was tough on you, I should have pushed back on that. But he was older, so assured, and I followed his lead with how to raise you. You and I got off on the wrong foot and by the time Lauren was born, it seemed too late to change all that. The new baby became my focus. I was tired all the time, and I didn't have the patience to coddle you. I was wrong. I'm sorry.

Something has changed. I won't be around and your father is going to need you. My kid, your sister, is going to need you because I'm not sure Jonah is going to do so well without me.

Perhaps he'll find another wife but I haven't had a chance to pick her, so no guarantees!

Whether you continue to be pissed at your dad or not, I need you to be in Lauren's life. She'll be angry that I've left, so it's important she knows you're there for her. She loves hockey and art, which means she's pretty well-adjusted—she's a creative like you, and even though you haven't been in her life, I feel as if she's the best of us, you and me. I'm hopeful she'll expend her rage on the ice and get in touch with her feelings with her charcoal. I need for her to be okay.

I have no right to ask you for a single thing, but I'll walk over hot coals for my kid.

I'm sorry I never made it right with you. I hope you can forgive your dad, and even if you can't, you can be there for our family. Your family. Thank you, Sadie.

Zoe

SADIE WIPED AT HER TEARS. All this time, they could have been friends, and her father prevented that. Was his rule over this household so strong that neither Sadie or Zoe could turn the tide? Or had Sadie been too caught up in bitterness to see this olive branch waiting to be delivered?

Sometimes people kept doing the same thing, going through the same motions because it was easier than admitting they were wrong. Sadie had always thought that sticking to her principles was important. Adaptability was all well and good, but flip-flopping signaled flightiness. Like her mother. She wanted to be the dependable one—for Allegra, for Lauren, even for Gunnar—but what if she was merely inflexible?

What is she was more like her father than she had thought?

JENNY STOOD in front of the full-length mirror in her bedroom, her lips stretching in a smile. She turned to check out her ass.

"Hey, guys, do I have curves now?"

"Yeah, ya do. That's abso-fucking-lutley gorgeous," Elle said. "Perfect for the wedding of the season."

For Jenny's dress, Sadie had gone with a cornflower blue fabric with a spangled sheen instead of the original Swedish print she'd come across in her attic. While winsome, it wasn't really suitable for a summer wedding involving a multi-millionaire pro-athlete.

For the last three days, she'd thrown herself into designing, cutting, and sewing. Jenny wasn't her only client. (And yes, she was calling them clients.) Harper had asked for something "to wear by the pool" and Sadie had gone out to Chase Manor yesterday to do a fitting, dragging a sullen Lauren with her because she couldn't leave her alone.

Sadie stood behind Jenny and placed her hands on the woman's hips. Pride in her work filled her up, evicting some of the ache in her heart. "You have really great shoulders and this strapless style looks so good on you."

"Va-va-voom," Jordan said. "One hot mama."

"What color wrap should I wear?" Jenny opened a closet and started rummaging. "This hombre one might work."

"Are you excited?" Sadie asked Jordan. Her wedding was just over a week away. Tonight was her bachelorette party and the girls were starting early on Brut Rose before heading downtown.

"Yes. Nervous, too."

"You're from DC," Sadie said, "so how come you're getting married here?"

Jordan sipped her wine. "It's for Levi. He doesn't have any family left and the team are his people now. Harper offered up Chase Manor. Apparently it's a tradition that team members can marry there if they want to, like the team's chapel, I guess. Levi's sort of superstitious and I don't mind where we do it."

The team's chapel. Sadie liked that, but then she liked everything she'd heard about the various Rebel couples and the family vibe surrounding them. She had heard the story, how Jordan's first husband was Levi's best friend in the Green Berets. He had died in Afghanistan and Levi had stayed away from Jordan for years, even though he'd always been in love with her. They reconnected when she was assigned to report on his rookie NHL season at the ancient age of thirty.

"Hockey players and their superstitions are so weird," Elle said. "Theo won't let me out if there's a full moon."

Sadie chuckled. "Should I even ask?"

"He said it's bad luck for the baby. Something Aurora told him." She rolled her eyes. "Sure, he's worse with his game prep. Between that and the special way he has to wrap his stick—"

"Nice," Jordan said and they high-fived.

"It's a wonder they get anything done," Elle finished.

"Knocked you up, didn't he?" Sadie said, around the pins in her mouth. "He probably thinks *that*'s getting it done."

"You know it." Elle shared a shifty glance with the others. "Speaking of hockey players getting it done, what's going on with Gunnar?"

"How do you mean?"

"Pretty sure that's him sitting in that car out on the street," Jordan said.

"But he's not staying with you anymore." Jenny twisted her mouth in apology. "Lauren told Jason and Sean."

Sadie infused la-la casual into her voice. "Oh, I told him his bodyguard services weren't needed anymore. The house goes up on the block soon, I'll be moving the personal stuff into storage, and I have our tickets for LA. The flight's on Sunday."

Jordan's eyes widened. "But you're coming back for the wedding, aren't you?"

"I wasn't invited."

"You are now!"

Sadie smiled. "That's sweet of you but I need to work things out with Lauren and get her settled. She's still mad as hell at me and I can't leave her alone for a second."

"Delay your travel plans and bring her. She'd love to hang with all the Rebels and their spawn."

"Ahem," Jenny said. "I think we're getting off track. What's the deal with Gunnar?"

Elle nodded. "Right. Quit yammering about your nuptials, Cooke. Sadie, I'm seeing a disconnect here. Bond has moved out of the house, but he's outside in the car. What gives?"

Sadie bent her head to the bodice of Jenny's dress. "Just a little tuck here, I think."

"Sadie!"

Startled, she jabbed Jenny with a pin and earned a yelp in return. "Oh, sorry." She turned back to Elle. "I-I screwed up."

"How?" Jenny pushed her down into a sitting position on the bed.

"Brought out the L word, didn't I?"

"Oh." A chorus of them.

"During sex."

"Ohhh!" Now a symphony.

"He freaked out and made it clear that's not what this is about. That's not what this will ever be about."

Elle chewed her lip. "Has he shared stuff with you? Painful stuff?"

"A little. Not much. He's still so bound up in his grief for them. He needed a distraction. That's what I was supposed to be. But—"

"You hoped it would be more?" Jordan sat beside her and held her hand.

He had warned her not to get too close. He had told her to keep her expectations at zero. Less than zero. But she fell for him anyway. She'd seen the way he looked at Lauren, with such tenderness, and assumed she was included under his wing. Every look, touch, smile he sent her way was water on her shriveled, arid heart. She hadn't realized how much she needed that attention. How lonely she felt. She weaved all these moments into a fabric, embroidered them with her hopes and dreams. But the seams weren't strong enough, the thread was too thin.

"I got pretty testy with him, saying it was his fault for being so nice to me. How pathetic is that? The guy's nice to me and I act like a lovesick puppy even when he's specifically told me *not* to be a lovesick puppy."

"Puppy can't help it," Jenny said. "Puppy's a puppy."

"This puppy's a dummy."

"But there has to be more. You guys go way back with the texting and all that."

Sadie stared at Elle who had uttered that immortal gem. "The what now?"

Elle's color rose. "He might have mentioned you had his wife's phone number. That he didn't know it was you when you guys met first at the hockey camp."

"When did he say that?"

"A while back, after he found out who you were. It really threw him and he came over to ours, got drunk, crashed on our sofa. I could tell he needed permission to go for it with you. That's what was holding him back."

Jordan waved in front of them. "Could someone explain what's going on here? His wife's phone number?"

After Sadie had told the story, they sat in silence for a moment.

She tried to explain his actions. "He's angry with me for interrupting the conversation with his wife. He's not stupid. He knows it's not healthy, but it's what he wants. He'd prefer to stay in that bubble with them. The thought of relying on someone for comfort is impossible for him. He doesn't want to make room for anyone else."

She knew this much: *you can't force someone to love you.* She'd tried it with her father. Was trying it with Lauren. Nothing real and lasting could exist on a bedrock of indifference.

Elle shook her head. "That's not what he wants. It's what he thinks he wants."

Which as far as intention went amounted to the same thing. Sadie could be persuasive but she didn't have the skillset to convince a man to love her. For now, she'd invest all the love she had to give in Lauren.

Jenny looked out the window. "So why is he out there? Does he really believe you're still being threatened because of your father?"

"Because he can't stay away," Elle said, "but he'd rather pretend it's because of some misplaced sense of duty."

"That's not it," Sadie murmured, though hope took seed in her heart because she was a sap.

"Let's find out." Jordan put her wine glass down and took a step toward the door.

Sadie sputtered. "What? You're going to ask him?"

"Yep. I'm a reporter. I ask things."

They watched her exit, then turned to each other.

Jenny made the first move. "Well, I'm not missing this."

∽

JORDAN COOKE WAS MARCHING toward Gunnar's car, closely followed by Jenny and a slower-moving Elle. No sign of Sadie, which he didn't like one bit.

He lowered the window.

"Jordan. Jenny. Elle."

"Afternoon, Gunnar," Jordan said. "Want to tell us what's going on here?"

"Just keeping an eye on Sadie and Lauren. Like I said I would."

So it sounded ridiculous, and the way Jordan's eyes softened told him she agreed.

He asked, "Where's Sadie?"

"In the house. Perfectly safe," Jordan said. "Surely you have better things to be doing."

"Not really." He held up his phone with his paused game of Bubble Ball.

Elle pushed Jordan aside gently. "Gunnar, this isn't fair."

Ah. So Sadie had confided in these women. He was glad she had someone to talk to. The only person he had was her and he'd screwed that up. He wanted to go back to before, to that time when he was alone in the woods. To morning funnies and the safety of a phone screen. Or back further, to a curvy stretch of road in California. He sure as hell didn't want to be here on a ludicrous bodyguard detail for a woman who didn't want anything to do with him.

"How is she?"

"Surviving," Jenny said. "She made me this dress for Jordan's wedding."

"It's pretty."

She nodded. "And she's wrapping up things so she can move back to LA."

Jordan squeezed his forearm. "You can't do this 24/7, Gunnar, and you don't have to. Sadie will be hanging with us for the rest of the day and the evening for the bachelorette party. Nick will be watching the kids later. We'll ask Levi and Theo to take it in shifts until she leaves in a couple of days."

"That's not their job."

"But it's yours?" Elle's look was pitying. "You know how she feels about you, so think about how hard it is to see you all the time. We'll take care of her until she has to leave for LA." She bit her lip. "I'm sorry."

She was right.

It wasn't his job to protect them, not when he'd checked out and made his position clear. Perhaps he was here because he'd fucked up with Kelly and Danny and Janie, and he had to put it right. Take action. He couldn't imagine ever living without that feeling of failure, and he shouldn't use Sadie and Lauren to fix what was wrong inside.

"Tell her I'm sorry. I've said it already but I need her to know."

Elle nodded, and they all stood back to let him drive away.

34

Gunnar walked into the Empty Net and nodded at Tina, the owner.

"In back," she said, thumbing over her shoulder.

Theo had invited everyone to meet here to kick start Hunt's bachelor party, the theme of which was a mystery. Gunnar hadn't been as involved as he would have liked because his mind was filled with Sadie.

He headed toward the back and stopped at a door with a sign that read: *If You Don't Know What This Is About, This Party Is Not For You!!!*

On pushing the door ajar, he felt the floor vibrate with the boom-boom bass of something he didn't recognize because he was too old. Was this what nightclubs looked like these days? He couldn't see a thing through an impenetrable haze.

A figure emerged ghost-like from the smoke. "G-Man! You're here!"

Gunnar blinked at Theo. "What the hell is going on?"

"Might have overdone it on the dry ice machine." He

waved away some of the haze and pulled Gunnar over to the bar set up. "You're the first person to arrive."

Gunnar squinted, trying to discern what might lie behind the smokescreen. "Is that a—shit, a mechanical bull?"

The haze cleared enough to show a brown legless bull torso surrounded by a padded wall.

"I told you I was going to set up something awesome! That Green Beret dude probably would have organized a bar crawl or maybe an army assault course. Which might have been fun, actually." He gave that thought a moment's consideration. "But a bar crawl? Like that's good enough for a Rebel. Don't think so. What are you drinking?"

Half a beer in, all Chicago-based team members but Hunt had arrived and were standing around, admiring the bull. Cal Foreman had started a book on who would stay on the longest.

"You sure Hunt hasn't just decided he'd prefer a quiet night in with his best man?" Gunnar took a swig of his beer and eyed Theo.

"You think you can hurt me with your cruelty, Double-O? I'm impervious to your blows. Hunt knows I'm the real best man, but he's got to give props to his army buddy. Dude probably saved his life or something." He pulled Gunnar aside to let Jorgenson get closer to the bull. "So, heard you moved out of Sadie's."

"I never moved in. I stayed over a couple of times to keep an eye on things."

"Riiiight. Also heard the ladies told you to take a hike today."

"Nothing gets by you."

Theo squinted, or maybe his eyes were filled with dry

ice. "Want to tell me what's going on before we get trashed and don't remember a thing?"

He opened his mouth to say "bring on the booze," but bit it back. Theo could probably handle some of the truth. As he seemed to share everything with Elle, maybe Gunnar could hear how Sadie was doing.

"I can't be what Sadie needs. She knows that, and if she doesn't, she'll figure it out. She's a smart girl."

"Is she? She thinks you're worth the trouble, so not sure how smart she is." Theo's expression was neutral, not matching the dig. Unsure how to respond to that, Gunnar moved on.

"Yeah, well, she's leaving soon. She has a life somewhere else."

"Maybe that life could be here. But then you'd have to get over yourself." He didn't even smile to soften it. Not like Kershaw at all. What was happening here?

"I never promised her anything." All the excuses were coming out, one by one. "She agreed to the terms." Now he sounded like his agent.

"God forbid anyone changes their mind, huh?"

That wasn't Gunnar's problem. He'd laid his cards on the table. If she didn't like the hand, she shouldn't have played it.

With the haze and the bull and the weird vibe, it felt like he'd entered an alternative universe with a different, less amiable Theo. "Kershaw, do you have a problem with me?"

"I don't get you, Gunnar."

Theo calling him by his actual name? "What don't you get?"

"I saw how you were around Sadie last weekend in Michigan. Sneaky looks. Handsy as fuck. Coffee in bed. You were so into her. And not telling her outright what day it was? That wasn't protecting her, it was protecting you." He poked a finger in Gunnar's chest.

Gunnar opened his mouth to protest, but Theo was still talking. "And this Secret Service detail is kind of ridiculous, don't you think?"

"I know. That's why I stopped."

Theo shook his head. "I mean it's ridiculous that it was your go-to in the first place. So you're not saying it, but you're doing it. You can't use your words to say how important she is to you, so you're doing all these things that *prove* she's important to you. You're so crazy about her that you can't help yourself!"

You can't have it both ways. I can't be important and unimportant.

So she was important. She was a fucking treasure, and he couldn't bear the thought of losing her. If that happened again ... Christ, he'd barely made it out the last time.

In fact, he hadn't. He was still pinned in place in that car three years ago.

"Hunt! About fucking time!" Theo squeezed Gunnar's shoulder, a gesture of conciliation, and moved forward to welcome Levi.

GUNNAR WASN'T DRUNK ENOUGH for this.

But everyone else was. Apparently the entire shindig would happen here which suited the crowd because this place had all a party needed: booze, buffalo wings, and a bull. The smoke had cleared—literally—but Gunnar's mind was still a fog.

He stood near the bar and watched while Kershaw held

onto the bull for dear life. Sensing a presence, he turned and found Dante.

"This must worry you," Gunnar said.

"Why?"

"Your valuable assets being thrown with considerable force from some height to the ground."

"Seems harmless enough," Dante said just as Kershaw was launched from the bull and hit the padded floor. He rolled over, holding his side and laughing his head off. Sure. Harmless. "Can't play it safe all the time," Dante added.

Someone else who wanted to poke that sore spot? "What the hell does that mean?"

Dante assessed him. "Heard you're not with Sadie anymore."

"Christ, you lot are chatty little fuckers."

"You seemed to be getting along at the party. To be fair, I noticed you didn't spend much time with her but you never stopped looking at her."

"So I liked looking at her." *Like.*

"And you stepped in pretty quick when Kaminski mouthed off."

"She was my guest and he had no right to talk to her like that. Of course I'm going to be there for her."

Dante smiled, a smug *gotcha* on his lips. "You know what else I noticed? Sadie never took her eyes off you. Whenever you got within two feet of a small child, she was ready to jump in."

"Really, that's your amazing conclusion? We made eyes at each other at a party?"

Dante half-shrugged. "That's simpatico couple stuff. Teamwork isn't just for sports, amico."

So they couldn't stop looking at each other.

So they had each other's backs.

So he might have made a terrible mistake.

Fuck.

Her last words to him echoed in his muddled brain.

When you're ready to talk, you know where to find me.

Why was talking so important? Actions had always spoken louder for Gunnar. On the ice, putting a ring on Kelly's finger, witnessing the birth of his children, protecting them with every ounce of his being.

But in the end, actions had proved squat. He couldn't protect them. Trapped in that car, he couldn't do a single thing. Hours had passed, with him falling in and out of consciousness, and every time he woke up—then and now —he was still fucked. He couldn't control a thing and that knowledge leaked like blood from his heart every single day.

Except.

He didn't feel as wrecked these days. He didn't feel as numb. Sadie had done that. She'd put her own needs aside to tend to his, and wasn't he the selfish prick? He couldn't give her anything, especially not the love she needed. He barely had enough for himself.

He barely had enough ... Something went flash-bang in his head, something he couldn't label, but it made him shake like that stupid mechanical bull.

"Back in a second."

Dante nodded absently, his indulgent gaze on Cade who was now in the saddle.

Gunnar headed to the restroom, but instead of going in, he wandered down a corridor until he found the exit to the alley. Then he left. For some air. For a quiet second to catch his breath and figure out why the status quo was bad and he couldn't just *be*.

He took out his phone and started typing.

For her bachelorette party, Jordan wanted less of a blowout and more of a chance to spend time with the significant women in her life. Sadie felt honored to be included, though this was more to do with keeping Sadie company than any strong feelings on Jordan's part.

They'd begun the night at Dempseys, a bar owned by the firefighter husband of Jordan's friend Kinsey (and appropriately populated by hunky CFD bartenders) then took a hired limo to Smith & Jones, a high-end restaurant in the West Loop, where Kinsey's brother-in-law was the executive chef. *Connections, I have 'em*, Jordan said.

The food was amazing. Apple-bacon pierogis. Burrata and butternut squash. Tandoori lamb chops. All night, the girls did a lovely job of keeping her mind off a certain someone. They talked about careers, goals, happiness, and largely skirted the subject of men. It was wonderful. Her heart still ached.

When would she feel like herself again?

Her phone pinged and she checked, worried about Lauren and hoping her sister would text to let her know she was having a good time over at the Isners.

She started at the identity of the sender. Not Lauren.

Her heart beat like a trip hammer as she scanned the first words of the text message.

Gunnar: You asked me once if I missed us. What we used to have and how we connected before. It seemed simpler then, just two strangers checking in, getting to know each other, becoming friends. I had no idea it would get so complicated. That knowing you IRL would hurt so much.

Sadie's hand shook. This was what she'd asked for—a

soul reveal—and now she had it she wasn't sure she could handle it. But she had to. Woman up!

She stood, a little too quickly, and Jenny reached to steady her.

"You okay?"

"Yes! Fine!" The words sounded squeaky. "I need to take a walk, get some air."

"Want company?"

"Nah, you stay. I'll be back in a few."

She left the table, conscious that everyone was watching the broken-hearted woman as she stumbled away. Her phone pinged with another message. When she got to the restroom, she locked herself inside a stall and read the text.

The thing is I didn't miss us. Because I felt like we had a new "us" in this moment, if that makes sense. I was two different people. The guy who talked his heart out to Angel in those texts, then the guy who wanted to lose himself in a gorgeous woman with a smile that slayed him. Combining the two would force me to take a step I wasn't ready for. Admit that I might be moving on. How could I do that to the people I love so much?

I used to dream about them all the time, but it stopped when I first moved to Chicago. Hockey helped. Drinking helped more. Then I met this woman, this bright, funny, amazing, annoying woman, who set my body on fire and my brain on empty. The dreams returned, but with variations. In these versions, I have chances to do things over. My arms aren't pinned and I can reach the door handle. My phone hasn't fallen under the seat but responds to voice commands. Kelly isn't breathing like her lungs are full of blood but is conscious and barking orders. (She was kind of bossy.) Janie is chattering on, wondering when Daddy is going to take her home. And Danny ...

Danny, his beautiful boy. Sadie swallowed, dreading what would come next.

I dream about my son in the backseat of the car, sucking his thumb. He's always asleep in the dream even though he wasn't that day. That day, he was chatting about the clouds. He loved clouds, was always seeing shapes and faces in them. In some versions of the dream, I can't see him. I know he's there but it's as if he's hidden behind a screen. In other versions, he's asleep before the accident. When we crash, when we go off the road, I hear Kel and Janie, but not Danny. I can't hear my son's voice anymore. I don't remember what he sounds like.

The coroner's report said he died immediately. They were both in booster seats, strapped in tight, but a branch knocked out the window and killed him outright. Kelly had internal injuries. She knew she wouldn't make it. She told me she was sorry she pushed back on a third kid. I wanted more and now, now it doesn't matter.

Janie lasted a couple of hours longer. My little princess had the heart of a fighter. I tried to sing to her that Johny Johny Yes Papa song. She used to love it when I'd sing it with her name instead. Janie Janie Yes Papa.

But after a while, she went quiet, too.

That was the worst of it, Sadie. How quiet it got. How the silence accused me when I was the only one left to hear it.

Sadie wiped away the wet on her cheek. She'd asked for it, hadn't she? If he could say it, she could read it.

That's why I went to the cabin in New Hampshire. For the quiet. For the accusing silence. So I could dream about them. But that wasn't enough and I started texting Kelly, needing to talk to her. Needing to pretend that she might walk in the door any minute and the nightmare was over. It felt good to keep that connection alive. It felt good to pretend.

Then you answered.

And I knew she wasn't coming back. None of them were. I only had the bad dreams where my daughter's screams still echoed in my ear, my son's refused to come, and my wife was definitely fucking dead.

Sadie clutched at her chest. Her thundering heart would break its confines any second now and splatter all over this restroom floor.

Should she respond? Did he need to know she was reading it right now? Could he tell? Probably.

Inserting herself wouldn't help. She wasn't his therapist. She was here to listen, not fix his problems.

Waiting for the next heartbreaking reveal was excruciating. So many times, her fingers hovered over the keyboard, ready to jump in. A painful two minutes later, he texted again.

You know what happened next. We started talking and I started looking forward instead of back. Forward to your bad jokes and check-ins. Forward to waking up instead of longing for the night to come. Forward. I hung onto every word of my guardian angel. That's you. Angel. The funny Angelino and my angel rolled into one. I returned to hockey, moved to a new city, kept busy. I acted because action kept me sane. Play, coach, eat, drink, fuck. Don't think.

Easier said than done. Have you ever tried to stop thinking? I mean, really try. It's impossible. Every day I wonder why I got pissed at that driver behind me. Why I didn't pull over to let him pass. Why I put my hubris above the safety of my family.

All these small decisions.

I wonder why you got Kelly's number. Why we exchanged texts instead of blocking each other. Why I came back to Chicago to coach a youth hockey team. Why we didn't have vegetarian sandwiches that first day. Why I believed Lauren's pretty outrageous story about her big bad sister.

Something beyond my understanding pushed us together, Sadie. Something within me, and completely knowable, pushed us apart.

The longest minute of her life passed while she held her breath.

I miss them and it hurts. With you, it didn't hurt as much, and I resented that. I resented the way my body reacted to you. I resented the way my heart awoke from a winter of hibernation. I resented pleasure and laughter and joy, all emotions I feel with you. I wanted the pain. It keeps me sane. Embracing happiness is a kind of insanity, don't you think?

If by happiness, he meant falling in love, she had to agree.

I don't know where to go from here. If there's even a place for us to go. I just know I don't want to do this without you. I can't do this without you.

Oh, Gunnar. She should text back, call him, something. While considering her options, another text came in, but not from him. This was from Jenny.

Where are you? We have an emergency. Lauren's missing.

35

SADIE JUMPED out of the cab, raced to the Isners' front door, and banged hard.

"Sadie, I've got this!" Jenny exited the cab and came up behind her. Before she could use her key, the door flew open. Nick stood there.

"How long has she been missing?" A screeching Sadie just about managed not to grab Nick by the shirt collar and shake him. They'd already talked to him on the cab ride over but she needed to hear it again.

His worry was palpable. "I checked on them last about an hour ago and they were playing video games. The hockey one. Jason said they got into a fight about something and she left. But he didn't come tell me immediately. He said she left about 10:30, so about an hour ago."

Sadie had stopped at the house to make sure Lauren hadn't gone home. It was time to call the police, but first things first.

"Can I talk to Jason?"

"Of course."

Sadie walked briskly into the house. Both Jason and

Sean stood at the kitchen island, looking like a truck had rolled over them.

"Hey, Jason, any idea where she might have gone?"

He shook his head. "She doesn't want to move to LA. She wanted me to run away with her. I told her I couldn't—" He looked over her shoulder at his mom and dad. "She called me a pussy and I was kind of mad at her. So when she left, we didn't tell anyone. I tried texting her but she won't answer. I figured she was just angry. But then Dad came in asking about her so I had to fess up. I'm really sorry."

Panic waved over Sadie. She searched each face before her. "Where would she go?"

"Maybe the practice rink."

Sadie turned at the sound of Gunnar's voice. She'd ended their text exchange with a few hasty words about Lauren. He'd come right over, and she was never so relieved to see anyone.

"Do you think that's likely?"

Gunnar rubbed his beard. "I'll call the facility security." He stepped away.

Sadie faced Jason again. "When she asked you to run away with her, what was the plan?"

Sean answered instead. "First of all, she wanted to hang out in our den like Eleven in *Stranger Things*. She thought we could build a shelter with blankets and keep it a secret."

That only worked in eighties-inspired kids' shows low on parental supervision, and Sadie's expression must have said so.

Jason frowned. "Yeah. I told her there's no way my mom would stay away from there. She's really nose—uh, involved."

"Anything else?"

Before he could respond, Gunnar came back and placed

a hand on her shoulder. "No sign of her. I asked security to keep an eye out."

Sadie turned back to the boys. "If you know anything at all, please."

"We don't! We've told you everything."

Nick stepped forward and put a protective arm around his son. "It's okay, Jason. We're not mad at you."

Jason squirmed. "She threw that rock through the window at her house."

Sadie gasped. "She told you this?"

"Yeah, she said you were, uh, kissing Gunnar and that was the best way to stop it. She likes *you*." The "you" was directed at Gunnar.

"What about the graffiti? Did she do that?" But she couldn't have. It happened while they were at the hockey game and Lauren was under her eye the whole time.

Jason slid a guilty look at Sean, who spoke up. "I did it."

"Sean!" Jenny threw up her hands. "How could you?"

"She said it would scare Sadie," Sean said, as if it were perfectly reasonable. Jenny had described her oldest son as the analytical one. "She thought Sadie might ask to move in here and then Mom and Dad might offer Lo a place to stay. Become her foster parents."

The weird workings of the tween mind.

"She misses her dad," Jason said. "She wants to stay in town for him."

Sadie sought out Gunnar, the only person she felt she could trust right now. He was watching her, not anyone else.

"Worth a shot?"

"Definitely," Gunnar said, knowing exactly what needed to be done. "Come on."

They headed out to the car, just as Sadie's phone rang with a call from Allegra, a follow-up to the ten-plus texts she'd already sent tonight. Sadie let it go to voicemail and called her father's lawyer to explain the situation. "I know it's outside visiting hours but would they let her in?"

The lawyer assured them that they would not. She hung up and turned to Gunnar. "Maybe she's waiting for Cook County Correctional to open tomorrow so she can slip in?"

"Try calling her again."

It went straight to voicemail.

"What about texting? Harder to ignore." He shrugged. "Can't hurt."

She wasn't so sure about that. She took a deep breath, thinking about how to begin. Then she put thumb to text.

Sadie: Hey Lauren, I'm worried. So worried. And I know you don't want to talk to me, but I need a word that you're okay. Say anything.

Nothing. "I think we need to call the police. This isn't working."

"Try again." Gunnar stroked her arm. "Tell her what's in your heart."

The bitterness, the recrimination, the blame she'd assigned to her father and Zoe—all valid, but not how to win over her sister. And after reading that letter from Zoe, Sadie saw now that it wasn't as black-and-white as her teenage memory had painted it. Zoe had her own problems and Sadie must have been a handful. After dealing with Lauren for the last few weeks, she recognized how hard that must have been for her stepmother.

She tried again.

Sadie: I know I haven't been there for you. I missed birthdays, celebrations, everything. I wasn't the sister you needed and now I'm the sister you don't want.

I'm going to be honest with you. My dad preferred your mom and you over me. I don't blame your mom. I did once, but not now. She married Dad and had a grieving, angry teenager to manage. I didn't make it easy on her and neither of us regretted parting ways when I turned 18.

Well, not entirely true. I had one huge regret. I left you behind. Sweet, baby Lo. You had just turned two. I remember checking in on you and your chubby little cheeks were so pink and pretty. I said a little prayer and put Iggy in your crib and then I left while I still had strength in my legs.

Each year on your birthday, I sent a card.

Now wasn't the time to tell her what happened to those cards. But she refused to pretend she hadn't tried, even if that effort was less than perfect.

When I tried to reach out ... well, that's another story. After a while, I stopped trying. I figured you wouldn't remember me anyway. The pain of rejection outweighed any hope I had that we could be friends. That we could be sisters.

"It says delivered, but I don't think she's reading."

"Give it a second," he murmured, so calm and soothing.

She typed in more. Better to let it out.

I'm not the best person. I was jealous that Dad loved you more. That he still loves you more. That hurts and I'm sorry I let it affect everything. I need to know you're safe. Please.

She waited. And waited.

"This isn't work—oh, the dots!"

"Really?" Gunnar grabbed the phone. "Knew it."

They both held the phone, shoulders touching, fingers brushing, and watched as the dots continued to taunt them.

Finally, a text came back with three amazing words:

I'm okay, dummy.

Sadie snatched a breath, but really she was choking back a sob. She hit dial and after two rings, Lauren answered.

"I'm at home," her little sister said, her voice rusty.

"Are you safe?"

Lauren sniffed. "Of course I am."

"We're a few minutes out. Is Coop with you?"

"Yeah, and he stinks."

"Well, he can't help it. Where did you go?"

"I walked around, but I saw you show up at the house, so I hid in the garden. I came back to get my stuff."

"What was the plan?"

"Go see Dad. I had planned to wait until tomorrow but then I had a fight with Jason."

Sadie heaved a sigh of relief as they pulled up to the house. She attacked the front door and made a beeline for the living room where Lauren was camped out on the sofa, Coop at her feet like the good doggo he was.

"I'm going to hug you so don't even think of stopping me, you little monster."

Lauren's teary "okay" was muffled against Sadie's shoulder.

"Tell me what you need, Lauren."

Lauren raised her head, her silver eyes brilliant with emotion. "To see Dad before we go. One last time."

Sadie couldn't stand it. She wasn't inflexible, like her father. She had the capacity to adapt and steer the course of her own ship.

"Here's what's going to happen. We'll go see Dad tomorrow. Then we'll figure out a plan for staying here."

"Really?"

"Yes. I thought—I thought LA was where I was supposed to be but it's just a place. We can be in any place, so why not here?"

Lauren's mouth fell open. "But this place will be sold, won't it?"

"Okay, not literally this place. But Chicago." She'd run

from this city and her past for too long. Time to stay put and figure it out. "I have to wrap up some stuff in LA, find a job here, and find a place for us to live. But from now on, we make all the decisions together."

Lauren wiped a tear away. "I have to tell you something."

"Shoot."

"I-I broke the window. That one." She pointed, as if the broken window was one of many possibilities.

"I see. Well, I expect you had your reasons."

She sniffed. "I was mad at you. For everything."

Sadie nodded, remembering what that was like. What it was still like. "Good reasons."

"And I painted graffiti on the door. Well, not me. I asked someone to do it."

"Which door?"

Lauren's expression turned questioning. "The one you— that Gunnar—painted."

Sadie shrugged. "No idea what you're talking about. That door needed a refresh."

Her sister gave a watery smile. "Did you really send me birthday cards?"

Sadie nodded. One day, she might give them to Lauren but for now she'd let her sister hold onto the faith she still had in her father. She had already lost so much.

Lauren picked up her bear. "And did you really give me Iggy?"

Oh, her heart. How would it survive this night? "Yes, I did. I sewed that heart onto his chest to make him more mine, but I wanted to leave something with you. Something that meant a lot to me and to let you know I hadn't forgotten you, my baby sister."

Lauren's tears fell more easily now. "I thought Mom gave him to me. She used to try to take him away to wash him but

I was worried she'd throw him out because he was old. She never told me he was yours."

Sadie had thought it a strange gift from Zoe, who could have taken it any time and disposed of it. But now, after reading Zoe's letter, she knew better. Her stepmother wanted to keep that sisterly bond alive, but perhaps she worried Sadie would only end up disappointing Lauren. Perhaps that's why she didn't fess up about Iggy's history.

"I'm sorry. I know it must be disappointing to hear he wasn't from your mom."

Her sister shook her head. "No, she gave me other stuff. I'm glad you gave Iggy to me. I'm glad he used to be yours."

Sadie poked at the heart she'd sewn on. "I should have asked if I could fix him up. That was wrong of me. I'm sorry."

Lauren thought on that for a while, then nodded her assent. "I'm sorry I called you a stupid cow."

"It's okay. We're going to fight a lot, because that's a sister thing. We'll figure it out because sisters do that, too."

Lauren wrinkled her nose, making her look a little like Sadie in that moment. "You can call me Lo. If you want to."

Sadie fought past the lump the size of Iggy in her throat. "Okay."

"There's one other thing we need to do," Lauren said, her lovely face as serious as ever. And then she told her and Sadie's heart eased for the first time in days.

GUNNAR SAT at the island in Sadie's kitchen, his mind clearer than it had been in months. His clothes smelled of smoke. His hands were scraped and grazed. At Lauren's request, they'd set the deceased Christmas tree on fire in the back yard. It would have had to go before the auction anyway, but this way, Lauren had a say in its exit.

Thank God she was safe. Thank God they both were.

Learning that Lauren was behind the property damage meant they were no longer in any danger. Never had been. Gunnar had no excuse to be here anymore, except the best excuse of all: he loved Sadie Yates.

Something had changed tonight. He'd told Sadie about the accident and what followed. It was a start, and with Sadie staying in Chicago, maybe they could use it as the first building block. Maybe she'd give him another chance.

She came into the kitchen, surprise on her face. "You're still here."

"Where would I go?"

"I thought you'd be done with all the drama." She walked to the fridge and took out two beers, then passed one over as she leaned against the island.

"Thanks for helping tonight. With everything."

"How is she?"

"Worn out. I hope I'm making the right call in staying here. I just know that dragging her to LA right now is not good for her."

"I'm glad you're staying."

Those silver-starred eyes studied him before she twisted off the beer cap. "Are you?"

"Did you read my messages tonight?"

"You know I did." She gave him that lovely smile, the sad one rather than the hooky one. "Thanks for sharing that with me. I know it can't have been easy."

"It wasn't. I'm not a talker."

"You don't have to be. It's always been easier for us to talk as if we were strangers. Meeting in real life was both the best and worst thing that could have happened. It halted the intimacy we were building before but ..."

"But what?"

"It had to happen." He must have looked confused because she went on. "As awesome as the texting versions of us were, we were hiding behind the technology. Only willing to take it so far. And when we finally met, we both got scared because we couldn't hide behind our screens anymore. I think we knew there was something there and we didn't want to give up on it, but neither did we want to open it up for examination. Better to compartmentalize. I knew I wanted more, I knew we could be more, but I agreed to take the crumbs you offered and stay in sex limbo because something was better than nothing."

"Sex limbo? What the hell is that?"

"It's the place you visit when you can't stay away from each other but you don't want to talk about it. Ever."

She had the right of it there. "But we're not there anymore. We've moved on. Haven't we?" He might have sounded a little too hopeful.

"I think so. I hope so. I want us to be there for each other. A team. We can't keep the sex part in one box and the talking part in another. At least, I can't."

He couldn't do that either. He'd tried but flings weren't his jam, sex without feeling didn't do it for him. Not that sex with Sadie had ever been without feeling. From the first touch, he'd been stripped to the bone, his nerves raw conductors for the energy between them. The potential of them.

"The boxes have been opened, Sadie." He waved his hands to indicate magical woo woo.

"I know."

Good, she understood. "So we're on the same page."

"If the same page is you getting the therapy you need."

The T word. Of course the Cali girl would bring it out. "I thought you wanted to be my therapy."

"I never said that. I said I wanted to be here for you, to listen, to be someone you can lean on. You were the one who worried about becoming a burden.

"But talking to me won't be enough for you, Gunnar." She closed the gap between them and placed a hand on his hip. "You need professional help."

"What? No, I-I don't. I'm getting through this. I've come further in the last three weeks than I have in three years."

"I know, but your grief is complicated. All those things you said in the text messages tonight—that's only the beginning."

No, this wasn't fair. He'd done what she asked. "I told you things." The accident. The pain. The soul-crushing guilt. "I haven't told that stuff to anyone."

She smiled, so serene. "I'm so grateful that you did. Do you feel better?"

"No!"

And still she smiled. "You're feeling raw right now. It's a good first step. A great first step. But you just said you didn't want me to be your therapy. You don't want to weigh me down with your troubles."

This reeked of a trap. "I don't."

"So, don't. Take some of those millions you've earned and pay someone to walk you through it. Talk to someone who understands a grief like yours. I can help but only up to a point. Show me you want to put in the work."

He'd come this far and it wasn't enough for her. He would happily talk his glutes off if she'd only listen, preferably late at night while he held her tight.

He had one more shot on the net, one more chance to claim victory. He launched the puck from his blade.

"Sadie, I—" *I love you.* This would win her. This is what she needed to hear.

But the words wouldn't come, probably because he'd never said them to anyone but his wife. They hit the pipe and he wasn't even in position for a rebound.

Not a wide eye from Sadie. Not an eyebrow raise. Not even a twitch of her lips.

She cupped his cheek and held it. "I know, Gunnar. But I need you to love yourself first."

Then she kissed him with a sweetness that broke him wide open before she left him blinking, wet-eyed, at her departing back.

36

Jonah Yates hugged Lauren tight, then pushed her away from him to get a good look at her.

"Don't ever do anything like that again, Lauren. You must have worried your sister sick."

"I just wanted to see you, Dad."

Her father looked over her head at Sadie, seated at the table in the prison's visiting room. For once, his usual disdain wasn't on display.

"I told Sadie to keep you away. I didn't want you to get upset, seeing me in this place." He kissed the top of her head. "We both want the best for you."

"I know," Lauren said, sniffing. "But I miss you."

A couple of minutes later, all the tears had been shed. Sadie asked Lauren if she'd wait outside while she talked to their father alone.

"She's gotten so big," Jonah said, his tone fond.

"She eats Pop Tarts by the caseload. But I promise, I'm throwing in some salads as well."

He nodded, placed his face in his hands, and spent a few seconds rubbing away his emotion. Sadie gave him the time he needed. Finally, he asked, "Are you really going to stay in Chicago?"

"Yes, Dad. But I'm not doing it for you. I'm doing it for Lauren. She's had too much upheaval and this is best for her."

"I expected you'd be like your mother. Vindictive."

She held up a hand. "Could you not do that, Dad? Mom cheated on you and died before you could divorce her. You never got your revenge on her so you took it out on me."

"Sadie—"

"I'm not a vindictive person, Dad. At least, I don't think so. Taking Lauren to LA was not a way to punish you for being a jerk to me after Mom died. I worried that I might be carrying this bitterness and making decisions for all the wrong reasons, but no. I have a life independently of your bad decisions. I don't owe you a thing." The words bubbled up, desperate to find voice now that she had a captive—literally—audience. "So I reminded you of Mom. What of it? So she did you wrong. How is that my fault? I was thirteen and you never had my back. My mother had just died and you never comforted me. I know you're hurting now but you've also doled out a fair share of pain yourself. Me, Lauren, and all the people you stole from. Man up and take some responsibility. I don't expect to have a relationship with you —it's probably too late for that but I won't ever poison Lauren against you. It's called being an adult."

All the things she could say. *I know about the birthday cards. I know about the letter from Zoe. Why the hell would you cut me out of your life like that?*

But she didn't say it. He knew what he'd done, and she wanted to put all that behind her. She stood, her piece said, not caring for a response. Any words spoken by her father would either be bitter or mealy-mouthed. She had Lauren to worry about, an apartment to find, and a business to build.

"Sadie, I don't know what to say." He sounded forlorn.

"That's okay, Dad. Take some time to think. I'll bring Lauren whenever she wants to see you."

He nodded, his eyes welling. "Thanks for looking after her."

"Of course. She's family."

Sadie turned, knowing it wasn't the end, but hoping it was a start.

SADIE STOOD BACK, placing a pin in her wrist pin cushion. "What do you think?"

Harper twirled in front of the mirror and moved her hands over the sateen fabric. The tulip skirt showcased her legs to perfection.

"Gorgeous." She fingered her cornsilk waves and raised an eyebrow. "Not bad for a mom of three."

The Chicago Rebels CEO always looked amazing, but Sadie liked to think her dress had peeled back another layer of her beauty.

"I can have it finished the day after tomorrow."

"I can't believe you have the time," Harper said as she walked into the ensuite bathroom to change. "When I asked, I never expected you'd be able to complete it so soon."

For the last week, Sadie had worked like a madwoman to complete Jenny's dress (done) and Harper's (almost). She was especially excited about Harper who was often snapped for Chicago society pages. Having the Rebel Queen herself, as everyone called her, wear a Sadie Yates original would be the perfect promotion. Assuming she could get her business off the ground.

Her phone vibrated with a text from Peyton in LA. *So Allegra wants bacon-flavored toothpicks even though she's vegetarian but the warehouse that stored them burned down (arson) and she thinks someone did it on purpose to mess with her. Have I made the biggest mistake of my life?*

Sadie laughed. She'd recommended to Allegra that she hire Peyton as her PA, though she suspected Allegra would eventually see Peyton as competition. Luckily Peyton would never take it seriously and would probably stand up to Allegra better than Sadie had ever done.

Tell her it's a conspiracy. She'll love it.

Harper came out of the bathroom wrapped in a floral-patterned robe. "So, I hear you're looking for an apartment."

"Where did you hear that?"

"Oh, not much gets by me."

Okay, then. Sadie turned away to organize her sewing supplies, but really to hide any reaction she felt should Gunnar's name be mentioned.

"I'm going to see one this afternoon." The third in as many days. She shouldn't be so fussy but she had to factor in school for Lauren and so many places weren't dog-friendly. Leaving Coop behind was a dealbreaker.

She sneaked a peek at Harper who was watching her curiously.

"I also heard that you and Gunnar aren't a couple anymore."

"Not sure we ever were." Except she knew Gunnar cared about her, maybe even loved her in his way. "He needs to work on himself."

"Don't we all?"

Sadie didn't like where this was going. "You think I'm abandoning him when he needs me most?"

Harper was silent for a few seconds. "We all need people, but we also have to do what's right for our own mental health. You have a lot going on in your own life, so that definitely limits your bandwidth. And as for Gunnar ..." She made a shrugging gesture with her hands. "You can lead a hockey player to the ice but you can't make him see a therapist. Well, *I* could. I could make it a condition of his continued employment. But I'd rather he chose that for himself."

Sadie agreed, though it was strange to not call or text or see someone who had become such an integral part of her life. It would be so easy to lean on him to help her through these next few weeks. He'd do it, too. But she had to make her own way. He had to figure out his, and maybe they'd reconnect further along on their journeys.

Allegra would be very proud of that piece of Cali-spun philosophy.

Mostly, Sadie hated that she couldn't hold him after he'd awoken from a bad dream and smooth away some of the hurt. But maybe she could help another way.

"This might seem weird, but I wondered if you'd help me get in contact with someone. I could find them but it might sound better coming from you."

"I'm intrigued."

Harper listened to Sadie's request and promised to make a call. "But before I do that, I have something to show you."

∽

FRESHLY SHOWERED after a two-hour workout in the Rebels' gym, Gunnar pulled on his shorts. Training camp started in less than a month and while running down pucks with kids was good cardio, it didn't contribute much to his strength regimen. His muscles felt tight, his skin with it. He could blame the workout but he knew it was more.

He missed Sadie.

He would have missed her if she'd moved back to LA, but knowing she was merely a few miles away was a particular cruelty. According to Theo, they would be staying with the Isners while they looked for an apartment (Lauren had got her way in the end). Several times over the last few days, he'd suppressed the urge to drop in, just to see how Jenny and the boys were doing. Right.

Sadie wasn't the only person who'd suggested therapy. Harper had mentioned it when he came into Rebels HQ to discuss his scuffle with Kaminski. She hadn't pushed but he could tell she was disappointed. It had been three years. He was finally on the mend—yet no-one believed him!

His phone buzzed with a text from Kurt. They'd been talking more lately. If Gunnar couldn't knuckle down to some $200 per hour shrink, he could make a start with his family. (He suspected *that* would be the first thing a therapist would order him to do anyway.)

Kurt: Hey, I wanted to send you something. A video. That okay?

Gunnar: What of? And why was he asking permission?

Kurt: Thanksgiving, a few years ago, here in Maine.

Gunnar gusted out a breath and looked around, though he knew he was alone. Was this some kind of immersion therapy? Blast him with memories and watch him crumble?

Gunnar: Send it.

It took a couple of minutes to download and Gunnar paced the room, waiting for the circle to complete, psyching himself up for what he was about to watch.

The video opened on the dinner table at his brother's place in Maine, which could seat an army. It was half-set with dishes and flatware, and then he heard it: his own voice.

"C'mon, Danny boy, let me show you how it's done."

In this clip, Gunnar picked his son up and placed him on one of the chairs so he could reach the table. Danny always wanted to help. In the kitchen, at the grocery store, wherever humans set their mind to things. On this day, he would have been three and a half. Gunnar distinctly remembered how proud he was of his little blue-checkered shirt and doll-sized jeans because he was dressed like his dad.

"Like this, Daddy?" He looked up and Gunnar touched the screen to freeze it. He'd wondered if it was a blessing or a curse that he was killed outright. Only a selfish fucker would want him to have survived the crash so Gunnar could hear his voice and commit it to memory.

He traced his index finger over the blond hair of his son, a little long and prone to curl, and marveled at how much he looked like his mom. The same hazel eyes, the same stubborn tilt to his chin. He hit the play button again.

"Exactly like that, bud." On the video, Gunnar straightened the fork and smiled at the camera.

"Just like Downton Abbey," a voice said. His sister-in-law, Carrie.

"Just like Down town Abbey," Danny said, taking a spoon from the basket Gunnar carried because they were a flatware-delivery team.

That was the end of the video and the end of Gunnar. He crumbled. His shoulders shook and he tried to play the video again, but he dropped his phone. Instead of picking it up, he stared at it until it blurred, an amorphous shape through his tears.

Minutes passed that felt like hours, but they couldn't have been because someone would have come into the locker room by now.

The phone rang and he picked it up. It was Kurt.

"You okay?"

"Fuck, no."

Kurt inhaled a sharp breath. "Wasn't sure that would be a good idea, but your friend seemed to think it was what you needed."

Gunnar straightened. "My friend?"

"Sadie. Well, she said she was a friend, but I got the impression there was more to it? Anyway, Harper Chase called and—"

"Harper Chase called you?"

"That's what I just said." Kurt sounded impatient as always, and for some reason, that made Gunnar smile. "Said this Sadie needed to talk to me about any videos I might have, especially ones of Danny. Carrie went back and checked the cloud. You know, I don't film any of that stuff."

"Yeah, me neither. Kel did all that." He'd started filming those kids at hockey camp, though, especially Lauren so he could sent it to Petrov. It was important to record those moments.

"Right. Anyway, she found this one and a few more. Said I should reach out to you and ask if you wanted to see it."

Gunnar closed his eyes, pondering this gift. *I can't hear my son's voice anymore.* He had told Sadie that, lamented it, and here she was, figuring out how to fix that one problem among a million.

"You said you have more videos?"

"Yup."

"Can you send them or put them somewhere I can view them?"

"Sure can. You could also visit once in a fuckin' while and watch them on the big screen in the den."

Gunnar smiled at that. "I will. I promise. And Kurt?"

"Yeah?"

"Thanks for this. Thanks for everything."

His brother snorted. "Jesus, we're family, aren't we?"

Yes, they were. Gunnar hung up, just as Dante walked into the locker room with a gym bag. He put it down on the bench and took a hard look at the current bench occupant.

"You okay?"

"No, I'm not."

Dante smiled, like that was the best news he'd heard all day. "Tell me how I can help."

37

I<small>T WAS A KNOCKOUT WEDDING</small>, perfect in every way. Sadie even managed to earn her hundred-dollar chicken plate by sewing a last-minute rip in the bride's gown.

"Have I told you how gorgeous you are?" she asked her plus-one.

Lauren rolled her eyes. "Only eleventy billion times. Give it a rest."

"Never."

Sadie had made a dress for Lauren from the Swedish print, the perfect fabric for a girl her age. Dark-haired and bright-cheeked, she looked just like her mom. But those silver-blue eyes were her father's—and Sadie's. They were sisters, no doubt about it.

In an astonishing act of kindness, Sadie and Lo were seated with the people they knew in Chicago. The Isners were on one side of her, Elle and Theo on the other. Also with them was a friendly guy named Joe, who fed slivers of the chicken to a cute dog called Cookie under the table. A handsome hockey hunk called Cal Foreman had flirted with her at the bar but was now feeling up his date three seats over.

The empty chair on the other side of the ten-seater table couldn't be more glaring. Sadie's eyes were constantly drawn to it.

Lauren nudged her. "Quit it."

"You quit it," Sadie mumbled.

The appetizer and entrée courses came and went, but still no sign of Gunnar. He wasn't at the church, either, and when Sadie asked Jenny if she knew where he was, she got a shrug of no. But his name was on a card at the front of the marquee tent, assigned to this table. He was supposed to be here, so why wasn't he?

Reaching out to his brother had seemed like a good move. A jarring, kick-in-the-ass move, but a good one all the same. Yet she hadn't heard a word about his reaction.

The desserts amazed, mini-tiramisus and lemon mousses and macarons by the truckload because the bride was obsessed with them. Toasts were given, tears were shed, and the first dance made everyone go aww!

As the guests headed toward the dancefloor, she saw him—finally!—headed her way. Her heart flipped like a landed fish.

He stopped at the table, nodded at Joe and his fellow players, and smiled at her. "Hello, Sadie."

"Hi," she managed. He'd shaved and wow, he looked so good. She'd seen pics of him in a suit online, but nothing impressed like in-the-flesh tailoring.

He peered down at Lauren. "Almost didn't recognize you there, Lo. Enjoy the desserts?"

"The lemon mousse was the best."

He took the empty seat beside her. "Heard you guys moved into the Chase Manor cottage."

Lauren lit up. "Yeah, Violet Vasquez used to live there and she painted these crazy murals all over the wall. She's married to Bren St. James but she's having a baby for Cade Burnett and Dante Moretti, which is really weird. But Harper says we can raid her fridge up at the main house any time. And Isobel invited me to join the U14 hockey team she coaches. She also said she'd put a good word in for me for school, but I wouldn't mind so much if I didn't have to go back. More time for hockey practice."

"Yeah, but you wouldn't get to learn about calculus and physics and geography, which are important. Or so I hear."

Lauren grinned. "You should dance with Sadie. She's been dying for you to turn up."

"Lauren! Don't put him on the spot. And I was not dying, just curious."

Gunnar stood and held out his hand. "She's right. Dance with me, Sadie."

Sadie's heart thundered like a jet engine in her chest. But she'd also been watching that damn chair for two hours, so she sure as hell would not be sitting this one out.

On wobbly legs, she stood and took his hand, feeling like she was on ice skates and he was the only thing holding her up. He led them to the dance floor, to the tune of Nat King Cole's *Unforgettable*. His big hand settled at her back, his other held hers, and their chests met in the perfect fit.

"You look stunning," he said. "That one of yours?"

"It is."

"And you've dressed a few of the guests as well."

"Business is looking up."

He smiled. She'd never seen him smile so much. Her heart *th-thunked* with joy at seeing him so at ease.

She gazed up at him. "You shaved."

"Well, the season's over." The way he said it made it

sound like season meant something else. "New one's starting soon."

She licked her lips, suddenly incredibly nervous. "You missed the ceremony. And the meal. And the desserts."

"Had a previous appointment. I only expected to take an hour. That's usually how these things go, to start, but once I started talking, it seems I couldn't shut up."

Her eyes welled with tears.

"Sadie, honey, don't get upset."

"You went to therapy? On a Saturday?"

He nodded. "Dante spoke with the team psychologist, but she thought it would be better to refer me to someone who deals with complicated grief. This therapist doesn't usually meet with patients on Saturdays but I didn't want to wait a minute longer. I wanted to be able to tell you immediately that I've started seeking professional help."

Sadie had never been more proud. "You're doing it, Gunnar. You're on the road."

"First step, though ..." He paused. Restarted. "Actually, I'm further along than I thought. The first step was about nine months ago when someone answered my text. A call for help, really. I didn't block that number. I continued the conversation. Then I gave up my summer to teach kids how to play hockey, mostly because I didn't want to be alone. All those decisions, every one a step toward you. Toward healing.

"And when you told me you loved me, Sadie, I panicked. I said things. I said awful things. Blaming you for what I'd lost, for cutting off that connection to Kelly. But then the night Lauren went missing, I thought I could do this. I could empty my soul on that phone. Pour it out like you want, and I'd be fixed. We'd be fixed. This woman loves me and hell, I know I love her. But I hadn't taken enough of those steps yet.

Like you said, I hadn't put in the work and telling that story was just the beginning. You knew that. You knew it before I did."

He was giving her too much credit. He'd merely needed a nudge to get there. "When I read those texts, all those months ago, I could have stayed out of it. I could have blocked that number. But I stuck my nose in. And then other things happened that set me on this path to find you. My father being a dumbass. Coming to Chicago to look after Lauren. All those decisions, every one a step toward you. Toward love."

His eyes softened with such tenderness she didn't think she could stand it.

"Kurt sent a video of Danny and it broke my heart, Sadie, but then it re-formed in that moment, stronger than ever. It gave me hope that I'm not numb or dead or incapable of moving on. You did that for me. I won't lean on you for everything but if I can rely on you a little ..." He squeezed her tight to him. "Maybe you can keep my heart safe."

She sniffed and tried to inhale, but her lungs had gone on hiatus.

"Sadie?"

"Sorry, it's just I ..." Her emotion got the better of her and she waved a hand in front of her face, a move that all women seemed to think staved off tears.

It did not.

"Hell, do I have it wrong?"

"No! Not at all, I'm just a mess." *Unforgettable* ended and Sam Smith's *Stay with Me* came on. She had all these words she wanted to use, things she longed to say, love she yearned to express, but nothing came out.

So she stopped dancing, snaked her arms around

Gunnar Bond's neck, and kissed him hard. His moan filled her heart and soul, and they stood there for an age, making out and up in the best possible way.

He pulled back and wiped her tears with those strong, talented thumbs. "I love you, Sadie. I know it's only been a few weeks in person but I've been falling for my angel for months in this other lifetime."

"I love you," she whispered. "And I'm so proud of you for getting the help you need. I'm here for you. For everything." And then she said the thing she had always been afraid to ask for from the closest people to her heart. "And I need you to be here for me. I need your strength and solidity, Gunnar."

Sam sung it out. *Won't you stay with me? 'Cause you're all I need.*

"It's yours. Everything I am, everything I have, is yours."

He initiated the kiss this time, his gift to her complete. She felt utterly loved, at peace with herself after a long time warring with her heart.

She looked over to Lauren who was chatting with Elle and Theo, but spotted her spying and gave a small wave before returning to the circle of friends that had welcomed them both. As they continued to dance, she sent up three prayers of thanks.

To Zoe for letting Lauren keep Iggy.

To Kelly for showing Gunnar how to love hard and long.

And finally, to those fuckers at AT&T.

EPILOGUE

REMEMBER *when we'd look at each other and you'd ask without saying a word: is this crazy? And I'd tell you silently: probably but do it anyway.*

That's how I used to feel when I texted you, Kel. Like I was hanging off the edge of a cliff by my fingernails. Like this was the only thing keeping my organs inside my body and my bones inside my skin. Texting you kept me sane but it also put me on this new path.

Texting you led me to Sadie.

You'd like her, Kel. She's no-nonsense and not afraid to push back when I'm being an ass. She calls me out when I'm down on myself and lifts me up when I need it. Like you, she's a smart cookie. And super talented. Harper is investing in her dress design business (Sadie wouldn't take a penny from me) and I know she's going to be a huge success. She already has a waiting list a mile long for orders.

I've been talking to Kurt more. Even went to visit him and the family. Carrie has a ton of videos of us, and you're just like I remembered you, with Janie and Danny. My therapist—yeah, don't laugh—says I need to embrace the good we had and recog-

nize it as one chapter of many in my life. An important one, of course. And while it's okay for me to re-read those chapters, it's healthiest for me to write new ones.

In these new ones, I'm creating a story with Sadie and Lauren. With Theo and Elle, who just welcomed a little one, Hatch. With Dante and Cade and their baby girl, Rosie. (They were born a couple of weeks apart so they're being labeled Chicago Rebel twins. Or an arranged marriage, per Kershaw.) With my new band of brothers. Harper's been there for me, too. I'd never have expected it from the CEO of a pro-hockey franchise, but that's what I've skated into. A new family.

Sometimes I wake up and you're not the first thing I think about. I don't dream about the accident anymore, either. I still feel guilty that you and the kids are no longer my constant, no longer part of my consciousness or even my dreams. The therapist says that's part of the process. We let go, then we labor over whether that's the right thing to do. My brain already knows it is and I expect my heart will catch up. It's the only way I can be the man that Sadie needs. It's the best way I can forgive myself.

Thanks for giving me some of the best years of my life. Thanks for blessing me with two beautiful children. And thanks for being the woman who shaped me into the man I am today, one that's strong enough to survive and generous enough to open my heart to someone else.

I love you, Kel. Always.

ACKNOWLEDGMENTS

Because she saved my butt big time on this book, my editor Kristi Yanta deserves both a dedication *and* an acknowledgment for the amazing job she did here. Let's face it: the first draft of this was a mess. But Kristi asked all the right questions and got to the heart of what I was trying to do. This book would be a shell without her insightful input. Thank you, K!

Thanks also to copyeditor Kim Cannon for not balking when I pushed back the delivery date and for working through a holiday to get it to me on time. I'm so grateful for her attention to detail and stellar work ethic.

To my agent, Nicole Resciniti, who always has my back. Thanks for supporting me on every path and detour on this journey and finding new opportunities for me.

And finally, Jimmie, I'm blessed to have you in my life. Thanks for being my support, especially in this crazy, upside down, is-it-over-yet year.

ABOUT THE AUTHOR

Originally from Ireland, *USA Today* bestselling author Kate Meader cut her romance reader teeth on Maeve Binchy and Jilly Cooper novels, with some Harlequins thrown in for variety. Give her tales about brooding mill owners, over-sexed equestrians, and men who can rock an apron, a fire hose, or a hockey stick, and she's there. Now based in Chicago, she writes sexy contemporary featuring strong heroes and amazing women and men who can match their guys quip for quip.

ALSO BY KATE MEADER

Rookie Rebels
GOOD GUY
INSTACRUSH
FOREPLAYER

Chicago Rebels
IN SKATES TROUBLE
IRRESISTIBLE YOU
SO OVER YOU
UNDONE BY YOU
HOOKED ON YOU
WRAPPED UP IN YOU

Laws of Attraction
DOWN WITH LOVE
ILLEGALLY YOURS
THEN CAME YOU

Hot in Chicago
REKINDLE THE FLAME
FLIRTING WITH FIRE
MELTING POINT
PLAYING WITH FIRE

SPARKING THE FIRE

FOREVER IN FIRE

COMING IN HOT

Tall, Dark, and Texan

EVEN THE SCORE

TAKING THE SCORE

ONE WEEK TO SCORE

Hot in the Kitchen

FEEL THE HEAT

ALL FIRED UP

HOT AND BOTHERED

For updates, giveaways, and new release information,

sign up for Kate's newsletter at katemeader.com.